ANCIENT TALES NEWLY TOLD

KING OF KINGS

Based on the meeting of King Solomon and Makeda, queen of Sheba

⊗

THE GRAVE AND THE GAY

Based on the 17th-century English folk ballad "Matty Groves"

By Jason M. Rubin

Copyright © 2019 by Jason M. Rubin

All rights reserved. This book or any portion thereof may not be reproduced or used in any manner whatsoever without the express written permission of the publisher except for the use of brief quotations in a book review.

Print ISBN: 978-1-54396-278-9

eBook ISBN: 978-1-54396-279-6

INTRODUCTION

I never intended to write a novel, let alone two of them. Novels are works of fiction and fiction has never been my bag. I was born on Abraham Lincoln's birthday and my first post-Dr. Seuss books were biographies of Lincoln written for early readers. I grew up with a strong interest in history and in college I majored in journalism. Eventually, I became a marketing writer and a freelance arts critic. The articles, reviews, brochures, white papers, web content, and such that I've written for more than thirty years qualify as nonfiction. I read and enjoy novels but it had never occurred to me to write one myself.

And then I was dared.

It was the end of October in 2006. My second daughter had been born in August. In spite of that, my marriage was failing. Meanwhile, at work, a colleague came up to me one morning and asked if I was "doing NaNoWriMo." I had never heard of such a thing. But it didn't sound like a fun thing to do.

NaNoWriMo, she explained, stands for National Novel Writing Month, which takes place every November. The goal of the effort is to motivate people to finally write that book they'd always been meaning to write. From November 1 to November 30, one is expected to put forth the effort to compose a 50,000-word novel; that comes out to an average of 1,667 words a day for thirty days.

I was right: It's not a fun thing to do.

Furthermore, I didn't have a novel in me I'd been meaning to write. But I was challenged to do so and so I figured, why not? The only problem was that November was just a day or two away and I had no idea what my novel should be about.

Fortunately, I quickly seized on a source. There was a song I loved with lyrics I always thought were particularly dramatic, and I'd long thought it could be turned into a play or a book or a film. (By someone else, needless to say.) The song was called "Matty Groves" by the legendary British folk-rock group Fairport Convention. It appears on their 1969 album *Liege & Lief*, and according to the album's liner notes, it was one of the old folk ballads of England and Scotland collected by Francis James Child, an American scholar who published several volumes of these ballads in the late nineteenth century. This particular song dates back to the seventeenth century, and is officially listed as Child 81 (being the eighty-first entry in Child's collection).

Excellent as "Matty Groves" is, it has only four characters and all the action takes place in a single day. If I was going to novelize this song, I would need to create additional characters—two of which were Alexandra McLean, the given name of Fairport vocalist Sandy Denny; and Thomas Richardson, a tribute to Fairport guitarist Richard Thompson—conceive backstories for them all, come up with additional plotlines, and, of course, write the damn thing. This required research, something that I learned to do as a journalism major and did frequently as a professional writer. There were many questions I needed to answer: When does the story take place? Where does it take place? What does the area look like? What were the local customs back then? How did people talk, act, dress? While as a novelist I was expected to invent this stuff, it had to be believable, rooted in some not insignificant measure of fact.

It was around this time that I came upon the wonderful word *verisimilitude*, which is the quality of seeming real (it sounds like "very similar, dude"). The idea is that I couldn't just let my imagination go wild; my story needed to appear authentic. So no cell phones, no pink elephants, no Martians. Instead, much of my writing would have to be fueled by research. This greatly appealed to my inherent inclination for factual storytelling.

Anyway, I began writing my first novel on November 1, 2006, and was doing well for a couple of weeks. Then my infant daughter decided to stop sleeping through the night. When NaNoWriMo ended, I was barely halfway to the 50,000-word goal. I didn't touch it again until January 2007. After some fits and starts, I started to regain my momentum, but then it again became plain to me that writing a novel is hard. Things that are hard require one to get psyched up in order to tackle them. And with a needy baby and an unhappy wife, there wasn't a lot of time or energy or enthusiasm for me to get psyched up for writing—especially considering that my day job involves writing as well.

It took a while, but eventually my home life got so bad that I felt a strong need to focus my attention on something personal, positive, and productive, and that something turned out to be the novel. Being that I was left alone night after night, I wisely chose to devote myself to the manuscript. It took three years in total, but I eventually completed it. When I finally got my own apartment (a room of my own, as it were), I spent another three years rewriting it while trying to interest an agent or publisher. Finally, in 2012, *The Grave and the Gay* (the phrase comes from a Lincoln speech) was published by a small midwestern outfit called Vantage Point that I later learned specialized mainly in erotica. I gave away more copies than I sold, but it was a rush holding a book with my name on the cover, and it made my family and friends very proud and happy. Good enough. End of story, in fact. Or so I thought.

Nobody dared me to write a second novel. I can only blame myself for that.

As with the first one, inspiration came from a song; in this case, "Solomon Sang" by the jazz singer Cassandra Wilson, from her 1995 album *New Moon Daughter*. From the lyrics, it was obvious that the Solomon in question was King Solomon of Israel, son of David, known for his wisdom and for Biblical writings such as the Song of Songs. I had learned all about Solomon in religious school growing up, but Wilson's lyrics included a line about him laying down with someone named Makeda. I could not recall ever hearing a person with that name associated with Solomon.

Curious, I Googled "Makeda" and learned that it was the Ethiopian name for the queen of Sheba (she is not named in the Hebrew Bible, is referred to in the New Testament only as "the queen of the south", and is known in the Quran as Bilqis). I learned that there is a sacred Ethiopian text called the *Kebra Nagast* ("Glory of Kings"), in which the meeting of Solomon and Makeda is central. In this telling, the two rulers end up doing the dirty deed and having a son named Menelik. Further research showed that Ethiopian emperors right up to Haile Selassie I in the twentieth century traced their lineage directly to the fruit of that royal union. Once again, nothing I had ever learned from my Sunday School teachers.

I opened up my handy Bible and went looking for the section where Solomon and the queen of Sheba meet (I Kings, 10:1-13). In the thirteen verses describing their time together, there is nothing about them having sex. The whole story is just that the queen of Sheba hears about Solomon's wisdom, comes for a visit bearing gifts and tricky questions for him to answer, is delighted with his answers, and leaves for home with a bunch of loot from Solomon.

I decided that the *Kebra Nagast*'s version of the story was much more interesting and that it would be fun to unpack their courtship, their intimate exchange, and its aftermath—chiefly, how was it that a queen from southern Arabia heard such great things about a king of Israel, what were their respective backstories, what was the basis for their attraction, and what was it like for Menelik to have two powerful parents (one of whom he didn't meet until he was twenty-two years of age) and to have to choose which throne to inherit? Toni Morrison once said, "If there's a book that you want to read, but it hasn't been written yet, then you must write it," so I realized I was not to be a one non-hit wonder in the fiction world.

I made an early decision that while the main bones of the story would come from the *Kebra Nagast*, I would make use of everything worth gleaning from the Hebrew Bible, the New Testament, and the Quran, as well as folk tales and, of course, my own imagination. There are many Biblical writings attributed to Solomon that he may not actually have written; aside from the Song of Songs, they include various psalms, proverbs, and the book of Ecclesiastes. I decided that I would make them Solomon's and use excerpts as things that he thought and spoke, as well as wrote, so long as they were relevant to the story, which I eventually titled *King of Kings*.

Because of all the research required and my life having become more stable and happier than when I wrote *The Grave and the Gay*, it took about twice as long to write *King of Kings*. Upon its completion, I realized I had written two books that work as a set. Both are based on ancient texts and are written so as to appear to be contemporaneous accounts. They both have unusual romances that lead to major consequences for the characters involved, and they both were inspired by songs. And so rather than publish *King of Kings* on its own, I decided to publish the two together in a single volume under the banner, *Ancient Tales Newly Told*. I also took the opportunity to review the original manuscript of *The Grave and the Gay* to correct errors and make minor changes, so if you already own that book it hopefully will be better this time around.

JMR
Boston, Massachusetts, 2019
www.jasonmrubin.com

TABLE OF CONTENTS

Introduction ... v

KING OF KINGS

Prologue I: Menelik ... 9

The First Book of Solomon ... 15
    Chapter 1 ... 17
    Chapter 2 ... 23
    Chapter 3 ... 31

The First Book of Makeda ... 37
    Chapter 1 ... 39
    Chapter 2 ... 44
    Chapter 3 ... 51

The Book of Tamrin ... 57
    Chapter 1 ... 59
    Chapter 2 ... 64
    Chapter 3 ... 69

Prologue II: Makeda ... 75

The Second Book of Makeda ... 81
    Chapter 1 ... 83
    Chapter 2 ... 87
    Chapter 3 ... 92
    Chapter 4 ... 98

The Second Book of Solomon	103
Chapter 1	105
Chapter 2	111
Chapter 3	117
The Third Book of Makeda	123
Chapter 1	125
Chapter 2	130
Chapter 3	136
Prologue III: Solomon	143
The First Book of Menelik	149
Chapter 1	151
Chapter 2	157
Chapter 3	162
The Second Book of Menelik	167
Chapter 1	169
Chapter 2	175
Chapter 3	182
The Third Book of Solomon	189
Chapter 1	191
Chapter 2	197
Chapter 3	203
Epilogue: Tamrin	209

THE GRAVE AND THE GAY

Chapter 1	219
Chapter 2	228
Chapter 3	237
Chapter 4	242
Chapter 5	252
Chapter 6	259
Chapter 7	271
Chapter 8	279
Chapter 9	285
Chapter 10	292
Chapter 11	300
Chapter 12	308
Chapter 13	315
Chapter 14	325
Chapter 15	333
Chapter 16	339
Chapter 17	345
Chapter 18	353
Chapter 19	362
Acknowledgements	369

KING OF KINGS

By Jason M. Rubin

EXTRACTS

[1] *And when the queen of Sheba heard of the fame of Solomon concerning the name of the Lord, she came to prove him with hard questions.*

[2] *And she came to Jerusalem with a very great train, with camels that bare spices, and very much gold, and precious stones: and when she was come to Solomon, she communed with him of all that was in her heart.*

[13] *And king Solomon gave unto the queen of Sheba all her desire, whatsoever she asked, beside that which Solomon gave her of his royal bounty. So she turned and went to her own country, she and her servants.*

> 1 Kings 10:1-2, 13, *The Bible*, King James version

[5] *I am black, but comely, O ye daughters of Jerusalem, as the tents of Kedar, as the curtains of Solomon.*

> Song of Solomon 1:5, *The Bible*, King James version

[16] *Awake, O north wind; and come, thou south; blow upon my garden, that the spices thereof may flow out. Let my beloved come into his garden, and eat [its] pleasant fruits.*

> Song of Solomon 4:16, *The Bible*, King James version

[7] *Many waters cannot quench love, neither can the floods drown it: if a man would give all the substance of his house for love, it would utterly be contemned.*

> Song of Solomon 8:7, *The Bible*, King James version

[19] *Wisdom strengtheneth the wise more than ten mighty men which are in the city.*

[20] *For there is not a just man upon earth, that doeth good, and sinneth not.*

Ecclesiastes 7:19-20, *The Bible*, King James version

[13] Solomon reigned in a *time* of peace, and *God* gave him peace all round so that he could raise a house to his name and prepare an everlasting sanctuary.

[14] How wise you were despite your youth, like a river, brimming over with intelligence!

[15] Your *mind ranged the earth, you filled it with mysterious sayings.*

[16] Your name reached the distant islands, and you were loved for your peace.

[17] Your songs, your proverbs, your sayings and your answers were the wonder of the world.

[18] In the name of the *Lord God, of him who is called the God* of Israel, you amassed gold like so much tin, and made silver as common as lead.

[19] You abandoned your body to women, you became the slave of your appetites.

[20] You stained your honour, you profaned your stock, so bringing retribution on your *children* and affliction for your folly:

[21] the empire split in two, from Ephraim arose a rebel kingdom.

Ecclesiasticus 47:14-21, *New Jerusalem Bible*

[42] *The queen of the south shall rise up in the judgment with this generation, and shall condemn it: for she came from the uttermost parts of the earth to hear the wisdom of Solomon.*

Matthew 12:42, *The Bible*, King James version

The honouring of wisdom is the honouring of the wise man, and the loving of wisdom is the loving of the wise man. Love the wise man and withdraw not thyself from him, and by the sight of him thou shalt become wise; hearken to the utterance of his mouth, so that thou mayest become like unto him; watch the place whereon he hath set his foot, and leave him not, so that thou mayest receive the remainder of his wisdom.

Kebra Nagast, chapter 24 (translation by E.A. Wallis Budge)

[22] *...I have come to you from Sheba with certain news.*

[23] *Indeed, I found [there] a woman ruling them, and she has been given of all things, and she has a great throne.*

[24] *I found her and her people prostrating to the sun....*

The Quran, Sahih International, "Surah An-Naml," 27:22-24

EXPLANATION

This is a work of fiction, inspired by and drawing from ancient texts of diverse traditions (including Ethiopian, Jewish, Christian, Muslim, and Masonic), none of which are completely substantiated by historical evidence. I have therefore taken great liberties with these texts to offer a story that borrows what is of most interest to me from the various traditions, without treating any of them orthodoxly. To these elements I have added ideas, characters, and subplots of my own invention. I was always respectful of my sources, even as I refused to be bound by them. To those who adhere to the literal content and interpretation of their respective liturgical and cultural texts, I apologize in advance if anything in this book causes offense. My purpose is to tell an entertaining story, not to make any political or theological argument. The original texts are always available to those who seek them.

INSPIRATION

The inspiration for this book came from the song "Solomon Sang" by the brilliant jazz vocalist Cassandra Wilson. In her lyrics I came upon the name Makeda for the first time. From Googling the name, I came to learn about the *Kebra Nagast*, in which the meeting of Solomon, king of Israel, and Makeda, queen of Sheba, is central to Ethiopia's sociopolitical history and cultural and religious beliefs. Copyright laws prohibit me from quoting the lyrics here, but I urge you to seek out the song on your own. Google, and ye shall find.

DEDICATION

To three secular teachers—Stephen B. Oates, Ernest Chamberlain, and Herbert Stearns—and four rabbis—Robert Miller z"l, Lawrence Kushner, Tom Alpert, and Keith Stern—who have inspired and influenced me throughout my life. Thank you for your teachings and your example.

APPRECIATION

Sarah Jensen dared me to write my first novel—and edited this, my second novel. I suppose I could blame her for both, but instead I'll just say thank you!

Prologue I:
MENELIK

Menelik was still a young man that day, that day he had the lion in his belly, and with this courage he went to his mother to ask a question he never before had dared to ask, seeking an answer he never before had needed to know. He was twelve years removed from his mother's womb, and the full-grown man he would become was apparent in his features already. He was handsome, his fellow villagers would say, like his father. Wise as the man from whose seed he had bloomed. A shade or two lighter in skin color than his mother, who loved him, and his peers, who teased him because of these characteristics.

As a child would, Menelik accepted his life as mostly normal, with his home, his family, and his relation to the community all as it should be. But, as a child would, he also was sensitive to the taunts of his friends and the remarks he overheard the older people speak. Not that anyone ever was mean or malicious in their teasing or their talk; in the whole of his life, Menelik experienced only the highest level of respect paid to him and especially to his mother.

Which is to be expected, given that his mother was Makeda, the queen of Sheba, the wealthiest nation in southern Arabia, situated on the Red Sea's southeastern shore. By virtue of Sheba's sophisticated merchant marine, which enabled its people to traverse that lean body of water in large ships for trade and emigration, Makeda also served, as did her predecessors, as ruler of Ethiopia, located west of the Red Sea. For that reason, gaining an audience with her at the height of the day, while important visitors waited in the sun to discuss large matters with her, to ask her a question cloaked with the weight of personal discomfort and curiosity, was difficult—even for Menelik, her only son.

I know this, for I was Makeda's most favored servant and many were those who waited while she and I discussed matters of trade and other subjects. I am Tamrin, the trader. I undertook other responsibilities on behalf of Sheba, but I always considered myself just that: a trader. It was enough for me. And thanks to my closeness with the queen, I had the privilege of watching young Menelik grow up. How well I remember.

Though he had his father's pleasing facial features, Menelik was not thought by some elders likely to inherit his father's wisdom or his mother's strength. As he grew older, though, his body started to mature, turned leaner, revealed the contoured musculature beneath his umber skin. Still, he stood on the unsteady plank of adolescence, with one foot in childhood and the other in young manhood. Play still consumed much of his time and his interest, and mostly he saw his mother only during morning meals and at bedtime.

Though it was just the two of them, Menelik did not complain about his limited access to her. He understood that his mother was important, a great woman, a leader who was strong yet fair, admired if not feared by people who came from lands where strange languages were spoken, whose clothes bore the dust of long voyages, all to request her blessing to engage in trade. Menelik was proud that his mother commanded such attention and respect, though he understood little of the details of trade between nations, knew nothing of negotiation or the strategies with which one could gain an advantage over the other. No, that was my domain. And no one knew better than I of such things. As for Menelik, he knew only that his mother was not available to him as other mothers were to their children.

But Menelik's life now had spanned twelve harvests, and he was of the age when he was expected to spend more time learning from his father than being cared for by his mother. Servants had attended to his every need, and they were kind and caring, but they could not hold him in their arms, caress his head, look deeply into his searching eyes, and tell him the stories of his family. These stories would fill Menelik with the knowledge of who he was and where he came from; they would arm him with awareness of the skills and strengths, traits and talents, of those who had come before him, and through that knowledge he would understand that those characteristics were in him as well.

But he knew none of that. He had not been told. He knew only his name, Menelik. And he knew its meaning: son of the wise man. Who was this wise man, this father he didn't know and had never met? He long had wondered, yet until now any appetite for knowledge he may have possessed had been sated by the fact that all his other needs were met by his loyal coterie of servants. His moments alone with his mother were so rare and so treasured that he feared angering or disappointing her by asking such questions. There must be a reason she had never told him of his origins. He had accepted that until the day when he noticed his body changing. Hairs were growing where none had grown before. His voice was as the unreliable tone of a cracked ram's horn. And that part of him that was boy had suddenly come to have a mind of its own. It, too, was growing, and sometimes would transform itself from hanging flesh to jutting bone, yet he knew not why or how.

Yes, Menelik was becoming a man, this he knew, and he wondered who and where was the man that he might look like. What kind of man could he become if he did not know what kind of man had sired him? The time had come. Finally, Menelik needed to know the answer. Finally, he was willing to risk asking the question of the one person who held the knowledge he sought: his mother, Makeda, the queen of Sheba. And so one day when his years numbered twelve, he left his companions, left the stifling heat of the midday sun, left the once-comforting balm of ignorance, and approached the room in the palace where she sat upon her throne.

THE FIRST BOOK OF SOLOMON

CHAPTER 1

In the time of Solomon's reign in Israel, Ethiopia was under the rule of Makeda, queen of Sheba, and was home to a wealthy merchant named Tamrin, son of Abat. Abat was a farmer and craftsman who was skilled with his hands and generous with his heart. Much of what he grew and made he gave to his friends. Masks, decorative gourds, stone jewelry, and delicious oils and breads came from his small piece of land. He was loved and respected for his skill and kindness.

Tamrin, lean and short-bearded with soft hands and practical mind, loved his father but did not love the work Abat tried to train him to do. He was not as skilled as his father, nor had he the patience to learn to be better. He also did not understand why his father so freely gave away the fruits of his labors. Abat expected Tamrin to work for what he got; why should others who were not family receive such desirable gifts with no compensation or favors performed in return?

Tamrin saw an opportunity to earn a living in a way more suited to his skills. Tamrin was outgoing and friendly, enjoyed meeting new people, always engaged travelers passing through in conversation. He was curious about other lands and how people there lived. He, too, wanted to travel, and he got the idea one day while grinding chickpeas in a bowl Abat had made from a calabash. Tamrin knew that his calling was to be not a farmer and craftsman like his father, but rather a merchant who could sell or trade Abat's foodstuffs and handiwork far beyond the village in which they lived. That was how he could best honor and support his father. Understanding all this, Abat blessed his son's enterprise.

Such was the quality of Abat's products and produce that Tamrin soon found his inventories insufficient. He asked his father to make more things that he could sell, but Abat had all the work of raising animals and cultivating crops and had no assistance now that Tamrin was a traveling merchant. Tamrin had no mother and no siblings and no desire to stop selling, so he began to expand the variety and sources of his offerings. Everywhere he traveled, he offered to help other people sell their wares, be they cattle, grains, spices, clothing, wood, or other items he could sell or trade to willing customers. He visited open marketplaces and soon became a trusted partner to many farmers and artisans.

Tamrin treated all people fairly, and when negotiating a price or his own commission, all parties completed their transactions with smiles on their faces. His compensation was more than enough to sustain his needs, and he shared his earnings with Abat, thus fulfilling his intention to support his father using his own unique skills.

In time, Tamrin established himself as an important and successful man. And so it came to pass that the queen of Sheba herself became aware of his name and his abilities and sent across the sea a ship so that she could meet with him. It was a short journey from the port near his home to Sheba. And then he found himself in her palace, in her presence. Tamrin was comfortable in the company of powerful people, but this queen was different. *So tall, so beautiful*, he thought. Hair as luxurious as her lustrous robe. Her speech was gentle yet authoritative. Her demeanor warm yet serious. When she asked him to represent her officially in matters of trade with other nations, he thought he gladly would go anywhere and do anything for her, be it trade or warfare. With gratitude and humility, Tamrin bowed his head and accepted.

Thus, with her investment and support, he soon commanded a caravan of five-hundred-twenty camels and seventy-three ships, taking him into many lands far from his new home in Sheba and realizing his greatest desires. Tamrin grew wealthier still and continued to give a substantial portion of his earnings to his father, who remained in Ethiopia to the end of his long and blessed life.

Whenever Tamrin journeyed on behalf of his "lady," as he referred to his sovereign and benefactor, he returned not only with payment for the goods he sold—or gifts and goods that he had received or bartered for—but also with stories of what he had seen, the people he had met, and the rulers with whom he had negotiated. Like Tamrin, Makeda had an intense curiosity about the world and its unknowable size and diversity. She knew that if one traveled for a week, the differences in topography and the type of people one would meet were few. Yet if one traveled for a month, one could come upon people of different customs and complexions, tongues and teachings, stories and songs. She dreamed at times that she was half as large as the world itself and that from her throne she could peer one way and the other, seeing in one astounding vista all the peoples and treasures therein.

The world is too large, she complained, *or people are too small. It is not fair that humans should be flung here and there, disconnected by mountains and oceans, canyons and forests. There is too much that I am missing. What great heroes, what inconceivable wonders are there that I may never know?*

Power she had, beauty and wisdom unmatched, but she could not know what lay at the ends of the world. This expansive land that is interrupted only by water: Were it to be traversed over months and years, where might it lead? Who might rule over such distant places, and might that king or queen also be wondering about a land too far away to see, a beautiful land called Ethiopia ruled by a queen who has much and wants more—not possessions, but knowledge? Unlike many other rulers she heard tales about, Makeda was not so interested in conquering other lands as she was of conquering her own ignorance of other lands.

In this she envied Tamrin, whom she sent on faraway journeys to benefit her government and her people through trade. And Tamrin understood well that his visits to foreign lands and his audiences with foreign rulers carried a double purpose: to increase the nation's wealth and to spread Makeda's name and reputation. From his new base of operations in Sheba, Tamrin had easy access to the Red Sea to the immediate west, the Gulf of Eden to the south, and the Arabian Sea to the southeast. With such an advantageous location, he was able to travel to much of the Ethiopian empire—even as far north as lower Egypt—and the Arabian peninsula. Thus word of Makeda's rule, as well as of her wisdom and her beauty, took root in many faraway lands.

Through those same channels, news of other lands came south down the Red Sea and reached her court. And so it was one clear, sweltering day that ships sent by King Solomon of Israel stopped in ports along the Arabian coast with word that trade was requested: the finest materials were sought for a massive temple, a house for the God of the Israelites who had worked miracles for His people. This God had led the Hebrews out of bondage in Egypt to occupy what once had been the land of Canaan, then the tribal lands of Judah and Israel, which were united by David the warrior king and ruled now by David's son, the wise king Solomon.

Makeda sent for Tamrin. She was intrigued about the scale of the temple that this Solomon was building and wanted to know what her trusted trader may have heard about it in his journeys. As Tamrin stood before her, he already was excited about his newest mission.

"You sent for me, my lady?"

"Yes, Tamrin," said Makeda. "No doubt you have heard that the king of Israel invites nations to offer him their goods."

"Indeed I have. And he promises to pay generously for those that meet his standards."

"Sheba never before has had contact with Israel. What do you think of this?"

"I believe it is a wonderful opportunity for us," said Tamrin. "We have much of value to trade with this king who wishes to build a temple to his God. Our black wood is impervious to worms. We have spices and incense to burn and jewels as numerous as the stars in the evening sky. Surely, the king of Israel will welcome your humble servant and pay well for our exceptional products."

"I trust that this is so, Tamrin," said Makeda, "but what manner of man is this who travels so far to buy things he can get at an arm's reach? If he wants fine wood, there are the cedars of Lebanon a day's camel ride away. Jewels he must have in sufficient quantity. Spice buds grow plentifully everywhere. How can you explain this? What more might he be seeking?"

"I can only speak from what I have heard in my travels and from the sailors of Israel who have just arrived at our port, my lady," Tamrin replied. "Solomon's father, King David, was a mighty man of war, devoted to his God and deadly with his sword. Having won his people's security, he desired to erect a temple where he could pay honor to his divine benefactor. But the blood he had spilled rendered him unfit for such a sacred task. Thus it fell to his son, Solomon, given not strength but wisdom, to fulfill his father's work. When completed, this temple will surpass anything that man has made on earth—even the pyramids of Egypt.

"So his messengers claim," Tamrin hastened to add.

"I bid you go to Israel," proclaimed Makeda after just a few moments of thought. "Bring with you large quantities of whatever you feel would be most valued; I desire that the products of Sheba be the centerpiece of this noble undertaking, that all who worship there know it is the treasures of our land that sanctify their praise songs. Negotiate a fair price—do not be greedy in the face of Solomon's wealth, even though he is prepared to open his vaults—but stay awhile and observe him. Learn the form and extent of his wisdom that I may know him as a man worthy of my respect."

And thus did Tamrin assemble materials, men, and provisions for his long and hopefully profitable journey to Solomon's kingdom of Israel. He prepared five ships to bring his party up the Red Sea. This august body of water, where a great miracle had enabled the Israelites to cross with neither boats nor rafts from servitude in Egypt to freedom in Canaan, was oddly shaped, resembling the meat of a snail without its shell. The long narrow inlet separated the southern Arabian peninsula in the east from Ethiopia in the west; farther north, and inland to the west, the Nile River mirrored its path like a growing boy challenging his father. Upon reaching the jutting southern tip of the Sinai Peninsula, the Red Sea split like a snail's two eyestalks, the one to the west forming *Bahr Suez*, the Gulf of Suez; and the one to the east forming *Bahr Aqaba*, the Gulf of Aqaba.

Tamrin would enter the narrow and relatively shallow entrance to the Gulf of Aqaba and sail on until he reached the port city of Eilat, part of the southern Negev Desert. From there, he would journey on foot due north toward Jerusalem as his camels, mules, and asses pulled wagons filled with gold, ebony, and sapphires from the mines and forests of Sheba and surrounding areas. Thus he must load his ships with men, animals, jewels, spices, food, and wood—and quickly, for the journey was long, the rewards were great, and his lady, Queen Makeda, was impatient. She loved to learn, and the subject she now was most curious about was this Solomon. Tamrin would be her eyes and ears in Jerusalem, but until he returned to Sheba, it would be his tongue and the tales it told that she would impatiently await.

CHAPTER 2

The kingdom over which Solomon ruled and ruled wisely had been united under his father, David. Long years of wind and sand, of blood spilled and battles won, tended to obscure the original lines delineating where the twelve tribes of Israel once occupied parcels of the land. Such lines went back to Jacob, the grandson of the patriarch Abraham and the son of Isaac, whom God mercifully had spared in testing Abraham's fealty.

Jacob had been given by God the second name of Israel when he wrestled successfully with an angel; this encounter occurred just prior to a happy reconciliation with his brother Esau who once had vowed to kill him in a dispute over birthright. God thus blessed Jacob, saying to him,

> BE FRUITFUL AND MULTIPLY; A NATION AND A COMPANY OF NATIONS SHALL BE OF THEE, AND KINGS SHALL COME OUT OF THY LOINS. AND THE LAND WHICH I GAVE ABRAHAM AND ISAAC, TO THEE I WILL GIVE IT, AND TO THY SEED AFTER THEE WILL I GIVE THE LAND.

Jacob had twelve sons who were the ancestors of those who would inherit and inhabit the land promised by God. In order of their birth, the sons of Jacob, the sons of Israel who would be one day the people and nation of Israel, were Reuben, Simeon, Levi, Judah, Dan, Naphtali, Gad, Asher, Issachar, Zebulun, Joseph, and Benjamin. Driven by pride, ego, selfishness, and disloyalty, they were a model of disunion, notoriously selling their brother Joseph into slavery in Egypt. But when long months of parched land brought famine, Joseph's brothers suffered with all the peoples in that region, while Joseph had earned a position of power thanks to his ability to divine the meaning of the Pharaoh's dreams.

So it was that Jacob and his eleven sons sojourned in Egypt, where there was food thanks to Joseph's foresight. There again did brothers reconcile as Jacob, on his deathbed, had desired. Not long after, Joseph also died, bequeathing all he had to his sons Ephraim and Manasseh. In Egypt the families prospered and grew for many generations, until all the pharaohs who remembered Joseph had long passed, and the latest pharaohs grew mistrustful of the burgeoning Hebrew population and so enslaved them. But everything is noticed, and God through Moses delivered the Jewish people from bondage. Moses carried the bones of Joseph out from Egypt. And as the people set out from Sinai with the Laws of God to take possession of the land of Canaan that was promised them and to rebury Joseph's bones there, they did so as a tribal nation.

Thus, the twelve tribes that inhabited the land were of Reuben, Simeon, and Gad in the south; Judah, Issachar, and Zebulun in the east; Dan, Naphtali, and Asher in the north; and Ephraim, Manasseh, and Benjamin in the west. The descendants of Levi dispersed among the other tribes, owning no land but occupying cities where they performed priestly duties for the Israelites.

The twelve tribes were bereft of consistent leadership, God tending to send warrior judges to protect them in times of crisis and lead them in battle. The growing need to defend their land led the Israelites to appeal to the prophet Samuel to establish a monarchy over the various Israelite nations. Thus it was that the Benjaminite Saul, victor over the Ammonites, was anointed the first king of Israel. Yet Saul twice disobeyed God and, because everything is noticed, God found disfavor with Saul and sent Samuel to find his successor. Samuel was directed to look within the tribe of Judah, from the house of Jesse, whose father was Obed, born of Ruth and nursed by Naomi.

Jesse was blessed with several sons, but only the names of four have endured in memory: Eliab, the oldest, tall and handsome; Abinadab; Shammah; and David, the youngest, also fair of face and working as a humble shepherd boy. Yet when David's older brothers, each after the other, were rejected by Samuel, he was summoned by his father Jesse to leave the field where he was tending his flock. The word of God entered Samuel's ear, declaring that young David would be the successor to Saul's throne and instructing the prophet to anoint him in the presence of his brothers. Being still a boy, David was not yet to be king. But his future soon would be revealed to all.

One night, Saul was visited by an evil spirit and in the morning felt unwell. He requested soothing music to be played for him. A servant had heard David's skill with a harp, which he played while his sheep grazed. A second time was David summoned from the field, this time to perform for the king. Saul was greatly moved by David's music, and so the handsome, talented shepherd boy with skin the shade of earthen olives and hair colored with the ink of the midnight sky became a valued member of Saul's court.

In a few years' time, there came to be a conflict between the Israelites and the Philistines. The enemy's champion, a behemoth named Goliath, stood more than twice again as tall as any of Saul's soldiers. The size and strength of Goliath put fear in the hearts of those who would defend Israel, and no one in the army or any other man in the land would accept the giant's challenge. But David had no fear. He spoke to Saul, saying, "Many are the times a lion or other beast has tried to take one of my sheep for a meal, but always I have fought them off, leaving them dead or discouraged from trying again to harm my flock. As I have done to them, so will I do to the Philistine."

David met Goliath in the valley between the encampments of the Israelite and Philistine armies. Armed with a sling made of calfskin and rounded stones the size of the young man's fist, David accepted Goliath's challenge. To observers who stood a safe distance away, it appeared he had no weapon at all, while the giant's sword and spear gleamed in the light of the day's high sun. Neither the disparity in size nor of armament intimidated the challenger, who stood his ground like the *alon*, or oak tree. The hulking enemy took offense at the spare competitor and cared not to delay the inevitable outcome. He charged toward David, and just before he was close enough to strike a blow, the courageous boy delivered a stone with such force and aim so true that it lodged in Goliath's skull and felled him. David took the Philistine's sword and removed his head, thus claiming victory.

Saul was much pleased by David's valor and strength. Adding to his several duties, David then became for Saul a warrior as well. Yet as David, now older and stronger, won more victories, the people sang his praises with such fervor that it brought feelings of shame and anger to Saul. David, they rejoiced, slew tens of thousands, while Saul's kills numbered only in the thousands. Thus began several attempts on David's life by Saul. But everything is noticed, and the God of Israel was with His favored David at all times, giving him victories—complementing the gifts of beauty, talent, courage, and strength He already had given the popular warrior—and keeping him from harm.

Finally there came the day when Saul, leading his troops into battle, suffered defeat. Rather than being taken prisoner, he impaled himself on his sword. Saul's son, Ish-Boshet, immediately took over the throne as king of Israel. Yet the tribes of Judah and Simeon, desiring the protection of David's proven strength, cast their lot with him instead, and the prolific warrior became their sovereign, taking Judah as his ruling perch. With two kings ruling a common people, dissention was inevitable. Ish-Boshet and David fought for supremacy. Unsurprisingly, it was David who emerged victorious, and at thirty years of age, he became sole ruler of a newly united kingdom. Under his reign, the nations of Judah and Israel were one.

Because of its ideal location, bordering on—yet independent of—both Judah and Israel, Jerusalem was chosen by David as the capital of his kingdom, and he declared it to be known as the City of David. Thus was the "city of peace" (as Jerusalem may be translated) renamed after a man of war.

Among the first of the neighboring sovereigns to recognize David's primacy as ruler of Israel was Hiram, king of the Phoenician city of Tyre. Situated on the eastern coast of the Mediterranean Sea, Tyre was known as a powerful trading center. Seeking an alliance, and mindful of David's many military successes, Hiram arrived in person to deliver words of honor and to make a generous offer.

"Your victories are great, David, king of Israel, and your strength impressive."

"My strength and my victories are granted to me by *Adonai*, the God of Israel," David replied. "All that I am is because of the Lord's will."

"Then I praise your God and beg you to honor me with your friendship. May Jerusalem under your rule know only peace."

"If it is so, it will be because God wills it. If it is not so, then I pray He will continue to guide my hand in battle to defend this place where I will build my palace."

"If it is here you wish to live, King David, you will need an architect. You will need cedar. You will need carpenters and stonemasons. The soil of Tyre nurtures the finest cedar to be found anywhere. The artisans of Tyre are admired far and wide for their skill. I will supply all of this for you as a sign of my friendship and my loyalty to you."

"I accept your friendship and your gifts, Hiram, with the gratitude and respect of all my people," said David. "You will forever be a welcome and honored guest in my home and throughout the land of Israel."

So it was that the friendship between Hiram and David was sealed and remained in force until the end of David's days. Hiram had initiated the relationship not out of fear of a mighty neighboring military but because he was a peaceable ruler who knew that the more nations he was friendly with, the more nations he could trade with. And given that Israel stood between Tyre and the Red Sea, his friendship with David would ensure easy passage to Eilat, from which Hiram's traders could sail south. Still, many a journey veers from its initial course, and as David proved loyal to Hiram and sent gifts to reward the Tyrian ruler's generosity, Hiram began to feel true kinship with David.

When construction of David's palace was finished, the king ordered that the holy Ark of the Covenant, which had been built and carried for years in the desert, be brought to Jerusalem from its temporary location in Judah. The Ark was placed on a cart, a new cart built especially for this sacred purpose, and taken into the City of David. On its approach, David and many thousands of his people danced with joy to the ringing and beating of timbrels.

A feast followed the requisite sacrifices and all went home to sleep. In the morning, David was visited by Nathan the prophet, who found the king far more somber than he had been on the day before.

"Why do you look troubled, my son? Is this not a time for joy?"

"It is that, Nathan," said David. "But I fear my work is not finished. Here I sit in a house of marble and cedar with every comfort attending me, while the Ark of the Covenant is but a box upon a table, with little more than sun-whitened curtains adorning it."

"What would you propose to do about this, David?"

"I wish to build a temple for the Lord. A sacred space for the Ark and a home for God Himself, a place where He might dwell and observe as we make our offerings to Him. Would such an undertaking be blessed, Nathan? Would God find me in favor to build such a temple to Him?"

"The Lord has been with thee many times. I cannot find a reason why He should not be with thee still."

Nathan's answer pleased David, and the king entered a restful sleep. Yet that very night, Nathan was visited by the presence of the Lord. And God's words were harsh, especially for one so favored as David.

Nathan liked David; they had known each other when they were children in the land of Judah. Only recently had Nathan been chosen by God to be a prophet of His word. However, Nathan had not yet been called to spread His word to the people at large; rather, God chose him to be His intermediary with David, for only the great Moses had known the Lord directly.

Moses, after the first year of the Israelites' wandering in the wilderness, had been instructed by the Lord to build a tabernacle to house the Ark of the Covenant while they traveled. When the people pitched camp, the tribes would erect their tents around it. When it was time to break camp and continue their trek across the desert toward the Promised Land, they would break it down and set it up again the next time they rested. The tabernacle was then both a visual reminder of God's glory and presence, and the physical and spiritual center of the community.

It had been given to Moses to build the tabernacle; now, David sought to be the one who would build the permanent house for the Ark and for the glory and spirit of God. Yet though he brought the Ark of the Covenant from Judah to Jerusalem, no further could he advance his desire. God gave a message to Nathan, that he should return to David with these words:

> ART THOU TO BUILD FOR ME A DWELLING PLACE? FROM THE TIME THAT I BROUGHT MY PEOPLE OUT OF BONDAGE IN EGYPT TO THIS VERY DAY, HAVE I RESIDED IN ANY HOME OR TEMPLE? I ALLOWED MY SPIRIT TO SETTLE WITHIN THE TABERNACLE ONLY SO THAT THE ISRAELITES WHO NEEDED TO SEE WITH THEIR EYES THAT I WAS WITH THEM SHOULD HAVE THAT SIGN. BUT A TABERNACLE IS NO HOUSE OF CEDAR AND MARBLE. CAN ONE WHO OCCUPIES THE HEIGHTS OF HEAVEN, WHO LOOKS DOWN THE TOPS OF MOUNTAINS AND SEES EVEN TO THE DEPTHS OF THE OCEANS, DWELL WITHIN A STRUCTURE MADE BY MEN?
>
> I LOVE THEE, DAVID, AND I AM WITH THEE. FROM A LEADER OF SHEEP TO A LEADER OF MEN HAVE I MADE THEE, AND I HAVE DELIVERED THY ENEMIES INTO THINE HANDS. I HAVE MADE THE NAME OF DAVID A GREAT NAME, AND I WILL GIVE THY PEOPLE WHO ARE MY PEOPLE A HOME FROM WHICH THEY NEED ESCAPE NO LONGER. TO THEE I GIVE A HOUSE, THAT IS A DYNASTY OF KINGS FROM THY NAME, SO THAT WHEN THY DAYS HAVE ENDED, THY SEED WILL CONTINUE TO THRIVE IN THE KINGDOM I HAVE ESTABLISHED.
>
> AND THIS SON WHO WILL SUCCEED YOU, HE SHALL BE A MAN OF PEACE AND HE WILL BUILD A HOUSE FOR MY NAME. I SHALL BE AS HIS FATHER, AND HE AS MY SON. IF HE COMMITS A SIN AGAINST ME, I WILL PUNISH HIM HARSHLY, BUT MY MERCY SHALL NEVER LEAVE HIM AS I TOOK BACK MY

MERCY FROM SAUL THAT THOU MIGHT SUCCEED HIM. THY HOUSE AND THY KINGDOM, DAVID MY SON, ARE THUS ESTABLISHED NOW AND FOREVER. BUT THE HOUSE THAT THOU WOULD BUILD FOR ME IS NOT THINE TO BUILD. THE HANDS THAT WILL BUILD MY HOUSE ARE NOT THY HANDS.

These are the words that were given to Nathan that night, and those words did Nathan relate to David the next day. Though the words were a rebuke to David's ambition, they also were a blessing to him, and David's love for God was such that he understood the message he was given. He was neither angry nor heartbroken, but grateful that God continued to find favor with him and would establish his dynasty such that the house of David would rule Israel for generations to come.

David approached the Ark, made a meal offering to the Lord, and prayed aloud a praise song thanking God for His benevolent mercy and kindness, both upon him and upon the people of Israel, blessing the Creator of the world that His name may be magnified and sanctified for all time, for there is but one God that rules over heaven and earth. Though God would ever be with David, David would not always walk God's path and so one day would pay a dear price.

Because everything is noticed.

CHAPTER 3

David was a brave warrior who exuded confidence and faith in God every time he fought an intruding army, and his fearlessness extended off the battlefield, as well. His passions plunged him into rash decisions that brought stern rebukes from the God he loved and otherwise served so faithfully.

One night, while the ugliness of war smoldered around Israel's borders, David climbed to the roof of his palace to meditate under the canopy of the heavens. From his vantage point, he espied a beautiful woman bathing nearby. David, who had seven wives already, had never been so struck by the loveliness of a woman. He had to have her, no matter the consequences.

He learned that she was Bathsheba, the daughter of Eliam of Giloh, a respected and decorated soldier in David's army, and granddaughter of Ahithophel, a trusted advisor to the king. Yet even more important than that, Bathsheba was the wife of Uriah the Hittite, a soldier currently fighting at the behest of David and for the security of his kingdom.

No matter. David sent for Bathsheba and lay with her, impregnating her with his seed. To cover up the act, he ordered Uriah home from battle. His plan was that Uriah and Bathsheba would have intercourse, and then the soldier would believe he himself was the father of the child. But Uriah was loyal to David and intent on maintaining his strength. He twice refused to enter his house and instead spent consecutive nights with the king's slaves, ready and eager to return to the fighting.

This frustrated David—not because his soldier was loyal and committed to defending the kingdom, but because his dedication threatened to expose the king's own misdeed. Finally, David ordered that Uriah be sent to the region where the most intense fighting was taking place. There, Uriah fell in battle, loyal to his sovereign unto the end.

Thus was David able to take Bathsheba as his eighth wife. He was with her as she bore their son, but the judgment of the Lord was that the child would die for his father's sin. And so it came to pass, and the baby took his final breath while the mighty warrior king stood helpless. David grieved not only for his son, but for his own failings as well. In time, David and Bathsheba had another son, whom they named Solomon. And while David would in the future have troubles with his other sons, Absolam and Adonijah, each of whom would plot to seize their father's crown, the chosen one would again be the youngest one: Solomon.

Everything is noticed.

After three and thirty years' reign over the united kingdom of Israel and Judah, David died. Word soon reached Hiram on his throne in Tyre, where the sadness he felt at the death of his friend was lessened by the knowledge that the Davidic rule would continue with the ascension of Solomon as king. Hiram sent envoys to Solomon with a message of unbroken friendship and loyalty, and the assurance that the son would be in Hiram's eyes the equal of the father, and the promises made to one would be honored to the other.

And yet Solomon was different from his father in almost every way. Though carnal pleasures were not to be unknown to him, David's heir to the throne sought wisdom over war and to bring forth justice in earthly matters just as God did in matters eternal. This gift did God grant him one day in a dream. With no temple, sacrifices were made at various hill-shrines, local sanctuaries built on elevations around the city. Thus it was that one day Solomon came to the hill-shrine at Gibeon, the largest of the hill-shrines, to make there a burnt offering to the Lord. It was late, and he decided to rest before offering his sacrifice. He fell asleep and was visited in his sleep by God. God asked Solomon, "What is it that thou desireth of Me?" And Solomon responded humbly and truthfully:

"O Lord my God, you bestowed every blessing upon my father, David, as he walked with Thee, even to give to him the son who now sits on his throne. Though I am a grown man, I feel as a child occupying the place of my father, your steadfast servant David. How am I to rule over Your people? For indeed they are Your people and not mine. A great people whom You have chosen and blessed, and whom ultimately You will judge. But for me to govern them on earth, to lead them in accordance with Your will and Your unending mercy, I need an open and understanding heart. Help me to distinguish between good and evil, that I may be equal to the task of leading Your chosen people."

This appeal greatly pleased the Lord, who responded to Solomon,

MANY MEN ASCENDING A THRONE SEEK THE DEATH OF THEIR ENEMIES, PHYSICAL STRENGTH AND FORTITUDE, GREAT WEALTH, AND LONG YEARS TO ESTABLISH AND EXPAND THEIR POWER. BUT THOU HAVE ASKED FOR THE ABILITY TO MAKE DECISIONS THAT ARE JUST AND FAIR, WHICH REQUIRES A HEART THAT FEELS COMPASSION AND A MIND THAT ALWAYS KNOWS TRUTH. I WILL GIVE THEE THESE THINGS FOR WHICH THOU ASK IN AN ABUNDANCE THAT EXCEEDS THAT WHICH I HAVE ALLOWED FOR ANY OF MY CREATURES. THY WISDOM WILL BE RECOGNIZED AND REVERED THROUGHOUT THE EARTH.

Then Solomon awoke and made his sacrifice at the altar at Gibeon. And from that time forward, David's son was known as the wisest of the wise. Though settling disputes was thought to be beneath the dignity of a monarch, no other authority was as respected as his, for no one was more intelligent than he, nor was anyone known to be equally so. Therefore, many people came to Jerusalem to hear his verdict on their matters, be they of great importance or small. Thus was the prophecy of Isaiah fulfilled:

"And there shall come forth from the house of Jesse a king for all of Israel. And the spirit of God shall be within him, granting him wisdom and understanding, counsel and might, knowledge and the fear of God. With

righteousness shall he judge the poor, and with compassion shall he deal justly with the humbled of the land."

Which is not to say that Solomon was incapable of defending Israel from attack. After all, he had at his disposal the well-trained and well-tested army that had been built by his father. Indeed, shortly after assuming the throne he was threatened by an old foe, the Philistines. Yet now Israel had a powerful ally—and an unlikely one at that.

Siamun, sixth pharaoh of Egypt, last ruler of the twenty-first dynasty, was unlike pharaohs of the past. He was more interested in building alliances outside Egypt than monuments within. The Philistines saw the transition of power in Israel as an opportunity to avenge the many defeats they had suffered at the hands of David since the time of Goliath's slaying, but Siamun offered the strength of his own forces to quell any Philistine offensive.

As it transpired, Siamun did not wait for such an attack. Instead, he invaded and lay waste to the Philistine city of Gezer, located thirty kilometers northwest of Jerusalem. With a rough landscape of caves and boulders, Gezer was not well-fortified by the Philistine army and fell easily. Siamun never intended, however, to claim the spoils for himself; rather, he presented Gezer to Solomon as a token of their alliance. By occupying Gezer, Solomon was able to secure Israel's southern border—which, by virtue of Israel's partnership with Siamun, protected Egypt's lucrative trade route to Phoenecia. Disrupting that trade route had been part of the Philistines' far-ranging strategy of regional domination, which now was upset by Siamun and Solomon's new friendship.

In the joy of their successful venture, and as a visible symbol of their mutual allegiance, Siamun offered his eldest daughter, Kanika, to Israel's bachelor king. Solomon accepted eagerly and with gratitude, for Kanika was young and beautiful. He thought little of the irony that his people, having escaped the slavery imposed on them by a long-ago pharaoh, now had familial ties with an Egyptian ruler. Or that the Israelites' leader on earth, Moses, who with God's arm had brought them from slavery to freedom, was himself saved by the daughter of that long-ago pharaoh who five centuries earlier had raised the Hebrew babe as his own son. And just as that daughter lifted Moses from the Nile, so did

Solomon take Kanika from her Nile kingdom to Israel, building a tent for her near the river Sorek, where Samson had been seduced by Delilah, a Philistine operative more deadly in her own way than even Goliath.

With a valuable new ally in his arsenal, Solomon reached out to an older one. For as David's body was now buried within the clay of the land God had provided to the Israelite nation, Solomon's eyes looked to build upon it. Having received Hiram of Tyre's message of condolence and continuing friendship, he was ready to reply. He drafted a message thanking Hiram and pledging that Israel would always be a friend to the people of Tyre, and to their enemies a foe.

And further, the note that Solomon bade his envoys to deliver in person said:

"You are aware, Hiram, that my father, David, desired to build a temple unto the God of Israel, but he was not permitted to do so while the land remained under siege by enemies all around us. As my father told us both, God wished that I, his direct descendent, should build that temple. You provided David with the materials needed to construct his palace in his time. And so I request that you send me architects, workmen, wood of cedar and of pine, and other materials of which Tyre is well known, that God's will be done in my time."

Solomon made it clear to Hiram that he could set any price he wished; Hiram asked merely for food for his people, because an infestation had ruined a substantial portion of Tyre's crops. Though his kingdom was still wealthy, Hiram saw that his people were hungry. What's more, the agricultural crops that they used for trade, including timber, were less plentiful and so did not bring much food in return. Solomon agreed to provide yearly twenty thousand kor of wheat and twenty kor of olive oil, a kor being roughly one bushel in dry measure and ten gallons in liquid measure.

Because the infestation in Tyre affected both the quantity and quality of the timber, Solomon sent out word to other trading partners to supplement what Hiram could not provide. Ships and caravans went out in all directions, including down the Red Sea. Thus it was that Makeda learned of Solomon and the temple he wished to build, then bade Tamrin to set sail to do trade with Solomon, that Sheba might have a share in the glorious work that was becoming the talk of the entire Mediterranean. And then, with this deed done, the region would talk as well of Sheba and of its young but impressive queen, Makeda.

THE FIRST BOOK OF MAKEDA

CHAPTER 1

The law predated the memories of the elders, who knew through generation upon generation of oral tradition much that transpired before their time on earth. All that was known for certain was that the law had been followed for centuries, such that for all most people knew or cared, it had been this way since the creation of the world. It was the law that said only a woman could reign in Ethiopia, and that the queen must be chaste. Yet this was not so in Sheba, a wealthy and independent kingdom in southern Arabia with strong ties to Ethiopia. There, kings had ruled for centuries, and a single family had maintained the throne for three-hundred-fifty years—the last fifty of which had been under the rule of King Za Sabado, who successfully leveraged the wealth and strong arms of his homeland to establish Sheba as the seat of power over all of Ethiopia.

Za Sabado and his wife, Queen Ceres, had one child, a daughter they named Ismenie. When the princess grew to womanhood, she married Kawnasya, who served as chief minister to Za Sabado and thus was next in line to the throne. Makeda, the only child of Kawnasya and Ismenie, was but six years old when her grandfather died, making her father the new king. With no sibling, the young girl was herself in the line of succession, a fact that amused her for she was but a child.

Makeda grew up privileged, not only in wealth and power but also in beauty and wisdom. Yet she knew hardship as well, for her mother died from an illness when Makeda was barely ten, and she was only sixteen when her father also died—he from injuries suffered in a failed coup attempt. Her grief accompanied her to the throne of Sheba. That was not all. In his final words to his daughter, Kawnasya told Makeda to rule justly, to increase Sheba's influence and wealth in the region through trade, and, finally, to follow Ethiopian tradition and rule as a virgin queen.

This last instruction took her aback. Not that Makeda wouldn't do whatever her beloved father told her to do, but her fledgling, untested sexuality had never before been discussed. Her mother having died before Makeda began to develop the physical characteristics of maturity, she had no instruction in what it was to become a woman. Yet because she grew up in a royal family, numerous servant women watched for and attended to the onset of Makeda's puberty: the growth and shapeliness of breasts crowned with carob nipples and the menstrual flow that signaled her young body's readiness for a maternity she was to be denied.

If her father had taken notice of Makeda's emerging maturity, he never mentioned it to her. And whether his instruction to her about maintaining her virginity was the unreasonable reaction of a guarded, wifeless sire or a well-considered political statement to the surrounding kingdoms the young queen would have to rule alongside, was unknown. But it was the final utterance of a king to his successor before transitioning into the infinite beyond, and thus it carried the full force of law.

Thus it was that Makeda, hymen intact, became the queen of Sheba. Strong-minded and adventuresome, she nonetheless vowed to remain just, chaste, and resourceful, in keeping with her father's wishes. Though still young, she was already more worldly than most, as she had been born in the Red Sea port city of Ophir—a gold-laced area whose docks frequently welcomed the ships of Hiram of Tyre—and had been educated by the most respected teachers in Ethiopia. She therefore took the throne with confidence, poise, and conviction, as befitting her name, Makeda, which meant "great one."

And a great one she was. She was tall for her age and would be tall for all her ages, tall as many men and taller still than some. As a girl, even as a princess, Makeda learned to casually stoop so as not to look down on a shorter male, especially a visiting dignitary or other important man of her father's court. Now, as queen, she could straighten her back and let her head—crowned with long, thick black hair—reach its tallest plateau, for the greater her height, the greater her perceived strength and power. Though young, Makeda was not frail; in fact, her physical strength was unusual for a girl, and she never backed away from a challenge.

As she was tall for her age, so Makeda was wise beyond her years. The very act of learning, the process of gaining knowledge, was exciting to her. If passion and reason were two goblets of wine to drink, she would always choose the latter, greedily lapping every last sweet thoughtful drop. Her teachers stretched her brain with riddles, yet soon her own questions outnumbered and outwitted their own.

For many years, since before the reign of Makeda's grandfather Za Sabado, Sheba had been a regional center of knowledge about the stars and heavenly bodies. The sun and moon were worshipped as gods to be feared and placated, for they held the cycles of the days and seasons in their mighty, radiant hands. Shams was the sun god, Ilumqah the moon god. The reigning monarch was expected to be able to interpret the positions of the sun and moon, as well as the stars that dotted the ebon skin of evening, and explain what they meant, what they foretold.

"*Astamari*," she inquired one day to her teacher, one day about a year before she became queen, "how is it that we know of the sun and moon and stars? There is no one who can reach or hold them in their hands. I look up and wave my arms but they give me no sign. I ask them questions, yet they remain mute."

"My student, they make themselves known to us," her teacher answered patiently, "not the reverse. Their positions in the sky change over time, their brightness strengthens and weakens throughout the seasons. They tell us when to plant and when to reap. They tell us when to travel and when to seek shelter. The hot light of the sun and the cold light of the moon are as parents to us: one who provides for us and one who comforts us; one who shows us the way, one who gives us to rest."

"And what of the stars, *astamari*?"

"The stars above our heads, my student, are as the sand beneath our feet. Just as this is the ground on which we stand, the stars in the firmament support Shams and Ilumqah."

"Last night I lay on the ground and looked up at the sky," said Makeda. "And I saw a star leave its place and tumble down to earth, leaving a trail of sparks in its wake."

"Yes, my student, I saw it, too. What is your question?"

"Do the gods visit us, *astamari*? Do the stars come to earth to create a ground on which Shams and Ilumqah can perch and be among us?"

Her teacher was silent a moment. He smiled, then responded. "This is a good question, my student. My answer is this: The lights of heaven are farther away than you can ever imagine. No caravan with the wings of eagles could reach them in a hundred lifetimes. Yet they do reach us. Their light illumines all of Ethiopia whereas a wood fire we make for cooking, hot as it may be, lights the ground for only a few paces in any direction.

"The lesson is this, my student: You need not seek the gods we worship, though they look at us from far away. They are with you always. They and all our ancestors, who in death are blessed with eternal life among the spirits in heaven. All of them are guides for you. To find them, all you must do is pray and they will respond."

"Then why do we learn their positions in the sky, *astamari*? Why do we chart them?"

"So that we might understand time and the cycles of the seasons, my student," said her teacher. "One day you may sit upon your father's throne and rule over Sheba. You will need to know when our festivals begin, when rain will feed our crops, when is the right time to conduct trade, and when is the right time to do battle. These the gods tell us indirectly, that by our own ability to decipher the meanings of the celestial positions, we gain an advantage over other peoples. As queen, your power and the prosperity of your people will depend on your knowledge of the sun and moon and stars that fill you with wonder today."

Makeda looked up. The sky seemed peaceful, perfectly arrayed. She looked forward to mastering the lessons her beloved teacher taught her. She desired this knowledge greatly, much more than being queen, which seemed as far away in time as Shams and Ilumqah were in space.

As for her beauty, it was not something she recognized or thought of. Many had told her she was beautiful, but what value did that hold, compared to strength and wisdom? *I can make myself stronger by working my body*, she would often tell herself. *I can make myself smarter by working my mind. But I cannot change the face I was given, so why give it power over me?* Being sworn to chastity, the only physical attributes she deemed worthwhile were muscular arms, a strong back, and legs that could take one from place to place. All these Makeda possessed, cloaked in perfect skin that in sunlight shined of deepest bronze. Taken together, her strength, wisdom, and beauty drew interest to Sheba as never before, and despite her relative youth, those traits brought good feelings throughout the Ethiopian empire over which she ruled.

CHAPTER 2

Makeda inherited a wealthy kingdom, thanks to abundant natural resources and a reverence for learning that made Sheba a leader not only in astrology but in agriculture and engineering as well. While her people were worshipfully subservient to the sun and the moon, they sought to tame the earth and the water. They built dams and wells and fashioned a system of irrigation that enabled them to produce lush crops despite the tropical heat that encrusted the ginger soil.

Among these crops were spices of abundant variety, widely desired both for sacrificial offerings and for cooking. Indeed, many a trader stayed in Sheba an extra few days for the sake of enjoying the local hospitality. They returned to their lands of origin with the scent of saffron still in their nostrils. Within the earth and rock were found gold and precious stones from which the artisans of Sheba made jewelry. Saffron and cumin, sand and stone, gold and grain—many of Sheba's most precious resources and valuable assets shared amber hues of varying degrees from the most holy sun god. Surely the land and people of Sheba were blessed.

Adding to their riches was a beautiful, young, and charismatic new queen, one that her people felt they knew well. For as a girl, Makeda had been everywhere, playing, learning, exploring her world with the other children out in the open, and with no guards or guardians keeping watch over her. Her parents, King Kawnasya and Queen Ismenie, encouraged her to be no different from the other children. The kingdom had been largely at peace with its neighbors for years, Sheba's trading partners were satisfied, and there was no need to fear that harm could come to their daughter from threats either within or outside the country.

And yet harm did come. One day when Makeda was nine years old, as she ran through a grove, she inadvertently came between a black-backed jackal and its prey, a mole rat separated from its secure subterranean tunnel. The jackal, its animus fueled by hunger and instinct, lunged at Makeda's left leg, tearing the flesh and tendons from her ankle nearly to her calf. She went down quickly and hard, the jackal's jaws still locked on its catch. Maintaining her wits, Makeda grabbed a stick within reach and began striking the beast's head. The jackal released its grip and, remembering its original target, ran off in search of the mole rat. Despite her serious injury, Makeda slowly began to make her way back to the palace on her own, leaving a trail of blood.

A farmer coming back from the market with his mule saw her limping along with a look of anguish marring her sweet face. He ran to her, lifted her into his arms, carried her back to his mule, and gently placed the princess on the creature's back. He removed his *keffiyeh*, unfolded the traditional headdress, and wrapped it around her wounds. Then he struck the mule's rump and walked swiftly alongside until they were in sight of the palace guards, who burst forward and took the princess inside to be treated by the king's physician. King Kawnasya himself later returned the cleaned *keffiyeh* to the compassionate farmer; inside the folded cloth were twenty gold coins and a pouch of myrrh for ritual burning.

Makeda recovered from the attack, but her leg was permanently scarred, the only flaw in her great beauty. Following the injury, she learned to disguise her limp by walking more slowly and she kept her wanderings closer to home to avoid straining her leg. Once she ascended to the throne, the virgin queen dressed in long robes so that the defiled limb would not be seen.

As a child, Makeda's closest companion was a girl named Eleni. Shorter, not as pretty, but just as smart and curious as Makeda, Eleni was a first cousin, the youngest daughter of Ismenie's brother, Tefere, who was first a soldier and then an advisor to Makeda's father. There was not a little jealousy between Tefere and his younger sister, whom he considered inferior to him, yet there she was, occupying the prestigious space beside the king. Despite his relation to the queen, Tefere held no special position or influence; his being named an advisor to the king was in actuality merely a courtesy. He and his family lived in tents woven from goat hair just as the common people did, not in a house made of mud brick and stone as befitted those with higher status. And certainly not in a palace.

Tefere's jealousy was known to Eleni, in the way that children uncover secrets about their parents that they find humorous but know never to mention aloud to others. It mattered not to her anyway, for she and Makeda had enjoyed being together ever since they were babies. They dug in the ground together in search of treasures, learned together with their beloved teachers, ran together through the plains and forests, climbed trees and sampled their fruits. They were nearly inseparable.

Yet on the day of Makeda's unfortunate experience with the jackal, they were apart. Eleni was sick with a stomach ailment. With no chores to do or lessons to study, she was enjoying quiet time with her mother, drinking an herbal tea that her mother had brewed for her to help ease her discomfort. Queen Ismenie had sent an inquiry to ask how she was feeling. Considering how ill she felt, Eleni was comforted by the attention she received.

Her reverie was disturbed by a commotion in the street. People were shouting about something. Eleni's mother went out to see what was wrong. After several minutes, she returned to the tent in a state of panic with a deeply concerned look on her face.

"What is wrong, Mother?" asked Eleni.

"It is Makeda," her mother replied, drying her eyes. "She is hurt."

"Hurt? How?"

"I don't know, my child, an animal I think. A farmer brought her home with a bloodied leg. She was then carried into the palace to be seen by the doctor. That is all I know."

"Was she out in the woods where we play, Mother? If I was not sick, I would have been with her. I might have been hurt as well."

"Well, thankfully you're not hurt, Eleni. I'm sure she will be all right. I must make some lentil soup for her."

"Ooh, *yemisir shorba*," cooed Eleni. "That is my favorite. Will you make some for me, too, Mother?"

"Eleni, Makeda is badly hurt, and she is the princess of Sheba. We must think now of helping her and the king and queen. You have a sour stomach, and it will be better soon. Makeda may not walk again. You mustn't think only of yourself."

This advice did not sit well with Eleni. She *was* concerned about her friend. But she also knew that whenever they were together, in good times and bad, whether healthy or infirm, regardless of who might be the instigator and who the follower, always Makeda was treated more favorably than she. If Eleni performed better in a lesson, still Makeda was the one praised for her wisdom. Makeda never acted like a princess when she was with Eleni; she was only too happy to dirty her knees, throw rocks at camels, and explore forbidden areas such as caves and deep woods. But Eleni was ever aware that they never could be equals.

It was only after two days had passed that both Eleni and Makeda were well enough to see each other again. Makeda's leg was wrapped tightly in a linen bandage that had to be changed thrice daily. For fear of continued bleeding, she was not yet permitted to walk, but she sat up and happily welcomed Eleni's company.

"How did it happen?" Eleni asked, eyeing the wooden crutch leaning against Makeda's cushioned chair, which had been provided so the princess could go to an adjacent private room to relieve herself in a limestone commode.

"I'm not sure," said Makeda. "It was so sudden. I was walking through the grove looking at the flowers, and from nowhere that I could see, a jackal lunged at me and bit hard on my leg."

"Were you afraid?"

"Only after the attack. Then I realized I was alone, bleeding badly, and far from home. I don't know if I could have made it all the way had a farmer not kindly put me on his mule."

"I'm sorry I wasn't with you to help you," Eleni said, turning away from her friend, "but I was sick with a very serious pain in my belly. I couldn't eat anything. My parents were very worried about me."

"I know, I heard," Makeda said. "I'm so glad you feel better."

"Usually, with a pain as bad as mine, one would not be able to leave one's bed for a week. But you know how strong I am," Eleni said, now facing her friend proudly. "I amazed my parents by being able to recover so quickly."

"Not me," said Makeda. "I can't walk for a few more days, until the doctor is sure that my leg won't start bleeding again."

"If you were as strong as I am, you could do it. Look, it is so tightly bandaged, what could happen to it? Perhaps the pain is too much for you to bear."

"There is no pain, but the jackal's teeth made deep holes in my leg. It will take a while for them to heal."

"Well, as I was walking over here, I noticed that there are ripe guavas on a tree down the road, near my home. I'm going to go pick one and eat it with my lunch. It's a shame you haven't the strength to come along and get one for yourself."

"You won't bring me one, Eleni?"

"Oh, I would, Makeda, but it's so close to my home and it's almost time for me to help my mother with lunch anyway. I just don't have the time to come all the way back here. So I'll visit you again tomorrow, if it pleases you."

"Wait," Makeda called as Eleni turned to leave. "A ripe guava sounds so good. Let me try to get up. It's not that long a walk."

And slowly, with no help from Eleni, Makeda did bring herself to a standing position. She took hold of the wooden crutch and took a step, grimacing in pain. But resolved not to let Eleni get the better of her, she took another step and then, gingerly, another until she and Eleni were walking out the door and down the road.

Makeda enjoyed being outside again in the fresh air and sunshine, and though she knew that Eleni was trying to shame her into an ill-advised activity, she was glad to defy her doctor, especially if the reward was the juicy semi-sweetness of ripe pink guava flesh. As they walked, she recalled a legend about the guava that she had heard from a Philippine sailor who had arrived in Ophir to exchange goods. It went like this:

Pleasurable as it is now, the guava fruit was once just as poisonous. Such was its power to kill those who ate it, the king declared the guava forbidden. It was allowed to grow wild, but none could cultivate, harvest, or serve it either to man or beast. One family owned a fruit orchard rich with many varieties, including one guava tree. The father picked what he could from the edible fruits to sell in the market. The mother picked what she could from the edible fruits to make pies. Their son was fond of playing in the orchard, which was on the edge of their property alongside a busy road.

Every day, hungry people would walk slowly by, looking with want and desire upon the fruit. The boy was generous and kind, and would give whatever edible fruits he could reach to the poor and needy he met. It came to pass one day that all the edible fruits were gone, and among all the bare trees, the only fruitful one was the guava tree. Soon enough, an aged woman came by and asked the boy if she could have some fruit. Her thin, withered face was in need of nutrition. Her eyes, nearly blind, could not see that only guava fruits remained. The boy, not wishing to refuse the old woman, picked a guava and said over it a prayer to the gods of the forests, that this fruit's poison be driven out, that it should provide sustenance to the woman.

Having uttered this simple, silent prayer, he gave the woman the fruit and wished her peace and long life. The woman ate the fruit and not only did not die, she became all the stronger for having eaten it. Her back, once stooped, straightened. Her eyes, two squints, became round and saw clearly. Her face, once a raisin, now was as full as a plum. Such was her transformation that the boy picked another guava and ate it himself. He, too, became stronger. From that time, the guava fruit, blessed with the prayer of a boy whose goodness was pure and plentiful, became a delicacy, satisfying to king and beggar alike.

They were but a few paces from the guava tree when Makeda lost her footing on a raised root and fell, her crutch of no use, her friend a passive witness to the accident. Makeda cried out, immediately regretting expressing her pain in front of Eleni. For her part, Eleni, recognizing that the cry brought attention to the princess' unfortunate situation, knelt to help her back on her feet. But she was stopped by the call of her mother, who was nearby and astonished to see the two girls together on the road.

"Eleni! What are you doing? Why have you brought Makeda out when she needs rest?"

"We wanted to pick some guavas, mother," Eleni replied hurriedly. "Makeda wanted one, and I said I would help her."

"You run and fetch the wagon, girl," rebuked her mother. "We must take Makeda back home at once. Look, her wound is bleeding again."

Eleni began to protest but understood it would change nothing. Though she was not at fault, she would take the blame for Makeda's accident. As ever, when it came to her and Makeda, Eleni could not win. Not even with her own family. She went off to fetch the wagon parked nearby, which contained a basket of papaya, three sacks of grain, and loose straw.

When she returned with the wagon, Eleni saw her mother tending to Makeda's wound, adjusting the bandage so that the blood spilled out on a clean portion and wiping away her privileged friend's tears with the back of her hand. Wordlessly, Eleni brought the wagon to rest beside them.

Eleni's mother arranged the straw and a sack of grain to make a bed and pillow, then picked up the wounded princess and gently laid her down in the wagon. Eleni couldn't help but marvel at her own mother's physical strength, for Makeda was large and had to be lifted over the side of the wagon. For some reason, Eleni had never acknowledged that her mother was so strong, though she had seen her pull full wagons and carry cauldrons of water.

"You stay here and put lunch together," Eleni's mother ordered the unhappy girl. "Your father will be home soon. You tell him what happened and that I took Makeda home."

With that, Eleni's mother pulled Makeda as quickly as she could and asked a child who stood nearby watching her to run as fast as he could to the palace to give word that the doctor was needed. Eleni watched them go, her mother in service to her friend, more deferential and caring to the princess than to her own daughter, she thought. Eleni turned and saw the guava tree directly in front of her. She reached up and pulled off one piece of fruit, then bit into the bitter outer skin until she reached the juicy flesh within.

CHAPTER 3

Makeda had been on her throne for a little more than a year when she received the merchant Tamrin as a visitor. She had sent for him, having heard of his reputation as a fair and respected trader. Makeda was interested in building on her father's success in growing the kingdom's wealth. With no threats to her rule, she sought to invest in the things that made Sheba great: agriculture and irrigation, the design and structure of public buildings, new processes for developing textiles of exceptional quality, and the mining of precious stones and minerals. For every tree felled, she insisted two be planted. Teachers and healers were subsidized to ensure that everyone was self-sufficient and strong.

As for Tamrin, he had hoped for an invitation from the queen and had helped to stoke the fires of his increasing fame by encouraging his customers to speak well of him to others. The more good business he did, the more people knew of him, such that a farmer or weaver would hear his name spoken by two or three others, not just one. The talk multiplied upon itself until the din was inescapable. Makeda heard the name "Tamrin" in several circles and soon decided that he might be well-suited to representing Sheba in markets abroad.

So it was that Tamrin, desiring a commission to trade with other nations on behalf of Sheba, was granted one by the end of that first audience with Makeda. The interview, as such, was short; the conversation, though, had depth, as the two discovered their shared passions for learning about other lands, other peoples. In truth, Makeda envied Tamrin, for while she had sought and gained knowledge of the world from books, maps, and teachers, Tamrin was making his dream real by taking himself across deserts, seas, and borders, gaining knowledge with his feet on foreign soil and his hands in the friendly clasp of strange new people.

"If you will represent Sheba in trade, Tamrin," spoke Makeda, "you must promise me to always be fair and to trade with anyone who will trade with you. It is of sacred importance to me that Sheba is seen as a nation in happy concordance with all the peoples of the world."

"I would have it no other way, my lady," Tamrin responded.

"I also ask that every time you return from your journeys, you first bring the money and goods you have received to the treasury. Immediately after, you come to me and tell me everything you saw, everything you learned. The people you meet, I must know their names, how they talked, dressed. What they eat, what they believe, how they live. You must describe everything in detail, so that I can feel the sand they walk on within my own shoes, so that the taste of their food is on my lips and the song of their voices is in my ears. Do you promise me this?"

"I do, my lady. Nothing I observe will be hidden from you, nor shall I speak to you of things that are not so. To this I swear on my own name, for the name of Tamrin has always been respected, and the words of Tamrin have always been honest and true."

And with this promise and significant advance monies to acquire the necessary supplies—including sailing crews, work animals, food for the journeys, and goods to be sold—Tamrin set about on his trade expeditions. For the next two years, he sailed along the Red Sea and ventured across deserts, stopping in ports and villages not only to buy and sell, but to stay and learn, that he would have diverse treasures and testimonies to bring back to his queen.

It was on such a voyage to Egypt that he learned of an unusual marriage, that of the daughter of the Pharaoh and the new king of Israel. One, a descendant of enslavers, the other, a descendant of those enslaved. When Tamrin returned from Egypt and stood before Makeda, he told her of the new queen in Israel. Yet it was but one small and seemingly insignificant piece of information, and not much more was said of the wise king who was no longer a bachelor.

Of course, this was well before Solomon invited nations to offer their goods for his temple. Over time, Tamrin would share more of what he was hearing about Solomon—how he settled disputes with ingenious logic, for example—such that Makeda would become intrigued by the amazing stories of this wise king. But for the present, she had other concerns than that of an Egyptian girl losing her virginity to an Israelite king. Still a child herself, Makeda now had the responsibility of making national decisions, meeting with official visitors, and maintaining the peace and prosperity of Sheba. Not even her old *astamari* could teach her how to do these things. She had to rely on her intellect and her instincts.

They were more than sufficient. Yes, it was proven that Makeda was effective at all the tasks that were expected of her. Still early in her reign, progress came quickly. She gave her beloved teacher the resources to create a center of learning so all the people of Sheba could know of science and nature, the majesty of the sun and moon, and the mysteries of the earth. Favorable weather brought crops both strong and plentiful. And Tamrin proved reliable in delivering goodwill to his trading partners and bringing back wealth to his lady the queen. Her people were pleased, both with their lives and with their ruler.

But for all her success, Makeda was lonely. When she had assumed the throne, her friendship with Eleni had begun to suffer. Already jealous of Makeda as a princess, Eleni could not hide her anger at Makeda the queen. And yet she had to for the simple reason that she was a subject and her former friend was her sovereign. So it was that Eleni decided simply to avoid the palace and any place she knew her friend the queen would be.

Makeda knew she was losing Eleni—and she knew why—but beyond an initial twinge of regret she felt no further remorse over the loss. Ever the pragmatist, Makeda knew that this was as it must be; though she had never thought much about what it would be like to one day rule Sheba, she understood now that her fate, as Eleni's, was inevitable, and to dwell on their changing status would only impede her and the country's progress.

And so, with both her parents dead and her friend estranged, her teacher engaged in work, and even Tamrin sailing abroad, Makeda had no one to advise her, entertain her, keep her company. Her father had always maintained an austere level of governance, with few official advisors and servants, and she was inclined to follow in his ways. Of course, his request that she remain chaste ensured that there would be no potential suitors. So there she was, a queen possessed of great beauty and wisdom, young in years but capable and strong, sitting in her palace, alone.

Her closest companion became her personal servant. Thuni was responsible for preparing her meals and escorting her to places throughout the kingdom. He was tall as she but thin; if a boulder blocked their path, some people teased, it would be the queen who would clear it rather than her servant. Thuni was quiet and obedient, and if he lacked warmth, he at least was loyal and reliable company. Makeda grew to like him but maintained the required personal distance between them.

Daily she enjoyed being taken to review Sheba's soldiery. As it was a peaceable kingdom, Sheba's forces numbered only a few hundred men, about one-third of whom were assigned to protect the palace. The rest were divided into small groups engaged in various improvement projects throughout the land. They helped farmers prepare their fields for planting, felled trees, cleared roads of the detritus left by storms, and delivered official proclamations throughout Sheba and beyond its borders to all of Ethiopia.

Sheba's soldiers, most of whom had served under King Kawnasya, were loyal to Makeda. In fact, the only negative thought of her among many of the younger ones was that she was chaste. Though rarely had any of them a need to use their weapons, there were those who dreamed of winning her hand by bringing back the head of a dread enemy. And while those dreams were forever banished to the realm of fantasy, the soldiers were willing to assume any risk to protect the throne upon which she sat. And with so few risks to face, they welcomed her visits and presented themselves in as impressive a manner as possible so as to please her.

One day, while Makeda prepared to leave with Thuni to inspect her troops. the commander of the force posted at the perimeter of the palace entered with an urgent message. The message came from King Solomon of Israel and had been delivered from ship to shore up and down the Mediterranean. It was a request for goods, not typically a matter for the queen, save that the quantity and scope of the materials requested was unusually large, and the purpose of the request—to build a temple for Israel's God—was noble. And there again was the name "Solomon." This, she realized, was an opportunity to make contact with this compelling monarch.

Makeda sent for Tamrin, but he was not expected back from his latest trade mission until the next day. When he returned to Sheba, lightened of the goods he took with him but possessed of two large sacks of money and fine linens gained for his trouble, word was waiting that the queen wished to speak with him at once. On his journeys, he, too, had heard of the request from Solomon and had considered it a good sign of his own success that news from and about the distant land of Israel should continue to reach him. His name was known in faraway places, and he intended to use his success as a trumpet for his sovereign and her nation.

Tamrin was granted the commission to travel to Israel, and he immediately set about hiring a crew and assembling ships and goods. Makeda ordered all soldiers who weren't protecting the palace to aid Tamrin in his efforts. There would be much competition to fulfill Solomon's request and Makeda intended Sheba's offerings to reach him first—which meant that Tamrin would reach him first. This was frustrating to Makeda because her interest in Solomon had grown so much from the stories she'd been told that she longed to meet him herself. She wanted to know if Solomon was as wise as his reputation foretold. And if he was, how would she compare with him? And what might he think of her? For so few were Makeda's equals. And so few were the men she would allow herself to meet, lest she invite unnecessary temptation.

THE BOOK OF TAMRIN

CHAPTER 1

A long journey should always be preceded by a long sleep. Thus had been the professional philosophy of Tamrin the trader since an embarrassing incident during his first expedition, when he slept clear through arrival at his destination port after spending the late hours of the night before finalizing details. Many treks had he taken since on land and on sea, and gladly so, for he loved to travel and to ply his trade. Whether walking in his own sturdy sandals, riding atop a resilient camel, or sailing on a durable sea vessel constructed by Sheba's skilled shipbuilders, he had proven capable of traversing large swaths of geography without succumbing to sickness or despair.

Yet travel was but the preamble to the work at hand; his success as a trader came from his quick wit and nimble tongue, both the products of a well-rested brain. No matter how far he had to travel, every venture would need to begin with a good night's sleep.

Such an untormented slumber eluded Tamrin, however, the evening before he was to launch from his home port to Jerusalem, where he was to offer Sheba's fruits to the wise King Solomon himself. It was not for lack of preparation. He had secured five ships and a crew of well-trained, able-bodied sailors for each. Beasts of burden were selected for the journey—more than were needed in case some died during transport—and sufficient grain and straw to feed them. The hulls of the ships were filled with large sacks containing gold and sapphires. Trimmed lengths of ebony lay lengthwise on the decks, and satchels of wool and linen rested on the earthen wood. Animals for eating on the journey and to trade waited in a pen on the shore until it was time to board.

All had been perfectly planned and efficiently executed by Tamrin in advance. Now, lying in the tent he had set up near the ships both to guard them and to save himself time in the morning, he should have surrendered to a comfortable sleep; instead he lay the night before his departure with eyes alert and mind in full gallop. Unlike his past trade missions, where the deal and the payment were of paramount interest, this time Tamrin was also expected to make an impression on his trading partner—to leave Solomon not only with the goods he required but also with interest in and respect for Sheba and the Ethiopian empire ruled by Makeda.

This added responsibility was no great burden to Tamrin, for he had met and conducted trade with important men before and had never felt intimidated. No, Tamrin found something of value in all people, whether powerful or not, and was at ease in the presence of royalty as he would be with his own father. The only difference now was the great interest in Solomon that Makeda had exhibited of late. Tamrin shared this interest, yet he took special notice of Makeda's growing curiosity for him. He had long wondered what sort of man might stir the attentions of the virgin queen. He knew he was not the only man among her subjects who was drawn to her beguiling presence. Yet since becoming queen, she had always remained aloof to men, be they common or powerful.

As Tamrin's influence and fame increased, as meetings between him and Makeda grew more common, there were those who were envious and even suspicious of his uniquely fluid access to Makeda. With no apparent attempt to besmirch his name or disrespect their beloved queen, utterances such as these were made in hushed tones through the kingdom:

"This Tamrin, he is free to bend the queen's ear at will. What else of hers does he so move, I wonder?"

"Queen Makeda will have no man, yet she allows this trader free passage throughout the palace. Where does he venture and for what aim?"

"I do not know which is more the object for Tamrin: to lie alongside the queen's body or to sit beside her throne."

Tamrin's ears were sufficiently attuned to local gossip to hear of these whispered speculations. He would admit only to himself that he enjoyed this talk, for it elevated his stature, even if his personal reputation bore a small stain. Still, none of it was true, and if the need ever arose, he knew that Makeda would move quickly to quell the rumors. Though their relationship was purely professional, it was also warm, stoking his own desires and motivating the trader to do all in his power to please her.

Was Tamrin jealous of Solomon, then? He considered the question himself. *Who isn't jealous of royalty? Who wouldn't dream of having a throne, a crown, power, and wealth?* Intellectually, Tamrin had no reason to believe that Makeda's interest in Solomon was sexual in nature. He had finally to admit to himself, however, that he well enjoyed his special relationship with her. No one else could so easily gain an audience with her at any time of day or evening and never have to wait for her to complete the business in which she was currently engaged. Their professional relationship felt to him like a personal one. And for that reason, he did feel jealous of Solomon. Yet he had a job to do, and to fail at his responsibilities, to disappoint his queen, was unthinkable. Intolerable. Impossible.

At Makeda's request, Tamrin had sent couriers to bring letters giving advance notice of his imminent arrival, "with the hope that the Israelite king would be most pleased with the quality and magnitude of goods the kingdom of Sheba has to offer to aid in his holy task of building a temple to his God." So he knew he would be welcomed to Solomon's court. The challenge lay in selling to him the greatest offering he had, one that he could not bring with him: the good will and deep respects of his lady.

Tamrin, having comfortably been in the company of many important and powerful leaders, had a facile tongue and found it easy to make conversation. Yet he wondered what would it be like to converse with a man so wise as Solomon. Could the king ensnare him in some sort of mental trap, where he was made to reveal things he would not otherwise? Or would Solomon adopt a strategy of revealing little of himself that Makeda would wish to know?

Confident as Tamrin was in his own skills of ingratiation and negotiation, he knew that Solomon would be his greatest challenge. Makeda was also very wise, and he had no trouble in any of his dealings with her. Yet, she was a kind, patient, and generous person. What was unknown about Solomon, what Tamrin tried to ascertain in lieu of sleeping, was the level of this king's cunning. For the wise may be compassionate and generous with their wisdom, or they may wield it as a weapon to give themselves an advantage. Tamrin knew that he would not be punished if Solomon forced him to accept a lower price for the goods than they were worth, but if he failed to defend and burnish the queen's name and reputation, or revealed too much and learned too little, he knew Makeda would be deeply disappointed.

He already has won, thought Tamrin. *He is in my head, disrupting my thoughts and delaying my slumber, and he still does not even know who I am!*

Surrendering to his failure to sleep, Tamrin decided to rehearse his overture to the king. His first attempt: "King Solomon, ruler of the Israelite nation, whose wisdom is as great as the expanse of the heavens, I bring you the bountiful blessings of my sovereign, Queen Makeda of Sheba. On her behalf I offer you the iron friendship of our land and its people. May our nations be forever allies and know only peace and prosperity until the end of days, and may your God bless your every endeavor."

Too obeisant? he wondered. *Every king enjoys flattery but too much of it sounds false. Surely Solomon, with his legendary wisdom, would see through such a long and fawning introduction.*

He tried again: "Greetings, King Solomon. I am Tamrin, come from Sheba with the blessings of Queen Makeda. We offer you goods of the highest quality from our land and its craftsmen, with our affection and respect."

Better, he thought. *But Makeda's name should come first, for it is the bond between them that I must secure.*

Once more: "Greetings, King Solomon. Queen Makeda of Sheba has sent me, Tamrin, with her greatest respect and affection to offer you the friendship of our nation and several ships of our highest-quality goods to trade for your most holy undertaking."

Good enough, thought Tamrin. He knew he would forget these words by the time he arrived in Jerusalem. He was not a speechmaker;

he did not engage people by memorizing a script but through the sheer force of his outgoing personality. Based on the stories Tamrin had heard of Solomon's wisdom, it was easy for one to become intimidated. But he had traveled long enough in time and topography to know that most stories were exaggerations. This giant that Solomon's father had bested was probably simply taller than the boy. The Egyptians' claim that the Nile River is the most important in the world could not be true; after all, who has sailed every river in the world?

It is foolish to lose sleep over stories from someone's imagination, Tamrin assured himself. *I must end this self-inflicted torment. Surely this Solomon is wise, clearly he has impressed many. But he is a man, not a god, and I have never let a man get the better of me. And I shall not now. My lady's interests will be served.*

Satisfied with his argument, Tamrin pulled a woven blanket over him and turned to his side. He faced a dwindling fire whose dull orange glow lay just beyond the opening of his tent, and his thoughts slowed and excitement ebbed. His mind became finally as quiet as the calm evening shoreline, and at last his eyes closed, his breathing softened, and he entered the realm of dreams. Dreams that could never compete with the reality of the adventure awaiting him come the morning light.

CHAPTER 2

"The beasts are secure in the holds, sir. At your word, we are ready to sail."

The declaration from Umar, Tamrin's most trusted aide, was unnecessary, for Tamrin had risen early to oversee the transfer of the animals from the pen on the shore to the ships, the last task to be performed before departure. Yet Tamrin appreciated efficiency and Umar's never-wavering attention to duty.

"Thank you, Umar," he said. "You have done well, as expected. We have our goods, all the provisions we need, and most important, the blessing of Queen Makeda. It is time to begin our greatest journey. Prepare to cast off."

As Umar went to deliver the message to Tamrin's pilots—the most skilled in southern Arabia—Tamrin took up his satchel of personal effects and boarded the lead ship. The voyage to Jerusalem would be among the longest he had ever taken, at least three weeks if conditions remained favorable and stops were brief and infrequent. Tamrin knew well that there were dangers in long trips. Disease, death, bad weather, spoiled food, ship damage—all were very real possibilities on any sailing voyage; the longer the journey, the greater the chance of any of these dangers befalling them.

While some lightening of the cargo was expected during the course of a long voyage over land or sea—especially where live animals were concerned—contingencies were always planned for: If the goal was to sell twenty lambs, for example, twenty-five were brought. But Tamrin was fortunate in that never had he suffered any major losses. He knew others, however, who through bad luck or ineptitude never returned home, fearful of retribution from investors and sponsors. And there were those who never returned because of the hazards along the way; their bones lay bleached in the desert or bedecked the ocean floor.

As Tamrin's maritime caravan left shore and began its lengthy northward course, he was at peace. In truth, Makeda could have had no better emissary to make her country's first contact with Solomon. Confident, professional, loyal, Tamrin had all the tools that made a successful merchant: an engaging personality, a tenacious pursuit of business opportunities, and a deeply ingrained sense of fairness and propriety. Indeed, he had no greater ambition than to sustain his success in his chosen profession. While some men given the trust of and access to their sovereign might harbor desires to someday supplant their superior, Tamrin wanted only to maintain and strengthen the faith that Makeda had in him.

And yet, on this long voyage, Tamrin had much time to spend in the company of his own thoughts. He thought of Makeda and Solomon. He thought of them individually. He thought of them together. And he thought of himself with them. As a subject, he was devoted to his service; as a man, he could not help but be attracted to Makeda's beauty, wisdom, and strength. And if he had any further trepidation about his current mission, it was that Solomon himself—if the stories about him were true—was perhaps the only man alive truly worthy of Makeda's gifts. And Makeda must know that, too, for her intense interest in Solomon was well beyond that which she ever had shown for another man.

Still, Tamrin knew as a businessman that you take the best deal that you can get. And as far as he knew—and certainly the rumors bore this out—his relationship with Makeda was closer than any man had ever enjoyed with her. While he never sought nor was impressed by power, he liked to be in the company of leaders and even considered it a high form of intimacy to be able to know and share in Makeda's thoughts, plans, and strategies before they were common knowledge. If he desired other forms of intimacy, he knew from his wealth of experience that foreign maidens were an easy spoil of the itinerant trader. Yet none could compare to his lady's beauty, and anyway this voyage was too important to indulge in such inessential whims.

At the same time, Tamrin was wise enough to know that Makeda was on an exalted plane and he, for all his success, was born into a life of labor. Ambition and intelligence had taken him far, but his upward trajectory would forever be limited. He could do no better than to be known as the best trader in the Arabian peninsula. After all, Tamrin was Makeda's most favored merchant, and his reputation was solid as granite. The only way to elevate his status further would be to marry Makeda, which, though he allowed himself the fantasy, he knew was nigh impossible.

But perhaps there was another way to further elevate himself. What, he pondered, if he were to become the most favored trader of Makeda—*and* of Solomon? What if his present mission were to be executed so successfully that a great alliance resulted between Israel and Sheba? Between Solomon and Makeda? *Surely that is part of what Makeda seeks anyway*, he thought. Tamrin had always done his duty with the personal detachment of any order he was given to fulfill, with the primary goal being the advancement of the empire's wealth and the queen's stature. But now he realized that he stood to gain in this enterprise as well. If he was able to bridge these two powerful kingdoms with unusually compelling and charismatic rulers, he could travel farther, conduct trade at the very highest levels, be known as the greatest trader in the entire known world. He would also have earned the confidence of perhaps the two wisest rulers who ever had lived.

This gain he desired was not merely about money, though surely he would be rewarded well; it would not be about power, for he would continue to be subject to already-occupied thrones; it would not result in a betrothal to the object of his affection, as he could not compete with Solomon—or with Makeda's vow of chastity, for that matter. No, the gain would be in terms of his reputation, his name, which he valued over everything. As much a self-made man as he was, his name was one thing he could not have given to himself. He had received it from his father, and he was ever mindful to protect it, to honor it, for to do so was to honor his parents. And given how hard his father, Abat, had had to work all his life for minimal rewards, Tamrin was driven to make sure that his own name was the greatest of all gifts that Abat ever had bestowed on another person. Thus, while he delighted in his own good fortune, much of his pleasure—indeed, of his ambition—was in the knowledge that his success had brought blessings unto his father and to the mother he never really knew.

"May I disturb you to give a report, sir?" It was Umar.

"Of course, Umar. How goes the sailing?"

"Very well, sir. All our ships are in sight of one another, the weather is clear, and the sea is still except for the action of our own oars. Also, the wind pushes us along from behind, so our speed is very good."

"Excellent, Umar. Thank you for the favorable news. It would appear that our journey is blessed."

"I can report that the men are as excited about this journey as is their leader," said Umar.

"I have not been good about hiding my emotions," Tamrin replied. "No matter. It is well that everyone is strong in spirit. I do believe that this expedition will result in great things and will be written about in ages hence."

"Would you like the men fed in shifts, so that our pace does not suffer too much during meals?"

"Yes, Umar, for we are in haste. But start it early so the men on the last shift are not famished. We will rest in shifts as well and sail through the night. Spread the word."

Umar left Tamrin to alert the pilots of the other ships. Through a series of blasts from the horn of a kudu and the waving of a large, brightly colored woven blanket, he was able to communicate with them so long as they were within range to hear and see him. To be entrusted as the pilot of the ship required strong navigational skills and the ability to maintain pace while remaining just behind the lead ship (the one on which Tamrin rode, helmed by Umar) so as to make such communication more practical.

These ships were ably constructed from the finest woods and materials. Sturdy cypress planks made for strong hulls, and masts were carved from long straight lengths of pine. Oak was carved into oars and split for the benches on which the oarsmen sat and sweated. Sails were fashioned using Egyptian linen traded for by Tamrin himself. The shipbuilders applied tar or wax to open seams in the hull to ensure their seaworthiness.

The benches were arranged in two rows on either side of the ship, two men to an oar, twenty-four benches on each side, ninety-six men altogether. With five ships, that meant four-hundred-eighty men had to be hired by Tamrin just to propel the vessels through the water; in addition, each ship was helmed by a pilot. It was an epic undertaking, but entirely justifiable given the circumstances.

The pilots navigated by eyesight when they could—staying close enough to shore to identify landmarks—and by the stars at night. Sheba, after all, was advanced in the study of the heavens; like the Phoenicians, the people of Sheba looked to the sky with not fear but curiosity. With keen observation and sound logic—not to mention faith in their gods—they learned to identify and assess the position of key stars, and so make order out of the seemingly random array of lights in the dark expanse overhead.

Tamrin was correct when he said that their journey was blessed. It was as if Shams and Ilumqah themselves delivered his small yet heavily stocked fleet to its destination with the most care and the greatest speed possible. No animals were lost, no crew members fell sick, the food remained fresh and plentiful, and the skies themselves must have marveled at the smooth straight lines that Tamrin's ships cut swiftly into the sea. The three-week voyage was completed in just eighteen days, and the entourage was welcomed into the Israeli port of Eilat by workers sent by King Solomon himself to bring the prized goods of Makeda's native land ashore.

CHAPTER 3

Steering deftly across an expansive coral reef, Tamrin's ships had entered the port of Eilat safely, yet the journey was not completed. Jerusalem, the ultimate destination, was still two hundred miles away. Solomon's anticipation seemed as great as their own, however, and Tamrin was delighted to find teams of men and ox-drawn wagons ready to help bring the goods of Sheba northward. Scores of hardy Israelites and their equipment were already in Eilat working in the extensive copper mines there. Tamrin made a mental note to inquire about including copper as partial payment in the negotiations to come.

It took the better part of five days to reach Jerusalem over land. Losses were minimal, and Tamrin hoped that Solomon could be convinced to shop heavily. Upon arriving, he was told that Solomon had prepared tents for his men to stay in and meals for the duration of their stay. First they were to rest after the long journey. Solomon would meet with them on the following morning.

That night, Tamrin had none of the difficulty in falling asleep that he had had prior to leaving Sheba, and he realized that Solomon was certainly wise enough to know that exhaustion is not the ideal state in which to conduct business. The food he and his men were served was plentiful and delicious. Solomon's hospitality was both gracious and generous. Or was it but a price-softening tactic meant to lull the Shebans into accepting a poor offer? An important question, to be sure, but not so urgent as to keep Tamrin awake his first night on Israeli soil.

He received his answer the next day in the heat of the midday sun. A small group of soldiers escorted Tamrin to Solomon's palace—built by David—where the wagons of Sheba's goods had been parked. He was led inside, where he marveled at the forest of pillars, the ocean of marble, the sheer size and luxury of the building, so much greater and more majestic than the palace of Makeda. Tamrin steeled himself that he should not be intimidated upon meeting the king, though the splendor of his surroundings surely bespoke the grandeur of the man with whom he was about to do business.

They came to a door two times as tall as the tallest man. One of the soldiers opened the door just wide enough for him to pass through, and the door closed quickly behind him. In a few moments he returned, motioning to the other soldiers that Tamrin was allowed to enter. As he walked in, Makeda's most trusted servant tried not to look at the tapestries, statuary, and other decorations; he did not want to appear overwhelmed, and indeed he was no stranger to the manifestations of great wealth. But he felt, perhaps feared, that he would need his full attention and awareness when conversing with Solomon, and he did not wish to be distracted by the things in his periphery.

"King Solomon," spoke the soldier who had entered first, "upon your orders, we present to you Tamrin from the land of Sheba in southern Arabia, who brings goods for trade with the authority of the queen of Sheba." *My introductory speech is already given for me*, thought Tamrin.

"He may come forward," said Solomon. Tamrin was led toward the throne, stopping about thirty feet from the seven steps leading up to it. He bowed his head and knelt in obeisance. "You may rise," the king instructed.

For the first time, Tamrin looked upon the face of the man he had heard so much about. It was a kindly face, framed to the south by a trimmed black beard nearly obscuring his neck and to the north by long, wavy hair of the same color, with a golden crown at the crest. He wore a robe of crimson and violet, stitched with gold thread and adorned with jewels of red, green, and blue. Solomon was a sight more pleasing than imposing. Tamrin swallowed, then spoke.

"King Solomon, I bring you the highest respect and warmest regards from Makeda, the queen of Sheba. We have traveled the length of the Red

Sea in the hopes that you will find favor with the goods of our land and will desire them to build your holy temple."

Solomon rose from his throne and descended the steps until he and Tamrin were standing at the same level. The king was tall and thin. He motioned that the trader should walk toward him. Tamrin was unsure about breaking protocol, but for his hesitation he got a tap from the spear of one of the soldiers standing behind him. Tamrin walked forward but stopped five feet before he reached Solomon. The king laughed and walked forward two steps, extending a hand that was smooth and soft to the touch.

"So you have made me meet you in the middle, Tamrin," Solomon said. "A trader's strategy."

"No, I—I—," stammered Tamrin.

"Be at ease, my friend from Sheba. I received word that you were venturing to Jerusalem and so asked my advisors to make inquiries about you. Your reputation for fairness in trading is impeccable. You are honest and upright in all your matters. All reports say that you are a man worthy of respect, and so I welcome you in friendship to Jerusalem and offer you my fullest hospitality."

"Thank you, King Solomon. I have heard that you are the wisest of all men. You are also the most kind and generous; my men and I are grateful for the food and tents you prepared for us. And now it is my honor to offer you the finest materials for your temple, which we have brought you from our long journey to your land."

"There will be time for trade later," said Solomon. "My builders will inspect all that you have brought, and I am confident they will find them entirely suitable. Please be assured I will pay a handsome price for all that we take. I promise you your ships will return to Sheba much lighter than when they left, save for the payment you will bring back to your queen."

Tamrin was shocked. For all the importance of the project, Solomon seemed calm as a desert breeze. Did he even care to view the goods himself? Was this a sly and subtle negotiating tactic, designed to catch Tamrin off balance and slow-footed? The compliments, the relative informality—were they an attempt to gain some advantage over him?

"Tamrin, I should like you and your men to stay a few days," Solomon continued. "I wish to learn more about your Sheba, this matriarchal land that you journeyed from, and of your queen—Makeda is her name? Our nations do not know each other, and I am interested that we should be friends. I trust you have no objection to that?"

"No, of course not, King Solomon. I only wish not to be a burden to you. We already have taken too much of your hospitality in the comfortable tents and delectable food you have provided for us."

"Nonsense, Tamrin. My temple will stand forever as a tribute to God. The materials from which it is constructed will be the finest available anywhere. I need to know the land from which they spring, I must understand the artists and craftsmen, the miners and farmers, who created the fine things you have brought. I cannot find out about Sheba myself. You must teach me."

"I am not worthy, King Solomon," Tamrin protested respectfully.

"You would not be here if you were not worthy," replied Solomon. "My navy is more than capable of turning around ships that we do not wish to land in Eilat. No, Tamrin, you must stay and share with me all there is to know about your land. And I wish to show you Israel as well, its people and its ways, so you can tell your queen about us with words informed by your own eyes and ears. I expect she possesses a mind most curious."

"Very much so, your majesty," said Tamrin. "About the moon and sun, the rains and tides. And about you, King Solomon."

"I am flattered. But please, return now to your men. Tell them of my wishes and that they are welcome here and should feel as though they are at home. Come the dawn, I will send for you and we will spend days and nights in conversation."

True to his word, Solomon's builders were much impressed with the quality of the wood, cloths, jewels, animals, and spices that had endured the extended journey by ship and wagon to the palace. When Tamrin met Solomon the next morning, Solomon offered a price considerably higher than Tamrin would have asked and would not accept any negotiation. It was no large share of Solomon's coffers, and further, Solomon insisted that the work on the temple begin immediately, so there was no time to engage in the sport of haggling.

Instead, Solomon and Tamrin spent the day and days after that touring Israel. Solomon explained about the northern kingdom and Judah, and how they were united by his father, King David. He gave a history to his visitor about the Hebrew people, their enslavement in Egypt, the revelation of the Law on Mount Sinai, their forty-year trek through the desert, and their arrival in the land promised them by God, the same God who had freed them and enabled them to survive as a people through generations of challenge.

So it was that for a fortnight Solomon and Tamrin were nearly inseparable. The Sheban was permitted to witness as Solomon ruled on matters of state, settled disputes, gave direction to servants, and conversed with builders. Tamrin was entranced by all he took in, not least by the humility with which Solomon received others' respect and affection. Most important, Tamrin found in Solomon an eager and curious listener. He spoke at length about his lady, and Solomon seemed genuinely interested in all that he learned about Sheba and Ethiopia. Surely, Tamrin would have an even more appreciative listener when he returned home and shared what he had seen, heard, and learned from and about Solomon in Jerusalem.

And so it came to pass that Tamrin—having much good news to tell Makeda and fearing his extended stay in Israel was testing her patience—expressed to Solomon his desire to set sail back to Sheba.

"Your majesty," he said one morning as they partook of breakfast together in the palace, "the days since I arrived in Jerusalem have been the most extraordinary of my life. But I must beg you now to grant me leave so I can return to Sheba and report back to my queen."

"I understand, Tamrin," said Solomon after a short pause. "I have expected this, and though I will miss my teacher, I know I cannot retain you longer. I ask only that you deliver to your sovereign my deepest respects. Please extend to her a personal invitation from my court that should she care to visit Jerusalem herself, I would be most honored to receive her."

The next day, preparations were made to transport back to Eilat Tamrin, his crews, and the sizable amounts of goods and treasures that

Solomon provided as remuneration for the excellent materials brought to him from Sheba. With a bow, Tamrin offered an affectionate and respectful farewell.

"Blessed are they who hear your voice and perform your commands, King Solomon. May you reign in peace all the days of your life."

"And may the sea bring you safely home, Tamrin. Each day that I enter the temple of the Lord, I will think on the fine man who made it possible. As well as the fertile land whence he came."

The same wagons that had brought the convoy from Eilat to Jerusalem took them back to the port city, and Tamrin, ably assisted by Umar, began the journey back to Sheba. As the ships headed southward, Tamrin felt a sense of success far greater than any he had experienced before. If he never set forth on another voyage, he knew that his name would be revered both in Sheba and in Jerusalem for ages to come. And the pleasure he knew he would bring to Makeda made him smile as his men rowed home on the accommodating waters of the Red Sea.

Prologue II: MAKEDA

She sat on her throne, alone in her palace, having left her bed because sleep did not join her there. It was not the first night that this was so. From the day that Tamrin sailed toward Israel until Makeda received word through a network of far-flung messengers that he had arrived and been invited to stay for a time, she was beset with anxiety and inconsolable with uncertainty. For her, this was most unusual. Though she had full faith in Tamrin as a trader, far too much was unknown to her. And there was nothing at present she could do about it.

Has Solomon found favor with our goods? she wondered. *What are he and Tamrin doing? Discussing? What is Tamrin learning and what—what does Solomon think of Sheba? Of me?*

By day and by night, Makeda tried to imagine what was taking place in Jerusalem, tried to picture herself in Tamrin's stead, discoursing directly with Solomon, testing his wisdom and demonstrating her own. She wished she were there, was frustrated that she could not be.

If only the mission was completed already, she thought, rising from her throne and walking over to the eastern wall to look out the window at Ilumqah the moon god. *If only Tamrin was just now at home port, on his way to tell me of his adventures, of what he learned from Solomon. The sooner then that I could follow his journey with one of my own.*

Yes, Makeda was decided already: She would travel to Jerusalem herself. She could not wait for an overture; as the sovereign of a state not in conflict with Israel, she required no invitation, merely to send word that she was coming. She must. For no matter what Tamrin would tell her about what had transpired during his time with Solomon, she knew she would have to experience it all herself. Not because she didn't trust Tamrin, but because she needed—had always needed—to gain wisdom firsthand, by observation and interaction. So restless was Makeda with the waiting she had to endure that she had begun to make plans for her own trip to Jerusalem. It was the only way to settle her mind.

Because the best ships and pilots were already in use and would be too worn upon their return for another long voyage so soon, Makeda endeavored to travel by land with an extensive caravan. This would also give her an opportunity to meet the peoples of Southern Arabia along the way; such personal interactions with people unknown to her, she hoped, would help quell her impatience and make the lengthy journey more bearable. If through sorcery she could fly there like a bird through the air, or simply appear as a new shoot that rises through damp soil to meet the sun, the queen of Sheba would be before the king of Israel even now.

But no, she had no such mystical means of transport, though Makeda's arrival would be no less sensational. She intended it to be the grandest caravan that ever crossed the plains and deserts of their world, and so she let her imagination be as unfettered as the wind. *We will journey with camels, asses, and mules, eight hundred in number*, she thought in impatient reverie. *Every beast will carry treasure, gifts for my host: precious stones, rare metals, extraordinary linens, and spices from Sheba's fertile gardens. Solomon will be more than impressed: He will be entranced.*

As Makeda imagined the reaction of Solomon to her arrival, she moved her hand to her chest, fingering the jeweled amulet she wore around her neck. The jewels were peridots, glistening and green like seagrass from the Red Sea. It was her favorite gem, and Sheba had a large store of them, thanks to Tamrin's many trade ventures in Egypt. There it was called the gem of the sun and was used to ward off nocturnal demons. The amulet belonged to Makeda's mother; when she died, it was given to her by her father. But it was too precious for an adventurous ten-year-old to wear. Only when she became queen did Makeda decide to wear it herself, and she never removed it from her neck.

Touching the peridots eventually broke Makeda's reverie, and she remembered seeing the amulet on her mother. It had impressed her even then. She recalled how being given the amulet helped to assuage the grief she felt at her mother's untimely passing. Makeda treasured it now because it kept her mother's spirit close to her. And yet, she would never be able to give it to her own child. *I will be buried with it*, she supposed. *For my father swore me to celibacy, and I will have no offspring to pass things down to.*

And instead of sadness, the thought filled Makeda will resolve. *I live my life for myself and for my people. And I will be fulfilled, and fulfill my duty to Sheba and all of Ethiopia, only by meeting the wise King Solomon. This is my duty and my desire. When Tamrin comes, I will go. I must go. I must journey to Israel. As soon as Tamrin returns. Just as soon as he returns. It will be soon—soon, but not soon enough for me.*

THE SECOND BOOK OF MAKEDA

CHAPTER 1

With Tamrin away, Makeda, still feeling lonely, thought to confide her plans to her old friend, Eleni. Though their friendship had surely ebbed since her ascension to the throne, Makeda hoped that fresh wind against the graying embers of their love would be able to restore the warmth they once had shared. It also would be good to speak with a woman; though she ruled a matriarchy, all of Makeda's official staff and visitors were men. It had been so long since she had been able to sit and talk with another female. Given Eleni's emotional distance, Makeda felt certain that her former playmate could provide more or less dispassionate counsel. Considered neither a false friend nor a bitter enemy, Eleni would be a most welcome visitor at this time.

And thus one evening she sent her servant Thuni to deliver a formal invitation to Eleni. Makeda was careful to word it not as an order or summons, but as a request that the two estranged friends meet to talk over food and drink. Sheba's ruler did, however, instruct Thuni that a refusal was not to be accepted. Though surprised and somewhat skeptical to be so approached, Eleni agreed to meet with her old friend.

The meeting was to occur the next day, and Makeda was sufficiently filled with uncertain anticipation that she had difficulty falling to sleep. She requested from Thuni a cup of heated water infused with seeds and leaves of anise. Sometime after consuming the aromatic drink, she was able to cross into the realm of sleep as the sky turned from black to violet, from end of night to early day, only to stir awake again when the stars dissolved into the sapphire sky of morning.

Though tired, Makeda was truly excited when Eleni arrived that afternoon. She herself, in fact, assisted Thuni in preparing the food and arranging an attractive table for their meeting.

"*Sadiqati!*" exclaimed Makeda when Eleni was brought to her. "I have missed my old friend. Welcome!" The two embraced, but Eleni's hold was decidedly weaker than her royal friend's.

"Why did you send for me, Makeda?" was Eleni's cautious response. "I should think you would have more important things to do than to break bread with me after so long a time."

"I do owe you an apology, Eleni," said the queen of Sheba, becoming, she sensed, the first Ethiopian ruler to ever utter such a sentence. "From the moment of my father's death and my suddenly becoming queen and learning to rule, I have been so preoccupied. I have little rest and no leisure. My days are spent not with friends but with soldiers, advisors, visitors. I need my friend, Eleni. I need someone who knew me and loved me when I was just Makeda, the little girl."

"You were never Makeda the little girl. You were always Makeda the princess," said Eleni. "And now you are Makeda the queen. And I? I was a plaything for you, something to occupy your time outside of your studies so you didn't bother your parents. My mother took care of you more than your own mother did."

Makeda smiled. She knew and understood Eleni's feelings. That didn't make them proper, and her tone was most inappropriate. But what was protocol between old friends? Makeda sought to assuage Eleni's anger and rebuild their bond without shaming her, or worse.

"Eleni, you speak to me as if we are enemies. And maybe you think that we are. But we are blood. We are cousins. And we are friends. And I can prove it. These things you say to me, the way that you say them, the callous way you refer to my mother who died when I was but ten years old. You know I could put you to death for your brazen conduct here. Yet you fear not such a punishment. For you know I have no heart to punish you.

"You are angry with me," Makeda continued. "Disappointed as well. You are justified to feel that way. Yet here we are. We have food and drink to share and much to catch up on. You have said your piece. I have apologized. Now I offer you again my friendship, and I pray you will accept."

"I am here because I was forced to be here, Makeda."

"Yes, I insisted you come. But I do not insist you stay. If you wish to leave, do so now and no more invitations will I send you. But if you stay, you stay because you wish to be my friend. What is your choice?"

Eleni chose to stay. *I am here already and this food tempts me*, she reasoned to herself. But also, Makeda clearly had things to say to her and she was curious to hear them. And, yes, for all of Eleni's anger at being abandoned by her childhood friend, the void left behind had never been filled. Eleni was now more and more caring for her own parents, and she regretted what she said about Queen Ismenie, her aunt. So she stayed, and in staying declared her acceptance of Makeda's friendship.

The two proud women, their skin as dark as the ebony wood even now being cut to length by Solomon's builders, their minds as deep and rich as the mines in which Sheba's precious stones were extracted, their hearts each yearning for something as distant and burning as their sun god, spent the afternoon together talking amicably about the past and the future. Empathy was expressed for the other, promises made for more times such as this. As dusk settled about the palace, Eleni took her leave with a kiss and an embrace. Truly, she was exempt from all protocol concerning how one acted before the queen of Sheba. *It is good that this is so*, reasoned Makeda, knowing also that Eleni would accept nothing less.

Makeda had enjoyed her time with her erstwhile confidante, particularly when she broached the subject of journeying to Jerusalem to visit Solomon. Eleni was enthusiastic about the idea, insistent that Makeda must make real her desire.

"How could you live with yourself, wondering always if what is said about this wise king is true?" she asked her old friend with far more enthusiasm than she had expressed at any other point during her visit. "You have never accepted knowledge without first questioning it and finding the truth on your own. If you don't go, you would regret it with the last breath you draw in this life."

"You know me so well, Eleni," said Makeda. "My mind was already made up on the matter. Your words have strengthened my resolve as a coat of tar girds a ship's hull from the water's attempts to break it. It will be a long journey but it will be worth it. Thank you, my friend, for your love and your support."

Yes, a long journey, thought Eleni, as she walked from the palace toward her own home. *A year or more to get to Israel and back. Long enough for me to take over the throne of Sheba. Then we will be equal. At long last, Makeda and I will be equal in every way. And I will avenge my father Tefere's shame in not being treated with respect by King Kawnasya and Queen Ismenie. Though they were Makeda's parents and my father's sister and brother-in-law, they wronged my father. Yes, I will rule in her absence. And after, as well.*

For Makeda's part, the visit with Eleni accomplished its modest goal: to pass the time in a casual manner with someone she could be herself with. She understood early on in their meeting that Eleni was not a friend—she had been once but was no more, and there was nothing to be gained in attempting to change that situation. She certainly did not need another advisor, and in any case, Eleni's counsel would not be worth following. Just as her own father did not seek out Eleni's father's advice, Makeda had no need for what little Eleni could ever wish to offer her.

Like his daughter, Tefere was impulsive and ambitious. He was prone to saying the wrong thing at the wrong time to the wrong person. Because he was family, he had been given a position within the palace. But King Kawnasya never trusted his judgment, never allowed him to have influence. Ever mindful of her father's example, Makeda understood she should keep Eleni at a distance as well. She knew her childhood friend would consider any of the menial positions in the palace that were available to a woman (who was not the queen) to be beneath her, and Makeda never offered one. But she had felt it was important to know what Eleni thought, how she viewed things going on in Sheba. The visit proved her correct. The queen would have to plan how to protect her throne while she was away in Jerusalem. For what good would it do to meet Solomon if only to be wearing an impotent crown?

CHAPTER 2

Another half-day's sail would bring Tamrin's fleet to shore. As the sun set, he ordered his ships to drop anchor until the early morning. He did not want to arrive in the middle of the night, did not wish to disturb his lady the queen. Also, there were many valuables to unload—treasures from Solomon's deep vaults—and it would not be wise to do so in the blackness of the hour. The men ate the last of their provisions and went to sleep in preparation for an early last leg of their wildly successful expedition.

When Tamrin's fleet reached land the next morning, he had no need to send forth a messenger to alert the queen. For the last few days, Makeda had ordered solders to stand watch at various sites along the coast. She was to be notified as soon as Tamrin's lead ship was sighted. Once it was spied, the giddy citizenry shared in spreading the information, and it was as if all of Sheba learned at the same time that Tamrin had returned. And for the first time in the memory of even the elders, the reigning sovereign of Sheba came personally to welcome arriving ships.

Though Tamrin was honored and pleased to hear the clamor of the crowd and to see Makeda standing at shore, he did not especially welcome her. Not only did he fear disruption of the hard and lengthy work of unloading the ships, paying and releasing the men, and turning over the vessels to the shipwrights for inspection and any needed repairs, she also preempted the dramatic presentation he had planned to give at the palace. Her appearance at the docks did, however, serve to make clear to the people of Sheba that Tamrin was held in Makeda's highest esteem, and that none in the land—save the queen herself—was as worthy of praise.

Makeda understood that the real treasure to be unloaded was Tamrin's own testimony of his time with Solomon, and that such riches were to be revealed in private. Thus, after welcoming the honored trader home, she soon left the area, leaving a retinue of trusted soldiers and staff to bring the gifts of Solomon securely to the palace. Tamrin was to be the queen's guest at dinner, and then would his presentation be made.

Even with the labor that Makeda provided, the unloading was a long and arduous process. It was of no boon to the enterprise that Tamrin and his men were weary after the voyage home, which was maintained at the same aggressive pace of the journey to Eilat. In fact, upon conclusion of the task, Tamrin barely had time to return to his house to bathe and change into clean clothes before six of Sheba's most senior soldiers arrived to escort him to the palace.

Tamrin's house had been made for him by Makeda's masons in recognition of the great wealth he had brought to the country in his trade missions. For one who traveled as frequently as he, less permanent shelters were more common. And Tamrin had long been satisfied living in a tent. With no wives or children, he had more space than he needed and all the privacy he wanted. Yet Makeda insisted that his importance to Sheba (and to her reign in particular) warranted a domicile that told to everyone who passed it that a highly valued and respected man lived within.

Tamrin changed into a clean woolen tunic and his finest robe made from heavy cloth dyed green and blue. As he reached for his leather sandals, Makeda's soldiers arrived to take him to her. In his rush, he hadn't had time to rehearse his presentation, though as they walked to the palace, he realized that she might well be too impatient for a formal accounting of the journey's success. He had never worked so hard at his job—planning for the voyage, traveling quickly to his destination, meeting Solomon, representing Makeda through his agency for the entire length of his stay as Solomon's guest, returning safely and swiftly back to Sheba, and discharging his cargo and his men. Now, at last, was the final responsibility.

He needn't have worried, for the news he had to share was all good. Surely the testimony he would reveal about Solomon's character would bring her only joy. Yet he also feared that as a result of his report, Makeda would want to travel to Israel herself. She would be gone a long time, and Sheba had never had a ruler who had been absent for more than a few days. With no spouse or offspring, who would lead in her stead? Who would commission his future trade missions? Who would be as kind and respectful to him and as accommodating to his needs?

The walk from his home to the palace was short, proof again of Tamrin's status. He was led directly into the dining room, where Makeda already sat and waited. Dressed in her royal robes, she made it apparent without uttering a word that this was no informal meeting as she had endured with Eleni. Rather, Tamrin would be treated as a visiting dignitary, and their discussion over the evening meal would be at the level of the most important state business. Aside from servants, no one else was present, not even the musicians and dancers Makeda often enjoyed having perform while she dined. Her expression, not unfriendly, was serious, and as much as she rejoiced in Tamrin's return, this meeting was less about celebration than revelation.

"My lady," was Tamrin's simple greeting, uttered with a mixture of deference and relief as he bowed.

"Welcome, Tamrin," said Makeda, a smile arching her lips, a smile she had hoped to keep inside, away from view. "I have never before been so pleased to see you. And I know how weary you must be after your long journey so I appreciate your meeting me with minimal delay."

"My journey was indeed long, my lady, but any fatigue I feel is a small sacrifice for what I experienced abroad. My mission was a success for Sheba and for Queen Makeda. And if I may, it was something I will never forget and forever treasure. My gratitude for your trust in me is eternal."

"The food is being served," said Makeda. Her words were not yet true, but they had the effect of an order as the servants quickly went about the task of bringing in wine, breads, roasted lamb, fish, and a stew of goat, carrots, and potatoes, sweetened with dates and perfumed with cardamom and cumin. "I wish you to regain your strength by eating, but please do not keep your lips still otherwise, for I must hear all that you have to tell."

Tamrin nodded, tore a piece of the bread, used it to sop up a portion of the stew, and ate it. A sip of wine followed. Then he spoke uninterrupted for a long time, during which neither he nor Makeda ate. In truth, it was Tamrin who provided their feast. This was the substance of his testimony:

"In all my travels, in all my experience, of all the men I have met, spoken to, broken bread with, there is no one like Solomon, king of Israel. He is known for his wisdom, and I will speak on that subject. But first is his person, his character. Solomon is a most righteous man. He is kind and just and fair. He treats everyone he meets the same. At no time does he remind the person he is with of their station relative to his, not with his words nor with his acts. Whether speaking with me, or a mason, or a servant, or an accused criminal, or a friend, he consistently makes the other to feel that they are worthy of respect.

"And when he speaks, his words! They are sweet as this wine before us. They provide sustenance just as does this food. They bring light, they heal. He makes himself understood to all and every word is a nugget of gold that glides from his mouth, hangs in the air to be marveled at, and slowly evaporates until it reappears among the stars in the sky. Of all the words I have heard, all the songs that have caressed my ears, there never has been music to match his speech.

"As a judge, he is impartial, doing everything in his power to allow justice to reign in his court. He listens with great care, asks important questions, considers all the facts, and renders a just decision. And every decision is Truth. The innocent are disrobed of their accusation, naked of suspicion forever after. The guilty are treated fairly and humanely, and they accept their punishment with mute dignity, for to protest would be to question Solomon's judgment, which is inviolable. Those permitted to live never repeat their crime; the families of those who are put to death or banished from the kingdom bear no stigma from the rest of the citizenry.

"Solomon is both a teacher and a student. He shares his wisdom freely and in doing so never makes his student feel unintelligent. Yet he also seeks to learn more. In humility, he asks questions of the stonecutters and woodmen, to learn their craft so that he sees what they see and understands what steps they will make next to complete their task. And he is pious, which I feel is the source of his humility. He is deeply loyal to the God of Israel and prays and makes sacrifices to Him faithfully and with solemn countenance. This he does, and his house and his kingdom do likewise, for they ascribe their blessings not to the valor of their kings but to the mercy of their God.

"The result of all these aspects of Solomon's personality, and the way in which he rules over his people, is that Israel lives in a state of peace—both within and from without. It is fitting that his throne is installed in Jerusalem, for in their language, Jerusalem means 'city of peace.' All are content there, happy with their king and with their lives.

"As for me, I was treated as if I were his kin. Within two days in his company, he was as a father to me. Two more days passed, and I felt like an Israelite myself, ready to go into battle for him if called upon. Only my duty and desire to share with you, my lady, all that I witnessed in Solomon's company motivated my return. Excepting that, I would be there still and grateful to be so."

For a full minute then, they both sat silent. Tamrin took another drink of wine, as his tongue had become dry as the Negev desert he had crossed to reach Jerusalem from Eilat. Makeda, who had yet to taste either food or drink, maintained a fixed gaze on her guest. Finally, she spoke.

"And what, Tamrin," she asked, "did Solomon say about me?"

CHAPTER 3

"This Solomon intrigues me, Thuni," Makeda confided to her most trusted aide the following day. "Here is a man, a king, who appears to lead from the heart and the mind, not the sword-wielding fist. I would wish to know such a man face to face."

It was a quiet, clear morning in Sheba. Another sleepless night for Makeda. All her life she had been in search of truths. If something she thought would be true were proven false, it crushed her. When as a child her favorite tree, an acacia, was struck by lightning, she believed that the inherent medicinal properties of the gum its sap produced would enable it to grow back its broad canopy, under which she took shade. Instead, its blackened frame withered, and it offered neither shade nor sap ever again.

Yet here was a rare instance of something she had thought would be true proving to be even truer than she had imagined. It was as if a goat that was sold with the promise of a bucket of milk a day had instead produced five buckets, or that a loaf of bread fed not one family but multitudes. It excited her imagination, and now the only disappointment would be not meeting Solomon in person.

"The land of Israel is far, Queen Makeda," Thuni replied. "The journey could take as long as six months by land, taking camels along the Red Sea coast; it would be much faster by ship, but we would need to build accommodations for you."

"No," said Makeda. "If I go, it will be by land. I wish that it should take a long time. I must see other villages, other countries, other people. I will die if I am destined to stay only on my throne. My mind will wither and break like the boughs of an aged tree, barren of fruit."

"So you say, my queen. But we do not yet know if the way is safe for you. Or even if the trip is worthwhile. After all, what more is there for you to learn?"

"You do not understand, Thuni. Since I became queen, my mind has been taxed but not stretched. I will test this Solomon, fully anticipating he will prove himself. And then his answers, his wisdom, will enter my ears and fill my brain. I would be satisfied beyond every happiness I have ever experienced if he is all he is said to be."

"You are wise as well, Queen Makeda," said Thuni. "You need not feel as though you are inferior to anyone."

"The student is never inferior to the teacher, Thuni, for a good student *makes* the teacher successful. My *astamari* taught me that. Learning is not about increasing your status, it is about becoming whole. We are born as vessels, and some die as empty as when they first came from the womb. That is not me. I wish to be full, to overflow with wisdom. As much as I have, I can have more. But who is there to teach me? No one in Sheba. No one in all of Ethiopia, of Arabia. Not in Egypt, with their emphasis on magic rather than reason. No, it must come from the Land of Israel, from their king, the wise man Solomon."

Of course, Makeda had decided to make the journey long before the previous night's meeting with Tamrin. His testimony about Solomon only confirmed what she already knew: She could never be satisfied unless she traveled to Israel to meet this most intriguing man herself. This was more than just a state matter; it was important to her personally. After all, she had everything the outside world could give to her: power, wealth, respect. But Makeda's inside world—her mind, perhaps even her heart—was not yet complete. She had more to learn, a will to feel, to be touched by greatness and to grow from it. For this reason, she would set out on a journey unprecedented by a monarch for its length—some two thousand kilometers—and for its purpose: to seek friendship and inspiration rather than trade or conquest.

"You will be gone a year, at least," said Thuni, "and that assumes you face no troubles in your travels. What will become of us in your absence? How will we keep Sheba secure with an empty throne? You must give us time to plan."

"No, Thuni, I cannot delay. As you say, the trip is long; already my goal is far from me. I must not wait any longer than necessary to begin this journey. Tomorrow evening, have all my advisors assemble at the palace to receive my orders. The leaders of our army must be there as well. Most important, Tamrin must attend."

Makeda used the time until the meeting to make her own plans. She had to select clothes and personal effects, make sure that most of her jewelry and valuables were placed in Sheba's guarded vault, and write and sign the orders she would give. Complex though the undertaking was, she had spent many nights conceiving it in full detail. On those nights she was robbed of sleep, she had filled the void with her sharp and motivated mind hard at work on ways to make her intentions possible.

At the appointed time the following evening, Makeda was joined in her throne room by those whose presence had been requested. There, she laid out her plan, which took all by surprise for its scope and urgency. She would go to Israel, she said. That was already known to—or suspected by—all present. She would go not by ship as Tamrin had, but by land. It would be a long, arduous journey of half a year each way. She and her entourage of soldiers, assistants, and servants would travel by camels, with horse-drawn wagons bearing gifts for Solomon. The time it would take to complete the journey was a factor not only of geographic distance but also the need to rest their beasts of burden—and to replace them if necessary.

The caravan would cross the Arabian desert, follow the eastern shore of the Red Sea through Dedan—an ally both of Sheba and Tyre, and thus a secure link between Sheba and Israel—and into the kingdom of Edom. From there, it would enter Israel from the south near Beersheba and head due north to Jerusalem. This path would not require water crossings, which were dangerous, yet bodies of fresh water would of course have to be accessible along the route for drinking and bathing. In areas where no above-ground source of water was nearby, wells would have to be dug.

Word was to be sent immediately to inform Solomon of her arrival in the coming months. Messengers would be dispatched as well to surrounding allies so that they would be prepared to offer assistance if such was needed along the way. At home, the army would remain on alert. But from whom would they take their orders?

This was indeed the most important question, for no creature disjoined from its head could survive. Makeda's answer was unequivocal.

"In my absence," she said, "I am appointing as my temporary successor one whose service to Sheba has long been exceptional. While I am away, the throne will be occupied by Tamrin, and he is to receive the same respect and loyalty that I have enjoyed, and his words will have the same strength and standing as my own. There is to be no question as to his status. So long as I am removed from Sheba, Tamrin is the one and supreme sovereign of my entire dominion."

This news surprised all, not in the least Tamrin himself.

"M-my lady," he stammered, agape, "I am honored by your faith in me, but...but…but who am I to assume your throne? I am a trader. I know nothing of how to rule and decide on matters of state. Surely there is someone more qualified in Sheba to serve as your substitute."

"No, Tamrin. There is no one I trust more than you, no one who is so dedicated to Sheba's interests. No one who would rule as I would rule, for you know so well my values and priorities. It is you who will sit on my throne, and with you so installed, I will not fear for my country while I am away."

"But what of our trading, Queen Makeda? How will we maintain our business with other nations if I am to be in your place rather than my own?"

"You have good men, Tamrin," said Makeda. "You will promote the best of them as I have promoted you. They will make Sheba proud, as you have made me proud.

"It is decided," she continued. "But before you assume the throne, Tamrin, there is one more task you must do for me. You must prepare the caravan for my journey to Israel, just as you did for your own. And I pray you make haste, for I wish to leave within the week. And then you will be the ruler until I return."

From that night until the morning she departed five days later, Makeda and Tamrin spoke only twice: first to confirm her needs and wishes in terms of what she wanted to bring and how she wanted to travel; and second, on the evening prior to her departure, when Makeda assured Tamrin of her confidence in him and told him that he would be honored in Sheba to the end of his days and beyond for his excellent service.

And with that, she left. Tamrin had split her caravan into three teams. One would leave the night before and maintain a frontal presence so as to be able to report back in the event of trouble and enable Makeda's team to avoid danger by pursuing another route or returning to Sheba; the second team would be Makeda's, including most of the soldiers and most of the treasures; and a third would travel at the rear, bringing with them supplies and extra, riderless horses and camels to be used in the event of attrition. In each team, the beasts were tethered to one another by ropes spun of goat hair and strengthened with wax; on their backs they bore saddles of oak covered with cloths dyed in rich hues of red and purple. The edges of the cloths were adorned with gold chains and jewels.

Every place the teams traveled, people came out to watch them pass or to invite them to stop and enjoy their hospitality. Makeda was happy to see such excited expressions from people she had never met before, and when the time could be spared, she was only too happy to dismount and engage with them. Though she had not been queen for very long, still she could not understand why she had not traveled more since assuming the throne. She realized that contact with people energized her, fed her soul. Solomon was her ultimate target, but making personal connections on a wide scale had always been her desire.

On the move, she saw that ruling over an empire was no longer an abstract notion; her charge had been to keep the people over whom she ruled happy and strong, and here they were, demonstrating that she had been performing her duties well. And when she passed into lands beyond her power and influence, many lined the path to glimpse the virgin queen of Sheba. She received the respects and gifts of other rulers: kings, judges, chieftains. Some were documented allies of Sheba already; others pledged their friendship. Within the first two months of travel, Makeda understood that her journey was already more successful than she could have dreamed. Her more personal goal of meeting and getting to know Solomon remained, yet despite the long travel still ahead, her optimism sustained her from horizon to horizon.

If she had known what was soon to transpire back at Sheba, however, her outlook would have been far less hopeful.

CHAPTER 4

As Makeda traversed the desert, Tamrin assumed the throne, and his trusted aide Umar took charge of trade missions, which, given the many resources deployed for the queen's trek, would be focused solely on neighboring villages and states within southern Arabia. The wealth gained from the transactions with Israel meant that Sheba could afford to suspend its more ambitious trade routes for the year or more that she would be away.

Tamrin had full confidence in the soldiers who traveled with Makeda to ensure her safety and the successful passage of the caravan through its long and challenging journey. He also had unshakable faith in Umar. In fact, Tamrin had offered to send Umar along with Makeda, but she understood that the temporary ruler would need people he trusted closer to home. If Tamrin lacked confidence in anyone or anything, it was in himself and his ability to govern.

Still, he understood that Sheba was a land that had long been at peace with its neighbors; the chance that a threat would come from outside its borders was very small. For this reason, he felt assured that at the very least, he would not likely find himself in a position to have to mobilize troops into battle against an enemy invader. Yet little did he suspect that a threat was mobilizing from within.

In her excitement to leave, Makeda gave no notice to the fact that missing among those who came to see her off was her old friend, Eleni. She knew that their recent meeting had not mended the divide between them. But she had neither the time nor the space in her thoughts to ruminate on their relationship, for there was a new relationship to be forged with Solomon and that was clearly more important, both to Makeda herself and to Sheba. She was pragmatic enough to know that no words she could utter, no actions she could undertake, would ever please all those under her rule. If Eleni wished to hold a grudge, that was her choice. Makeda had not the luxury of dwelling in the past; it was hers to press forward.

Eleni felt differently. Though she did not come out publicly to wish Makeda a successful journey, she was overjoyed at the prospect of the queen's absence. Indeed, even as Makeda's caravan took its first steps northward, Eleni was completing her own plans for advancement. Through her father, Tefere, now old and frail and weak of mind such that he no longer remembered when he had served in the court of King Kawnasya—did not even recall the name of his own sister, Queen Ismenie—Eleni knew some of the older soldiers of Makeda's army. She would bribe them with honored positions in her court if they agreed to mount a coup against Tamrin, allowing her to take over as queen.

To do so, they would have to turn a majority of the soldiers against the temporary monarch, which was not as difficult a task as it normally would have been, since their ranks were diminished by the absence of those accompanying Makeda to Jerusalem. Still, the army had no reason to be disloyal to Makeda or her appointed successor. But there was tremendous wealth in Sheba's vault, thanks in no small part to Tamrin's extraordinary successes. Eleni desired respect and power over wealth, but surely the common soldiery could be swayed with money. She would be more than willing to share the nation's riches with Sheba's soldiers if it meant the end of Makeda's reign—not to mention revenge for Tamrin rising to a higher position than her own deserving father had ever had a hope of achieving.

Eleni waited several weeks to ensure that Makeda and the soldiers she traveled with were too far away to return quickly. When she felt the time was right, she approached Sharaf, whom she knew as one who had been trained by her father. He was nine years older than Eleni and had served with honor in Makeda's army. But she knew Sharaf was also loyal to her father, for he continued to visit him even after the old man no longer recognized the soldier who bowed before him and offered him gifts of fruit and bread. Surely Sharaf would understand that the ultimate honor he could show Tefere would be to help supplant Makeda's reign.

As for Tamrin, he knew nothing of Eleni's plot; in fact, he knew not Eleni at all. Never had Makeda mentioned her to him in their meetings. Makeda knew that Eleni could not be trusted but could not have guessed that her old friend would be so desperate as to mount a coup. Had she suspected that Eleni would conspire to take her crown, she would have warned Tamrin before she left and alerted the army that remained behind while she was away. Tamrin did not yet know many of the soldiers by name and did not think there was any reason to, for he could not conceive of threats for which he would need to engage them. The throne of Sheba seemed quite invulnerable.

Yet Eleni was blinded by her own bitterness and greed and did not recognize that Makeda was nearly without enemy in her own land. And so it came to pass one night while most slept under blankets of darkness that Sharaf stood guard at a post one thousand paces south of Makeda's palace. Around his waist he wore a belt; held within the belt was a sword on his left side and a ram's horn on his right. Thus armed, Sharaf was the first point of security, able to give warning to those guarding the perimeter of the palace by blowing the horn upon sight of an approaching enemy. It was a quiet night, lit by the second full moon to appear since Makeda had left on her journey. Though the risk of invasion was low, the well-trained soldier was alert and instinctively reached with his left hand for his horn upon seeing someone approach. In the clear moonlight, Sharaf was soon able to recognize the figure as Eleni. He took his hand from his horn, yet he remained poised and in position as she came near enough to greet him.

"Sharaf, it is I, Eleni."

"Why are you here? It is late. You should be home with your parents," he responded with concern. "Is there a problem? Is your father in need of assistance?"

"No, he is fine. Thank you for asking. You always have been so kind, so loyal to him."

"Tefere trained me, guided me as a boy into becoming a man. His kindness helped me to become a soldier. As you know, my own father died before I was born. Until your father took an interest in my welfare, I was adrift. Like dried thistles in the wind. As a soldier, I finally felt that I belonged, that I had a purpose. I owe that to him. But if he is not ill, why then have you come to me?"

"Sharaf, you know that my father's sister was Queen Ismenie, mother of Makeda. Despite his close relation, my father received no favors, no rewards from her or from the king. He remained a soldier, and the only promotion he received was to be allowed to serve as one of a number of advisors to the king. But he was never asked to provide counsel on important matters. This humiliated him, and to this day he feels the sting of the disrespect his own sister and brother-in-law showed him."

Sharaf did not speak, nor did his expression betray any sense that Eleni's words were moving him emotionally. She decided to get to the point quickly, to force Sharaf to respond instinctively from his sense of loyalty to her father.

"Makeda took over as queen and my father's health declined. He sits in his tent all day, not knowing who we are, who he was, what day it is, what is going on in the land. And yet Makeda enjoys wealth and power, while my father, Tefere, your mentor and friend who served his king and queen with nobility and pride, eats dry cakes and water."

"Eleni—"

"Sharaf, the time has come to avenge how my father was treated. We must have change. We must take down she who has demeaned my father."

"Eleni, what—"

"We must seize the throne from Makeda. Should she return, let her come back a peasant. I will be Sheba's new queen, and my father will have his honor and his dignity restored."

"No, Eleni."

"Yes, Sharaf! And you will help me. You will help me turn the army against Tamrin."

"No, Eleni!"

"There will be riches for those who join us. Sheba is wealthy, and we will share that wealth. You will be a rich man."

"Eleni, you must leave, return home. What you are saying is treason. I would be justified in slaying you where you stand, but I could not raise my sword to you, the daughter of my *astamari*. So please, go and speak nothing more of this insane plan."

"Sharaf, do you not see that Makeda is evil?"

"It is you who do not see, Eleni. Makeda is a just ruler for Sheba. Our country grows stronger with her as our queen. And we, her army, have pledged our loyalty. There is no soldier who would accept your bribe to turn against her. Until she returns, we are sworn to protect and serve Tamrin; and when Makeda's journey to Israel is over, she will again sit on Sheba's throne, and we—I—will remain devoted to her and pay any price to shield her from harm. From anyone."

"You are making a mistake, Sharaf. And you dishonor my father by not taking his side. You will see. Makeda will fall, and then you will take your orders from me."

As Eleni turned to leave, Sharaf reached for his sword but never touched it. He watched her go. With his hands at his side, his gaze fixed upon Eleni's hasty strides in the growing distance, he was for the first time distracted from his duty. For a brief moment, Sheba was vulnerable from the south, but then he resumed his attention and position, and Sheba again enjoyed the security of a loyal and alert sentry.

Should I report this? Sharaf wondered. It was a foolish question. *Of course I should. Someone has threatened Makeda's rule. I am honor-bound to take action. But it is Eleni, my mentor's daughter. How could I do so, when he relies on her to care for him? Tefere once was strong, confident. Now, with a weakened mind and withering body, he is helpless as a freshly born lamb. I will remain silent this time. But if there is another attempt at treason, Eleni must pay the price. For I serve Makeda and Tamrin, not Tefere. And certainly not his daughter.*

Everything is noticed.

THE SECOND BOOK OF SOLOMON

CHAPTER 1

In half a year, much can change. Seeds planted when the days are long will have their fruits harvested well before Ilumqah the moon god completes six cycles around the heavens. A kid born on unsteady feet and wholly reliant on her mother's milk will be well on its way to becoming a yearling goat that can breed. In half a year, an elder's vision may fade, a tree's canopy may fall to earth, secrets told may be forgotten, a dragonfly may be born and die.

In the six months it took Makeda and her camel-driven caravan to travel the many arid miles from Sheba to Jerusalem, numerous things had changed. Hair on faces, heads, and legs had grown long. Animals had died, either for the sake of food for the queen and her party or due to exhaustion, illness, or injury. One soldier had died as well, having been bitten by a poisonous snake while foraging for berries. The sheer size of Makeda's caravan kept most animals of prey from any attempt at attack, though man and beast coexisted fairly well at the sparse bodies of water they encountered, hydration being an essential salve for the desert heat.

One thing had not changed from the time that she set out on her journey and left her throne in the care of Tamrin: her resolve to meet Solomon. If anything, her desire had only deepened over the many days she had to think about what that meeting would be like. Quite opposite to her character, Makeda had allowed herself to believe only in a positive outcome; she entertained no thoughts or fears that he may disappoint her, or she him. She took on faith Tamrin's testimony as fact and believed that something of historical importance was soon to take place. Solomon and Makeda would be like Shams and Ilumqah, the two reigning lights that all the world would recognize and revere. Together, the two leaders and their nations would put an end to war and institute a meritocracy based on wisdom and justice. Even mighty Egypt would be in envy of their powerful alliance.

At present, Egypt, large and prosperous, was neither interested in nor concerned about the meeting between Solomon of Israel and Makeda of Sheba, though Shishak, the reigning pharaoh, eyed Solomon's wealth enviously. Sheba's closer neighbor, Aram, home to the mighty cities of Damascus and Aleppo, likewise took little notice of this unusual diplomatic mission. In fact, any leaders in the region who knew of Makeda's long journey by land would have said it was a foolish undertaking. Who would leave one's throne vulnerable for such a length of time? Why put oneself through such discomfort when there were subordinates who could serve as intermediaries in making international connections? Especially when one had a trader as respected and trustworthy as Tamrin, who was known far and wide as a fair and honest man.

One leader who knew of Makeda's journey and welcomed it was Solomon himself. The lead party of Makeda's caravan had reached Jerusalem and was accorded the same gracious hospitality as Tamrin had enjoyed. Solomon recalled Tamrin's words as he had described his lady to the wise king.

"She is tall and strong like an oak, with dark skin and eyes that defy her blackness like midnight stars," the trader had told the king. "Beautiful as a sunrise. Deep as the Nile. If I may go on,"—Solomon nodded—"she is also wise and just in all matters, the same as you, great King Solomon. Stories of your inestimable qualities and morals are told reverently in our land," Tamrin continued. "Though my queen would never claim to be your equal, she so wishes to meet you because she shares and respects those qualities and morals. You would do Makeda and all of Sheba and the Ethiopian empire over which she rules a great honor by receiving her."

"If she is all that you say she is, Tamrin, then I should be worshipping her, not merely receiving her," an intrigued Solomon had replied with a gentle laugh. "If she is half the noble creature you have described to me, then she has my respect and affection already. Upon your return to Sheba, please tender unto her my official invitation and personal request that she be my guest here in Jerusalem when it so conveniences her."

And thus it was that after Tamrin the trader—and soon-to-be interim king—left Jerusalem for the port of Eilat, Solomon sat upon his throne and tried to create and retain a picture in his mind of the black queen that anxiously waited to meet him. Tall, strong, beautiful, wise. He imagined her skin as smooth and beguiling as that of the black desert cobra. *This is not a woman to take lightly.* Solomon in his wisdom knew that as the leader of a sprawling land, Makeda was worthy of the highest respect. Yet he was his father's son, and a woman of beauty was irresistible to behold. Like his counterpart in Sheba, Solomon was growing impatient for their anticipated meeting. He hoped to see a ship in Eilat carrying the queen within a scant few months.

It took somewhat longer for Makeda to arrive than the few months Solomon had imagined, for she chose to cross the anhydrous desert sand rather than the quicker currents of the Red Sea. But eventually came the day when she arrived in Israel, coming to the outskirts of Jerusalem as the sun was setting. Thanks to the advance team that had preceded her arrival by two days, Makeda found an honor guard of troops waiting to escort her caravan into the city. Word spread quickly that the black queen of Ethiopia had finally appeared, and throngs came out to see the visiting dignitary. Makeda, though exhausted from the journey and the sleepless nights that preceded its end, was delighted by the attention and reassured by the cheers and excited, welcoming faces.

As her caravan moved into Jerusalem proper, she looked around and was impressed by the view. The architecture was magnificent, the people well-dressed. Carts carried goods revealing a fine crafts tradition, and others were filled with fresh produce, indicative of a thriving agricultural system. It reminded her of Sheba, until she saw Solomon's palace. Only the reported splendor of Egypt, known throughout the world for its opulence, could rival the majesty of this home for the wise king. Her own throne stood in a structure that could barely be called a palace in comparison with this. Not that she was covetous of the building itself, for what is a building but cover for the people who live and work within, and surely the lives and the works of people are more important than the inanimate envelope in which they dwell. But she could not turn her gaze from the palace for the simple reason that inside it was the man who had consumed her thoughts for so long, and who now was so close.

He would not get closer, however. Not this night. The lead soldier of the honor guard, named Amnon, halted the caravan, bowed before Makeda, and helped her down. He had been instructed to welcome Makeda thusly:

"Great Queen Makeda of Sheba, King Solomon of the united kingdom of Judah and Israel welcomes you. With the lateness of the hour, and the rigors of your long journey, he invites you all to rest, bathe, eat, and sleep until morning, when he will greet you in person."

"Thank you—"

"I am Amnon of King Solomon's army, Queen Makeda."

"Amnon," repeated Makeda. "Thank you, Amnon. I am most pleased to be here in Jerusalem at last. I hope our arrival has not proven inconvenient for King Solomon."

"Not at all, Queen Makeda. King Solomon is humbled by your journey to meet him and is anxious to welcome you himself. But first he wishes you to enjoy his hospitality. There are tents for your people. Your animals will be cared for by our own handlers. There will be no limits to your food and your comfort."

"Again, I am most grateful. Where shall I be staying?"

"You will have your own tent, which has been erected within the grounds of the palace of King Solomon. There you will be attended by his servants. All you desire will be yours. You need only ask it be so, and it shall be so."

Everything spoken that had to be, Makeda's caravan scattered; her servants were shown to their tents, her animals brought to the stables and pens, her stores and gifts brought to a secure place within the palace where they were kept under guard. And she was escorted to her tent. A tent? It seemed to be half the size of her entire palace at Sheba. A large bed with a mattress made of skins stuffed with straw and covered in fine linen, with pillows containing soft feathers. An enormous tub of marble. Walls as tall as cypress trees adorned with tapestries. A small army of servants to draw and heat well water for bathing, laundresses to care for her clothes that had become all but encrusted by the miles of sands she had crossed, maids to help her dress, food preparers and servers, wine stewards, and messengers to make her wishes known to those who, duty-bound, would fulfill them.

I have everything here, she mused while reclining in the tub of warm healing water that buoyed her weary bones, her first priority upon entering her quarters. *Everything but one, the one thing I traveled so far for.* She inhaled deeply, exhaled slowly. Her naked body, the proud and powerful vessel for her intellect and her dreams, lay warm and wet, the water drawing out the strain of her journey, resuscitating her spirit, making her clean, drenching her hair, which soon would be ready again to hold her crown, frame her face, spring out like a black blossom.

Tomorrow, she thought. *Tomorrow I will see him and he will see me at my best. Until then, though I am weary with travel, I fear another sleepless night.*

Standing close to a window in his bedroom, a dark figure in a room lit by a single taper on a table beside him, Solomon looked down onto Makeda's tent. He could not tell that she was then in the tub, though, as the tent's roof prevented Solomon from seeing his guest the way his father David had spied on the bathing Bathsheba a generation ago. He was anxious to meet Makeda but not at night, not in dim light, not with the low store of energy he had at the close of a day—and that surely she would have at the conclusion of her journey. No, better to wait until morning. Thus he gave Amnon the words of both greeting and regret for him to utter to Israel's latest guest from Sheba.

To know that she was there but for her to be hidden from his view was frustrating to Solomon. Like a fact known but not instantly recalled to mind, it seemed a senseless inconvenience. Something that surely soon would pass but made the intervening moments uncomfortable. Yet this was of his own doing and so he demanded of himself patience and restraint. *Your decision was rational and correct,* he reminded himself. *Let not the mystery below cloud your judgment. Tomorrow. We will meet tomorrow.*

That night, Solomon and Makeda willed themselves to sleep. That first night was a still one, and as it began to change into morning the sky beheld both of Sheba's heavenly gods, Shams the sun god and Ilumqah the moon god, who could look down and see through any structure, and so for the first time saw the king of Israel and the queen of Sheba, separate but together in the same land.

Their first meeting would take place under the watchful eye of Shams.

CHAPTER 2

A learned woman, Makeda understood how the sun god and the moon god shared dominance over the heavens, amicably taking turns showing themselves to the mortals on the brown, green, and blue world below. She could speak of the moon god's mischievous inclination to gradually withdraw from sight night after night until invisible, and then reveal himself again gradually until fully exposed. And how the sun god exploded in regal oranges, magentas, and purples upon rising and retiring. She knew of rains and winds and tides, the seasons of sowing and harvesting, the silver-speckled stars and the cotton-coated clouds.

Yet she had never learned about lightning. Those intensely flashing veins that connected heaven and world in a frightening show of force were a mystery to her: what they were made of, what they meant, how they burned the things they hit, such as trees. Though they studied the sky and benefitted from their knowledge of it, the Shebans knew nothing of what caused the lightning to strike.

Perhaps the only other thing Makeda was ignorant of was romantic love. After all, she had sworn herself to virginity at the request of her father before she had reached the full flower of physical maturity. Within a few short years of taking over as queen, however, she began to see that most of her peers—Eleni excepted—had both mates and children. Each birth was greeted with celebration and ceremony. Food and drink, music and dancing heralded the arrival of new life, and the blessings of the ancestors were invoked to protect the child, the family, and the community. Yet to Makeda, this world of carnal desire and procreation was closed.

But now, perhaps, the veil was lifting. Makeda's persistent thoughts about Solomon had been so all-consuming that they had gathered input from all parts of her being. While at first it was intellectual curiosity and respect for wisdom and wealth that drew the queen to the man beside whose palace she had eagerly awakened, now it was something more. Now she wanted to be beautiful for Solomon. The quality of her intellect was still the part of her that she valued most. *But should not the finest wine be kept within the most attractive vessel? After all, Solomon will make a judgment of me before I even have the chance to speak. Perhaps softening his eyes will help to open his ears,* she reasoned. At the same time, Makeda hoped that his physical form would be as pleasant and perfect as the beauty and bounty of his wisdom. For that which is seen provides the first and most enduring impression, like the daunting enormity of Solomon's palace.

There was, however, also a feeling that caused her inner thoughts to be manifest on her body. A flush in the face, an ache in the gut, and tingles below that. An unexpected heat. *Could this be what it feels like to touch the flaming veins in the sky?* she wondered. Impatience took hold of her. *I crossed deserts over six moons to be here, and yet now I feel sick, feverish. And still I am alone!* But not for long, for a bell announced the arrival of five servant women, there to fulfill the king's order to help Makeda dress, provide her with fruits and breads to break her fast, and bring her at the appointed mid-morning hour to the great hall in which stood Solomon's throne to meet the wise king in person at last.

I have no appetite, she told herself upon being given an overflowing bowl of food. And yet she had. She dressed quickly and soon was ready to go. But there still were more than two hours before she was to be escorted to the throne room. With no orders to give, no troops to review, no arguments to settle, Makeda began to pick at the fruit and flatbreads she'd been brought. *I will eat that I may also consume time*, she reasoned. *Perhaps it will settle the discomfort I feel in my stomach.*

"Queen Makeda, the time has come. Are you ready?" The voice was that of Amnon, who had arrived after what seemed an interminable wait.

"Yes," she said abruptly. *Over-anxiously*, she thought. She held her ground a moment longer than she wanted to offset the eagerness of her verbal response, then walked slowly to Amnon. Makeda was clad in her finest green and yellow robe. On her feet were jeweled sandals, on her head, her gem-bespeckled crown. Her neck and bosom were scented with oil of myrrh. The time had come, and outwardly she was ready to be received.

Step upon step. There were not many to take in order to reach the palace, yet Makeda took each one slowly, deliberately, as if savoring the steadily shrinking distance between Solomon and herself. So slowly did she walk that Amnon out of respect was obliged to slow his own pace, although the order from his sovereign had been to bring the visiting queen to him at once. No matter, there was not far to go—by design— and so they arrived with but a modest delay.

"We are here," said Amnon, stopping before a wooden door so large that a creature three times Amnon's height and eight times his width could comfortably fill its frame. The door's tall wooden planks were painted a brilliant red and held together by broad bands of gold, yet Makeda did not allow herself to be awed by the scale and luxury of her surroundings. No, her focus was on something life-sized, something—someone—who would truly fill her with awe.

"I will enter first and announce you," Amnon continued. "When I hold out my arm in your direction, walk in and stand beside me until King Solomon invites you forward. Then walk across the white marble floor until you reach the black marble." Makeda nodded, her mouth too dry to speak.

Amnon grasped the door handle and with a firm jerk opened it fully. Instinctively, Makeda looked downward. She could not bring herself to steal a glance at her royal counterpart, her host. Not yet.

Solomon, however, stared straight at the door and when it flew open he saw his faithful soldier Amnon standing beside her. She was tall, regally clad. In fact, her crown was most of what he could see of her, not any part of her face. *Why does she bow her head?* he wondered. *She has not even entered the room.*

"Your majesty, King Solomon, son of David, God's favored child, I give you Queen Makeda of Sheba, ruler over the entire southern Arabian peninsula and the empire of Ethiopia, who has traveled over two seasons and many deserts to honor her host." Amnon held out his arm toward Makeda, who did not see the gesture because her face was still turned downward. He gently tapped his spear on the floor to gain her attention. Surprised and embarrassed, Makeda took two swift steps into the throne room then regained her composure and walked more slowly, but with her ever-present slight limp, toward Amnon. Her face now raised, she could see Solomon's face at last.

At last, thought Solomon, *I can see her face. She is all that Tamrin described her as being, yet even his trusted words were insufficient to portray the beauty of her deep black face, the strength that her tall and substantial body suggests. Could there be within that fine head as exquisite an intellect as well?*

The face of the wise king, thought Makeda. *It is not as I thought it would be. It is kinder. The eyes express joy, the lips a silent welcome. It is said that a beard makes a man look older. Not so with Solomon; the black hair smartly decorates his face, rather than obscures its shape. He is handsome. He looks directly at me; what are his eyes whispering to his brilliant mind?*

"Please approach, Queen Makeda," said Solomon.

Makeda walked ten paces forward, until she stood on the line where white marble met black marble. There he was, so close, another ten paces and they could touch hands. His hands. They rested on the arms of his throne. *Beautiful hands*, she thought, noticing his long, thin fingers. Solomon's throne sat atop a platform six steps above the floor. On either side of each step was a golden lion, twelve in all, representing the tribes of the united kingdom. At the very top of the throne, also carved in gold, was a bird of prey holding in its claws a smaller bird, symbolizing the victories of Israel over its enemies.

Makeda bowed deeply, then slowly righted herself to speak. She was shocked upon raising her head to find that Solomon had descended from his throne and was standing directly in front of her. Again, she called upon her inner strength to maintain composure, and then she spoke.

"Your majesty, King Solomon of Israel, it is my honor to be your guest. I bring you considerable treasures as a sign of our nations' friendship, and the affection and respect of all my people."

"It is I who am honored to have you in my court," said Solomon. "If I may?" He held out his hand to receive hers. Upon giving it, she trembled as he cupped it in both his warm hands. "I pray you will stay long, for there is so much I wish to learn about you and your people and the land you inhabit. Let us begin now."

With that, Solomon gestured that he be left alone with his guest, and all but a small group of four guards assigned to protect the pair everywhere they went began to depart. Though she had much to say and ask, Makeda felt it essential that she not suggest a topic of conversation to Solomon. As the visitor to his kingdom, she must be deferential to him and wait for him to speak first. The clatter of dispersing guards created a din that did not make conversation easy, and the two monarchs stood momentarily in the gummy awkwardness of their silence. Though each smiled politely as the throne room gradually emptied, their eyes betrayed a difference in their respective comportments: Calm and at rest, Solomon's eyes showed his smile to be genuine, while Makeda's arched eyebrows and unfocused view of what was happening told of her impatience in waiting for their conversation to begin.

At last they were alone, a minute pair of figures among the majestic cedar and bronze columns of Solomon's palace. He looked at her, and his honest smile was as it had been before. For her part, Makeda turned only the merest of glances toward him, her eyes and brows unchanged. It was an interminable moment, it seemed, until the wise king finally spoke.

"Shall we walk?" he asked, his right arm extended to the side in invitation. "Shall we talk?" is what Makeda would have preferred to hear, but it did at least give her the permission to do so.

"Yes, please, King Solomon."

"If you please, when we are together I should like to invite you to call me simply 'Solomon.' And may I call you Makeda?"

"Yes, please—Solomon." She cursed her tongue for failing her.

"I would like to show you my palace and the plans for the temple, which the rich bounty of your land has made possible for me."

"I would enjoy that very much. I—I have so many questions to ask of you, so much I wish to know."

"I do not doubt it, for I have many for you as well. But we have time. We needn't be rushed. You will visit with us for some days—weeks, I pray. Let us be well-paced in our mutual discovery, gradually getting to know each other the same as the way the leaves of the date palm must be pared back one by one to reveal the sweet fruit."

"Of course, Solomon, a wise approach. Why should I expect anything less? I apologize for my impatience. Please show me the way."

And so they walked, and he showed her the architectural marvels of the palace, the golden mountains that could be seen from the portico, and the site of the temple where Sheba's cedars and stones were finding their purpose. They spoke of unimportant matters, enjoying the bright sun and clear sky, until the stars began to show themselves as the day grew late and the blue bowl of heaven turned from sapphire to onyx. They dined together then retired each to their own quarters, and it was evening and then it was morning. A new day.

CHAPTER 3

The second day passed as the first had, and the third as had the second. Soon it was a week, and all the days had been spent walking and sightseeing, eating meals outside when the sun was not too searing, inside when the cool marble floors ensured their comfort. They spoke about their respective countries, their customs and beliefs, their hopes for the future of their people.

Through these talks, they began to learn about each other. A prized student in her youth, attentive always to the *astamari* she adored and his lectures that she so joyously absorbed, Makeda was accustomed to a more didactic way of learning. Solomon, she began to understand, saw wisdom and learning as being less a quantitative accumulation of facts than a philosophical engagement whereby mind and heart together considered what they observed and sought to harmonize its meaning and measure.

When Makeda told Solomon about Shams the sun god and Ilumqah the moon god, Solomon paused to think about this new information. He understood the sun and moon as being opposite elements and did not find it strange that a people should deduce that they were, in fact, not only separate entities but also separate rulers who shared their power. For the sun enabled plants to grow, and the moon directed the tides. One without the other would make life impossible. And yet, he did not, could not, share her belief in their divinity.

In fact, Solomon responded by sharing with her his devotion to the One Eternal God, in whose hands the sun and moon are tools He placed in the heavens to make His Creation work. Solomon did not tell Makeda that he was right and she was not, because her belief was her Truth, and no one can own another person's Truth. But he continued to speak to her of the God of the Israelites, for Whom the children of Israel owed their freedom, their sustenance, and their land. Makeda was fascinated by his tales. She thought it interesting that Solomon's God was a jealous god, for the sun and moon gods that she worshipped each happily ceded their part of the day to the other and would never deny their counterpart the worship that the Shebans so willingly gave to both.

And yet, while Solomon could speak at great length about the miracles that the Israelites' God had done for His people and point to writings and artifacts that testified to the difficult history and blessed deliverance that this God had caused to happen, Makeda realized she had no such proof of her own celestial deities interceding in the lives of the Shebans, other than their effects on light and darkness, sunshine and rain, earth and sea.

"We worship the sun as our fathers have taught us to do," she told Solomon, "and we think of him as the king of the gods, greater even than the moon."

"And there are gods even beyond the sun and the moon?" Solomon asked with genuine curiosity.

"My kingdom is large and spreads far into other lands," Makeda replied. "In fact, I have not even seen some of the places in Arabia and Ethiopia over which I rule. But I know that among our people, there are those who worship mountains, trees, and the ocean. And there are many who worship a variety of figures, some carved of wood, some forged of gold or silver."

Solomon responded with stories of Abraham smashing his father's idols and of the golden calf through which the newly freed slaves disgraced themselves before the Hand of their deliverance. But always he was respectful to Makeda's testimony. For that is how he learned, and Makeda was now learning this way as well—and by being moved by Solomon's complete fidelity to his God.

Another thing that moved Makeda about Solomon was his kindness. In every interaction that she observed of him with any other person, be they common laborers, the *kohanim* priests, or, gladly, herself, he was consistently kind in his manner and his speech. One day while they were out walking, she asked him how it was that he could be so great a king and yet act so unlike a king, that orders were delivered as patient requests and the well-being of others was so much his concern.

As Makeda expressed her query, there passed not far from the two of them a laborer. He carried a large stone on his head, steadied by his hands. In spite of the obvious burden, he carried also on his shoulder a skin of water; around his waist was tied a small bag of cakes and fruit for his midday meal. His clothes were dirty and moist, having absorbed the copious perspiration they could see glistening on the muscular man's face and neck.

Solomon called to him. "You there. Please set down your work and come to me." The laborer did so, gratefully yet apprehensively. He walked to the two rulers with head bowed.

"What is your name?" asked Solomon.

"Gershon, my king. What do you ask of me?"

"For one thing, Gershon, please help yourself to your water. The sun is high and you are clearly weary from your work."

"Thank you, King Solomon," said Gershon, removing the skin from his shoulder. Before refreshing himself, he offered the vessel to the royal pair. They gently refused. As he drank, Solomon spoke to Makeda.

"Look at this man. In what ways am I superior to him? Where comes the favor that is mine and not his, and for what cause and what purpose? Are we not both born of dust and fated to become ashes? I am the son of David, and I sit upon his throne in the palace he built for himself. Gershon here is the son of another man, another laborer, no doubt, and he takes his father's place as I have taken mine. We are of two stations from what you can see, but we are both feeble and weak in comparison to God. So we are more alike than different, and what right do I have, therefore, to act as if I am his master? I may have more wisdom than he, yet he has greater strength than I. God wills that he is to do his part, as I am to do mine.

"Why, then, should we not exercise kindness and love upon each other?" Solomon continued. "You saw that this dirty man, wet with toil, scorched by the sun with thirst, offered us his water. Yet I walk in comfort, so why should I take what he needs? Are we not all like grass of the field, which is hearty and green in its youth, and dry and withered at the end? My fine robes and jewels: I cannot wear them after I die. These material things that we covet and crave, they lead us only to sin and selfishness. To get them, we turn to magic and sorcery, we worship idols, and then we find they have led us astray and we are no richer for our transgressions.

"This laborer here, this Gershon, he is a man I admire. I envy his honest reward of wages for his work. When the temple to the Lord God is built, it will be his honor not mine, for he has made something to appear on the earth, while I have merely watched it happen. Oh yes, I commissioned the work, financed it, chose the materials, but worshiping God does not require clean hands. God does not ask us to come to Him in fine clothes and sumptuous jewels. God knows what is in our hearts, and ultimately it is with our hearts that we worship Him. Gershon's heart is no less than my own. God loves those who are humble and who walk in His way. And the man who knows compassion and the fear of God knows wisdom."

At the conclusion of his remarks, both Makeda and Gershon stood silent, neither knowing what to say.

"You may return to your work," he said to the laborer, who promptly did so. To Makeda, he apologized.

"Forgive me for my rather lengthy pronouncement," he said. "Your question was an important one, important for understanding me, my people, and the important work that has brought you here to visit. My people have known much turmoil, much displacement. Only through our faith in God's peerless power can we hope to be able to assume the difficult task He has given us, of living according to His laws in full sight of the world. Because of our love for one God, none of us who live on earth can claim to be better than our fellow man. We have different responsibilities, but even then, our greatest responsibility is to worship God. You flatter me by calling me kind. I am simply being what God commands me to be."

That evening, after sharing dinner and an entertainment with Solomon and his court, Makeda retired to her quarters and thought about God. The one God. *Had this God brought me here?* she wondered. *Is this God the One I must thank for enabling me to reach this moment in my life? If so, I do thank Him. For without His intervention, the Israelite people could not have survived to be a free nation, and there would be no Solomon.*

But what of this unseen God? The sun god was plain to see by day, the moon god was revealed at night. Solomon's God was never seen, yet always present. So said Solomon himself. *It is a puzzle*, she thought. *Yet to believe in something based on tradition rather than visual representation requires great faith. Great love. Am I capable of that? Worthy of it? Could I give that to this God? Could I give that to the wise King Solomon?*

Before retiring, Makeda wrote a note to Tamrin that in the morning she would give to a messenger to deliver. It expressed her gratitude to him for preparing Solomon to receive her and for his willingness to rule in her place until she returned. She hoped that all was well. *I am enjoying myself immensely*, she wrote. *The lives of so many people will be enriched because of this meeting. Mine has been already. And the best surely is yet to come.*

THE THIRD BOOK OF MAKEDA

CHAPTER 1

The next two days, Makeda was on her own. Solomon wanted to inspect the goods and gifts that she had brought, and check on the progress of the temple construction that had been continuing apace since even before Tamrin's visit with his five ships' worth of fine Sheban materials. While the king met with his architects and builders, the stone masons and carpenters, his advisors and the priests, Makeda spent time with her own people, those who had brought her to Israel on that long journey. The men spoke of Sheba, wondered what was transpiring there in their absence, and when they would be taking the moons-long southbound trek home. Yet such was Makeda's pleasure in being in Solomon's company that she did not even think about the rigors of the return trip to Sheba. She was not ready to leave anyway, for she still had many questions to ask of him.

These questions she had written down during her journey to Israel. She searched her mind for questions that were challenging, as well as philosophical problems that she could not answer convincingly. They were puzzles, some of them, riddles that required not just wisdom but cleverness. Makeda knew that for some, there could be no one true answer, but she also knew that Solomon's answers would give her great insight into how his mind worked. Now that she had spent several days with him, however, she felt unsure about asking some of them. She thought they would sound naïve given what she knew of him now that she had not known when she conceived the questions. And yet she also now realized that his answers would reveal not only his mind but his heart, for anyone can learn and remember an absolute truth, but the more subjective relative truths reflect character as well as wisdom. And so Makeda was emboldened to go on with her inquiries as she had planned.

It was after lunch on the next day that Solomon was again available to her. Their lunches were their most pleasant time together, she felt, for after eating they would go on walks—and lately, the deferential distance they would stand and walk from each other was shrinking. The last time they had walked together, they were close enough that their robes kept brushing against each other, occasionally his hand would graze hers, and her breadspice scent flew into his nostrils. At first Makeda would pull away, yet she gradually found that just as stars occupied their fixed position in the sky, so their physical closeness was impossible to break once it had been established. One could look at their footprints in the cumin-colored ground and suspect that an oddly configured four-legged beast had passed by.

Their meal digested, their walk just commencing, Makeda requested an interview with Solomon.

"If it pleases you, Solomon, I have prepared questions for you, challenges that only you in your peerless wisdom could respond to successfully."

"You are testing me, Makeda?"

"Oh no, Solomon—" but her protest was waved off by Solomon's pleasant countenance.

"Fear not, my dear friend. I understand. You have heard stories of my judgments, and you wish to know how I arrive at my conclusions, yes?"

"Your wisdom is apparent in each utterance," she said. "I thought of these questions as I crossed the deserts to reach you, and now they seem inadequate. But my own curiosity is too great. Would you be so kind as to hear them?"

"It is my honor to receive your work, Makeda. I pray that I am equal to the task you are about to place before me."

"Thank you, Solomon. Forgive me if any are the interrogations of a lazy child. Here now is the first. Tell me, wise ruler of Israel, what is evil?"

Said Solomon, "Evil is the counterpart to good, is the enemy of good. The greatest good is God, and so evil is His enemy. But as we cannot see God, we cannot see evil; only God's eyes can see God's own enemy. Yet just as we can feel God's presence as a light that helps us to see, we can sense evil; it is the shadow that obscures the way and confuses our minds. Good and evil, God and His counterpart, are in eternal opposition. The more we stand with God, the more we stand against His enemy. Thus we will know evil when evil is defeated and all that remains is good."

Then Makeda, seeking to draw Solomon off guard by moving from eternal matters to mortal, asked which was the most powerful organ of the body.

"The tongue," replied Solomon, "for death and life are in its power."

"What when alive does not move, yet when its head is cut off, it then moves?"

"The timber used to build a ship." Solomon smiled. He was enjoying this.

The queen of Sheba, blushing noticeably, then asked, "What are the seven that issue and nine that enter, the two that offer drink, and the one that drinks?"

Solomon answered, "The seven that issue are the seven days of a female's monthly impurity. The nine that enter are the months of her pregnancy. The two that offer drink are her breasts, and her child is the one who drinks."

"Tell me, Solomon, what is the ugliest thing in the world, and what is the most beautiful? What is the most certain, and what is the most uncertain?"

"I will answer the last questions first and the first questions last," said Solomon. "The most certain thing in life is death; no matter what else happens, all creatures that live must pass away. What is the most uncertain is one's share in the world to come, because that is known only to God, and none who reach that destination are permitted to return to tell us their story.

"As for the other two questions, the ugliest thing in the world is the loss of faith within the once-faithful. The most beautiful thing? For that, I have two answers. One is that the most beautiful thing is the sinner who repents."

"And what also is the most beautiful thing in the world?" asked Makeda.

"She who this day asks me such challenging questions," said Solomon.

Makeda looked up at her host, and for the first time her eyes met his fully. His face betrayed no sense of his having made a joke or an intentionally false answer. And as she knew not how to respond, she asked no more questions, but thanked him and begged to return to her quarters to rest. And so they returned, he to his palace and she to her tent, and they spent the rest of the day with their separate affairs—and silent thoughts.

When she was summoned to dinner, Makeda had already spent hours wondering if she had made a great error in asking her questions. At minimum, his shocking final answer gave her reason to refrain from asking the remaining questions she had prepared. She was embarrassed, afraid of having done something wrong, and yet flattered and pleased all at the same time. How Solomon would welcome her at dinner would determine how she acted and what she said.

"Welcome Makeda," said Solomon as she appeared at his table, chaperoned as always by two guards. "I trust you had a relaxing afternoon."

"Yes, thank you, I did."

"I wish it were so that any discomfort you may have felt was due to Jerusalem's oppressive heat as opposed to my rash yet well-intentioned words."

"I am feeling fine, Solomon, and I apologize for cutting short my interview. It all was so overwhelming to me."

"And why is that?" he inquired.

"For so long, I have heard reports of you in my own land, and for many months I journeyed to see with my own eyes and hear with my own ears if indeed there was any man who could match the descriptions that had so enthralled me."

"Have I then passed your test?"

"You tease me, but I deserve it. King Solomon, my heart is full in the knowledge that the reports I had of you were not half the truth of your actual greatness. I dared to believe that you could approach such lofty tales as I was told, and yet you have exceeded every wondrous hope I have had of you.

"Happy are all who serve you," Makeda continued, "and all who hear your wisdom and receive your just and fair rulings. And I must add, Solomon, with my whole heart, that I bless your God, your one eternal God, Who delights in you and Who set you on the throne of Israel. Your God truly loves Israel, because He made you king to give judgment and do justice for His people. And I thank you for all you have taught me, and all the kindness you have shown me."

"All that I have shared with you today and every day since we have met is the truth as I know it, Makeda. I am grateful for your visit and for your kind words to me. I pray you stay long and that the friendship we have begun may grow stronger, just as the sapling matures into a mighty tree. And now, let us eat."

They dined in relative silence, as no more was said about Solomon's compliment to Makeda's beauty, and no more needed to be said by either to the other. Let the greater world know, and the heavens witness, that the kingdoms of Israel and Sheba, the Hebrew people and those of the Ethiopian empire, were allied. Bound by affection and respect, matched in intellect and compassion, the respective sovereigns were as perfect a pair as Adam and Eve, or Shams and Ilumqah. What they stood for could inspire all nations to forgo war and petty battles over land or gold, for the true treasure was in the head and the heart. Given that, and faith in God, what else was needed? What else had value?

And yet, the world did not know this, for it did not notice the blossoming friendship between Solomon and Makeda. It did not understand that the promise of Eden was taking root in the soil of Jerusalem. That is how it may have looked that night, yet not all that is sown grows to be reaped. And while Israel was doubly blessed having both Makeda and its king in country, Sheba was currently ruled by one not born to rule. If a balance of power was ideal, its center had yet to be established. The fulcrum was on Jerusalem's soil, the lever on which it rested was pointing there as well. But as day becomes night, and seasons change one to the next, winds also shift and forces unseen may bring forth events that are unforeseeable. But in the cover of night, and that night in particular, all was possibility.

CHAPTER 2

Another night, another night awake. In spite of all that had been pleasing to her earlier in the day, and what she had told Solomon at dinner, Makeda was concerned, frightened, unsure. It was his remark about her beauty. It was the message in his eyes. Inexperienced as she was in romantic love, she knew its intense stare. Even though Makeda was born into royalty, she had been subjected to lustful looks since she passed through the age of maturity. She knew she was tall. She knew she possessed both physical strength and exceptional intelligence. She knew her mother had been a beautiful woman. Yet no man had ever called Makeda beautiful before. None had dared, for she had forsworn marriage and become queen so young.

Yes, she knew that the men of Sheba desired her, that they lamented her father's deathbed order that she remain chaste. Their appreciative stares had always been to her a curiosity; she neither rejoiced in nor regretted keeping her virginal vow. Devoted to her father and to her duties, Makeda thought little about such things as the intimate acts between a man and a woman. If they had not been taught to her by her beloved *astamari*, then it could not be important to know of them. She ignored the subject and ruled as she wanted. Whether the respect she received was due to her appearance or to her abilities was impossible to know, and she would not let that rare instance of unknowing disturb her self-esteem.

In the past year, however, Makeda sensed that she was learning something new about herself. For the first time, a man truly excited her. At first, it was strictly due to his reputation for possessing peerless wisdom. *Such an astonishing creature, this Solomon!* The very idea of actually meeting an immensely learned man gave her mind to wander. *What must it be like to be with such a man? What might we discuss? What might we do?* The closer the possibility came to reality, the greater the shift in the locus of her excitement.

First it was Tamrin's tales, his descriptions of how Solomon spoke, how he led, how his wisdom presented itself in the course of a day. Then, once Makeda had made up her mind to go to Israel, she began to imagine him physically. She was so tall; would she have to look down to him? Was he strong? Did he have a kind countenance? Was he—handsome?

It was then that she knew that she was capable of having these strange, churning feelings, the feelings of physical attraction that she had heard of but never experienced herself. A desire to be with a man not merely because of his skills and knowledge, but because of his personality and how he looked. She was for the first time thinking of a man in the way that unvirginal women thought of their husbands. That had always seemed to Makeda to be a limited perspective. A man, for all his political and social power, was to her mind a useful sort of beast of burden. Someone to send into battle. To build a bridge. To drive caravans. But not someone to be adored and to dote on. Having romantic feelings for a man would only make it harder to use him to greatest effect.

And yet, now that she had met Solomon face to face, had spoken and listened to him, walked and dined with him, and taught and learned from him, she felt as if rough waters had caused the ship of her heart to heel from one side to the other. For it was her heart and not just her mind that Solomon excited. But with the joy of this new feeling came that of fear and uncertainty, because of her oath. If she had to, she could control her impulses, she could self-sacrifice. She knew that of herself. But could she control Solomon?

Yes, she had seen in his eyes, had felt in his seemingly accidental touches, and now heard from his sweet honey voice that he was in love with her. Did he know that she was chaste? She didn't recall speaking to him about the law in Ethiopia that all rulers be virgins, that even though Sheba's was an inherited crown, she had sworn herself to chastity out of loyalty to her father. Yet how could she tell him now? Now, when her resolve was weakening? And besides that, were not the stories true, that Solomon had many wives and concubines? *How, then, could his heart, or his chambers, have space for me?*

Unbeknownst to her, Solomon in his bedroom was likewise awake and his thoughts also were of his counterpart, Queen Makeda. He had a harem, yes, but they were mere entertainment, spoils even. His first wife, the Pharaoh's daughter, had helped him forge an alliance with hated Egypt; others were gifts bestowed upon him as a result of successful business dealings or through treaties. Though these women did not fulfill him emotionally or even sexually, he knew that they were a sign of stature, that the number of women he attained would in some foreign leaders' minds be as illustrative of his power as the weight of the gold and jewels in his immense vaults.

His father was different, of course. David had loved women, and he had been happy to use their bodies to satisfy his desires. Surely, Solomon knew, he himself had to have inherited some of his father's notable lust. But for Solomon, a woman's body was not merely a pleasure in itself but also a vessel wherein her intelligence existed. Yet where was the intelligence? Not so close to the mouth, he sensed, because so few of his wives and concubines had anything to say that could tempt the wise king's mental lust. In fact, Solomon despaired of ever finding a woman he would be attracted to both for her beauty and for how well she thought.

Makeda was different. Not merely different. Superior. *The ideal woman*, he thought. Tamrin's tales had intrigued him. But Solomon was well-accustomed to hearing traders exaggerate the fineness of their wares, the value of their materials, the strength of their sponsor. Truth was not a commodity to be found on many a trader's tongue. And yet Tamrin did not oversell the cargo he brought to Solomon. It was indeed very fine, very valuable. And as for his most precious asset—Queen Makeda—Tamrin expertly whetted Solomon's appetite and delivered fully on his promise.

Yes, all that Tamrin had told Solomon about Makeda was true. She was beautiful, she was strong, she was intelligent. *And all three in equal and overabundant portions*, Solomon mused. *This queen of Sheba, tall and black and solid as the ebony tree, with a rushing river of hair and a* mind that reached to the heights of the sun and spread as wide as the ficus tree's boughs, is someone to whom I must continue to get closer.

But does she feel the same way about me as I do about her? She came to me, Solomon reasoned. *She endured a journey of great distance and difficulty. All to meet me. And she has been such wonderful company. Our conversations are deep and meaningful. She must stay. She has given me no notice that her departure is imminent. She is curious, eager to know, to understand. I must keep her stimulated, interested in Israel. In Jerusalem. In me.*

He regretted telling her she was beautiful. It was true but was it too soon to say so? And not just that she was beautiful, but the most beautiful thing in the world! It was unlike Solomon to be so loose with his language, to betray his feelings so clumsily, so overtly. Where was his composure of the first days, when he had set the pace for their mutual discovery? He had begged her not to probe too quickly, for a hole dug in sodden ground right after a rain will simply refill itself with water; better to wait a few days, when the soil is dry and breaks up easily.

We will talk in the morning, Solomon reassured himself. *I will apologize more formally, I will speak more soberly, be more patient. The time to share our feelings will reveal itself to us. I only pray she will forgive my rash words and will in time think as kindly of me as I do of her.*

They met again at breakfast. Solomon attempted to apologize, yet because of her comfort in his presence and her need to confess her status, Makeda dared to interrupt the king in his own home. He permitted it.

"Forgive me, Solomon, but I wish to speak first today. I must tell you about the conditions by which I wear my crown, which I pray will not form a wedge in our friendship."

"I was foolish to speak to you of your beauty yesterday, Makeda. Not because it is a lie, but because it was forced on you. I gave you no chance to prepare for me to express myself so boldly, and I must apologize and ask your forgiveness."

"There is no need for you to apologize; in fact, it is I who am in the wrong."

"I do not understand," Solomon said.

"It is the law in Ethiopia that all rulers must be women, and all must be chaste. It has always been that way."

"This I have heard and this I understand, but you yourself have told me that you inherited the crown from your father and he from his. So Sheba does not follow the ways of Ethiopia, correct?"

"No, we do not. Sheba has been ruled by kings for many hundreds of years. It is because of our wealth and our armies that the throne of Sheba rules supreme over all of Ethiopia. Yet we have allowed the other nations within our kingdom to govern themselves according to their own traditions. The only requirement is that they recognize their subservience to Sheba."

Solomon had a question to pose at this time, but rather than ask it—rather than risk being rash as he had been the day before—he remained silent, allowing Makeda to finish her explanation when she was ready.

The pause in conversation was palpable. It was a weight on Makeda's chest, compressing her lungs and making speech difficult. She thought she had rehearsed sufficiently for this moment, but the combined force of historical fact and her innermost feelings was almost too much to bear. She wished that Solomon would say something, but he did not. The air between them was empty and he was ceding to her the right to fill it. With a deep breath, dislodging the weight of silence, she made the words come.

"My father, as he lay dying—in the final moments of his rule and of his life, he drew from me a vow—that I should be as the other female rulers in our portion of the world—and remain chaste.

"I have been a virgin queen from that moment to this," she continued, "and I am sworn never to take a husband."

Another silence. Makeda was sad. She looked down. Solomon wore the small, silent smile of understanding. He indeed wanted Makeda for a wife but, even more important, he needed an heir and who better to birth his son than the extraordinary Makeda? This was an obstacle but one that was more riddle than immovable object. If he put his mind to it, he was sure he could find a way to get what he wanted. The proper strategy was not to press the issue but to keep Makeda feeling comfortable, cared for, and happy.

"Thank you, Makeda. Once again you have taught me, and I am grateful. Today we will visit my weavers. Let us have new clothes made for you. And then, let us plan a grand feast for all of your people who are here. It is time for Israel and Sheba to make their friendship as solid as the Sinai mountain."

"Yes," she replied. "That would please me very much."

They commenced to eat. But Makeda put down her bread and spoke again.

"Solomon?"

"Yes, Makeda?"

"Thank you. I am most honored to have your affection."

Solomon smiled, and between them bread was broken.

CHAPTER 3

The weavers were visited. The clothes were made. The day passed, and the night. Many other days and nights passed, stacked in measures of weeks and months like fragrant cordwood. Happiness and comfort between the two rulers returned swiftly. Though Solomon guarded his words and Makeda her space, they were united in genuine affection. The hardest times were late at night, when Makeda lay awake in wonder about what could have been and Solomon visited wives to whom he gave all but his heart.

Yet the grand feast proposed by Solomon the night of her confession to him had yet to transpire, so full were their days together.

It came to be that Makeda's stay in Israel equaled the time it had taken her to travel there. Though she felt fulfilled in Solomon's company, she knew she must return to Sheba. It already was an entire year since she had left her homeland—even if she left that very day, her total absence would be longer than anyone had predicted. Though messages had been sent back and forth via ships on the Red Sea, and by all accounts the kingdom was as peaceful and prosperous with Tamrin on the throne as it had been when she was its occupant, Makeda was not ready to abdicate her inheritance and forsake her people.

Thus it was that Makeda approached Solomon one morning and begged leave to return home.

"This day was always to come, of this I was aware," said Solomon. "Yet I must admit it pains my heart, for in spite of your oath, I have sustained the desire to make you my queen."

"I cannot be queen to one man, but only to my people," she replied. "Long have they been without me, and me without them. I, too, am sad to leave Israel. I came here in search of your wisdom, and I will leave having found your friendship. Truly, my riches have trebled in these months that I have had the honor of being in your company."

"I cannot follow you," said Solomon, "though my heart says I ought. I cannot leave Israel vulnerable. We have many enemies."

"I know."

"So we may never see each another again."

"I know."

Solomon stepped a few paces away from Makeda, then turned and walked back. He needed to be the strategist, not the lovelorn, and in the short pause he created in their conversation, a strategy had come to him.

"My dear Makeda, I fear my wisdom has failed me. No judgment I give could keep you here, and no order of mine are you bound to obey. But I cannot let you leave without a feast to commemorate our friendship. I spoke of this some time ago and never fulfilled my promise. I pray you will allow me to entertain you and your caravan this evening, that you all may embark on your journey tomorrow morning with satisfied bellies and warm remembrances."

"It would indeed be our honor, Solomon. I only wish it was in my power to reward you for all you have done for me and my people. No gift of gold or jewels could repay you for what you have taught me. I can only give you my word that should you ever be able to visit Sheba, that it would be a festival for the entire duration of your stay."

As Makeda left to speak with her retinue, Solomon called for his chefs. He insisted on a specific menu. Fish coated with pepper, spiced lamb well-done, root vegetables cooked without oil over fire. Makeda's wine was to be lightly diluted with vinegar. Nothing to be dipped, no condiments, but salt bowls at every table. Makeda's goblet was to remain full.

As evening fell and the guests assembled in the palace, Solomon rose to speak. Makeda sat at his right, wearing a dress of many colors made by the weavers on that day that seemed so long ago.

"The queen of the south came to us six months ago," he announced. "She brought us the finest goods from the land of Sheba, that we may complete our temple to the Lord our God. She came in peace, in friendship. She leaves tomorrow with many gifts from our stores—with wagons and camels, jewels and textiles, grain and meat, and the deep love and affection of all of Israel. Her time with us will not be forgotten; it will be a memory we will cherish to the end of days, and we do thank her for gracing us with her visit."

With that, all raised their mugs and drank. Many more toasts were offered, the food was served, Makeda's cup was filled and refilled. All were in the most pleasant of spirits. There was entertainment as well: harpists and timbrel players, singers and dancers, magicians and storytellers. It was the grandest feast ever to occur during Solomon's rule.

It grew late. Solomon announced that the feast had come to an end. As servants went to work and guests left for their tents, Solomon came to Makeda with a request most earnest.

"Makeda, it is your last night in Jerusalem. We may never see each other again in this world. I pray you, will you not spend what remains of the evening in my personal chamber with me?"

"Solomon, we have spoken on this subject before."

"No, we have spoken on a different subject, many different subjects, in fact. But as to your virtue, I am not asking you to defy the laws of your kingdom or your oath to your father. I am not asking you to willingly submit to my desire. I am merely asking you to share my room. My room, that is, and not my bed."

"You want that I should make my bed in your chamber, but that we remain apart? And you swear not to approach me?"

"That is my request, Makeda."

"And you place no other conditions or guidelines on this arrangement, by which I might risk forfeiting my virtue?"

"Surely, Makeda, you are the wisest one in Jerusalem today. Or maybe the most cautious? It is true, though. There is one condition. You see, to share my chamber is an honor, an honor I have granted to few others. In my rooms are many valuables, many precious items that are dear to me. By having someone spend the night within this space, I am the one at risk. Many are the temptations for a thief."

"A thief? You think I would steal from you, Solomon? You grant that I am wise, and I am grateful for such acknowledgement. But you do not mention that I share another trait with you: I, too, am wealthy. And while your vaults are enormous and overflowing, I have no need to take anything of yours that you do not choose to give to me freely."

"I have many wives, Makeda. I have no need to take anything from you that you do not give me freely, either. Yet still I know desire. I understand temptation. It may lie dormant in a person from a distance, but with proximity, that temptation grows, that desire becomes unquenchable. Your riches are many, Makeda, but inside my chamber, you may find you have an appetite for more. So you would not object to my making just one condition in order that I may sleep soundly tonight?"

"What is that condition?"

"If you steal anything inside my chamber, take anything within my sleeping quarters that does not belong to you, you will permit me to have your virginity as payment."

Makeda took some moments to consider this condition. *Is he trying to trick me?* she wondered. *What is his game? Surely there is nothing at all in his palace that I would want or need so badly that I would take it without asking. And in the course of just a single evening, what are the chances anything should tempt me so? It is, after all, our last night together, and I will be sad to leave. I would value spending as much time with him as possible. But is it worth the risk? Is there a risk? I do not see it.*

"I accept, Solomon," said Makeda. "I accept because I want to be with you as much as possible before I leave for Sheba. I want nothing from you but time and will take nothing with me but wonderful memories."

Makeda returned to her tent to prepare for spending the night in Solomon's chamber. She was excited—curious still, questioning his motives and the condition he had set, but indeed also excited. She understood that their meeting, their friendship, was historic and fruitful. Tonight would be the last of her stay in Israel. It was right that they share it together.

Sufficiently prepared, Makeda walked back to the palace, where Solomon himself escorted her inside. A bed for her had been set up twenty paces from his own. Between the two beds was a table, on the table a vase of flowers, a jug of water, and a cup. The two rulers spoke briefly with each other—she thanking him for the feast, he expressing gratitude for her willingness to share his space. He recited poetry to her. She sang him a song from her land. And then they retired, separately yet together, in the silent night.

Makeda had difficulty finding sleep. Not unusual for her, but this time was different. Her throat was dry, her mouth heated by the spicy, salty food served at the feast. The drinks she had consumed were insufficient to quell the prickly feeling on her tongue. She turned in her bed from side to side, tried to draw saliva into a pool that she could use to lubricate the affected areas. She deployed her mind to will herself to sleep, to ignore the hot-sand sensation in her mouth that irritated her so intensely.

Eventually, she sat up in her bed. In the dark she could make out the shape of Solomon's bed and in the foreground, the table with the flowers. And the jug of water. Relief. Her only thought was that she mustn't awaken Solomon, so she arose slowly, silently stepped toward the table, carefully poured water into the cup, and drank it. It was cool and soothing, and she began to pour a second time when suddenly Solomon stirred.

"And so, temptation reveals the thief," he said.

"What do you mean? I am no thief, I am merely drinking the water you provided."

"The water belongs to me, Makeda. It was drawn from my well by my own servant, poured into a jug that is mine, which sat on a table I own that stands in my room. You never asked permission to take it, you had no thought of replacing it. I now have less water than when the night began, and it is because you stole it. You have broken the condition, and unless your integrity has been lost in this warm black night, you are thereby honor-bound to accede to my desire."

"I didn't—" Makeda began to speak, but she knew she had been tricked and that she had willfully entered into a challenge that she lost. She could argue with Solomon, but she could not win. Solomon would spin logical assertions more deftly than his most productive weaver could assemble cloths. He would wear her out. In the end, the result would be the same. She owed Solomon her virginity, and she gave it to him shyly but, ultimately, not reluctantly. Solomon peeled away the mysteries of romantic love for her along with her clothing, and, praising her garden, did feast and sow in it lovingly. As every day had been for Makeda since she had arrived in Israel, this night was about expanding her knowledge and soaking in the wonders of Solomon. As he completed the act, she held him tightly, her strong arms and legs binding him to her. He had never experienced her strength so directly, and she, having allowed him inside, was not about to let him depart so easily.

They awoke the next morning, still entwined in her bed, the water cup still wet, the rising sun falling upon the curtains and giving clear form to the shapes inside Solomon's chamber. They looked at each other, smiled, but said nothing. Soon, out of necessity, they stirred. The sun was rising and it was time for Makeda to leave.

Prologue III: SOLOMON

He sat alone in his new home, his palatial home that was built immediately following the completion of the house of the Lord, the holy temple that was the first duty and accomplishment of his reign. While for years he had been content to live in the palace his father, David, had built, with Makeda gone Solomon felt the urge to start anew. Inside this new palace was the Hall of Judgment, where he conducted official business; south of the temple stood the House of the Forest of Lebanon, where military equipment was stored. Together they comprised a wondrous complex of grand structures rivaled only by Egypt's gargantuan monuments.

Constructed largely of stone and cedar, the palace was notable for its numerous pillars: three rows of fifteen pillars each that traversed its length, plus a colonnade paced with pillars, and in front, two truly remarkable pillars cast in bronze by Huram-abi, a Tyrian craftsman recommended for the task by Hiram, the king of Tyre. To crown the two bronze pillars Huram-abi had made bronze chapiters, adorned with carved lily-work and pomegranates. The bronze pillars were of such a splendor that they were named by their creator: The one on the right was Jachin and the one on the left was Boaz.

Vanity of vanities, he thought. *All is vanity.*

Solomon sat alone in his home, not in the presence of its pillars but on the throne of the Hall of Judgment, in which each wall from floor to rafters was paneled in fragrant cedar. This was the room in which he would deliberate and deliver rulings on matters brought before him, where his greatest attribute—his wisdom—was on full and essential display. The Hall of Judgment was a sober room, built for contemplation and analysis, and it was empty this day except for his presence, for with no other business requiring his attention he chose to inhabit it to wonder silently when—and whether ever—she would return to him.

One generation passes, as yet another generation comes to pass. Yet the earth remains constant. The sun rises and sets as it will. The winds go this way and that, yet never are gone for good. All rivers run to the sea, but the sea never overflows. All remains in balance.

Solomon had lived for many years before meeting Makeda. Only God knew how many more years he would live without her. But how different those two spans of time were, for he had lacked nothing of meaning before she came. And now, having known her for six short but rich months, every day without her seemed to last a millennium. The palace was new, bold, luxurious, yet he could not enjoy it. Its massive pillars, its polished marble, its brass and gold, the servants, the guests, the wives, the concubines—they did nothing to cleanse his home of the emptiness he felt inside.

All the works that have been done under the sun, I have seen them. Yet there is no wonder or amazement in my eyes; all is but vanity and vexation of spirit.

For all its size and splendor, his home brought no joy to Solomon. All its mighty pillars could not replace the stabilizing presence of Makeda. It was as if his life had been sunrise, all potential and possibility, and then she came and the sun was at its highest point in the heavens, and the light in his mind and the warmth in his soul were at their peak, and all was clear and visible, clear and understandable, clear and unfettered, and his happiness was as complete as the sun was bright. Then she returned to her native land, and all was perpetual sunset, darkening and dismal, and the best of his days were behind him, and night, eternal night, lay in front, and what—if indeed anything—might be beyond that was obscured by dusk.

Sheba. That was her land. Whence she came. Where she returned. So far away a traveler on camel from here to there would miss both the planting season and the harvest season. Yet Makeda had willingly made the journey, just to see him. And just as willingly, she had journeyed home. And so he waited, months, years now, in his magnificent new palace where he took silent moments like this to sit and wait and wonder if, when, she might return. And if she didn't, could he survive?

There was another unknown as well. Was Sheba home now to his heir? And would that son ever come to Jerusalem to claim his legacy? *All my wisdom*, he thought, *and yet there is so much I don't know. What good is it then?*

He rose from his throne and walked to a window. He looked out as far as he could, until the horizon blocked his view of the world beyond it.

And then he looked up and he saw the moon. Surrounded by darkness, it radiated light. Was this Ilumqah? Was Makeda now looking at the same thing from her home? Could this moon god bring her back to him? Would Ilumqah hear his prayer? Solomon knew only that he could not will her to return. Just as he could not will his tears to stop.

I gave my heart to know wisdom. Yet I have found that in much wisdom there is much grief. He that increases in knowledge increases in sorrow.

THE FIRST BOOK OF MENELIK

CHAPTER 1

Makeda's departure became a stirring scene encompassing almost the full spectrum of human emotions. The happiest people were those in Makeda's caravan who had been separated from their families for a year now and would not see them again for six months more. Still, for them to be beginning the long trek home was cause for celebration, though all were careful not to show their feelings out of respect for their queen's mixed emotions at this parting.

Indeed, Makeda herself was experiencing a range of feelings: gratitude and joy, sadness and remorse, anticipation and relief, fear and guilt. The tearing of her hymen could not be repaired, but there was hope that from that regretful though ultimately pleasurable act, she might yet bear an heir to her throne—if not her father's express wish, at least assurance that the family and royal lines would be continued. From a diplomatic perspective, she knew her visit had been a great success, and the advantages to her people in terms of trade and political and military alliance with Israel would last for generations to come. She felt enriched by her time with Solomon.

Enriched, yes—yet also, to a degree, violated.

Even so, she had to believe that good would ultimately come of their sexual union. Why else would Solomon pursue her so aggressively? Had she even subconsciously allowed herself to be tricked? Had she intentionally taken the water, understanding that everything in Solomon's tent was Solomon's property? The idea of being pregnant with an heir was a satisfying one. Perhaps this was a dream of hers that she had never allowed herself to acknowledge, never believed could be fulfilled. She did not, after all, volunteer to be chaste. It was forced on her when she was too young to understand what would be its consequence when she became a woman. She was now grown, supremely intelligent and rational, and a powerful queen. Surely if she could rule a large kingdom as she wished, she could lead her own life as she wished.

Makeda also knew, deep down, that she had romantic feelings for Solomon. She had been afraid to act on them, and announcing her desire to leave Israel for Sheba provided a convenient means of deflection. Desire. Yes, desire played a part. If the timing was wrong, his approach more cunning than caring, in the end Makeda opened her legs for him unforced. Thus, as she approached Solomon to say goodbye, she did so with a curious blend of acceptance and defiance, affection and diplomacy.

As for Solomon, he, too, hoped that his seed would bear fruit, that from Makeda's garden would spring forth an heir to his own throne in Jerusalem. For all his wives, Solomon had only one son whom he acknowledged: Rehoboam, whose mother was Naamah, an Ammonite. Surely if a son of Solomon, and thus a future king of Israel, was to have a foreign mother, then Makeda was the ideal choice.

And yet his hope was severely tempered by sadness—more than sadness, grief. For he realized even in the cunning act he had undertaken the previous evening, that what once had been friendship was now something more. Always did he respect Makeda's intelligence and her desire for learning. Always had he felt a deep attraction to the tall, strong, black queen. But now the depth of his heartbreak was evidence enough that he had grown to love her. Yet he could not show his grief to his people—nor to Makeda and her people. So while Solomon may have been the aggressor hours before, now he felt as if a guilty subject to the queen of Sheba.

In the moment of their parting, ignoring protocol, Makeda spoke first, softly, though, so only they two could hear.

"I still hold that I did not steal anything from you, Solomon, but I do believe now that our union was willed to be."

"I would be relieved to have faith that it was so, Makeda. It was not how I had hoped it would be. Not as tender as it had played in my mind for so long. I know only that you are the one. You are the one I needed to mate with. The only one worthy. The only one I really care for."

"We shall know before long whether I am with child. If so, then that child will enjoy blessings that outnumber the stars."

"It is all within you, Makeda. You, like no other besides God Himself, has the power to create the world, the new world that will be built after we are gone. To be built by our child. I have done all I can do, the remainder is the work of your strong and capable body."

"I must go now. You have given me so much, I cannot ask for more. However, there *is* something of yours I intend to take with me."

"And what is that, fair Makeda? Though please know, before you answer, that there is no limit to what I would give you, and all you need do is to ask. I would deny you nothing, and put no limit on the quantity of the gifts you desire."

"Thank you, Solomon. I have all I need. I always did, and yet my cup now overflows with sweet abundance, thanks to you. But the thing I take with me now is not something that sits within your impressive vaults. It is far larger, and yet there is but one of it. It is your God, Solomon. No longer shall I worship the sun and the moon, only the One Eternal God, the God of Israel, which is to be my God as well. For I have seen how your loyalty to your God has given you wisdom, peace, and kindness, which you share both generously and with grace."

Tears came to the wise king's eyes. All observers felt impelled to look away, even as they craned to hear the highly personal, emotionally charged words of the two rulers.

"I am truly humbled by you, Makeda. I shall never forget you. And so that you should not forget me, I ask you to take this ring with my mark upon it. If you have a male child, he is to wear this ring when he comes of age. And should he journey to Jerusalem to seek me, by this ring I will know him to be our son. And all that I would do for you, I would do for him."

Solomon took the ring from his finger. Cast of gold, it felt warm to Makeda as he placed it in her palm. She closed her fingers around it and held it tightly. She imagined one day giving the ring to her son. *May it be so, please, God.* Thus was her first prayer to the God of Israel.

Solomon and Makeda embraced. Protocol be damned, they kissed, albeit briefly, their tongues quickly yet subtly taking in the other's salt upon their lips. No spice ever grown and ground by pestle could offer such intense flavor. They then released each other and all at once there was a flurry of activity, as wagons were loaded with supplies and plentiful gifts from Solomon—jewels, precious metals, food. Camels, also from Solomon, were bound to the wagons so as to pull them across the deserts on the long, dry journey. Makeda took her place in the caravan. With a wave of her hand they were in motion, and the Israelites who had gathered to see off the cherished guests cheered the Shebans as they set out on their way home. Solomon watched for just a few moments before returning to his palace. Makeda's trip, he knew, had an end; his wait, however, might not.

Makeda had decided that since they had traveled to Israel from the eastern shore of the Red Sea—logical, since that is where Sheba is located—on the return trip they should travel south along the water's western shore, which would take them through Egypt, Sudan, Eritrea, and Ethiopia. They would then board ships to sail across the narrow southern part of the Red Sea, near where it empties into the Gulf of Aden. This route would take somewhat longer, which did not please many in the caravan, as it would require first crossing the broad Sinai peninsula. But Makeda saw this as a unique opportunity to spread her name across the entire world of which she knew—and surely, as word of her long stay in Israel with King Solomon traversed the region, many would be interested in meeting the queen who was deemed his equal.

In time, unlike on the trip from Sheba to Jerusalem, the caravan faced problems—chiefly because of Makeda's increasingly apparent pregnancy. Her discomfort grew steadily as the phases of sickness and pain took hold. There were days when she couldn't take the bumpiness of riding on uneven terrain, nights of poor sleep. She required additional stops for food and drink and to relieve herself.

Knowledge of her pregnancy turned the journey home into something more like a pilgrimage, a spiritual undertaking but one with a difference: The destination was not a place, but rather a birth. It was not so much for them to arrive somewhere, but for the baby inside of Makeda's swelling abdomen to appear to them. Could the baby wait until the caravan reached Sheba? Not even Solomon could have told them with any certainty. No, the yet-unborn child—whether a son or a daughter, none could tell—was now in charge of the journey. The child decided when to stop, when to continue. When Makeda was joyful and content, and when she was distraught and distressed. The child, having no map to consult, would come when he or she wanted to, with no regard for where the caravan might be and how much longer it had to go.

And so it was at thirty-six weeks, just as the caravan neared Eritrea, that the child's growth made it so that Makeda could bear no more travel. She ordered the caravan to halt, requested and received assistance from the local healer, and resolved to have her baby there when the time came. A tent was erected for her comfort and privacy, a messenger was sent on ahead to alert Tamrin of the situation. The king of Eritrea took responsibility for Makeda's security. The watch began.

Finally, nine months and five days after she had left Solomon, beside the Mai Bella stream in the province of Hamasien, Eritrea, Makeda went into labor and began to know a pain exponentially greater than the jackal's jaws on her leg when she was a child. She would not give in to it. With the expertise and care of the local midwife, the queen of Sheba's birth canal pulsed and pushed, and a genetically superior baby began to appear head-first through the opening of Makeda's stretched vagina. Like Moses taken from the waters of the Nile, the baby was lifted from the rush of amniotic fluid by the midwife and swaddled in cloth.

"What is it?" pleaded Makeda, her voice hoarse, her eyes clouded by tears, her insides burning, her legs weak, her stomach rubbery, and her heart a galloping steed.

"You have been blessed with a male child, Queen Makeda," said the midwife, placing the boy on his mother's heaving breast. Makeda laughed. More tears. She kissed her son's head, smelled it. Thought of his father. Thought of her father. Said a blessing. *I praise you, eternal God, Who made earth and heaven and brings all life into being. I will sing Your praises all my life for this gift with which You have blessed me.*

She named the child Menelik, or Ibn al-Hakim: son of the wise man. On the eighth day of his life, Menelik was circumcised. On the tenth day, the caravan continued on to Sheba. Makeda was able to lie on a straw mattress in the back of a hooded wagon, where she brought her son to her nipple and he drank greedily of her milk until his brown lips stopped moving and the sleep of satiation overtook his small body. Also exhausted, Makeda nonetheless felt complete. All that remained was the return of her throne.

CHAPTER 2

Tamrin had ruled Sheba for two harvests and then some. Communications from the caravan were spare and came only about every three or four months. Therefore, there was little that he understood about what Makeda was experiencing in Israel, only that she was in no rush for that experience to end. This did not trouble Tamrin in the least; he knew this journey was important to his queen—yes, in spite of the fact that he sat on her throne, and had for so long that he now wore a long beard to give him a greater sense of seriousness and piety, Makeda was always his queen. He also knew that the longer she stayed, the more she was gaining from being in Solomon's company. And yet he knew that she would return.

He did not know, however, until the caravan made an extended stop in Eritrea that Makeda had become pregnant and was to give birth imminently. This was news of the most extraordinary nature. For so many had desired her, Tamrin included, yet it had always been an impossibility. She had promised her father the king as he spoke his last words, and Makeda had always been fiercely loyal to him. What had changed? And who—well, surely it had to be—but could it be true? And if it were, how then would *he* allow her to leave?

While the kingdom had remained peaceable in her absence, it was not bereft of trouble. Eleni, spurned by the loyal soldier Sharaf, had attempted to assassinate Tamrin herself so as to take Sheba's crown for her own. This act took place six months after Makeda left for Jerusalem, about the time, Eleni determined, that Makeda would arrive there. This meant that the queen was the farthest from Sheba that she would go and so could never return in time to mount her own defense; at the same time, if she decided to return at once it would mean her desired alliance with Solomon would never have time to form. For Eleni, however, it meant she would have plenty of time to entice the army to pledge their loyalty to her and she would be well ensconced in power by the time her rival made it back to Sheba.

Sadly for Eleni, she was clumsy and obvious, and her wine-fueled, one-woman attack on the palace—with a sword in one hand and a torch in the other—was thwarted well before she was in striking distance of Tamrin. She was promptly separated from her weapons and detained. Upon learning of her act, Sharaf went to Tamrin and admitted that he knew of her plans and had failed to stop her. He told his ruler that Eleni approached him because of his relationship to her father. With bowed head and his own sword laid on the floor before his prostrated body, Sharaf surrendered himself to Tamrin's mercy. Which he received.

"You have always been loyal to Queen Makeda, Sharaf, and just as you and Eleni's father have an important relationship, so I know well that Eleni and our queen also have a long relationship. I am disinclined to punish you, because while you did not arrest or kill this person who had evil plans for Sheba's throne, you did refuse her request and so proved your loyalty to your country, as you have to Eleni's father.

"At the same time," Tamrin continued, "I am unsure what to do about Eleni, for while she has clearly moved from discussing plans to overthrow my rule to taking action against me, she is still not only a friend of my lady—er, our queen—but her cousin as well. Raise yourself, Sharaf, and take up your sword. Eleni is to remain confined to her tent until further notice. You are to recruit three others and stand guard outside her tent at all times, day and night. She is permitted to receive food, but may not venture outside."

Sharaf bowed and went off to obey Tamrin's orders. *Here, then,* thought Tamrin, *is a puzzle for Solomon himself. What to do about a friend who becomes an enemy? How do I keep the throne secure and yet spare Makeda the pain of having her own cousin and childhood playmate put to death?*

Tamrin needed to rule with authority, that the people and neighboring nations would knew that Sheba and Ethiopia were not vulnerable, that law and justice would prevail during Makeda's absence, and that the country was capable of responding to threats. At the same time, he did not wish to do anything that could not be undone if it were to come to pass that Makeda would have handled things differently. Even though Eleni was intent on capturing not Tamrin's interim crown so much as Makeda's birthright, he could not enable Makeda to show mercy at some later date if he showed no mercy in the present. The queen might choose to overrule Tamrin's judgment in matters of property or lesser punishments, but she could not bring back to life someone who had been executed.

So it was that the lives of both Eleni and Sharaf were spared—at least until Makeda returned. And in a crushing irony, Eleni now was impatient for her old friend to return, in the hopes that she would be freed from her confinement.

On the day that the caravan rode into Sheba, there was a nationwide festival. Though no official proclamation had been made about their queen having become a mother, many had heard and were eager to see the child. And while Makeda was still trying to reconcile the reality of her motherhood with her expectations for her life and the responsibilities of her crown, the people she ruled were, by and large, overjoyed. As she told Tamrin later, after the crowds had dispersed and the transfer of power back to her was done, she had not wanted people to be informed too soon, lest it cause upset and disruption of the country's peace. Seeing and hearing their enthusiasm and affection—both for herself and for Menelik—lessened the burden she had placed upon herself, as she understood that she would bear no shame nor be haunted by what she had allowed to happen to herself.

"It is so good to be back in Sheba, Tamrin. I was not sure how I would be greeted. You and I have both changed since we left," she said with a smile as she reached out and touched Tamrin's beard.

"Perhaps, my lady," Tamrin replied. "But I am now merely a trader just as I was before and can cut off these whiskers, whereas your change cannot be undone."

"That is true, but I have no regrets over it. I believe this was meant to be. I felt it when you came back from your visit with Solomon and when

I made my own journey and learned firsthand that everything you told me about him was true. I could not bring him here, could not stay with him there, but now with Menelik we are connected."

"What I said just now, about a change that cannot be undone—"

"Yes, Tamrin?"

Tamrin told Makeda about Eleni: about how she had approached Sharaf but that he had refused her and warned her not to attempt a coup, about Eleni's bungled attempt to carry out the deed by herself, and about Tamrin's reluctance to order the ultimate punishment carried out against Eleni and Sharaf.

"My queen, do you wish to question or change my judgments?"

"I never doubted my choice of you to rule over Sheba in my absence, Tamrin. I knew you were fair and trustworthy, and loyal above all else. As I sit here now, I agree with what we said earlier, that I have changed and cannot change back to the way I was. For I have studied with Solomon, and I have witnessed his approach to justice, his belief in the value of every person. I hope that the lessons I have learned from him will continue to guide me for as long as I rule.

"So as to the matter of Sharaf," Makeda continued, "I know him well, and I know his relationship to Eleni's father; for that matter, I remember my uncle Tefere and the trouble he tried to bring to my father after my mother died. Yet Tefere was good to Sharaf, and Sharaf's concern and loyalty to him is praiseworthy. As is Sharaf's own admission of guilt and willingness to accept the consequences of his decision to take no action against Eleni. I agree, then, that Sharaf should receive no punishment.

"As for Eleni, she has always been a jealous friend and an unloving cousin. I have forgiven her many times for many offenses because she is both friend and family to me. But I can do so no longer."

Tamrin was surprised. His mouth opened and he was speechless for a moment before he asked, "Are you sure?"

"Eleni tried to launch a conspiracy against me and failed," said Makeda. "If that were her only crime, then I could forgive her once more. But then she made a direct attack on her own. Though it was thwarted, it is reasonable to presume that she may attempt it again in the future. I do not fear for myself, nor doubt the strength and loyalty of my army, but now I am not alone in the assassin's eye. If Eleni would kill me, she would also kill Menelik. If she killed me today, Menelik would have the right to reclaim the crown when he came of age. But if she were to kill both of us, then the line of my father ends. I will not allow that. Eleni, then, is to be put to death immediately.

"Please understand, Tamrin, that in overruling you, I do not criticize you in the least bit," Makeda continued. "Your judgment was both cautious and compassionate, which is appropriate given the unusual circumstances. You will always been an honored man in Sheba and my personal friend."

Makeda dismissed Tamrin and gave the order to execute Eleni and to have two guards dedicated to protecting Menelik at all times. She had nursed her son since birthing him in Eritrea, but now that she was back in Sheba and returned to her throne, she felt it was impractical to continue. The next day, she appointed two women to serve as nurses and caretakers, to feed and care for him while she attended to her royal responsibilities.

Makeda never questioned her ruling as to Eleni's fate. The traitor's death came swiftly and silently, and Eleni made no protest nor pleaded for a mercy she knew would never come.

As Makeda sat on her throne with Menelik in her lap, she spoke to him softly about his father, the wise man; about his future as ruler over all Ethiopia; and about how he, this tiny baby boy, made her feel like the most powerful woman on earth, for she had taken Solomon's seed and created within her own being this beautiful and remarkable creature.

The transition of power from Makeda to Tamrin and back to Makeda had been smooth. For that she was grateful. Even before meeting Solomon, she was proven wise in her choice of Tamrin to occupy the throne in her absence. She also knew that in the future there would be a transition of power from Makeda to Menelik, and she prayed to the One Eternal God that when that day should come, it should be likewise easy as well as successful for both her people and for her son, the son of the wise man.

For with God, everything is noticed.

CHAPTER 3

What had the sun to do with this? she asked herself while examining the five small yet exquisitely detailed fingers on each of his delicate hands. The symmetrical lengths, the engraved lines, the thin, tiny nails that crowned each one. *For that matter, what had the moon to do with this, other than mutely witnessing the conception? Where did this perfect creature come from? Inside me, of course, but how? I know how, but HOW? How did that act, that combination of reckless lust and resigned surrender, sweaty, messy (and my thirst barely quenched by that damned water!), create a perfectly formed baby with jeweled eyes and sculpted nose, round knees and stringy hair, pink tongue, and earthen complexion? This young boy who breathed on his own, who would one day think on his own, walk on his own, rule—.*

No, this was not the work of Shams or Ilumqah. This was not merely the result of a man's seed and a woman's flower. This was not about magic or agriculture, science or construction. This was something more, something mysterious yet undeniably powerful. *This must be God. Only God could do this. Humans are the ingredients, but God is the cook. It happened inside me. Somehow. God worked within me. God took from Solomon and within me made Menelik. He formed in my body, entered the living world through my opening, and now is nourished by me.*

Though Makeda had assigned nurses to take care of Menelik's infant needs, she could not bear to be without him. And while she may still have been concerned about how she would be perceived if she tried to lead with a young child at her side, Makeda would not deny her son his mother's own milk. For the next month, she did as much nursing and caring for Menelik as she could. In truth, she was still recovering from the physical trauma of birth and so kept her official duties to a minimum as her body healed.

In time, however, the baby was returned to the primary care of the nurses and only was brought to the palace when official visitors came to see and bring gifts for the small heir. Makeda was there for him in the mornings and the evenings, sometimes rising in the night to quell Menelik's crying but more typically taking the rest she needed, knowing that he was in good hands whenever he wailed his needs. *Had I been like this?* she wondered. *Had my mother felt this way about me? Had I been fed with her milk? Had she come to me at night?*

By his third year of life, Menelik's features were set. He would be handsome indeed, with his large eyes, strong nose, and sweet smile. He was precociously curious, chasing lizards, collecting rocks of all sizes, shapes, and colors, testing his voice and his growing mastery of words. At five years, the way his arms hung beside his lean body suggested he would be tall. He was active, running everywhere, trying to climb everything. He got into mischief, but he was honest. If he did wrong, he admitted it. He liked to run, but he did not run away. Makeda was proud of her son and could not help seeing shades of Solomon in him—and of herself as well.

She knew it was time that Menelik had a teacher, an *astamari* of his own. It was time for him to learn about the world, about the sky and the earth and the waters and all the living things they hosted. So much to learn. Everything but the identity of his father. Not yet. Makeda did not want her son to be affected by the knowledge that his father was so special, lest he feel that he need not work to become a worthwhile man himself. Her love of learning had driven her to excel even though she was the daughter of royalty; Menelik, too, would become worthy of his birthright through his own efforts.

There were other reasons that Makeda sought to keep Menelik's patrimony from him until he was older. One was her fear that he would want to meet his father, and if he did so, perhaps he would want to stay with Solomon, and her son would be lost to her. She knew she could never make such a long journey again, but Menelik was young and had the same inclination for adventure that Makeda had had when she was younger. Another reason was that she wanted Menelik to rule over Ethiopia, even though he also was entitled to become the next king of Israel. She needed time to impress upon him the honor of ruling his true homeland as his maternal grandfather had done. Though to be fair, Menelik's paternal grandfather, David, had ruled over his own homeland as well. But this was not to be spoken of. Not to Menelik. Not yet.

It was not easy keeping such an immense secret from him. Certainly in his first year of life, everyone in Sheba talked about Makeda and Solomon's union. That talk largely died down as he grew older since it was well-known and accepted; in fact, most people had been excited by the news and proud of their queen for having won the heart of the wise king. Yet children were not creatures adept at keeping secrets, and Makeda was afraid Menelik's playmates, having heard the truth from their parents, would tell him who his father was. And it was true that some children took to calling him "the wise prince," though the deeper meaning of the tease had escaped Menelik.

At the same time, Makeda did teach her son that while her people had long worshipped the sun god and the moon god, she was devoted to the One God that had a special relationship with the children of Israel. While she wanted Menelik to also follow the God that Solomon had spoken so passionately about to her, she hoped that he would not question why he had to worship Israel's God instead of the many native gods to which people throughout Sheba and Ethiopia still prayed.

As it turned out, for all of Menelik's innate curiosity, he wasn't particularly inquisitive. His new teacher aside, he preferred learning about things on his own, through experience and activity, rather than by asking questions. If he saw a shrew burrowing into the ground, he would take a stick and begin to dig, hoping to find how it lived down there. Noticing a woman making paints from flowers and roots, he copied her and came to enjoy painting pictures of things he would see on his walks. Through his first ten years, the secret of his patrilineage seemed safe.

By the time Menelik had reached the age of twelve, however, things had changed. Instead of exploring the world around him as he had done with such joy and purpose as a youth, he began to question his own identity. He noticed the changes happening to his body and to his voice. He became more attuned to what older people said in his presence. He was not a particularly fast learner in his lessons with his teacher, and so the name "wise prince" began to cause him discomfort. He knew what his given name meant: son of the wise man. *Who is this wise man? Will I become wise one day as well?*

He asked his teacher if he could tell him who his father was, but the teacher demurred.

"There is information I cannot provide you, Menelik," the teacher said. "Both because there are some things I do not know, and because there are some things you cannot learn from me. When the time is right, you need to ask your mother."

"When will the time be right?"

"When you can live not one more day without knowing."

"I think the time has come, my teacher."

"Maybe it has. But that doesn't mean you will learn what you seek to know. Some knowledge is dispersed like weeds on the earth and all you have to do is pluck it from the soil. But other knowledge is like a jewel in a vault, and merely desiring it will not get it for you."

"You are saying my mother won't tell me?"

"I do not know if she will tell you or not. But if not, she will have her reasons and you must respect that. Remember, no vault is locked forever. There is a time to live in knowledge and there is a time to live in mystery."

"But you still think that I should go to my mother and ask her who my father is? That is your advice?"

"Questions always come before answers, Menelik. That is why you do not know the answer today. You have not yet asked the question. You may not get the answer you want from the queen, but you surely will not if you do not ask her."

"And if I lack the courage to ask her?" A worthwhile question, since Menelik had only now been able to summon the courage necessary to raise the subject with his teacher, let alone his mother.

"Then you lack the courage to know," his teacher replied. "Understand: In gaining knowledge you gain responsibility. Simply knowing is never enough; you must then find meaning in that knowledge and put it to use constructively. Babies are ignorant because they cannot do anything with knowledge. You are becoming a young man, Menelik. There is much you can do with the knowledge you gain. Your question is important. The answer will be important. So your first question is to yourself: Am I ready to know?"

Menelik looked down at his feet, then up at his teacher. He bowed and walked away. His heart raced, but his pace was slow and deliberate. He was headed for home, to the palace where his mother, Makeda, sat on her throne. A throne he would one day inherit, so he believed. *What king never knew his father*, he wondered. His teacher's words echoed in his head. *Am I ready to know? Am I ready to know? Am I?*

The palace was in view. The question continued to ring. It could not be ignored. He could not escape his need to know. Menelik looked up at the sun. The light caused white glimmers to appear in his vision. The palace appeared spotted. In a few moments, his full unfettered vision was restored. In that instant of clarity, he knew what he must do. He knew it was time at last to learn the mystery, to bring what was hidden into the light. He knew now the answer to his teacher's question.

I am.

THE SECOND BOOK OF MENELIK

CHAPTER 1

"I knew this day would come, my son," said Makeda with lips that were dry and eyes that were wet. "Yet still I feared it. I was not sure I could bear to face the moment, and now it has come to be."

She turned away from Menelik but quickly turned back. She did not want to give the impression that she was refusing his request. She just needed time to compose herself—and her reply.

"With so long to prepare for this, I find myself feeling quite unprepared. So what am I to say? What do I tell my beloved son on this bittersweet day?"

"All I ask is your blessing," replied Menelik. He was twenty-two years of age now. A man. It was time and he was ready. Ready at last to sail to Israel, to enter Jerusalem, to meet King Solomon, his father. He was a man now. He didn't need his mother's permission. Yet that is precisely what he sought.

"My blessing you have, my son, but what then is left for me?"

"I don't understand."

"It was ten years ago that you asked me the name of your father. I knew that day would come as well, but it was different. I had no intention of denying you the truth, once you had acknowledged your need to know the truth. And I told you, proudly, that King Solomon, the wisest and fairest man in the world, was your father. And that he favored me to provide for him an heir, and that you grew in the soil of my deep love for Solomon, whose teachings were so important to me. I always hoped that you would emulate him when you became a man. And you have."

"I am honored that you think so, Mother."

"Yes, in many ways you are his exact image. Handsome, sensitive, compassionate, creative. Not as wise, of course, but no one is. How I wish I could tell you all you ever wanted to know about your father, and—and—"

"Yes?" Menelik softly asked so as to gently break the pause in his mother's halting, haunted speech.

"And still keep you near me."

Menelik looked down. He had feared it would come to this.

"I am not leaving you forever, Mother."

"Perhaps not, but perhaps you are. I know what it is like to ride into Jerusalem and see the magnificence of his kingdom, the magnificence of Solomon himself. I knew you would one day want to visit him, and I knew that I would have to let you."

"Mother—"

"And I knew that if you went there, tempted by Solomon's wisdom, the majesty of the land, and the promise of his throne, you might never return."

"Mother, I promise you that I will return. If you like, you may send old Tamrin with me to enforce this vow I make to you."

"That is an excellent idea, Menelik. Perhaps you are wiser than I had allowed." The two shared a smile. "But no. I must trust you and allow you this journey, this journey not of miles but of years. It is important that you know where and from whom you come. You must go to Solomon."

For Menelik, relief. No tears—not many, anyway.

"Thank you, Mother. Please don't be troubled by my wish. I will return. I swear it to you. And I will be a better man for the experience."

"I know you will. But first, I must give you something." From her third finger, she pulled a ring. "This was given to me by your father on the day that I left Israel. His instructions were to give it to you, and should you one day travel to visit him, by this ring would he know you. Take it. He will not deny you are his son."

Menelik took the ring and examined it. Jewels, gold, an engraved pattern, the seal of Solomon, he assumed. It was a beautiful ring. *Where had she been keeping it? Had it been on her hand all the time and I never noticed it?* He placed the ring on his own finger and embraced his mother, the queen of Sheba. In two days' time, he would be sailing north to Israel.

His mother was correct, of course, in that this was a long time in coming. From the day he had drawn the courage to ask her who this "wise man" was who had sired him, Menelik knew he would meet his father face to face one day. But he had to wait. This was not a journey for a twelve-year-old boy. He needed to grow. If he was to meet a man as great as Solomon, he required maturity, experience, judgment, and strength of purpose—not merely to undertake such a long voyage but also to prove himself worthy of his lineage. Menelik would wait ten years, until he was twenty-two. Then he would go.

On the day that his mother told him the name of his father, she had kept nothing from him. Not the feast, not the water, not the forfeiture of her virginity.

"That proves you are special, my son," she told him. "That is the one and the only time I have ever been with a man, and it was so you should come to be. Only Solomon could have made me do it, and only Solomon was worthy of my prize. As I was his."

Menelik was proud, delighted even, to learn that his father was such a great man. He did believe he was special. After all, his parents were the wisest people in the world. His mother contributed strength and beauty, his father bestowed kindness and fairness. From Makeda, he had also gained a love of learning. Thanks to Solomon's example and her influence, he had grown up saying prayers to God. He was a prince of two nations, was ensured of wealth throughout his days. Truly, it was a burden relieved when he learned that his father was the king of Israel.

The only thing that frustrated him was not having Solomon near. Not being able to learn from him directly, to see firsthand the amazing feats of judgment and wisdom of which his mother had spoken. He wished he had known sooner. He hadn't fully understood the reason for his advantages, not knowing his father's identity. Yet he did not wish to disrespect or trouble his mother; he could tell this subject was difficult for her, so he did not press the question. He merely asked for stories, which she happily shared with him. It was, for all the uncertainty surrounding his asking, a happy and painless occasion, one of the most meaningful and enjoyable times that Makeda and Menelik had ever spent together.

Sun and moon set and rose twice, and then he was on a ship with a modest crew of men and rations for the journey. Few of the crew had even been born when Tamrin made the same journey by water. Yet unlike Sheba's prior travels to Jerusalem, Menelik would arrive unannounced. No message had been sent in advance to Solomon. No official greeting would be arranged when the ship reached the port of Eilat. This was not a state visit, this was not official business. This was a most personal quest.

All the same, when he did arrive just two days past a fortnight later, Menelik attracted the stares of everyone he saw. *I am not so young that they should be astounded that I have undertaken such a journey*, he thought to himself. *My clothes are not inappropriate. And no one knows who I am or that I was coming, so why do they stare?*

He asked a pair of fishermen the way to Jerusalem and then hired a camel-drawn cart to take him there. When he reached that place that he did not yet know was also called the City of David, named by and for his paternal grandfather, the stares only increased. More and more people stopped what they were doing, their travel ceased, their work came to a halt. Could it be only his imagination that even the animals paused in their activity?

"I wish to meet with King Solomon," he told one of the gawking men. "Please tell me where I can find him."

The man directed him to the palace. As he entered the grounds, he was stopped by guards.

"What is your name? Where are you from and what do you want?" asked one of the guards.

"I wish to see King Solomon."

"What is your name?"

"My name will mean nothing to you, but I wear this ring," he said, lifting his arm to show the back of his hand.

Another guard stepped forward and lowered Menelik's arm.

"That is not necessary. It is plain who you are. Please wait here. I will go and alert the king."

With that, Menelik finally understood why so many people stared at him. Everyone could tell merely by looking at his face that he was the son of Solomon. And everyone knew how much their king yearned for the day when they would meet. It took only a few minutes for the guard to return and hastily bring Menelik inside the palace.

Solomon was in haste as well, and met them at the door. His eyes widened as they reflected back the image of the young man standing before him.

"I was told there was a man here to see me," he said, "a man who wears the face I had when I was younger. But in truth, you are handsomer than I am, and your features remind me of David, my father, in my earliest memories of him."

"King Solomon, I wear this ring that was given to me by my mother—"

"I know the ring, and I know the mother. I need not see the first, and I will never again see the second. Pray tell me, my son, what is your name?"

"I am Menelik, prince of Sheba, King Solomon."

Solomon went to his knees and closed his eyes.

"I praise you, O Lord my God, for You have brought my son home to me. Just as You favored his ancestor David, please shine Your blessings on Menelik, that he may know only health and strength and long years. Amen."

Solomon stood and embraced Menelik tightly. Menelik returned the embrace. He had longed to know his father, and finally he had met him face to face. He only knew of Solomon what his mother had told him, and now he knew for certain that his father truly loved him. The king looked older than he had been described; that was to be expected, a decade having passed since Menelik's mother stood where he stood and saw what he saw.

But Solomon's gentleness of spirit, his honest and earnest tone of voice that Makeda had spoken of—it all was true.

Yet in the same moments, Menelik could not help but think of his mother, and his heart spasmed with regret as he realized he would never have both his parents together, in one country let alone in one home, and therefore only one of them would get to have his presence in their life, and only one would be a part of his life. He did not come to Israel to make a choice; he was not there to audition his father—or for him. And yet he knew he could not live in two lands. He could not sit on two thrones. But for now, Menelik had to be in Israel because completeness was there, the chance to make his life whole was there. He sensed that he would leave Israel a changed man. If indeed he left Israel at all.

CHAPTER 2

"What did your mother tell you, my son?"

"That you are the wisest man who ever lived," replied Menelik to his father—though he was not yet comfortable using that word. "Son" came easily to Solomon because Menelik was not his only male offspring, but Menelik had never had a father before. He decided to maintain a respectful and decorous—if not distant—tone, at least until he felt more of an emotional connection to his long-hidden sire.

"Also that you are fair and just in all your dealings, that your judgments are unerring, and that her most fervent wish for me is that I grow to be all the things you are."

The words sent a rush of blood pulsing through Solomon's body, though his speech remained calm and sober.

"That is very kind of her to say. And what did she tell you about how you came to be?"

"All she told me is that she came to meet you, stayed in Jerusalem for six months, learned by your side, felt a deep connection to you, and when she left to return to Sheba, I was already in her belly." This, of course, was not the full truth but it was enough until Menelik felt more comfortable with Solomon.

"Are you satisfied with that explanation?" his father asked.

"Is there more I should know?"

Few words, much confidence, thought Solomon.

"No. So Menelik, what did you feel when you learned I was your father?"

"I was younger at the time. I didn't know about you, didn't know about Israel. I believed everything my mother told me about you, and I worshipped your God as she taught me to."

"Really? The queen of Sheba still prays to the God of Israel?"

"Yes, quite faithfully."

"That is truly wondrous." Solomon's mind reeled with this information, rendering him briefly without speech. *A gift from across the miles. Two gifts. Adopting my God and sharing my son. Such generosity. Makeda, you are—*

"Your mother is amazing. I will never know her equal. Not in beauty, nor in strength, nor in learning. You are indeed a lucky young man to have been raised by her all these years."

"Thank you. I agree. I owe her everything."

Solomon and Menelik were enjoying lunch outside Solomon's palace. Lamb and bread and chickpeas. Wine and dates. The sun was high and hot, but Menelik found the weather quite comfortable. It was his first full day in Jerusalem. He had spent the night in the same tent that his mother had occupied when she had visited. A guard had whispered to him that the king had never allowed another person to dwell in it since the day that Makeda left.

Menelik liked Solomon, respected him of course, yet could not feel warmth for him. He did not blame Solomon for being absent from his life; after all, his mother had made the decision not to stay with him. To some extent, he was now uncomfortable having such a great man as a father. His mother was powerful and impressive enough, but to have two such parents was intimidating. *Too much to live up to*, he thought. *Too many expectations. I am not like them. I have done nothing special to distinguish me. I am just what Solomon said: A lucky young man.*

"So you are here, Menelik. You wished to meet me, and you have met me. As for myself, I am pleased by what I see. You are a fine young man, handsome and solid, confident and bright. I pray that you also have a positive impression of me. But now that you are here, what is it that you seek?"

"Is it not enough that I wished to meet my—father?"

"You came in secret, giving no advance notice that you wished to visit me. That means you were willing to risk my not being here when you arrived. I do not doubt that you desired to meet me, but to undertake such a long journey knowing that I might be away or otherwise occupied, you must have been seeking something else as well."

Menelik had to smile. "How foolish of me to think that I could keep anything from you. Indeed I am here for more than just to meet you. I wish to know my history, my ancestors. I know my forebears on my mother's side, but she was not able to tell me very much about my grandfather David and the line of Israeli kings into which I was born. I was hoping you could tell me, but in truth I knew that I could probably get the information from any elder in Jerusalem. Tamrin told me once that speaking with elders was the best way to learn."

Solomon smiled in the memory of Tamrin's visit, which had set all of this in motion.

"But mainly, I must admit to being intimidated by the thought of meeting you, King Solomon. And I was not sure you would want to meet me."

Solomon was most pleased. In truth, he had all but rehearsed the stories he would one day tell to his son. For a throne is a meager inheritance when compared to one's own familial history. Not to know one's forefathers, what they stood for and what they did, their glories and their teachings, is a poverty that no material wealth can assuage. *God blessed me when I asked Him for wisdom; I have much the same feeling of pleasure knowing that Menelik wishes to learn of his heritage.*

Now Solomon had an opportunity to make twenty-two years evaporate like a mirage by telling his son his stories—for they *were* Menelik's stories, as necessary for him to know as his bones were necessary for him to stand. In fact, it was said that the stories of one's family live in the marrow of their bones, and thus one didn't learn of one's ancestry so much as become awakened to it. And then one realizes that their ability to stand and walk and work and build and love is because of the deep presence of their ancestors in their bodies and in their lives.

And so Solomon made a plan for the next day. They would ride east out of Jerusalem to *Yam HaMelah*, "the Sea of Salt." There they would walk along the shore and Solomon would tell Menelik of the proud ancestral line of which he was a part. Along the way, Solomon would provide a history of the Jewish people: of Abraham who was the first to know God as spirit rather than man-made idol; of Moses who led the Israelites on their freedom journey to the Promised Land; and of David, the brave shepherd boy, sensitive musician, and mighty warrior.

On that day, at the appointed time and place, as the two men stood in their sandals beside the west bank of the sea, Solomon began his discourse to his son.

"David, my father, was greatly loved and greatly feared. He was a man of courage and passion, and he was the first to rule a united kingdom in Israel. All that he did, he did masterfully. And sometimes ruthlessly.

"Fitting for one as powerful as he, David took Jerusalem by force and built a palace there. But rest eluded him, for the Philistines attacked again. Over the course of three bloody battles, David's army cleansed Israel of the Philistines for good. The land then safe and at peace, my father brought the Holy Ark, the Ark of the Covenant, to Jerusalem, the City of David, where it belongs."

"What is this Ark that you speak of?" asked Menelik.

"The Ark contains three valuable artifacts representing our faith in and covenant with God. It had been carried from place to place throughout all our people's wanderings, from Egypt, to the Revelation at Sinai where the tabernacle was first built to house it, to Jerusalem. It is of the highest importance to us in terms of our faith and worship, and of our culture and nationhood. Yet because of its awesome power David did not bring the Ark into the city until the time was right.

"Look there," said Solomon, pointing northward. "Ahead the sea meets its tributary, the Jordan River. It was there that Moses and the Israelites crossed over into Canaan, the land promised to them at the end of their forty-year journey. The Ark was with them then as it is with us now, thanks to your grandfather. With the Ark safely brought to Jerusalem, David desired to build a temple to the Lord our God, to praise Him for the good fortune with which He had blessed us."

"But it was you who built the temple, was it not? Why was building the temple so important to David? And why was he not able to do it?"

"My son, building a temple, a permanent and prodigious tabernacle in which to give thanks and make sacrifices to God, has always been a dream of the Israelite people. Even while in the desert, Moses attempted to build one. He assigned the most talented craftsmen—Bezalel son of Uri, from the house of Judah; and Aholiab son of Ahisamach of the tribe of Dan—to build the Ark of the Covenant and to be the chief artisans of the tabernacle. Their skills were imbued with the spirit of the Lord, and their ability to carve, to engrave, to sew, and to weave was unmatched. And yet only now does the temple that our people have wished for, that God has commanded of us, stand.

"As for why my father, David, did not build it, God through Nathan the prophet made it known to David that the temple could not be built by hands that dripped of blood. That duty would instead fall to me, the son of a warrior but not a warrior himself. This was a great disappointment to David, but it was not a punishment. David was a warrior because the nation needed him to be so to ensure our survival and protect our land. His successes meant that I myself do not need to raise a sword. And so I was the one entrusted to build the temple."

"Did David die in battle?"

"No, Menelik, he was never vanquished in war, although strife from within his family and among his enemies consumed his remaining years of health. At last he became weak and often cold. He took to his bed but was unresponsive to care. He had promised Bathsheba, my mother, that I would ascend to the throne upon his death. But Adonijah, his oldest surviving son, birthed by his fifth wife, Haggith, took the crown as his birthright and proclaimed himself king. My father's final official act was to anoint me publicly—as Samuel had once done to him in front of his brothers—to demonstrate to the people that I was the true heir to my father's rule over the united kingdom. At that, Adonijah fled and my ascension was uncontested.

"And then he died. David our greatest king, my father and your grandfather, went the way of all who dwell on earth. He was seventy years old and had reigned for forty years. Indeed, I was forty years of age when I inherited the throne from him.

"And now that you have returned to your ancestral home, my son, that throne is yours upon my death, if you will agree to take it. You are my heir and my most favored child, for you were born of my truest love, Queen Makeda of Sheba. As Bathsheba was to my father, your mother is to me."

Menelik took a moment to digest all he had been told.

"I am honored—Father—and am pleased to know of your love for her and your love for me. I am also grateful to you for telling me my history, which I shall never forget. I am truly blessed to have such powerful and inspiring ancestors."

"Indeed you are, my son. Have you any questions for me? You have listened well but spoken little."

"I am overwhelmed by the stories you have shared with me so generously. I feel like David proved himself worthy through his success as a warrior, and you proved yourself by building the temple. It will be no small task for your successor to prove himself as well."

"God calls upon all of us, according to our talents, to be His partner in fulfilling the act of Creation," Solomon said. "David soothed Saul's soul with his harp and protected the kingdom against Goliath when he was but a boy. His fame as a warrior came later. I myself asked God for wisdom, that I may judge fairly and understand the world. Your mother is not so different from me in that regard. What you are called to do is yet to be known, my son. But God will make it plain to you when the time is right. You must keep your eyes open, your mind open, and your heart open. And when it is time to act, you must do so with all your being. God will bless you for your efforts."

Menelik was intrigued. *What would God have me do? Or has God already planted within me the task I am to perform, yet I do not see it?*

How can I ever measure up to the greatness of David and Solomon? I have no special talents, no deep insights. What if I prove myself only to be a failure? Several moments of quiet self-inquisition passed. At last, he spoke.

"King Solomon?"

"Yes, my son?"

"May I see the Ark of the Covenant?"

CHAPTER 3

From the time they left the site of their Revelation at Mount Sinai, everywhere the Israelites went they brought with them the Ark of the Covenant. Strong, pious men from the tribe of Levi were entrusted with the task of carrying the Ark when it was in motion and guarding it when it was at rest. Safeguard the Ark, they were told, and the Ark will safeguard our people.

Through the years in the unforgiving desert, the Ark needed protection from the heat and wind and rain. As well, the people needed a place where they, through the agency of the *kohanim*—the priests, descendants of Aaron, brother of Moses—could make sacrifices. Thus was the sanctuary, the portable tabernacle, predecessor of Solomon's temple, built.

Walled on all four sides with curtains fastened to wooden poles, the tabernacle featured an altar where burnt offerings were given to God, a laver cast of bronze where the *kohanim* would purify themselves, and a rectangular tent covered in skins that was the sanctuary. The front two-thirds of the sanctuary was called the Holy Place and contained a menorah holding seven oil cups, an altar for incense, and a table where cakes of grain offering were displayed.

A curtain separated the front part of the sanctuary—the Holy Place—from a smaller room in the rear, the *Kodesh HaKodashim*, the Holy of Holies. It was here that the *Aron HaBreet*, the Ark of the Covenant, was housed. It was here that God dwelt. When Solomon planned the construction of the temple, he adhered to the layout of the tabernacle that God had dictated hundreds of years earlier. Thus it was that a permanent Holy of Holies was built to be the place where the Ark of the Covenant would always be kept. And it was there that Solomon and the High Priest Zadok, a descendent of Aaron, led Menelik to view the most sacred relic.

Zadok drew back the curtain, but not even Solomon and the young prince were allowed to enter the room. Still, its beauty filled the small space and caused Menelik's eyes to grow wide with wonder.

The Ark was constructed of wood from the *shittah* tree, gilded in gold, and its golden lid was adorned with two wing-spread cherubim, also cast in gold. Its size was two-and-a-half cubits in length, one-and-a-half cubits in width, and one-and-a-half cubits in height. It could have contained a good-sized goat, yet, as the priest explained, its contents were actually the two stone tablets that Moses received at Sinai, as well as Aaron's budded staff, and a bowl of manna.

On each of the Ark's four corners was attached a ring of gold; through those rings were staves of wood, allowing it to be carried by four men. Now, the staves were arranged in a crossed position so as to keep the Ark off the ground. When on the move in the desert years, Zadok explained, the Ark was always carried in advance of the Israelites by a distance of two thousand cubits.

"It was before this Ark, which my father brought to Jerusalem, that I worshipped after God promised me the gift of wisdom," said Solomon. Menelik understood how solemn an act that was, for it was wisdom that made Solomon's name known throughout the world. Menelik meditated on the fact that his grandfather had brought this holy relic to Jerusalem and his father had built the temple in which it dwelt. *If I am to prove myself to God, is it somehow to do with this Ark?*

"When the priests came out from the Holy of Holies after placing the Ark here, the temple was filled with a cloud," Solomon continued. "That was the sign that the glory of God had rested here."

With that, Zadok closed the curtain and instructed them to leave. "Few are those who are not *kohanim* who are permitted to stand so close to the *Aron HaBreet*," he explained. "God speaks from the space between the two cherubim, and many unworthy and unclean people have been harmed or killed for touching or taking it. My presence has protected you, but one must not linger more than is necessary, for one cannot hear God's voice directly and live."

And so the king and prince, the father and son, returned to the palace. There were judgments to give, and Menelik would get to see Solomon's wisdom in action. That night, they dined together yet mostly in silence. Only near the end of their meal did Solomon speak.

"We have said little this meal, my son, but we have thought much. Do you agree?"

"Yes, I suppose so," Menelik responded.

"You suppose so? Why do you suppose so?"

"I just mean that you must be correct."

"But why must I be correct? I asked if you agreed with me. Therefore I did not assume that I was correct. I know for certain what *I* think; I want to know what *you* think, my son."

"I think you are correct," said Menelik, somewhat louder than he had intended.

"Must I mine for your words as if they were encased in rock, Menelik?"

"I don't know what you want me to say, Father." Menelik was testing the word to see how it fit, like a newly woven sandal.

"I want to know your thoughts. That is all. I simply want to know what you are thinking."

"I know that. But I am not sure of my thoughts. I have many thoughts, but they fight each other in my mind. They must lead somewhere, I know, but as of this moment I know not where."

"That is good, Menelik. That is the sign of a healthy mind. Knowledge does not flow like milk from a teat. It is the result of digging, sifting, examining, evaluating until finally you see if what you have had knocking around in your head is a jewel or just a stone."

"I fear what I have is a stone."

"From stones the temple to the Lord was built. Hide no more from me. Tell me what is behind your silence."

Menelik paused. *Why must I always summon courage to speak with my parents?* he wondered.

"I have enjoyed my visit here. I have enjoyed meeting you. Having briefly gotten to know you, I am deeply honored to be your son. Truly, I am. But I am also conscious of the fact that your land is not the land of my birth."

"You wish to return to Sheba."

"If it were as simple as that, I would not be troubled in my mind."

"You are torn, then. I understand. You have been raised in Sheba at your mother's side. You are heir to the throne of all of Ethiopia. You would rule over people you understand, over a land whose soil is in your skin, whose air has filled your nose since the day you were born. Who would not envy being in that position?"

Solomon rose, and continued to speak.

"And yet, you are my flesh and my blood, too. You are the son of a king, the king of a united Israel. Your feet may feel as strangers here, but this land of milk and honey that was promised by God to Abraham our forebear is in the blood that pulses within your heart. You are no alien here, Menelik; the history of the Israelite people is your history as well. This land is yours. These people are yours. And this—"

Solomon waved in all directions.

"—all of this is yours. The throne, the kingdom, the temple, all has been promised to you from the moment of your birth. It has all been waiting for you. I have been waiting for you. To give this all to you."

Menelik was without speech. He stared down at the table, not daring to make contact with his father's eyes.

"This is your conundrum, Menelik, is it not? Your mother and I each have a throne to offer you, but you can sit in only one. Whichever throne you choose, you will disappoint the parent holding the other. You may wish to have both, you may wish to have neither, but one you will have. And the time for your decision is soon at hand."

"I know, Father," Menelik said at last. "It is exactly as you say. What I have seen in Jerusalem in my short time here is beyond anything I have ever imagined could be possible in this world. It is magical. But my mother—."

"Yes," said Solomon. "Your mother. Not your mother's throne, but your mother. It is hard to leave one's mother. Quite difficult at birth and nigh impossible thereafter. I am reminded of one of my judgments."

Menelik sat up, for he understood that Solomon's judgments represented the peak of his wisdom and the full flourishing of his logical powers. The minor issues he had watched his father settle earlier in the day did not require great wisdom, merely authority. But now, to hear Solomon speak of one of his judgments at such an emotional juncture in their conversation was something that Menelik knew was going to be very important.

Said Solomon:

"There came to me one day two women with a serious argument between them. The source of the argument was a newborn baby, the maternity of which was in dispute. As for the women, they both were prostitutes. That is of no matter to the case, of course, other than that no man was there to speak for them or to support one or the other's claim on the child.

"I asked one of the women to tell me the facts of the case as she understood them. She said to me, 'King Solomon, this woman and I live in the same house. We became pregnant at the same time, and we both gave birth just in the last few days. Each of us slept with our baby at our side. But last night, this other woman lay on her child while she slept and suffocated it. She awoke first, saw what she had done, and switched our babies, so that when I awoke, the baby at my side was dead while she had the other baby already at her breast. When I looked closely at the dead baby, I saw that it was not mine. I pray you, please, make her give my baby back to me.'

"I then," Solomon continued, "asked the second woman if this testimony was true. 'No,' she insisted, 'this child is mine. He came from my body, and with me he should stay. This woman is the one who killed her baby.' Back and forth they went with their respective claims. O that the baby himself could talk and help me to decide the matter!

"I thought on the statements of the two women. How to choose which was telling the truth and which was not? Finally, I asked that a sword be brought to me. It was done. Then I said, 'As each of you claims the baby to be hers, and there is no evidence to verify one's testimony over the other, the only just and fair resolution is to divide the living child in two lengthwise, that each of you may have half of it. Then both will have some, and neither will have none.

"At that, the second woman seemed satisfied. But the first woman spoke out desperately. 'No!' she insisted. 'You must not harm the baby for my sake. Let the other woman have the child if it must be so to ensure this baby is not killed.' I put down the sword, took the baby from the second woman's arms, and gave it to the first woman. 'This is the child's mother,' I said. 'For a mother's compassion for her own child is stronger than any force known to mankind.'"

The story brought tears to Menelik's eyes. He rose and walked to his father and embraced him. Solomon returned the embrace and kissed the top of his son's head. Presently, the embrace was broken and Menelik again found the courage to speak difficult words.

"King Solomon—my father—I am sorry but it is impossible for me to abandon my country and my mother. I swore to her by her breasts that I would return to her. To succeed you as king of Israel is an honor I am not worthy of, and though you are so kind as to offer Israel's throne to me, I cannot accept it. I so deeply apologize to you. And may I never regret these words."

As did the mother, now does the son, thought Solomon.

"I understand, Menelik. I am not surprised by your decision, nor am I disappointed in you. In truth, I would be with your mother today were it not for the fact that God wills I occupy my father's throne. I wish for you, my son, all of David's talents, his courage, and his ingenuity. And may all the friends you make be loyal, and may your enemies hate you from afar and cause you no grief.

"I bid you leave, my son, and I ask only that you leave tonight, that the temptation to keep you here forcibly does not take root."

"Then give me your blessing, Father," Menelik implored, "that my leaving be right and your heart be comforted."

"Yes. Yes, my son. Though it pains me to do so, I will give you my blessing." Solomon put his hands on Menelik's shoulders and said to the future king of Sheba, "My beloved son, I release you to fulfill your destiny. May you live long and well and rule your people with wisdom, honesty, and integrity. Forget not the lessons of your parents and grandparents, and seek to emulate them in all your doings."

Then Solomon rested his hands on Menelik's head, and with moist eyes closed, uttered the priestly benediction: "May the God of our ancestors, the God of Abraham, of Isaac, and of Jacob, may He bless you and keep you. May God's face ever shine upon you and be gracious to you. And may our Lord lift up His countenance upon you and give you peace."

They embraced once more, kissed, and Solomon retired. Later that night, Menelik gathered all his belongings, and then some. He dispatched four of his crew to enter the temple, to enter the Holy of Holies, and to take with them the Ark of the Covenant.

"If God wills this to be, if this indeed is the test that I must pass to prove myself worthy, then no harm could come to us," he told them. The plan was to meet back at their ship. Menelik arrived first. He said a prayer:

Dear God, Who protected my ancestors and so blessed my grandfather, David, and my father, Solomon, may this deed be pleasing in Your eyes. I know not if this is the right thing to do. But I must return to Sheba. And I must have something that will connect me to Jerusalem and to the Israelite people as I rule another people in another land. I pray You will look kindly upon my act.

Menelik and his crew left that night with the Ark, which he brought back home to Axum, in Ethiopia, the land of his people, the land he would rule until his death. Yes, like his mother, he had headed south and west from Israel to Ethiopia before ultimately returning to Sheba. Whether in taking the Ark he had done right or done wrong, he could not yet know. But he and his men had not been harmed during or after their heist. He took this to be a good sign, for as he had learned from both his parents, everything is noticed.

THE THIRD BOOK OF SOLOMON

CHAPTER 1

Zadok the High Priest was beside himself with anger, fear, and sadness. Well he knew that the Ark of the Covenant had been captured once before. It was in the time of Samuel, when the Israelites were defeated in battle by the Philistines. His predecessor as High Priest at the time was his great-grandfather Eli, and two of Eli's sons—Hophni and Phinehas—were killed in the battle. But when he was told that the Ark of the Covenant had been taken by the Philistines as a spoil of war, Eli collapsed and died instantly. He was succeeded by Ahitub, son of Phinehas. Three other High Priests would serve before Zadok, a son of Ahitub, became the first High Priest of Solomon's temple.

Still, it was somehow easier for Zadok to understand the loss of the Ark to a vanquisher in war than to Solomon's own son in stealth. Clearly, he had to report this incident to Solomon, but he was wary of what the king's reaction would be. Solomon's mood had long been dark as the skin of the queen whose departure had caused his plodding depression. Only Menelik's arrival had restored to Solomon the hope and optimism he had once felt. With Menelik gone, surely the king's sadness would return. And then to learn that his son was a thief and his target had been the holiest item the nation had ever known? Zadok bowed and prayed.

Solomon himself had suffered through a sleepless night. He had long ago lost Makeda, suffering a certain kind of death in her leaving. And then after many empty years, life had returned in the form of his son, like a second soul come to inhabit his being. But it was not to last. And in some ways, the loss of Menelik was even harder to bear, for the loss of one's heir is a broken link—never to be mended—in a noble line. Makeda had never returned to Jerusalem. Neither, he now knew, would Menelik.

He did not blame his son. Solomon being Solomon, he understood. Menelik would be successful in Sheba. He knew his native country's history well. Solomon had tried to teach Menelik as much of the long and difficult history of the Israelite people as he could in a very short time. Menelik was attentive and respectful. He was smart. He would retain much of what he had heard. He would apply the lessons of Solomon as he sat on Makeda's throne. His people would know that their king understood their dreams and their destiny. They would never lose faith in the God of Menelik's paternal ancestors. They would seek to be an example of righteous living for the rest of the Arabian world.

All of this Solomon knew. None of it healed his heart. The rest of his life, he believed, would lack meaning, for it lacked hope. He would continue to rule as long as God allowed him to draw breaths. But what was there left to motivate him to use the gifts he had been given, the position he had inherited? The temple was built. The new palace was finished. The vaults were full. The law was upheld. Justice and peace prevailed in Israel. If he died that day or ten million days hence, it was all the same to the son of David. For Makeda and Menelik, he cared greatly. For everything else, he cared little or nothing.

In this hopeless state, Solomon received Zadok in the morning after refusing to eat breakfast. He could see the despair in Zadok's eyes, but the king remained unmoved.

"King Solomon, I have the most dreadful news to report."

"Speak."

"I went to the Holy of Holies this morning. The Ark of the Covenant—it has been taken."

Solomon's expression did not change. His lips did not move.

"I am sorry to say that I believe the thief to be your own son, Menelik of Sheba."

Solomon winced slightly, not so much at the information but at the phrase "Menelik of Sheba." But still, he said nothing.

"How he is dealt with is up to you, of course, King Solomon. But we must send out troops to track him down and return the Ark to us."

Silence.

"Do—do you not agree?"

Though it pained him physically to do so, to make his tongue and lips dance together in the geometric formations of speech, Solomon at last spoke.

"Zadok, I do not deny that Menelik was likely responsible for taking the Ark of the Covenant. But as he has done so, so we must let it be done. My father took it from one place to another, I took it from there to a new place, and now my son has taken it to where he belongs. And where he belongs is where the Ark of the Covenant belongs. He needs it. His people need it. Let the crime stand and the criminal be absolved."

"But King Solomon, surely we, the people of Israel, need it as well!"

"And we have it. We don't see God's face, but we feel God's presence. It has not left us. It is within us. We still have the temple. We still can perform sacrifices. We still pray. We still observe. The heart's belief in something, even when physical evidence is lacking, is faith itself. The *kohanim* will continue. Your role will not change. Let it be, Zadok. Let Menelik be."

"But, King Solomon—"

"Zadok, a sultan from Persia once came to me and asked if I could utter a sentence that would always be true, no matter how pleasant or how foreboding the circumstances. My reply was, 'This too shall pass away.' And so it shall."

Zadok acquiesced and left the king to his doleful repose.

And so passed the days and nights, the weeks and months. Solomon never forgot Makeda's voice, her face. It was all that he had of her. Though he had won her virginity, she possessed the ultimate prize: the son whom he loved and coveted. Fated to live without either of them for the rest of his days, he sought consolation among his numerous other wives and concubines. But even they were not enough. Forgetting the laws of God, he began to look elsewhere and took many foreign women as his wives.

Though his first wife had been an Egyptian Pharaoh's daughter, Solomon never took on her customs or observances. In fact, when the temple was finished and the Ark of the Covenant was installed in Jerusalem, Solomon built for her a house outside the city, for Jerusalem itself was consecrated by the Ark's presence, and his wife's foreign feet were not allowed to step in it. The exception made for Makeda was thus even more significant.

That fidelity to God's word abandoned Solomon now. He not only took wives from Moab and Ammon, he built shrines to their gods and worshipped them there. With his Ammonite wife, Naamah, Solomon had another son, Rehoboam. He did not place Naamah or Rehoboam on the same plane of feeling as he did Makeda and Menelik, but at least they were here with him. They would not leave. Where, after all, was there for them to go?

God became angry with Solomon, because his heart had been turned toward the gods of the foreign lands that were subservient to Israel. One night in a dream, Solomon was visited by an angel of the Lord, who spoke to him:

> WHAT YOU HAVE DONE IS ABHORRENT TO ME. YOU HAVE NOT KEPT MY LAWS, YOU HAVE BROKEN THE COVENANT I MADE WITH YOU. I GAVE YOU THE GREATEST WISDOM ANY MAN COULD ATTAIN, AND ALL I COMMANDED YOU WAS TO BE FAITHFUL TO MY WORD. AS YOU HAVE WORSHIPPED OTHER GODS, PUT THEM BEFORE ME, DEFILED MY TEMPLE BY PRAYING AT PAGAN SHRINES, I TELL YOU I SHALL TAKE THE KINGDOM AWAY FROM YOU AND IT SHALL BE WITH YOUR SON, REHOBOAM. BUT PROSPERITY WILL NOT FOLLOW HIM, AND THE KINGDOM WILL BE RENT UNDER HIS RULE. FOR THE SAKE OF YOUR FATHER, DAVID, I WILL NOT DO THIS IN YOUR DAYS. BUT IT SHALL BE DONE.

He heard me, thought Solomon upon awakening. *He saw me.* To him, this was comforting, despite the severity of the decree. For Solomon had felt alone in his grief, if not abandoned by God then at least ignored. He did not expect God to intercede in his sorrow. He merely hoped for a change, something to reengage him with the life he trudged through every day. *Day becomes night, night becomes day, seasons pass one after the other. That which is young and feeble grows large and strong. That which is old withers away. Only my sadness is unchanging. Only my pain stays the same.*

In truth, God's punishment was a gift to Solomon, for it revealed to him the end of his life and with it, the end of his grief. *There will be a change, and I will be glad not to see it. My troubles will be Rehoboam's. I am sorry for that. But it is beyond my power. The Greatest Power in the universe has seen to it that I will not suffer forever. It is in retribution for my wicked ways. Perhaps, it is also because I could not make Menelik stay to succeed me. As much as I love him, maybe God loves him, too. But God willed that he return to Sheba.*

For that matter—Solomon's thoughts raced faster now—*did God not bring Makeda to me? For what purpose? To lay me low? Was this all a test? To show me that my mind could not conquer every challenge? That my heart must also at times take up the fight? And yet my mind has never been defeated, while my soft heart took a fatal hit, pierced by the spear of Makeda's strength and beauty, and the wound reopened by Menelik's loyalty to his mother.*

I am not the warrior that my father, David, was. Neither a warrior of battle nor of love. Reason, peaceful reason, was my sword. But reason is cold like sheathed metal, and emotion burns like that metal exposed to the sun. Wisdom was the gift I requested, wisdom was the gift God granted me. What I should have asked for was passion. Perhaps with passion I could have kept Makeda, and then I would have her by my side this very day, and Menelik would be in my shadow. But no, all I have is wisdom, impotent wisdom, and the knowledge of both my pain and my punishment.

God saw my sadness and did nothing. Then God saw my sin and acted.

Everything is noticed.

The judgments of the Lord are true and righteous altogether.

Solomon sang. He sang a prayer to God, praising God's judgment. He sang a prayer for his sons, that God might keep them safe. He sang from his heart, with sweet tears of thanksgiving falling down his face, for he knew that his troubles would one day end. Yes, just as when he had laid down with Makeda, Solomon sang.

CHAPTER 2

Chastened by God, sure now of the limits of his suffering, Solomon passed much of the rest of his days in quiet solitude, his repose broken only by the writings that he began to compose by the score. Proverbs, psalms, poems, and a work of philosophy that reflected his conflicted feelings about his life and about life itself—they began to spill out of him like blood from a severed vein.

He found the privacy, introspection, and invention of writing to be exceedingly more pleasant than speaking with other people. As a consequence, Solomon spent much of his time in silence and isolation. Of course, he did the king's business when and how it had to be done, and with the same sense of fairness and consideration he had always demonstrated (one of the qualities about him that had most impressed his three visitors from Sheba: Tamrin, Makeda, and Menelik). But it was rote, based on pure logic and no imagination; these distracting duties he had to do felt more to Solomon like penance than privilege.

Despite his demeanor, his written works demonstrated that his mind was still keen. He was still the wisest man in the world, still able to finely grind the essential meaning out of a puzzle as though it were grain in a mortar, his mind the pestle. It could be said that Solomon's true calling was to be a teacher, like Makeda's beloved *astamari*. He was not the kind of monarch that other nations had, not a warrior or a pillager. He simply ruled fairly and intelligently, forming alliances with friendly kings who offered such useful things as food, skills, resources, and protection.

Solomon had never cared about ruling people; rather, he was interested in exploring people's hearts and minds. What did they think, and why did they think it? It was hard for him to learn these things because as he was the king, the people he would meet were not truly themselves in his presence. That frustrated him. It was also one reason Makeda moved him, even beyond her obvious beauty and intelligence: with her questioning and curiosity, her willingness to speak of her life and her land, she was an endless well of fascinating qualities and enviable characteristics from which Solomon gladly drew.

For many years now, she had been back on the throne in Sheba. And from that perch, Makeda ruled much as Solomon did, with intelligence and an unerring sense of justice. She thought of him often, never more so than the time during which Menelik traveled to meet him. How she wished she could have been there to witness their meeting. To see her son show Solomon the ring the king himself had given her for that very purpose. To see the two handsome men talking together, Solomon showing Menelik the land of Israel as it had been shown to her. And she wondered how it would be if all three were to be together in one place. As one family.

And yet she could not be there, and so she feared what may transpire. Feared that Menelik would want to remain there, to live in Jerusalem and one day to rule Israel. He had promised to return, but she knew how difficult it could be to leave Solomon. Makeda had felt guilty about keeping them apart for so many years, though she knew that Menelik had to grow up first. Yet she would feel no guilt at all if Solomon never saw his son again, because that would mean that Menelik had returned to her forever.

And indeed he had. But Menelik had decided to enter his homeland with the same stealth with which he had entered and left his father's. The reason was simple: He did not want his mother to know he had taken the Ark of the Covenant. This was partly for her own protection should Israeli forces show up determined to take it back. Partly, he feared her disappointment in his actions. Yet it also was important to him that he had done this for himself, not for any glory or honor, nor for notoriety, but rather just to prove to himself that he could do it. That he could do something bold without the knowledge or control of his two powerful parents. And so he hid the Ark in Axum, in a protective sepulcher of sorts, hidden in a barren field where no one would likely venture. This he did in the obscurity of night, and not until he and his crew had finished the plot under a violet sky did they sail back to Sheba, entering unannounced.

It did not take long for the palace guards to notice them and for Makeda to be notified that her son, the prince of Sheba, had returned. She was awakened from her early morning sleep and insisted he be brought to her immediately, despite her unreadiness. The crew, she ordered, were to be fed, paid, and returned to their homes.

When Menelik entered the palace, Makeda ran to him, royal decorum and protocol cast aside, and embraced him tightly for minutes until he complained that he could not breathe. There were tears in her eyes, and with her unkempt hair and sleep garment, she looked like a madwoman in the throes of a devil's clutch. And indeed impulse got the better of her breeding as she took her son again by the sides of his head and pressed him against her breast, as though refusing ever again to allow him to travel a hair's breadth away from her.

"Mother, I beg you!" he implored Makeda for his freedom. Reluctantly, she released him but only barely, as her hands now cupped Menelik's cheeks and she stared at him, looking for a change, for the mark of Solomon's powerful presence upon his face. *Menelik seems older than when he left, but is it true? Wiser? Might his speech have changed? He still called me "Mother."*

"I apologize, my son," she said haltingly, her lips glistening with the emotions that streaked down her face. "I—I wasn't sure—that you would—return to me."

And again her muscular arms took Menelik's tired body and clamped it against her own. This time, Menelik did not protest as he felt the throbs of sobs within his mother's chest. He returned her embrace and allowed her this spell.

"I told you I would return, Mother," he said into her clavicle. "Sheba is my home. I belong here. And even if I had accepted King Solomon's offer of succession, I would have come back here to tell you and spend more time with you."

Hearing those words, Makeda finally felt that she could let go of Menelik without fearing that he would run back to the port and sail off again. And so she let down her arms and asked him to follow her inside their home.

A table. Platters of food. Jugs of wine. Though assembled hastily by servants aroused from their slumber well before their usual time, the meal was enjoyed by an equally sleepy Menelik as he alternated chewing and talking with his rapt audience of one. Just as in her talk with Tamrin when he had returned from Israel, Makeda demanded to know every last detail about Menelik's time with Solomon.

"Was I afraid to meet him?" he began, responding to his mother's prompting query. "No, I don't think so. Nervous, certainly. But mostly curious, as I would be even if my father were an ordinary laborer. Yes, it was different because of who he is, but right away he offered only warmth and acceptance to me, so I was put at ease from the first."

"And the ring? Did you show him the ring?"

"I had no need to. From the moment I disembarked in Eilat, my features made my identity obvious to all. I was hurriedly brought to the palace—a new one, by the way, not the one you experienced—and when Solomon saw me he knew at once who I was. I must say I didn't find the resemblance quite as clear, but then I could not see behind his grey whiskers."

Grey? The passage of years, noted Makeda. To her, Solomon's face was fixed in time.

"You are indeed his son, Menelik. I see it in your eyes and your forehead. You are darker of course, and your hair is not straight and long like his, but there can be no denying that you are the fruit of both the king of Israel and the queen of Sheba. Were you treated like a prince in Jerusalem?"

"Once we had met, from that time until the night that I left, I did not meet many people. That is one reason I never felt a connection to that land. Solomon insisted that we should be together at all times."

"That is understandable, my son, not only his desire to get to know you, but also your feeling like a stranger in a strange land. After all, you never were a child there as you were in Sheba. Here you spent years playing and exploring and getting to know the young ones and the old ones who live in our villages. Like me, that is how you established your roots in this soil. Your first time in Israel, you were there as a prince of a foreign country, an emissary of Sheba. As much as you are Solomon's son, as much as you have been raised to worship Solomon's God, you are not of Solomon's land. Yet still, you were entitled to ascend to Solomon's throne."

"I was not interested, Mother," said Menelik. "I could not foresee the people welcoming me—an outsider—into their hearts, even as Solomon's son. It would take too long to earn their trust and their affection."

"And are you in such a hurry to become a king, Menelik?"

The smile through which Makeda's statement passed evaporated with her voice's breath upon hearing Menelik's reply.

"Yes, mother, I am. I am ready to become a king. And that is why I have returned to Sheba."

"What do you mean, my son? You are still so young, and I am in good health."

"I am six years older than you were when you became queen. I have energy, some wisdom, I have led a trip to a foreign power and shown myself to be mature and capable. It is time for me to take my rightful place. I leave it to you to prepare for the succession, but I ask that it happen within the coming year."

"And what, my son, is to become of me? Am I to be your servant? A cook? A laborer?"

"Of course not, Mother," Menelik tried to assure her. "You will be my most trusted advisor. I do not wish any dishonor to fall upon you. It is simply that I had two thrones to choose from, and I have chosen one. And so I must have one rather than none. You and I will rule together until your death, and I will be the king of Sheba."

The word "advisor" stung Makeda, for she recalled that Eleni's father, Tefere, had been her own father's advisor, and in that case it was not a position of honor. But could she allow her own son to stage such a coup against her? At the same time, could she stand in his way if the lion was in his belly—and could she bear it if because of her resistance he decided to succeed Solomon in Israel instead? Was keeping Menelik with her for the rest of her life worth losing her throne? She was young still, strong still, capable still. Everything she had been when she assumed the throne at age sixteen. With one exception: She was no longer a virgin. She had disobeyed her father's deathbed charge to her and allowed herself to be taken advantage of. Robbed of her hymen, she was given a son—her successor—as compensation.

So perhaps this was how it should be. Having violated her oath to her father, she would be allowed to keep her throne only until Menelik came of age. And in this way, the throne would remain in her family. *It feels right*, she thought. *I get what I deserve, Menelik gets what he deserves. The country does not suffer, and there is meaning to the mischief Solomon played on me. Yes. Yes, it feels right. Menelik was meant to rule Sheba after me. And so I will not stand in his way. Within a year, Sheba, like Israel, will be ruled by a king—and both men joined by blood.*

CHAPTER 3

Hurting and aware of the futility of his remaining reign, Solomon began gradually to recuse himself from many of the duties of leadership. Disputes were heard by empaneled elders, though rulings and sentences were approved by the king. Trade decisions were delegated to trusted officials; never again would he personally entertain a trader as he had Tamrin. The united kingdom of Israel and Judah he had inherited from his father, David, was still strong and well-defended and enjoyed the friendship of its neighboring nations. Solomon had never been a warrior, and there was no need for him to assume that ill-fitting mantle now.

Still, though, he was aware of what was going on in the world. He wished to be kept apprised of wars, uprisings, floods, droughts, unusual phenomena, and changes in leadership. So it was that word reached Solomon's ears from the traditional carriers of regional news and gossip—trading ships—that Menelik had succeeded his mother and now ruled over Sheba and the southern Arabian empire, as well as all of Ethiopia. At first, Solomon was taken aback, stricken with the thought that his beloved Makeda was dead. Then clarification from other sources turned his heart from grief to shock as he learned that she had abdicated her throne to her son so as to counsel him and return Sheba to a patriarchy.

Curious that she should do that. Had Menelik stayed with me in Jerusalem, he would have assumed the throne only upon my death. Maybe that is why he chose to return to Sheba. Still, she is alive. I am grateful to know that she is still alive. Thank God she is younger than I.

As he pondered the news, Solomon realized that he had seen the ambition of Menelik through the young man's futile attempt to cloak it in youthful innocence. *Yes, it was clear at the time, though I dismissed it. And now his ambition is in full flower, with his mother's blessing, apparently.* With only the most minute twinge of pride at Menelik's rise, the feeling in Solomon's heart turned to embarrassment, for his own son sat upon the throne of another nation in his father's lifetime. How could the great wise man not keep his cherished heir in Jerusalem? That must be the gossip among the Red Sea nations. And it shamed him. *Please God, do not tarry in carrying out your ultimate punishment. Take me before the pain is too hard to bear.*

A few more such joyless years passed, until finally, with broken heart and a mind strong enough to suffer it fully, right up to his last moments, Solomon died at the age of eighty. He had been sitting where he had always sat as of late, on his throne in the Hall of Judgment, alone and lamenting his loneliness. He was tired, so tired. His head sunk, chin to chest. His breathing became short, shallow. A spasm, then release. He was gone. Like his father, the great King David, Solomon had ruled for forty years. He would be the last king to rule over a united Israel.

With Solomon gone, his son, Rehoboam, who had impatiently waited for the opportunity, succeeded him. Though descended from the warrior David and the wise Solomon, Rehoboam was the fruit of his father's illicit marriage to the Ammonite woman, Naamah. God was angered that Solomon had worshipped the gods of his foreign wives, and His punishment was that the kingdom would be torn from Rehoboam's hands. And yet the brash new king sowed dissent from the very start of his reign, as if to prove to God that he was capable of failure all on his own.

Solomon had taxed the Israelites for many years, building a massive treasury that helped to pay for the temple and his new palace, but Rehoboam sought to tax them tenfold more. "If it must be so, use a conciliatory tone," the elders advised the new king. But Rehoboam and his friends, whom he planned to appoint to high positions in his court, wanted to show strength by ploughing his own way and sowing fear, and so he spoke harshly to the people instead.

"Understand, Israelites, that Rehoboam is not Solomon," he proclaimed at his coronation. "My father died a weak man, but the blood in my veins runs fast and hot. Indeed, my littlest finger is thicker than were my father's loins; likewise, your backs, which bent like reeds before my father's rule, shall break like straws at my own hand. Furthermore, while we shall worship in the ways of our fathers, we shall also adopt the Ammonite ways, for I represent the union of two powerful nations."

Ironic, then, that the ten northern tribes of Israel—being those of Reuben, Simeon, Dan, Naphtali, Gad, Asher, Issachar, Zebulun, Manasseh, and Ephraim—began feuding with Judah, where Jerusalem and the seat of Rehoboam's power was located. Led by the Ephraimite Jeroboam, the northern tribes officially separated from Judah, and the united kingdom was rent forever. Thus weakened, both Jeroboam, ruling over a new land called Samaria, and Rehoboam of Judah were vulnerable to attacks from other nations and lost key cities over the next decades. Other kings succeeded the two, but none were held with the affection and respect shown to David and Solomon. And, in Sheba, to Menelik.

Within a few months of Solomon's death, word reached the palace in Sheba, and Menelik was informed that his father was no more. He instructed that no one with such knowledge was to speak of it, lest his mother hear the news and be grieved. Thus in Sheba, the father of King Menelik was never officially mourned, though Menelik in private did mourn he who sired him. Makeda, while showing deference to her son and not questioning what was not hers to question, like her only lover maintained a sharp mind all her days. She knew of life and she knew of math, and after a span of time she understood that Solomon could no longer be alive. Though there was no word of his death, there also was no word of anything pertaining to Solomon. For a man who once was talked about frequently, this muteness must, she reasoned, signify that he had died. *Baruch dayan ha'emet. I praise you, God, the true judge.*

Makeda never spoke of this awareness to Menelik, but she, too, in private mourned. She praised God that Solomon had been king of Israel, had desired to build the temple, had invited traders from throughout the Red Sea nations to offer their goods, had met so warmly with Tamrin, had welcomed her into his palace, had given her his seed and in so doing had given her the son she had so proudly watched take her place. The blessings of Solomon were more than enough for her heart, and she was grateful.

As the years progressed, Menelik proved himself to be a fair and wise leader like his father, and also a capable warrior like his grandfather. Though wars were few, enemy advances were deftly deflected, and the spread of land over which he ruled grew rather than diminished. That said, he did not seek to make trouble for the sake of spoils that would enlarge his kingdom or his reputation. But he had a well-trained army and skilled weapons-makers and was not hesitant to use them.

Initially, Menelik continued to rely on Tamrin to conduct trade and relations with foreign countries, though as he grew older, Tamrin begged to be relieved of his duty. A great friend now of two generations of Sheban rulers, the legendary trader was granted his request. Menelik kept him close as an advisor, as his knowledge of the world outside the sprawling kingdom was unmatched. Trade missions continued to connect Sheba to other parts of the region under Tamrin's guidance and direction, and Sheba's wealth continued to grow.

Unlike the lustful David and disloyal Solomon, Menelik did not collect wives and concubines, but busied himself chiefly with affairs of the state. However, in time Menelik took to him a wife, a woman from Sheba named Eshe. He did not know her so well, but his mother insisted that he marry and ensure that the line of Solomon continued. In fact, Makeda went out among the people and made the match herself. As none could refuse her, Menelik and Eshe's family consented and had an elaborate wedding lasting three days. It was not long before the desired heir was born. He was named Yekuno and bore resemblance mainly to his mother's side.

Makeda was a doting grandmother, a role that suited her well in her later years. Her capable son had proven to have little need of her counsel, though she remained honored and respected by Menelik both in public and in private. As the years passed, Makeda, her hair the color of ash, her skin loose and wrinkled like a weathered tent canvas, saw less clearly, heard less well. Spoke little. Eventually fell ill. Though she received attentive care, she did not wish to fight for her life. Having seen all her dreams and wishes realized, she did not need more days. When she prayed, it was for mercy, not for health. Her last wish to Tamrin was to watch over Menelik.

Her last wish to Menelik was to remember his father and be like him in all ways. Her last words were, "God is one."

"They will rule together in eternity, as God's most favored partners," Menelik announced at her state funeral, it being the first public acknowledgement of Solomon's death. Thus the people of Sheba mourned them both and held Menelik, their sole offspring, all the more in their esteem.

The many generations before Menelik and the many to come after him form a balance, and he is the fulcrum, the point in the center that achieves harmony with the past and the future. Because he respected his forebears on both his mother's side and his father's, and lived a life of integrity, his legacy is one that goes from strength to strength, generation to generation, as long as God wills this world to continue.

Because from God's heavenly perch, everything is noticed.

Epilogue: TAMRIN

I was the only one who knew all three so well. My lady, of course, Queen Makeda, I was closest to her. She put great faith in me, and great responsibility, and it is the crowning achievement of my life that I can say I never let her down. My service to her was one joy after another. Thanks to her, I saw the world (and briefly ruled one small part of it!). All its wondrous sights, all its most powerful leaders. Including Solomon, the wise king of Israel, whom I was privileged to spend considerable time with. He, too, took me into his confidence and treated me fairly, and with far more respect than he needed to.

Yes, I knew them both, Solomon and Makeda, and I loved them both. They made me feel like I was their equal, which of course I was not. But such was their gentle manner and deep intelligence, and I was at my best when they saw the best in me. It fascinates me when I think of how similar they were. Each on their own was truly great, yet neither would ever dream of upstaging the other when together. Had they married, if somehow they could have ruled one nation as king and queen, it is almost unthinkable how mighty that nation would have been. Its equal would not be seen in one hundred generations.

I will go to the grave having never met two finer people, and it fills me with peace—not to mention pride—knowing that I served them well. And though I would have been happy to retire, my loyalty continued when Makeda stepped down and I was asked to serve Menelik.

Ah, Menelik. My only regret is that I was not there at his birth, for I was occupying Makeda's throne at the time. But from his first days in Sheba, I observed him with awe. After all, he was the only child of the greatest man and the greatest woman I have ever known or heard of. Even if he did not live up to the potential of his flawless antecedents—and, to be frank, he did not; could not—he clearly was a blessed being. Solomon and Makeda's God may have been the primary creator of life, but the ongoing miracle of birth worked through man and woman, and of all the sons on earth, Menelik had the best of each in his blood.

Had Menelik chosen to stay in Israel and succeed Solomon, might God have wrought the same punishment that befell Rehoboam, with a divided kingdom and bitter fighting among lesser kings? Ask instead this: Would Solomon have angered his God by marrying foreign women and worshipping their gods had Makeda decided to stay with him in Israel? Makeda was a foreign woman, but she accepted the God of Israel. Had she stayed and raised Menelik in Solomon's land, Israel would likely be the most powerful nation on earth to this day.

As it stands, Solomon remains the last beloved king of Israel, yet I can't help but feel that things would have ended up better had Menelik succeeded him. The ten northern tribes might not have split with Judah. Not with Menelik in Jerusalem. No, I think that if Menelik had been king of Israel, the dynasty of David would have continued to rule over a united kingdom in that holy land to this very day. Instead, it is now the Solomonic dynasty that rules over Sheba and Ethiopia. And may it ever be thus.

One story ends with Menelik, another begins with Menelik. And here am I, an old man, who has seen them both come to pass. Soon it will be my turn to go, but history will not remember me. I was a bit player on a grand stage, occupied by three remarkable people. King Solomon of Israel, the man of great wisdom, who built the most spectacular temple for his God. Queen Makeda of Sheba, with more beauty, strength, and intelligence than any single person before her or since. And Menelik, emperor of Ethiopia, the King of Kings, the Lord of Lords, the Conquering Lion of the Tribe of Judah.

May his glory, and through him that of his parents, reign eternal. And let us say, amen.

THE GRAVE AND THE GAY

By Jason M. Rubin

The tale that follows
Has long been told
By fellows with flute
Fiddle or lute
And though it be old
It continues to suit
And fill the hollows

DEDICATION

This book is lovingly dedicated to all my friends and family who have supported me through days and nights both grave and gay. It comes too late for some, but know that I carried your faith and belief in me into these pages.

ABOUT THE AUTHOR

Jason M. Rubin has been a professional writer since 1985 when he graduated from the University of Massachusetts Amherst with a degree in Journalism. He lives and works in the Boston area, where his daughters Hannah and Stella give his life deep meaning and endless joy. This is his first novel.

ABOUT THE BOOK

The Grave and the Gay is based on the 17th-century English folk ballad "Matty Groves." It is known by several variant names, including "Little Musgrave and Lady Barnard," and is one of the 305 ballads from England and Scotland collected and published in the late nineteenth century by American scholar Francis James Child. Twentieth-century recorded versions by Doc Watson (1966) and Fairport Convention (1969) are particularly recommended.

CHAPTER 1

Darkness. Stillness. Silence. Then cool air against exposed flesh, causing in the bed a slow rustle, a sightless reach for the goose-feather blanket. From this sudden instinctive response Lady Barnard's eyes roll up beneath their lids. The darkness no longer is absolute. It shifts, gradually, from black to brown, from red to orange. Eventually there is light entering the room, sunlight, stirring her emerging consciousness. Now voices, muffled. But not just voices. Songs. Birds. Her eyes open. Like a bear winter denning, she arises, aroused by the siren call of appetite. For after a long, lethargic winter, the air finally felt like—

Spring! Could it be? Yes, it must!

The calendar had promised. Each day had been a little warmer, a shade brighter. And now—

At long last, she realized in her still-waking mind, *spring is here!*

Convinced it was true, Lady Barnard sprung from her bed and strode towards her window. As her face hovered near the glass, nearly pressed against it, her exuberant breath created a moist fog on the interior-facing pane. Impatiently, she wiped the moisture with her hand, revealing only that the window's exterior was still wet with countless silver ovals of morning dew that the young day's low sun had yet to dry.

Not to be denied the sight and smell she craved, Lady Barnard thrust her small pale hands at the wooden bolts that had kept the window closed tightly against the winter chill, and struggled to work them loose. It took a few moments for they had not been disturbed for a number of months, but at last she succeeded.

Shedding for a moment her well-practiced gentility, Lady Barnard flung open the window and into her face flew the long-awaited guest: that southwesterly wind that clipped the green fields of Dublin, carried the moist, mossy aroma of peat over the Atlantic Ocean and round the Isle of Anglesey, and at last deposited this timeworn trace of spring to the thawing English county of Lancashire, and into Lady Barnard's bedroom.

It had been a brutally hard winter—dozens in the county had died of exposure or illness—and this much-anticipated change of season was as welcome to the weary Lancastrians as the sight of a branch in the beak of Noah's dove must have been to the survivors of the Great Deluge. Together with the increased chatter of returning birds and the reappearance of tight green buds on vines and shrubs, these heralds of spring inspired a restless euphoria in all.

Never mind that one's breath was still clearly visible at dawn and in the evenings, or that fires as much for warmth as for cooking still burned in people's hearths. No, impatience prevailed and folks were already out and about, preparing for the Eastertime celebrations to come.

Of course, in spring impatience is nothing if not a virtue. After all, it is the impatience of the crocus pushing through the damp, softening soil that calls nature again to life. It is the impatience of the sun, no longer intent to give way to darkness so soon after supper, that gives light and thus encouragement to all human and natural pursuits. And it is the impatience of time itself that stands not a day longer in a single season than it must, because tomorrow is never inevitable and each day, each season, is a gift to the earth and all who live upon it.

That the advent of spring and the festival of Easter coincided was Divine inspiration, so it seemed to Lady Barnard. For the very stakes that her father used to support his nascent tomatoes and peas in spring reminded her of the cross in her church upon which the wooden sculpture of Jesus was nailed, awaiting his own ripening in heaven. Even the Lord's nickname, the Lamb of God, reminded her of the fresh lamb that her father killed and her mother cooked and that graced their festival table on Easter afternoon.

In this season rich with tradition, small bands of enterprising young men gathered in taverns, on porches, in fields, and even in the rear pews on Sunday mornings, enlisting like-minded merry-makers to join their pace-egging troupes. "Pace", of course, is from the Latin *pacha*, or spring. And eggs are the common symbol of rebirth. In this part of the country, the pace-eggers journey from town to town each Easter Sunday in wild costumes and with a song of entreaty, requesting favors—usually eggs boiled in onionskin or coins of any value—in return for which they enact a farcical play.

The *dramatis personae* of this street-staged theatrical undertaking includes such characters as the Lady Gay, the Soldier Brave, and the notorious Old Tosspot, whose coal-blackened face gapes and guffaws above the basket he waves to hold the aforementioned favors. In his other hand, the stronger one in fact, he holds a straw tail stuffed with pins, which he swings madly towards those who either are slow in paying into the basket or who have the temerity to try and steal its precious contents.

Following the play—not the Passion narrative as such, although a comical death and a magical rebirth of sorts typically transpires—Old Tosspot again bullies the crowd for favors. When the audience then disperses for their own feasts, the eggs are eaten (and shells crushed, lest witches use them as boats to spread their spells and unholy mischief to other locales, so the legend goes) and the coins shared and pocketed, or else tendered in exchange for mugs of ale. The pace-eggers then make their way to another village and the entire act plays out again. By the end of the holiday, the pace-eggers would have consumed enough eggs and ale to keep them in their beds well into the following day.

Yet even as the men were organizing their bands; even as the women were cleaning their houses and making room in their kitchens for the game they would pluck and cook, and the pies and cakes they would bake; even as children dreaded the clean, newly knit clothes they had to wear to church, and the switch they knew would be taken to them if they misbehaved during the service; even with all this activity, this anticipation, at high pitch—still Easter was half a fortnight away.

Perhaps a milder winter would not have inspired such relentless desire for spring and all its vernal wonders. Yet rarely is spring met with indifference, especially here in Lancashire, still a Catholic stronghold, where the faithful greet this time of year with hope, for all have the capacity to change, to grow. And if the sun finds us and we strengthen in the warmth of its light, we, too, may be reborn in an eternal spring, a perfected flower in God's vast, loving garden.

It was in this happy and hopeful atmosphere that Lady Barnard drew the fresh peaty air deeply into her nostrils, and in exhaling released a winter's worth of loneliness and frustration. The crisp, invigorating breeze felt good on her alabaster face, framed as ever by dark straight hair she often drew tightly at the back in a bun. As she had just arisen, though, it now fell randomly about her shoulders with a few black strands strewn across her face. She closed her eyes, savoring the moment, and then opened them to see which persons were out in the crisp, clean air.

What Lady Barnard saw first were the few servants her husband employed out in the yard going about their morning chores: raking, sweeping, pruning, planting, mending, washing. She also saw townspeople passing her grand home on the winding dirt road. By all accounts, a typical morning sight. But today, instead of white, the endless, hopeless white of cold and imposing snow, there were colorful figures in motion against a deepening green and brown background. Faces were uncovered, revealing pleasant-looking people with things to do and the will to do them—not bundled creatures too cold to socialize, rushing from one hearth to another.

I bid you welcome, spring, she thought to herself, *and may winter not soon return.*

In truth, as cold as it had been out of doors the past few months, it had been just as frigid within her stately home—and for an even longer duration. Though she was not a prisoner in her house, her comings and goings were carefully controlled by Lord Barnard, who had an odd, intensely adamant dislike of people gossiping about what went on in each other's lives and homes. Concerned that Lady Barnard would reveal personal information about their lives, he stringently limited her trips into town and never let her go alone; though in truth, it likely was not so much what *did* go on at home that fueled his fears, but rather what did *not*.

After ten years of marriage, there had been no children. Furthermore, it had been far too long, in Lady Barnard's opinion, since the act of conception had even been attempted. Now, with the coming of spring, Lord Barnard would resume his hunting trips. She would be left alone for days and weeks, which, while not ideal, she found preferable to being ignored while in his company.

This day, however, as nature's insistent cycle moved one-quarter turn, as other people's lives were opening up like laurel buds, Lady Barnard wanted no longer to be so constrained, as if she were a mourning dove held in too cramped a cage. She desired to meet people, speak with them, and revel in the attention of the ladies who would envy her fine clothing; perhaps read in a young man's eyes that there was more to her appeal than that overly familiar visage that appeared in her looking glass.

Then a scowl formed on her face, as she turned away from the window. Lady Barnard knew she could never be like the young girls out there on the street, fluttering about and flirting in plain view, with no care nor shame. Raised with no special privileges in terms of money or station, she was the fairest of three daughters born to a small farmer and his oft-sickly wife. Despite their circumstances, it was her father's intention that she be well-married. As such, he traded sacks of cornmeal he had milled himself for lessons in etiquette and domestic skills for his daughter, that she would be a draw not only for her looks but also for her suitability in any social context.

She was taught to be polite, demure, submissive yet capable. She ably learned literature, geography, and mathematics yet was instructed not to volunteer opinions on these matters. It was better to possess knowledge than to demonstrate it, her teacher impressed upon her frequently and emphatically. Of these subjects, she was particularly enamored of the first two for they promised vistas beyond her reach, adventures that seemed otherworldly, and stories of courage and daring such as she could only imagine being close to.

When the match was made with Lord Barnard, she did as she had been prepared to do. She held herself with a dignity free from pomposity and a wisdom expressed in whispers of competence as a given situation required. Yet as Lord Barnard's constraints upon her grew more numerous, frequent, and intrusive, her only response was to become more silent, withdrawn, and resigned. Thus it was that Lady Barnard sadly turned back to the window, continuing to spy enviously on those who have fewer means yet far more freedom than she.

It may not be a good life they lead, she thought, *but it is a life they own, a life they control. I am no more in charge of my destiny than these French draperies are of theirs. In truth,* she admitted, *I am much like the draperies, the furniture, the china and silver. We all are affectations, mere decorations for my Lord.*

We are that, she thought, *all that, yet nothing more.*

Distressed again, as if spring were still just a distant dream, her focus became distracted. Though she continued to look out the window into the yard below, in truth she saw nothing; or rather, her mind did not acknowledge what was there within her view. Thus it was that she took no notice of the tall figure passing into the scope of her vision, the handsome man named by his long-deceased mother Matthew Musgrave.

To his friends and lovers, and he had plenty of both, he was Matty. Sporting fair features and a confident gait, Matty was Lord Barnard's stable hand, and had Lady Barnard truly seen him she would have thought him familiar-looking yet been unable to identify either his name or his role. The stable was but one of many places to which she never ventured—though in this case, it was of her own choosing that she avoided it.

Matty, however, looked towards the grand home as he crossed the yard and could see Lady Barnard's eyes facing his direction. He assumed she was looking at him, but as she did not appear about to give an order, he continued on his way.

Fewer than twenty paces hence, Matty came upon Alexandra McLean doing the Barnards' laundry under the calm mid-March sky. A red handkerchief held back her long, straw-colored, slightly curly mane. Beautiful even in damp, loose-fitting work clothes, she stood chest-high to her visitor. As Matty approached, she gladly suspended her work and placed a lid on the tall cast iron cauldron of water that sat on an open wood fire beside her.

"Good morning, Alexandra," said Matty, with a knowing grin on his strong and pleasant face.

"And to you, Matty," Alexandra replied, dabbing her moist forehead with her apron.

"Will I see you in the loft tonight, fair maiden?" he inquired.

With mock incredulity, she said, "Oh, is it my turn again so soon, then?"

"Whatever could you mean?" came another mock-incredulous reply, met with a bemused smile and a few shakes of Alexandra's fair head as she returned to her waiting work pile.

"I shan't promise you," she replied, not looking up. "I don't see myself finishing before supper, unless I collapse where I stand. The Lady instructed me yesterday to wash all the quilts today, though I'll never get to hers if she doesn't wake up already."

"Odd thing, she was just staring at me from her window as I passed along from the stable."

"It's not so strange for a woman to stare at *you*, now, is it, Matty?"

"Well, she's not just any woman, is she? And I doubt she even knows my name."

"Ah, but I'm sure she knows a pretty face. And I believe she has been lonely for a man's attentions," Alexandra added.

"What makes you say that?"

"I wash the bed linens," she whispered, raising her eyes from the steaming cauldron to her handsome caller. "Many a tale is told in soiled sheets. The Lord's and the Lady's are unusually clean, if you understand my meaning."

"Perhaps they employ that long dining table in place of a bed," said Matty.

"I would prefer hard wood or even cold marble to the straw you sleep on."

"Then accept this offer. Tonight you will ride me like a horseman and I will take the quills in my backside."

"You are a true gentleman, Matty. A true—"

The Grave and the Gay

At that moment, the occasional lovers were interrupted by Darnell, the Barnards' personal assistant. As a "house" servant, he boasted a more prestigious position than those like Matty and Alexandra, who toiled out of doors or in other quarters. Darnell even had a room of his own in the Barnards' basement, with a door for his ingress and egress so that he could enter and exit his room without having to go through the house proper.

"Matty Musgrave," Darnell called.

"I am here," replied Matty.

"Lord Barnard wishes to see you immediately."

"For what purpose?"

"I neither wish to know nor need to know," Darnell replied, without the disinterest he would typically choose to display. "It is my Lord's desire to speak with you and while I do not comprehend the affection he seems to have for you lately, I am merely fulfilling my duty in informing you of his urgent request."

Looking down at Matty's feet, Darnell added, "Might I suggest you change your shoes so as not to track manure into the house?"

"Lord Barnard loves his horses and he loves me," teased Matty. "How, then, can he be upset if my shoes bring both his loves to him?"

As Darnell stifled a shout and Alexandra muffled a laugh, Matty bid them good day. When the strutting stable hand neared the house, Darnell said to Alexandra, "He is a disgusting brute."

"Yes, though you have to admit he is honest about it," she replied.

"You're too good for him, you know."

"So you've told me. Thank you for your concern, Darnell. Now if you don't mind, I need to attend to the washing."

"I can do better by you."

"Can you, then? How? You work *in* the house, but you are not *master* of it."

"Alexandra, you know I have feelings for you. I am a decent man. I have a good position. The Lord and Lady treat me well. As my wife, you would improve your standing with them."

"Is that your offer, then?" she asked with a faint smile. "That I should be a servant's wife? Am I to be servant to a servant?"

"Well, what can Matty offer you?" Darnell demanded to know.

"Laughter, Darnell. Laughter and passion. And nothing more because I desire nothing more. You know Matty. He'll not be chained to a wife, nor I to a husband. It's enough for me that I can be out on a spring morning and earn a wage and a meal."

"You're a lovely girl, Alexandra. But you have no sense. I will not stop courting you, not until I have proven to you that I would be a better husband for you than that, that…stable hand."

"That 'stable hand' may not be cultured, Darnell, he may be nothing more than a raggle taggle gypsy, but he knows what he is, he's not ashamed, and he doesn't put on airs. You're a decent man, true, but you're not your own man, are you? You're the man the Barnards demand you be. That's the difference between you and Matty. You try so hard to please that it's impossible to distinguish between your position and your person. That's why even though I've known you longer than I've known Matty, I've no clue as to your soul. Yes, you show interest in me, but you've never shown passion."

Just then a bell rang, its bird-like warble emanating from the open window above.

"That's Lady Barnard," said Darnell. "I must go to her. Remember what I have said, Alexandra. I don't know how I will prove my love and my worth to you. But I will. I swear it upon all that is right and holy."

And with that, Darnell followed the same steps that Matty took into the house, looking down all the way to check for traces of manure. Alexandra watched wordlessly as he walked away, then returned her attention to the piles of laundry that had not lessened during her conversations.

She placed another log on the neglected fire down below and submerged a feather-stuffed comforter in the hot, soapy water, stirring it with a large wooden paddle as she thought on the disparate propositions Darnell and Matty had made to her that morning.

CHAPTER 2

The Barnards' residence sat on a large parcel of land, equidistant to the ocean due east and the Forest of Bowland to the west—an hour on horseback to either location. With the house situated close to the road in front, the bulk of the property was in the rear, out of the public's view. As such, the village square to which Lady Barnard longed to go was a short southward walk, made somewhat longer by her husband's obstinacy.

Though not a master horseman by any measure, Lord Barnard enjoyed taking morning rides by himself. Elevated and alone, he was comforted by the beautiful views that surrounded his property, venturing farther from home yet never getting too close to either the ocean (for he could not swim) nor the village (for he was not a sociable man). He hunted in the forest in every season except summer (too much heat, too many insects) and winter (too frigid, not enough game), but was a poor navigator and thus often had to hire a guide.

The impressive house, built by Lord Barnard's father and uncles when Lord Barnard was but a bump in his mother's belly, was large, a landmark in the area; no other home in the village had near as much living space. Strange, then, that so little of it was actually lived in. The Barnards were not wont to entertain and so rarely hosted parties. Business associates and relatives would come for dinner occasionally but on most days the house would hold the bare minimum of Lord and Lady Barnard, plus a few servants coming and going as necessary.

The couple employed just five servants, though two of them—a cook and a house cleaner, chatty people both—had recently been dismissed by Lord Barnard. The others were Darnell, who coordinated the maintenance and operations of the home and its occupants; Alexandra, the laundress; and Matty, who minded the horses. In the absence of the cleaner, Alexandra had been asked to mop the floors and dust the draperies in addition to her usual duties. These were the full-time staff; a gardener and a carpenter from the village were hired as needed.

Their meals in the interim were simple, prepared either by Lady Barnard or Darnell. It was beneath their means, yet neither Lord nor Lady Barnard was eager to replace the fired servants, preferring the increased quiet and privacy. (This was, after all, the house in which Lord Barnard had been raised, and he was disinclined to change it much, or to drive any more foot traffic into it than was necessary. At any rate, for most minor chores he would rather fend for himself than invite and involve additional persons into his surroundings.)

Such traffic, as Matty did now, generally entered by way of the wide front porch. With a waist-high wall in front and no chairs set out on the floor, the porch seemed more a buffer against the outside world than an entrée to the home. The unadorned front door opened to a great room that connected to a hallway on the left, with three rooms and a staircase accessible to the right. Directly to the rear were a plush, hunter's green sofa and four matching chairs with arms. Just to the side of them was an ornate spinet harpsichord purchased in Italy that was hand-painted and signed by its maker, the master craftsman Girolamo Zenti.

As Matty entered the great room he passed beneath a large round chandelier fashioned by Lord Barnard's father from a wagon wheel; the fine workmanship notwithstanding, the rustic piece contrasted with the elegance of the room's furnishings. Centered underneath it was a square crimson carpet spotted here and there with blobs of candle wax that had dripped from above. Matty's carefree steps pressed the wax deeper into the carpet's otherwise well-cared-for threads.

The hallway to the left led to two vacant rooms formerly occupied by the cook and house cleaner. (Aside from Darnell's quarters in the basement, no other servants had rooms in the house. Matty lived in a room outfitted with a wood stove and a makeshift slop sink—really just a half barrel set above a hole in the ground—that was attached to the rear of the stable, the comfort of which often depended on the direction of the wind. Alexandra was allowed a bed when needed in her cousin Andrew's home in the village. She hoped to be invited to occupy one of the empty rooms in the house, though such invitation had yet to be tendered.)

The rooms to the right were the kitchen, accessible through a door at the far left end of the wall, and a dining room and study that were essentially partitioned areas of the great room itself as opposed to discretely constructed spaces. With so few inhabitants and visitors, additional walls and doors were deemed superfluous.

The staircase to which Matty approached, also crimson carpeted with a railing painted white, led to a perpendicular hallway sitting atop the dining room and study. Once at the top of the stairs, to the left was Lord Barnard's bedroom; to the right was Lady Barnard's. From the start of their marriage, Lord Barnard had insisted on separate quarters. His he used for both sleep and study. Fastidious about its order and cleanliness, Lord Barnard further insisted that their sexual activities, such as they were, be confined to his wife's bed and bedroom.

As Matty ascended the staircase, a wooden sword rack rose to his view. Built by Lord Barnard's father, it hung in the center of the upstairs hallway. The cherry wood the elder Barnard used gave it the appearance of having been glazed long ago with actual blood, since dried and darkened. The four rungs held two pairs of swords: one pair, worn and dull, was originally owned—and apparently often used—by the senior Barnard; the other pair was purchased two summers prior by Lord Barnard when on business in Versailles. There he'd taken fencing lessons, though these swords, ornate and expensive, were for display only, and their silvery glint beckoned imposingly to Matty as he approached Lord Barnard's study.

Matty had been tending the horses for more than a year now; this was his second spring wielding brush and shovel in the stable. He had not come upon any person's recommendation, nor had Lord Barnard issued any broadside advertising such a position. After all, before Matty arrived Lord Barnard had owned but two horses and he had cared for the beasts himself.

It was early in March of the previous year when Thomas Erickson, a printer, had to sell off some of his possessions in order to avoid jail for nearly killing a young man named Henry Harrison, whom he believed had disgraced his eldest daughter. The weapon had been the steel poker with which the widower was tending his fire.

Despite the seemingly improvised choice of instrument, this was not a crime of passion but rather one very much planned and premeditated. The precipitating incident had occurred four days earlier, but Erickson had heard of it only the day before, and not from his daughter (who denied it) but from the man he'd hired to muck out his stable daily and perform a complete cleaning every Sabbath morning: one Matthew Musgrave.

The talk in the local tavern was that Matty and Henry had a disagreement between themselves, perhaps over Erickson's daughter, a common point of interest for the two men. Regardless of how and for what reason the accusation came to be made, Erickson invited Henry to his home one night under the ruse that he was eager to give a potential suitor his blessing. Once the poor lad crossed the threshold, however, Erickson came at him with the poker, and only his daughter's impassioned screams for mercy saved the young man's life.

Neighbors, alarmed by the girl's wailing, soon rushed in. One seized Erickson from behind, wrapping his arm around the deranged man's neck, while the other took hold of the weapon, now crimson-flecked. Henry, on the floor and barely conscious, was given a blanket and consoled. A large gash on his temple soaked through several cloths before a doctor could arrive with thread to close the wound.

Erickson, being a man of some stature in the business community, was held in a locked room overnight, chiefly to let his fury subside, but otherwise was allowed to remain free. However, he was ordered to pay restitution to Henry's parents (the boy being too young to collect the fine himself and in no condition at the time to make use of it) and so auctioned off his two horses to raise the money.

Lord Barnard attended the auction, though more out of curiosity to see the final act of a local tragedy than to acquire Erickson's mares. Yet Matty, who was also present and for much the same reason as Lord

Barnard, saw an opportunity for advancement and, perhaps, immunity, and so approached him with a proposition.

"Lord Barnard," spoke Matty with head bowed, "I beg your forgiveness but may I have a word with you? I am Matty Musgrave, Mr. Erickson's stable hand, and I know these horses well. They are fine animals indeed. I have seen your stable in passing and it is large enough to provide shelter for these two. Furthermore, the addition of these remarkable creatures would make you the largest horse owner in the village, which is fitting for such an important man as yourself."

That Lord Barnard was accustomed to flattery did not render Matty's brief soliloquy, made with such a sweet mouth on such a handsome face, any the less effective. Barely concealing a smile, Lord Barnard replied, "And an important man such as I has the time to care for four horses? How would I manage the doubling of my stable?"

"Well, sir, prior to this unfortunate incident Mr. Erickson was most pleased with my work," said Matty. "After today, the horses will be gone and my skills will be unneeded here. Should you choose to purchase Mr. Erickson's horses, it would be my honor to transfer my services to you, to care not only for these animals, but for your other two as well."

"Very well, then," said Lord Barnard. "I will pay you what Erickson paid you for one month. If I am satisfied with you, I will pay you one-and-a-half times your current salary. This assumes, of course, that I make the winning bid. If not, you have no job with me."

"If you don't mind my saying so, sir, as I look at the crowd assembled here today, I see not another man whose purse is as deep as yours, nor one whose honor and generosity are a match for yours," Matty said with an exaggeratedly reverent bow.

As it turned out, Lord Barnard did purchase the horses and gained Matty's services as well. After a month, Lord Barnard, as promised, raised Matty's wages. That summer, during which he spent considerably more time observing Matty's work (tiring work as it was in the summer heat, Matty often soaked through his shirt and removed it, baring a lean, glistening chest and stomach), Lord Barnard raised his wages again, now paying him double what Erickson had.

In the fall, Lord Barnard was away often, hunting and attending to business in other towns and villages. He returned two weeks before the solstice and every week or so after that would summon Matty to his office. He had no particular request or order to give to his charismatic stable hand. Rather, these meetings were a process by which Lord Barnard got to know Matty better. Occasionally, he would give Matty a gift, either a small trinket he picked up while on business or else an extra ration of food. Unbeknownst to him, Matty often gave both types of gifts to Alexandra.

Matty, accustomed to seizing onto advantages, did not question the Lord's generosity or interest in him. He attributed it to the quality of his work and indeed the horses were well cared for and the stable fairly immaculate. At the same time, he was careful not to give his benefactor reason to question his continuing employment and so judiciously engaged in half-truths and omissions when Lord Barnard asked about his background. What wasn't expressed, Matty reasoned, needn't be explained.

As Matty reached the door of Lord Barnard's quarters, he thought to look down and back, just to see if he indeed had tracked any detritus into the house. Not seeing evidence of such, he turned back to the door and knocked two raps.

"Enter," came the voice from inside. Matty opened the door and stepped in. Lord Barnard rose from his writing table and greeted Matty warmly, placing his left hand over Matty's right, which was in the clasp of Lord Barnard's writing hand. "It is nice to see you again, Matty," said Lord Barnard. "How are the horses this morning?"

"Eager to be ridden, sir, in this accommodating air," Matty answered.

"It is a lovely day now, isn't it?" Lord Barnard released Matty's hand and took a few steps past him to close the door. "Come sit here, my boy." Matty took hold of the chair next to Lord Barnard's writing desk and sat down.

"Matty, you have served me very well over the past year. I am most pleased with your work."

Matty hastened to interject his appreciation for the comment, but Lord Barnard stopped him with a raised hand. Matty's gaze fixed upon Lord Barnard's open palm, which faced him, and he noticed how much cleaner it was than his, how much smoother, without the calluses that the handles and shafts of shovels and pitchforks caused. *What things do these untroubled hands touch and caress,* he thought. *If I had such hands with which to touch Alexandra, how much more pleased would she be?*

"Please just listen, Matty," Lord Barnard continued. "In the year that I've known you, I've become quite fond of you. I think you know that." Despite the last statement, Lord Barnard arched his eyebrows in a silent query, which Matty acknowledged and affirmed—also silently—with a quick nod of his head.

"I must divulge some rather personal information to you. What I am about to say to you is very important and I want you to hear it. But I must ask you to remain silent about it. You must not utter a word about this matter to anyone. Do you understand?"

Again, a silent nod of assent.

"Matty, Lady Barnard and I didn't know each other when we married. As is the custom, our respective fathers made the match. But I accepted it because I respected my father and also was ready to build a life for myself. Every professional man needs a wife to manage his home and accommodate his, er, needs. So I married Lady Barnard and thus made a commitment to her. Now, when one undertakes such a commitment, one has certain hopes and ideals. Marriage, to me, was a way of enhancing my station, enjoying companionship of course, but also providing offspring. I suppose every man desires a son, an heir to his estate, someone whom he could look in the eyes and see a younger reflection of himself. Someone to impart his beliefs and values to, someone who would look up to him and be loyal to him. Who would be a friend to his father and share a special bond. Do you understand?"

Matty nodded, though such a relationship between a father and a son was foreign to him.

"Matty, I'm sorry, this is a difficult thing to say, particularly to one in my employ. And that is why it is so essential that you not share what I am about to tell you with anyone. Matty, my marriage to Lady Barnard has not fulfilled me quite as I had hoped it would. After ten years of marriage,

I have no children, and no—well, it is enough to say that I choose to wait no longer.

"Matty, I need to know that my possessions and my affairs will be maintained by someone whom I trust, someone whom I love. And I do love you, Matty, as I would my own son. Of course, I cannot leave my estate to a stable boy. And so I would like to make you into a gentleman, an educated man. There is much I can teach you, much that I want you to know—the proper dress, manners, knowledge of politics, business, history, and national affairs. I want to take you from the stable and make you presentable to people and institutions of great prestige. I want to make you worthy of being my heir, Matty. Do you understand? You will essentially be my son. In fact, legally you will be my next of kin after Lady Barnard. Do you understand what I am offering you?"

"I believe I do, sir—yet I don't know how to respond," said Matty, and this was as true a statement as any he had ever uttered in this room. "This is unlike anything I have ever heard to happen. What am I to do?"

"It is up to me to make this happen, Matty," said Lord Barnard. "First, I must confer with my solicitor. Then I must hire a new stable boy. Lastly, I will commence to teach you in the ways of sophisticated men."

Matty sat, stunned, as if he'd just been told of a dear personal loss, yet he was, in fact, being offered something of great value. *His son? I am to be his son? And he my—father?* Perhaps it was more the feeling of being given a fine coat made in some exotic land, like China, yet it is tailored to fit a man of much smaller or larger dimensions. A gift, then, that is precious yet not practical; or one that must be appreciated even if it is not desired. *Can this be so? Can this really happen?* Regardless, it was not a gift that Matty could easily refuse. In the whirl of his mind he thought of how he would benefit from Lord Barnard's largesse. Yet still he could not seem to register an emotion that even approximated gratitude. *How am I to live? And where?*

Lord Barnard disturbed his silent reflections. "I can see you have grasped the enormity of my offer," he said. "I do not expect you to be entirely comfortable with the idea of adopting a new life to replace your old one, limited though it is—at least not right away. But you will have time to think on it. For now, I want you to make sure the horses are ready for a hunting trip. I plan to leave three days hence and I will be gone past Easter. Darnell has all the details, yet I have not told him nor anyone else—not even Lady Barnard—that which I have revealed to you this morning. You have been uncharacteristically quiet these last few minutes. Remain that way about this matter, or else there may be severe consequences for both of us. Do you understand?"

"I do, sir," said Matty, now finding his voice again. "And I appreciate your, um, affection for me. May I leave now to tend to your horses?"

"Of course, Matty. Thank you." As Matty turned to leave, Lord Barnard added, "I wish I could take you with me on this trip. But there will be many opportunities for us to spend time together in the future."

"Yes, sir," replied Matty, still facing the door, which now he hurriedly walked through and down the steps, passing Darnell, who was answering the Lady's bell. Darnell looked down and behind, checking as Matty had done earlier to see if flakes of manure and pieces of straw had dropped from the stable hand's boots. Almost annoyed to find the carpet clean, Darnell continued to climb the stairs. As he neared the top, he saw Lord Barnard's door close, though he did not see Lord Barnard. It was as if a spectre or a sharp wind had done the job.

Darnell turned then to the right, past the sword display, and went down the hall to the room at the end, the private quarters of Lady Barnard.

CHAPTER 3

As aide to both Lord and Lady Barnard, Darnell had seen and heard many things that the people of the village would wish to have known. Yet he understood that to be a good house servant one must be discreet. And Darnell always wanted to be known as a man with whom one can entrust a secret. Even when Lord or Lady Barnard asked him about the other, he was very careful to give an appropriately vague reply. For even if, say, Lady Barnard wanted to know what her husband had been discussing with a certain visitor, it would not do to admit that he had been listening to the conversation.

In order for each to be confident that their own privacy would be protected, both the Barnards had to believe that Darnell had little to share with them about the other. Darnell cultivated that belief through his own admirable restraint.

And indeed there were things he had heard and witnessed that would give a gossiper many hours' worth of salacious details with which to command and satisfy an audience. For example, Darnell was witness to the fact that Lord Barnard had something of a temper, was fastidious about his personal space and papers, and was not entirely comfortable in the company of women. For her part, Lady Barnard could be moody and withdrawn, had a taste for wine at all hours of the day, and spent more of her husband's money on items of fancy than he was aware of—or would likely approve.

Though Darnell knew all these things (and more), to his credit in four years of service he had never spoken of them. Unlike Matty, Darnell did come recommended, though some deception was involved. A visiting Lord Sanders paid a call on Lord Barnard, bearing a note of introduction from a mutual acquaintance who was an advisor to the governor. Lord Sanders had brought Darnell with him, with the story that the boy's parents had been in his employ for many years, and he had promised them that when Darnell turned eighteen years of age Lord Sanders would arrange honorable employment for him. Lord Sanders had educated Darnell himself and the boy could be trusted to be loyal, prompt, and courteous.

This last sentence was true; the rest of his story was not. In fact, Darnell was Lord Sanders' son, although the mother was the cook in the Sanders household. Sadly, she died shortly after giving birth to him. Lord Sanders convinced Lady Sanders that they should raise the poor orphan themselves. Not knowing the identity of the father, Lady Sanders agreed. The boy grew up privileged and educated. When he turned eighteen, however, Agatha the housekeeper, an elderly woman who had taken sick and did not expect to live much longer, told Darnell the truth about his origins. Shocked, he confronted his father. This caused quite a row, and Lord Sanders decided it was time to grant the boy his independence. He secured his son's silence by threatening to harm Lady Sanders, who had raised Darnell with all the caring and love a woman can give to a child.

And so, Darnell willingly let himself be put in the employ of Lord Barnard. Since that time, he became known as a very capable worker, though unquestionably humorless and stern. In truth, he had long decided that he would exact revenge on his father for his deception and cruelty, all the while mourning for the mother he never knew. Lord and Lady Barnard were none the wiser about Darnell's background, yet it had left him with qualities they much appreciated in his role as their personal assistant.

Though he would never admit it to anyone, in his heart Darnell favored Lady Barnard greatly over her husband. For no good reason, simply on the basis of gender, he had projected Lord Sanders onto Lord Barnard and his deceased mother onto Lady Barnard. Which is not to say that he loved her, certainly not with the love of a boy to his mother or that of a man to his wife. Yet he did pity her. And as that pity did soften his heart, a certain attraction for her had but recently asserted itself within him. It was based largely on a sense that he should save her, as he could never have saved his own mother. He was, therefore, somewhat protective of her and often struggled to show Lord Barnard the honor and respect he was due without betraying his true feelings, either in the tone of his voice or the expression on his face.

All this, of course, is merely to give the reader an understanding of what is to transpire next. Darnell had not been waiting on this explanation. He already had knocked and had entered Lady Barnard's private quarters. She had handed Darnell a list of items for him to purchase for her in the village. He would have to go to the seamstress, to the market, and to Mr. McDougall, the old Scot who arranged flowers for the church, who had promised to make her a fine bonnet for Easter. Darnell agreed and asked Lady Barnard if there was anything else she wished of him.

"No, not really, Darnell," she replied.

"Then I shall attend to these tasks straight away."

"No," she said, a bit too quickly, perhaps. A bit too forcefully. "No, please, if you don't mind, I…I wish you to stay and chat for a few minutes."

"As you desire, my Lady," said Darnell, feeling rather pleased by the attention she was giving him.

"I'm sorry, Darnell, but it has been a long winter, hasn't it? One gets rather lonely during the winter, one stays indoors more. Of course, I'm not one to take rides or walk through the village. Lord Barnard wishes me to stay close to home usually, as you well know. But lately I feel I've been rather trapped, as if in a prison or something. Not just lately in fact, for a long time, a very long time now. And, well, spring is here and I've got it into my head that I don't wish to be quite so alone anymore."

"Yes, I see," Darnell lied, hoping she would elucidate further.

"I think this spring I should like to go out more from time to time," she continued. "To the village, I mean. Obviously, I will go to church on Easter Sunday, which is soon, but I don't wish to go out only then."

After a brief pause she continued softly, almost timidly, "What do you think of that idea, Darnell?"

"I should think it would be very good for your constitution to be out in the fresh air, my Lady," replied Darnell. "I imagine as well that it would give the villagers a great deal of pleasure to see you more frequently."

Lady Barnard was pleased with this response. "Do you really think so?"

"I do indeed, my Lady," said Darnell, lying again though with the most noble of intentions. "Please forgive my saying so, but without your presence the village itself is like a flower that has no scent or a bird with no song."

Darnell thought he saw his mistress blush. It was not readily apparent because she looked down shyly upon hearing his words, kinder words than any she had heard before in her marriage.

"That is very gracious of you to say, Darnell."

Then Lady Barnard summoned the courage to raise her head and look directly at Darnell, even taking a step towards him, so that they were but three paces apart.

"Darnell, I know I can trust you with this," she said. "Lord Barnard does not…visit me very often anymore. You know what I mean. At night. He is a very busy man. But I have wondered recently if I am…well, still attractive. Of course, you are a young man and your eyes are drawn to lovely young girls, as well they should. But I don't know whether anyone would consider me desirable anymore.

"Tell me," she continued after a short pause, "is it true that Lord Barnard is going off on a hunting trip over the Easter holiday?"

Sensing that this was not private information, he replied truthfully. "Yes, my Lady. Lord Barnard will be leaving with a small party three days hence and is not expected to return until after the holiday."

"In that case," said Lady Barnard, "I should like to ask if you would accompany me to church on Easter Sunday as my escort."

Now it was his turn to blush. "It would be my honor, my Lady."

Darnell would have said more, but his well-trained ears noticed that Lord Barnard was approaching. Indeed, he came swiftly through the door without knocking or announcing himself, startling Lady Barnard.

"Darnell, would you excuse us, please?" he asked.

"Of course, my Lord," Darnell replied.

Turning to Lady Barnard, he bowed, said "My Lady," and left the room, closing the door behind him.

Darnell stayed near the door for a few seconds, then walked down the hall and turned left to descend the stairs. His heart was racing with an excitement that he rarely had cause to feel. The house servant was glad to be sent into town, for he feared he could not yet conceal his racing emotions. A walk in the brisk spring air would be just right.

As he set off on his errands, Darnell quietly cursed his own lauded trait of discretion.

If only Alexandra could have heard our mistress' words just now. If only she knew the high regard in which Lady Barnard holds me. And if only Matty could see that he is not the only one so favored by those for whom we toil.

If only.

CHAPTER 4

It was not difficult to understand Matty's appeal to women, nor his success with them. Standing half a head above average height, he appeared strong and solid, yet not intimidating. His thick raven hair hung nearly level with his pronounced collarbone, though he took better care of the equine manes he brushed every day than of his own tousled locks. His eyes were dark as well, though lit from inside by an impish joy that contradicted one's first impression of them: that they beheld a deep melancholy.

His skin was a shade darker than that of his fellow villagers, and there was talk that he had Spanish blood, though his nose and profile suggested an Italian or perhaps even a Turk. His full, soft lips seemed ever to be smiling and his smile was broad and true. His hands and limbs were firm. Though he had worked with horses for a number of years, he himself was not a skilled rider. He came to his livelihood because he needed one, and because he realized that most ladies were very fond of horses.

Matty had an extraordinary appetite for women and it rarely went unsated for long. Yet any strong appetite is driven by a significant hunger, and hunger is a form of emptiness. So it was with Matty that for all the good fortune that fell upon his exterior, inside he tended a private void that he would permit no other person to see or know or inquire about.

Born in the dark heart of winter to poor but hardworking parents—his father a cobbler, his mother a mender—Matty was one from a set of twins. His brother emerged first, stillborn. So great was his parents' grief that until his mother felt a new strike of physical pain that nearly matched her emotional agony, it was little noticed that he was coming not far behind. Matty's first human experience, then, was of an encompassing sadness.

He was raised with care and tenderness by his parents, but the sense of loss in their lives was palpable. When they looked at him, they saw the empty space next to him as well. As a child, Matty was unaware that he had shared his mother's womb with a brother he would never know outside of it. He came to believe, therefore, that he was born incomplete, as if there were an organ or limb present in other children that was absent in him. He feared his deformity would cause him to be taken away like others he had heard about who had been cursed in the womb by witches or because of their mothers' sins.

When as a ten-year-old he was finally told the story of his birth, he at first was relieved to know that the problem was neither with him nor caused by him. Yet as he grew and matured, he understood that his parents had been in pain all his life. He began then to feel jealousy towards his dead brother. Never named, the blue baby would remain innocent forever, while Matty, who indulged in the merry mischief of all healthy boys, would occasionally receive the rod, the hand, or a sharp verbal rebuke.

And then, as a teenaged young man, his perspective shifted again. Seeking to know himself, it pained him to realize he would never know his brother. This sibling he had either despised or been ignorant of would have been his mirror image. Matty would have been able to observe and understand himself by watching his brother. In turn, his brother would have been uniquely capable of understanding and supporting him. Matty's closest friend was never to be known to him.

From that time to the present, Matty felt nearly the same sting as his parents had felt. Yet while they had been consumed by their misery, Matty vowed to avenge it. He would live, live well, and live for both his brother and for himself. He would not face the world with bitterness or despair. Rather, he would express the affection that he and his parents had not had the opportunity to bestow on his brother, and the simple satisfaction in being alive that his parents were unable to show to him—for he was a living and constant reminder of their tragedy.

The Grave and the Gay

Of course, it helped no small amount that Matty possessed both the physical assets and the force of personality that made fulfilling his goals no difficult task.

At age sixteen, his parents died of typhus—or perhaps they simply lost the will to go on living. Mere weeks apart from each other, his father and then his mother took sick and expired quickly. Matty left his parents' home to embark on a life that only he could provide himself. He took on any task for which he could earn even a pittance. When a slightly deranged widow hired him to repair a hole in one of her dining room walls, she paid him in flesh in advance and offered him room and board until the work was done. One would have thought that hole had been enormous, for a fortnight passed before he emerged from the house. And in looking back, one would not doubt that the dining room had been less fully transformed than he.

Word spread about "Little Musgrave" and his willingness and ability to please, and he was kept busy by maiden and matron alike, all the while refining his art while fulfilling his vow. More than two seasons had passed before a few fathers and husbands either heard the whispers or wondered why a skinny, uneducated boy with such a scarcity of skills should be so much in demand throughout the town. Thus threatened, the confident lad decided he had accomplished all he could there and set off for new opportunities. Thus he came to Lancashire.

When he arrived in the coastal county, now a man of eighteen, he decided it would be prudent to establish friendships with men before he began his conquest of the village ladies. He reasoned that the local tavern would be the right spot to engage with peers. A single inquiry was sufficient to lead him to one owned by a man named Thomas Richardson. From the outside, it was nondescript, a simple structure of stone and wood with a few windows through which little more than the glow of oil lamps was visible.

No heads turned upon his entry, chiefly because a disturbance was in progress within. Two men had squared off against one, and while Matty was unaware of the three men's identities or the nature of their disagreement, he instinctively sympathized with the lone combatant. For now, however, he stood still and stared along with the tavern's other patrons.

No blows had yet been struck; rather, the three men were shouting at each other, although their crouched postures suggested wild animals preparing to attack. As he listened, Matty picked up clues as to the offense that caused this row.

"I tell you, it was not my doing," said the lone man, clearly the one in the more defensive position. "Who am I, that Lord Barnard would heed my advice?"

"Then what explains his sudden change of heart?" challenged the taller of the two aggressors. "Two years in succession Barnard hired Phillip and me to be his guides, and paid us handsomely. We've prepared already for the next hunt. Now, the day before we are to leave, we are told he has hired you in our stead. You've taken money right out of our pockets. Tell us why, Quentin Wainwright, or your blood will mark the place that you stand!"

The lone combatant, a rugged, fine-looking young man whom Matty now knew was named Quentin, had apparently had enough of the accusations and decided he had little to lose by going on the offensive.

"Hear this, you ignorant swine," spoke Quentin. "A blind man can see that I am a superior shot than your brother. In fact, a blind man *is* a better shot than the two of you sops combined. Lord Barnard knows it, and now so does everyone present. Come at me if you dare, but know that I've a fist for each of you."

And the two offended men did just that. Phillip came in first and was easily brought down by Quentin with a swift blow to the chin. The other, more talkative one had a slight advantage in that he could attack while Quentin's momentum was still directed at his brother. And indeed he landed a punch to the side of Quentin's head. The force threw Quentin off balance but he was able to right himself and come back at the taller man. The two grappled and wrestled, each seeking an advantage of space and position so that a forceful blow could be struck.

Meanwhile, Phillip began to sit up. Rubbing his chin and seeing his brother in close combat with Quentin, he clambered to his feet. Matty saw him reach into his coat and withdraw a pistol. At that moment, Quentin created enough separation that he was able to deliver two punches in rapid succession to the nose and cheek of Phillip's brother. The taller man reeled and struck his head against the edge of the bar, knocking him unconscious. Blood immediately began to flow from his nostrils and forehead as he collapsed to the floor.

With that, Phillip raised his armed hand and took aim at Quentin. Instinctively, Matty reached for a bottle from the table he stood adjacent to, and hurled it at Phillip, standing no more than two body lengths away. Matty's aim was true and the whiskey-filled weapon hit the back of Phillip's head with a sickening thud. The would-be assassin fell forward, his firearm dropping and hitting the floor just ahead of him. Quentin rushed over and grabbed the pistol, tucked it within the belt of his trousers, and then dragged the two men out of the tavern and onto the street.

By now, all heads had turned in Matty's direction. And if the response was not quite what David received upon slaying the Philistine with his rock and kerchief, he was made to feel welcome. The gentleman whose bottle Matty had thrown ordered a replacement and offered Matty the first shot from it. A few introductions were made, although some viewed him suspiciously—not without reason, of course; after all, his first public act in the town was one of violence. This was not the impression Matty had hoped to make in his new dwelling-place.

Some minutes had passed before Quentin returned. Having taken the brothers outside, he called then for a constable. When one arrived and took the luckless pair away, Quentin went directly to wash up and compose himself. Upon his return, he ordered two drinks from Richardson and walked towards Matty, a dram of whisky in each hand.

"Sir, I am in your debt," said Quentin, offering one of the glasses to his unknown ally. "My name is Quentin Wainwright and I would be honored if you would accept this drink, a momentary refreshment, along with my unending friendship and loyalty."

"Matthew Musgrave," said he, accepting the gift. "I am called Matty by my friends and Little Musgrave by my lovers. My enemies have called me many other names."

Quentin smiled. "In that case, *Matty*, your enemies are my enemies, as you have already taken my enemies as yours. Come, let us sit and drink and get to know each other better."

The handsome pair sat down and talked for many hours, until they had outlasted all the other company and Richardson forced them to leave. On the way out, Quentin asked Matty where he lived. Matty explained that he had only arrived in town that day and had yet to secure lodging for himself. Quentin insisted then that Matty come share his home. Matty accepted and stayed for several weeks until Quentin introduced him to Erickson the printer. In that time, the two men became fast friends. In Quentin, Matty finally felt he had the brother he had lost; moreover, he had actually been able to save this brother's life. In Matty, Quentin found a spirit that was as contagious as it was unquenchable.

It should, then, have been a pleasant sight for Matty when, emerging from the house after his meeting with Lord Barnard, he spied Quentin and Alexandra speaking with each other. In truth, however, Matty's mind still reeled with the information Lord Barnard had given him. He wished to be alone with his confused thoughts, to wrestle with the prospect of a prestigious new future, of a station above and beyond that of his family, his friends, and his lovers.

Instead, he would have to engage in conversation, though it was with two people he cared for very deeply. Knowing he could not say anything about Lord Barnard's offer, at least not until he had digested it in his mind and settled on a response or resolution, he forced himself to adopt the carefree tenor and attitude that people expected of him, and for which they loved him.

"Ah, Matty," called Quentin, "just the fellow I seek. I have a favor to ask of you."

"I granted you a favor the day I met you," Matty replied. "Has that not proven sufficient?"

"I believe it is time to come clean on that score," said Quentin. "The fact is that even at point blank range, Phillip could never have hit me. Therefore, you didn't really save my life at all."

"Perhaps not," countered Matty, "but certainly I have improved it."

Alexandra laughed while Quentin smiled and nodded, and then he continued. "Quite so, Little Musgrave, quite so. But in all earnestness, I must ask you: would you be willing to take my place among the pace-eggers on Easter Sunday?"

"Pace-eggers? Bah, they're but beggars."

"And are you now a nobleman, Matty Musgrove?" asked Alexandra. The question caused Matty to flinch, but he righted himself quickly.

"A beggar begs for what he cannot get for himself," explained Matty. "All I need I can acquire through my own means."

"Aye," said Alexandra, with a knowing nod, "and you are a persuasive one, indeed."

"Why are you not engaging in the festivities this year?" Matty asked Quentin.

"Your master has scheduled a hunting trip over the holiday and, once again, he wants my eyes and my guns."

"I would like to help you, you know I would. But I must refuse. This holiday I feel the need to stay free of obligations. Please understand."

"I do, my friend," said Quentin. "I, too, wish I could be a passive spectator. But Lord Barnard is also a most persuasive fellow. I must find someone to take my place. I was to portray the Old Tosspot this year. Therefore, I must bid you farewell for now. Miss Alexandra. Matty." Bowing to each in turn, Quentin adjusted his coat and walked away.

"What troubles you, Matty?" inquired Alexandra once Quentin was well beyond earshot.

"Why do you think I am troubled?" replied Matty.

"Because I know you well, far better than you know yourself. I can always tell when something is weighing on your mind."

This may well have been true. Shortly after Matty began working for Erickson, he made Alexandra's acquaintance. She was in town purchasing soap for the Barnards' washing. Matty was instantly smitten. A lovely face, to be sure, yet in her posture and gait she clearly also was confident and strong. The sinuous curls of her hair, her large round eyes, held him transfixed. And even through layers of inconvenient garments, he could tell she had the figure of Venus.

Alexandra noticed him as well. In fact, she had heard of him already. A friend of hers had enjoyed a tryst with him once in Erickson's stable. Yet she allowed Matty to introduce himself to her. She betrayed no knowledge of him and gave off an impression of polite indifference. This merely served as bellows to the flame that had begun to consume his insides. He asked if he might take her on a walk sometime. She replied that she was busy but that he was invited to run errands for her if he cared to be a gentleman.

And so, for about three weeks, Alexandra fetched no water, bought no soap, and carried no baskets of clean laundry up the steps to the Barnards' porch. Matty came by every day to see what she needed. And he did so willingly, for no woman had ever cast such a spell over him without first having shared her treasures. Finally, she agreed to go on the walk with Matty and, as she expected, little actual walking was ultimately achieved. Yet a bond was indeed forged between the two.

For Matty, Alexandra was a lover to be respected. Knowledgeable and responsive, she distinguished between desire and need, could not be forced into anything, and did nothing out of obligation. Her father, a fisherman, had once arranged a marriage for her; the prospective groom's father, however, had tried to get to know his future daughter-in-law a little too intimately before the ceremony. She resisted with fingers to his eyes and a knee to his genitals. He then called off the wedding and from that time forward Alexandra decided that she would control her own body and destiny.

So Matty and Alexandra became lovers, yet, to their mutual pleasure, both rejected the shackles of exclusivity. Freedom was the watchword of their faith, and the virtue they most valued. So it was that the topic of freedom surfaced in their present conversation.

"So tell me what is occupying your mind so," said Alexandra. "I can tell something is the matter, because your dour demeanor is in stark contrast with your usual vivaciousness," she continued with a smile.

"You do know me well, Alexandra," said Matty. "And I know you. Neither of us was bred for a life of comfort or order, were we? We seek what we desire and ignore the rest, do we not? Our lives are about courage, not consequences."

"I'll not argue your words, Matty," she said, "not yet. But I do not understand your point."

Matty paused, his lips pressed tightly together. He looked down, inhaled deeply and exhaled slowly. Then he looked back at her. "Alexandra, I cannot help being who I am. And I like being who I am. I am responsible only to myself and to my employer. And that's the beautiful thing about you and me. We are free beings, and we shouldn't allow anyone to change us, either for good or ill. Don't you agree?"

"Well, Matty, I still don't know from whence comes this curious questioning. But you are wrong. You aren't free, and though you sometimes act irresponsibly you do have responsibilities and you perform them admirably. We both rely on others for shelter and a wage.

"Furthermore," she continued, "you and I are different. As a woman, there are consequences to my behavior. My body changes from moon to moon. And I cannot go and chase my fancy whenever I please. They talk about you, Matty Musgrave, and your reputation grows. It is that of a rake, a rogue, a rascal. But any talk about me and mine is one of shame and disparagement."

Matty stared at his feet, uncomfortable at Alexandra's frank testimony, yet unable to dispute it.

"Neither of us are free," she went on, "but you are more free than I. And besides, I don't think you are capable of changing or being changed. I say that with affection, of course. So whatever is troubling you, I beg you to dismiss it. There is no one quite like you, Matty, so I pity the person who would try to make you into something else."

"Something you have never tried to do, my dear sweet Alexandra," said Matty earnestly and with gratitude. "You truly are a blessing to me. I should like to kiss you here, in the open, where all could see. But my horses beckon and Darnell is somewhere about, so I must leave you now. I thank you for your concern. I suppose I shall be fine. But for now, until we meet again."

And with that, he turned towards the stable. Alexandra, watching him go, felt she had said too much, yet there still was much she needed to say but couldn't. It was hard to love Matty, and harder still sometimes to have his love. Furthermore, this talk of changing and freedom upset her. Though not for his sake, but for her own.

CHAPTER 5

Matty's face was handsome, all knew it was true. Most, upon first seeing it, thought it the face of Adonis himself. When Lord Barnard first gazed upon it, though, he was struck not simply by its beauty but by its resemblance to a boy he knew in school.

Lord Barnard had three older sisters, and they and their mother delighted in finally having a baby boy to play with. His father, whose own father before him had been one of the founders of the village and was appointed to serve as its first governor, was a strong yet gentle man who would have been as happy to work as a simple carpenter as to ascend to nobility. As the elder Barnard's responsibilities took him away from home for extended periods, Lord Barnard grew close to his mother, a kind yet illiterate woman whose breads and cakes were known to and craved by people a day's ride from the village. Within the village proper, she was also highly regarded as a compassionate and capable midwife.

Though his father was well known and his family well to do, the adolescent Barnard had few friends. He was not overtly ostracized by his school peers, but the other boys did whisper about him. Some thought him strange, perhaps a tad fey. He didn't go in for rough and tumble play, fretted about getting his clothing soiled, was quiet and enjoyed spending time alone to read and to contemplate. He was, quite simply, different.

Just as the other boys wondered about him, he also wondered about them.

Why must they be so boisterous all the time? he ruminated. *Have they no self-control? Is this how commoners raise their offspring? They are like chickens trying to elude the slaughterer. Even if they were to have me as their friend, I should not know how—nor wish—to engage in their frivolities.*

Mutual distaste eventually evolved into mutual dislike. Except for one lad, Peter Williams, who arrived in the village when the boys were twelve years old.

Peter was handsome like Matty, with thick dark hair and exotic features. Born of an English father and a West Indian mother, he was darker than their peers and also the target of their teasing. Lord Barnard and Peter took comfort in each other, shared their dreams and fears, and swore love and loyalty to each other. But just a little over a year after he'd arrived in the village, Peter contracted a virus. He had a high fever for more than a week, could hold down neither food nor water, and died.

Lord Barnard was inconsolable, so much so that the other boys actually began to show some compassion for him, inviting him to join their activities. But he couldn't bear to forgive his tormentors. Through grade school and even while at university, he had no true friend who could compare with Peter, either in looks or fealty. By the time he reached adulthood, Lord Barnard's social circle, such as it was, comprised business associates exclusively: serious men who valued wisdom and success.

If he was aloof around boys growing up, he was terribly shy around girls and had never so much as held one's hand until he took his bride's during their wedding ceremony. With Lord Barnard nearing the age of thirty, and no prospects in sight, his father arranged the marriage—"You are too old to remain single," the elder Barnard told his reluctant son—and the day of the nuptials marked only the third time he had met her.

Lady Barnard was from northwest Sheffield and she came with a modest dowry: five sacks of freshly milled grain, seven pewter goblets, a dozen chickens, and two goats. Fair and intelligent, her fitness to be a wife and mother were assumed, yet she always had her doubts. She had willingly served her father, but her new husband was more serious, less handsome, and certainly less familiar to her. However, she was raised to obey and she was prepared to uphold those expectations dutifully.

On their wedding night, the bed they shared for the first time shook, though more from their collective unease than from gymnastic exertions of passion. Neither had experience in this sort of thing, and it went badly. No words were spoken between them that night. The next night they tried again and managed to couple, though only for a few minutes before it had reached its conclusion. A third time took place two nights later, and for the first time Lady Barnard had a glimmer that the act needn't be merely functional—still, for Lord Barnard it was unwelcome duty.

He had sensed for some time that he was not like the other men he knew who yearned for a woman's flesh and spoke of their desire and their exploits, and often with braggart tones. He did not understand its appeal; the whole thing seemed messy, intimidating, embarrassing. He found greater satisfaction engaging in work and study, two areas where he generally did not have to come into contact with the other gender.

Lord Barnard had been quite comfortable in his virginity—not proud, necessarily, but also not eager to explore the alternative. When he married Lady Barnard, however, suddenly there were expectations, both between the married couple and among their respective families. He was expected to sire children, heirs to the family name and estate. After the first few weeks of their marriage, however, Lord Barnard realized he couldn't fulfill the duty of a husband with any degree of frequency or competency. He hoped each time for a successful issue that would lead to a pregnancy.

One child, he said to himself, *and I'll no longer have to play this charade.*

But no child came. To be fair, few were the attempts to conceive, and after a while each attempt had to be preceded by a few shots of whisky. This did not increase the rate of success, but it made Lord Barnard more relaxed and less put off by the chore. Lady Barnard shared the desire for a child yet also had managed to experience some degree of pleasure from the act—by sheer dint of pressure and friction she was brought near some invisible plateau she yearned to leap onto, but sadly the experience was never sustained sufficiently for her to reach that elusive point. Thus, she was increasingly distressed by her husband's lack of interest.

It is not surprising, then, that she came to view herself as unattractive, or as lacking the skill, sensuality, or seductive powers that women with faithful, passionate husbands must surely possess.

Soon Lord Barnard took up hunting as an excuse to spend time away from home. He organized parties of friends and business acquaintances, and hired guides to lead him and his party to distant grounds rich with wild game. In warmer months, the men would bathe together in a lake, both upon rising and after the day's hunt. There was mischief as always happens when boys and men are together, but gradually Lord Barnard began having feelings he could not define. He had no example to allow him to say, *This that I know exists is true as well with me.* These feelings troubled him, and he was mortified that his body could betray his feelings when he watched the other men swim and romp.

One day when Darnell was ill and confined to his quarters, Lord Barnard went himself to the village general store to purchase gunpowder. There, he met the young clerk, Quentin Wainwright. Quentin talked of his skill and experience hunting in the farthest reaches of the county. Lord Barnard listened intently yet could not look the man in the eye. Instead, he focused on Quentin's mouth, which seemed ever to be shaped into a smile, and the lips, the way they formed vowels and consonants, became moist with spittle, and rested with the upper jutting ever so slightly forward of the lower.

Lord Barnard had hired two brothers as guides already, but with fumbling language he offered Quentin an amount equal to the total of what the two brothers were due to receive—on condition that the clerk would agree to serve as his guide on a trip leaving the very next day. The money was much too attractive to refuse, and his employer granted him the time away from the store purely because it was Lord Barnard who had conveyed the offer.

Though Lord Barnard hired Quentin time and again, their only physical contact was a handshake and maybe a platonic embrace following a particularly exciting or challenging kill. Lord Barnard even took to rising early so that he could bathe alone while the others were asleep. He was content to view beauty rather than partake of it, like an art patron who wields not a brush himself.

The Grave and the Gay

In spite of Matty's friendship with Quentin, Lord Barnard never made his acquaintance until that day at Erickson's auction. While Quentin was a very fine-looking man, Matty was truly a sight to behold. It was not just his face that put certain people into a spell, but his voice, his hair, his build, his personality. People were drawn to him the way flowers reach for the sun's life-enabling rays.

It was clear that few women could resist his allure; certainly, some men felt the same. In the first year of Matty's employment, Lord Barnard had become all but smitten with him. He would look out of his window daily to watch him work in the stable and cross the yard on the way to town. Still, given the gulf in their ages, Lord Barnard did not view Matty as a potential lover, but rather as the heir he had yearned for, the son he sought to remove the constant pressure on Lord Barnard to have a child and thus continue having unsatisfying sexual relations with his wife.

None of this Lady Barnard suspected. To her, Lord Barnard's inability to become aroused was simply part of a larger pattern of his being distant and unpleasant. When they first were wed, she was expected to serve. As his wealth and position improved, and servants were hired, she no longer had a role. And without a role—be it homemaker, mother, or temptress—she was losing any sense of her own identity and worth. Wine dulled the sadness associated with this loss, but did nothing to restore what was slipping steadily away from her.

And so, as Lord Barnard entered her room and sent Darnell out, Lady Barnard—still embracing the notion that the house servant finds her attractive—steeled herself, for she knew this small, fragile bubble of good feeling would soon be pricked.

Facing his wife, Lord Barnard remained silent for several moments after Darnell left the room. He waited, in fact, until the servant left the house. When he heard the door downstairs close, Lord Barnard turned to look out the window, the same one through which Lady Barnard had earlier gazed. Satisfied that Darnell was beyond hearing range, he swung around to engage Lady Barnard. But she was not looking in his direction. She, too, had turned away and was facing her bed on the opposite wall.

Thus it was for this married couple, for little had they shared at all in these ten years gone. Days could pass and the only time they would interact would be at breakfast and supper. Of course, Lord Barnard had business and other interests that took him away to various locales, some requiring a journey of a fortnight or more. Yet whether he was far away or in the next room, Lady Barnard was more often than not sure to be alone, an unbound hostage inside an inhospitable house.

"I'll not have you commingling with the villagers," he would say when she expressed a desire to go into town. "You are far too fair. You would come down with the ague before nightfall."

Many such excuses were tendered, yet in reality Lord Barnard was concerned about what she might reveal to others about their lives, most specifically about him. And so came this morning's rant.

"I am leaving on a hunting trip this Thursday," Lord Barnard said, "and will be gone four days."

"I know," Lady Barnard replied. "You've told me."

"You will have to miss Easter services this year," he continued, "but I will ask Reverend Collins if he might drop by and offer you the Sacrament here."

"I have no intention of missing Easter services. Mr. McDougall is making a bonnet for me."

"That is of no matter," he said, his voice a little louder, a little higher pitched. "I am leaving and you are staying, and that is all."

"Why must you leave before Easter and why stay past it? You are my husband. You belong by my side. We should be going to church together."

"You belong where I say you will belong," Lord Barnard shouted. "When I want you beside me, you shall be by my side. When I want you away, you shall be away. And when I want you to stay at home, you—shall—stay—at—home!"

Lord Barnard began to march swiftly out the door, then stopped and looked back at his now-weeping wife.

"I will not have you cavorting about the town, gossiping like a mad crone," he yelled still louder. "Only when I desire your conversation will you speak. And when I do not, you will be silent. And in all cases, you will be here in this house, and not among the coarse commoners in the village. That is my last word on the subject!"

Then Lord Barnard walked out and slammed the door closed. Lady Barnard sat upon her bed, her head in her hands, her tears wetting her wrists. As sad as she was, she was assured now of one thing: It was not her fault.

CHAPTER 6

It was two days prior to Easter and the town was astir with excitement and activity. At church, the Reverend Sanford Collins was reviewing his sermon notes. Not yet thirty years old, he wore tightly cropped whiskers on his chin, keeping the space between his lips and nose hairless.

As a youth, against the advice of his parents and the village physician, he had embraced his younger brother, then near-mad with a raging fever. Unexpectedly, the boy's fever broke that night and the superstitious villagers were convinced that Almighty God had worked through young Sanford's hands directly. Thus, the precocious lad, a believer in any case, was coaxed into serving as the area's spiritual leader, though he had no pastoral training and had never undertaken Bible study of any depth. Nevertheless, he was liked and admired by his flock.

His theme, predictably, would be rebirth and resurrection. He would focus this year on the idea that we should prepare for Eternal Afterlife by letting go of the material items and negative traits that mark our human failures.

In becoming perfected, he had written, *we will become less than we are currently, not more. Just as Jesus lost his physical form and returned incorporeal, all those who are saved have taken from them all those things—sinful acts, bad habits, unholy urges—that had weighed down their mortal lives on earth.*

The Grave and the Gay

The young cleric's key point, then, was that people should give up those things now—things such as lust, possessions, hatred, and greed—that eventually will be taken from them anyway.

Do not desire things that degrade human personality, his text implored, *such as flesh and power. Live more simply and spiritually. Then when your time is due, your transformation will be that much more swift and sure.*

Meanwhile, in the field adjacent to the church, Mr. McDougall was selecting the flowers he would cut for Lady Barnard's Easter bonnet. In addition to the peonies and paperwhites, the bonnet would be adorned with a lace trim that his wife was making by hand. The Lady's bonnet was the one commission he anticipated most each year. She came out in public so rarely that to be seen in a creation of his would surely keep the women of the town clamoring for his flowers and crafts until the first frost settled on the ground.

Meanwhile, Quentin had succeeded in finding someone to replace him among the pace-eggers, and the troupe were attending to their costumes, practicing their songs and lines, and planning their route. From a room in the back of the tavern where they had been gathering the last several nights, passers-by on the street could hear the absurd verses sung in rowdy fashion, starting always with the first:

Here's one, two, three jolly lads all in one mind
We have come a pace-egging and we hope you'll prove kind
We hope you'll prove kind with your eggs and strong beer
For we'll come no more nigh you until the next year

As for himself, Quentin was checking surveys of the surrounding areas and stocking up on gunpowder for the next day's departure. Lord Barnard had told him that he didn't wish to go too deep into the woods, and that Darnell should be informed of the precise location of their camp.

Unbeknownst to Quentin, Lord Barnard was planning to enforce his order to his wife that she not attend church on Easter Sunday. He would ask Darnell, as yet also unaware of the plan, to find and inform him if his wife left the house that day. Of course, Lord Barnard was himself unaware that Darnell had already accepted his wife's invitation to serve as her escort to church.

For his part, Matty had spent the morning with the horses, preparing them for the hunting trip. Freshly cleaned and polished were the saddles, bridles, and bits. He had bathed and brushed the animals, and filled sacks with oats and straw. When the sun had reached its highest point in the sky and the warmth had filled the stable, Matty emerged to obtain a drink of water for himself. He walked over to the well near the center of the property and began to work the pump. He had perspired heavily in the stable, and his shirt clung to his shoulders and back, constricting his movements. He stopped and removed his shirt, then went back to the pump, more eager than ever to draw a ladle of earth-cooled water.

It was at this moment that Lady Barnard drew closer again to her window. This time, her gaze caught Matty's form squarely. She gasped audibly, half in surprise at seeing a seminude man in the yard, and half in admiration for the sheer aesthetic quality of the specimen he was. She didn't recognize his face—a face such as his she would not have forgotten had she seen it before.

Though Matty had worked and lived on her property for more than a year, Lady Barnard's ignorance of him should not be a complete surprise. She despised the smell of horses, feared them since seeing her youngest sister, then ten, thrown from one, breaking her arm. As such, Lady Barnard never spent time around the stable (in this, she and Darnell were alike, though Darnell's dislike of Matty also contributed to his avoidance of that structure).

Being confined to the house—and tending to further restrict herself to her room—Lady Barnard looked out on the yard often, though not so much to observe or notice people; rather, she typically focused on the expanse of the property and the woods and ocean beyond, or of the horizon itself, the boundless vistas she envied simply because they could not be contained. They reminded her of the places she had read about in books and dreamed of visiting in real life, a life that for all her wealth and station never had materialized.

Yet here was cause for shortening and sharpening her focus. She continued to watch Matty as he drew water and drank it, then drew more to splash on his face and dump on his head. Streams of water slid down his face and provided a cool caress to his muscular, hairless chest and stomach. Though he was heated by his exertion, and the day was at its warmest, it still was early spring and not summer; it was not, therefore, a hot day. And this was why the cold water on his bare torso brought a chill to Matty, causing his flesh to rise in countless tiny protuberances. This, too, was noticed and admired by Lady Barnard, aided with a spyglass she previously had used only to see stars more clearly.

Matty was unaware he was being watched; or perhaps he was so accustomed to being noticed that he didn't check to see whose eyes may be on him. Quenched and cooled, he replaced his shirt and ran his fingers through his dripping hair, pushing the strands behind his ears and away from his face. This last look afforded to the Lady triggered a sensation within her that she had not experienced before without first having been touched intimately. Aware as she was that there might be more to lovemaking than she had yet to experience first-hand, Lady Barnard sensed now that this man—dirty, no doubt malodorous, at the very least from a lowly station—might hold the key to her physical fulfillment and happiness.

This thought so held her imagination that she turned away from the window and stared at her wall, a silent witness that could only assent to her apparent resolve to know this man. To do so would require two things to happen. First, Lord Barnard must leave. Then, she must do likewise. It was always daring to disobey her husband; now, she felt there were greater consequences in continuing to dismiss her own needs and desires.

No longer looking out the window, Lady Barnard did not see Matty walk away from the well and leave the property. His destination was Quentin's home, to bid him good luck and farewell before his hunting trip with Lord Barnard. The walk was not long, though it was pleasant for a man popular as he. As he passed, women turned their heads. Men he had regaled at the tavern called out to him. He had been much more successful integrating himself into the community here in Lancashire than he had been before in other places. Though just as active, he had learned to be more discreet. He valued his friendships with men and endeavored to maintain them, even those with whose wives he had lain.

Upon arriving at Quentin's, Matty saw his good friend sitting beneath the shade of a willow tree. He was polishing a brass horn, such as the type used by soldiers and hunters to sound the call to arms when chasing their respective prey.

"Ho there," said Matty.

"Welcome, my friend," said Quentin, waving Matty over to join him on the ground. "May I offer you some shade from the midday sun?"

"Exactly what I was craving," Matty replied. He sat down next to Quentin. "That's a fine horn."

"A gift from your master it is," said Quentin, offering it to Matty for his inspection. "I'm planning on bringing it with me tomorrow. So what brings you here?"

"I wanted to wish you well on your journey," said Matty, as he handled the horn and thought of the gifts he had also received from his employer, "and to say I shall miss you over the holiday."

"And I you, Matty," Quentin responded. "I would rather join you in hunting fair ladies in their finest dress after church than in bagging foxes and pheasants with Barnard and his cronies."

"Never to worry, Quentin, for I shall be sure to capture and feast upon such a grand trophy that she would have satisfied the both of us."

"I'm sure you shall, Matty, but it is not in your manner to leave behind morsels for less-skillful hunters," Quentin said with a laugh.

"Then I shall think of you when I take my spoils," said Matty. "Tell me, who is in Lord Barnard's party?"

"Aside from he and I, there is a chap by the name of Finster, I believe. Barnard said he was his solicitor. He is also taking Dennis Upham the tailor and his banker friend Thomas something. That is all, a small party for the first trip of the year."

At the word "solicitor" Matty stopped listening. *So, it is to be set legal this very trip*, he thought to himself. *Away from me, giving me no chance to refuse.*

"Has Lord Barnard said anything about why he invited his solicitor?" asked Matty.

"Not to me. Why?"

"Nothing really," replied Matty.

"Are you all right?" asked Quentin. "You've suddenly turned white as lamb's fleece."

"No, yes, I'm fine, I was just curious is all."

"Well, your master, he's a strange one. I don't bother asking him anything about what he does and why he does it."

"Strange?" Matty asked. "How so?"

"Well, I don't know exactly. It's just that…well, he…he's rather standoff-ish, you know?"

"No, actually. I find him rather brusque myself, though he shows me much kindness. How exactly do you mean?"

"I can't find the words," Quentin replied, "but he tends to sort of… stare at people. Me, sometimes. You, of course, I've noticed that, everyone has. But other fellows as well. Sure, he engages in conversation, he takes part in the hunt. But he never relaxes. That's what it is. He's very intense, doesn't joke, laugh, smoke, anything. Just stands apart and stares a lot of the time. Makes me rather uncomfortable."

"Why do you think he does it?" asked Matty.

"Well, I don't know. I don't know what he means by it. What is he like at his home? Does he just stare at his wife?"

"Perhaps. Alexandra thinks they don't do much together, you know, personal-like," said Matty.

"You should ask your friend Darnell there. I'm sure he knows what's what."

"Oh yes, my 'friend' Darnell, we're close as cousins we are," laughed Matty. "He says as little as possible to me, addresses me only when he has to."

"Well, get him drunk and see if that brings his speech out," said Quentin. "I wouldn't mind knowing what goes on in there. And what doesn't."

Matty rose to his feet and handed Quentin back his gift. "My advice to you," he said, "is to put it out of your mind and rest well tonight. For I expect you to slay something particularly large and nasty on your trip, and I will look forward to hearing you tell of your kill. Godspeed, good friend." With that, Matty and Quentin embraced and went back to minding their respective tasks.

Returning to the Barnard estate, Matty mulled over Quentin's suggestion. While he was half-joshing, it was a sound idea. Matty needed to know some things about their lives if he was going to become a part of it. And if the testimony was decidedly unfavorable, then Matty would have to do something to ensure that this adoption of sorts would not play out. He could run away, but there was always the risk of recapture. As well, even if successful he likely would lose not only his livelihood but also his friends, Quentin and dear Alexandra.

Of course, he had no fear of starting over again in a new county, he'd done it before, but he had a feeling of belonging here in Lancashire that was not true of his previous surroundings.

Considering two poles of possibilities, one benign and the other outrageous, talking Lord Barnard out of the arrangement was unlikely to be successful while murdering him would not render Matty free. His only reasonable alternative was to make himself appear unworthy to be a nobleman's heir. How to accomplish this was a challenge, since he didn't consider himself worthy already.

What should I do? he thought. *Curse and be drunk all the day? Do some petty theft? Take something of value to him?*

No, he reasoned, *I must not let my mind race ahead of me. First, I must find a way to encourage Darnell to accompany me to the tavern one night. Then I can ply him with several pints and let the gossip pour out like draught ale from a keg. I shall attend to this tonight, after supper.*

And yet the very thought of the detestable page brought forth the outrageous realization that since Matty would become the *de facto* son of Lord Barnard, Darnell would be obligated to serve the former stable hand as well! Darnell taking orders from Matty—surely neither man would abide by such a thing for long.

Arriving on the grounds of the Barnard residence, Matty was so consumed by his thoughts and plans that he didn't notice Alexandra wave to him. She saw him preoccupied and worried for him. All men are entitled to their moods, but Matty—in so many ways—was not just another man. She had long expected that his boundless enthusiasm for a life that held little future promise (he was limited in trade skills, after all, and his looks wouldn't last him another ten years) was a masquerade. A magnificent one to be sure, yet no disguise, no matter how pleasing, could do aught but suffocate its wearer in time.

Many were the moments that Alexandra sought to peel back his mask and gaze upon his true visage. Yet she knew that would violate the understanding the two had with each other. Each was entitled to privacy, freedom, space. Alexandra respected and abided by this unspoken agreement chiefly because she craved it for herself; yet to what useful end it served was a question more troubling to her when it concerned Matty's inherent mysteries.

She remembered his arrival in town well. Never had a sober man been so forward with her. She'd have thought him rude but for his large, kind eyes that focused so intently on hers and the genuine pleasantness with which he made his introduction. Her feet were not so easily swept off the ground, however, and she saw that she could use his keen interest in her to her advantage. She made him her servant in essence, thinking that no man so intent on establishing relations with a woman would bear to wait and wade through countless tasks simply to prove his worth.

In fact, few men would, and while Matty could have been one of them, he was not suffering cold nights alone while he waited for Alexandra to accept his entreaties. Alexandra found this out, though not until after they had first consummated their mutual desire for each other. Rather than feeling hurt or betrayed, it attracted him to her all the more. Not because she favored rogues as a rule, but because he was so certain of what he wanted and knew how to get it. And the more he got, the more he seemed to want, yet without the desperation and overt deception that the insatiably needy typically demonstrate. His very confidence and independence was attractive to her, though in weaker moments she allowed herself to consider a life they could lead together.

The sun now was setting and thick ashen clouds confederated in the sky. With the wind rising and the darkness thus accelerated, it was clear that the night would be filled with the sound and scent of rainfall. As Alexandra looked to the rugs and linens on the clothesline, clean and dry but threatened by the advancing weather, Darnell emerged from the house.

"May I help you bring in the wash?" he asked, seeing both the foreboding sky and the vulnerable work of Alexandra's hands.

"Yes, thank you," she replied.

"Lord Barnard will leave tomorrow for his hunting trip," said Darnell as he pulled down an ivory-hued oval rug.

"That is what I hear," said Alexandra. "The poor Lady will be left alone on Easter."

"Without her husband, yes, but not alone," Darnell replied in hushed tones. "She has asked me to escort her to church services on Sunday morning."

"Well, well, Darnell. Your station is rising. And her husband approved of this arrangement?"

"I believe he is unaware," replied Darnell, "and that is how it should remain."

Alexandra smiled coyly as she bent down to lift her wash basket. As she rose and straightened her back, she got suddenly dizzy, dropping the basket and nearly collapsing rearwards. Darnell dropped the rug he was holding, making it dirtier in seconds than it had been before Alexandra expended so much energy beating and washing it. He lunged to catch her as she reeled, and he held her in his protective embrace, his pulse racing both from the unexpected crisis and the fact that he finally had Alexandra in his arms.

"Alexandra, what is the matter? Are you ill?" he managed to speak through his gasping throat.

Tired, weakened, slightly nauseous, yet otherwise feeling normal after a long day of work, Alexandra was more embarrassed than alarmed. She accepted his arms around her for a moment, then patted his shoulder and gently pushed against it, signaling that she was ready and wanting to stand independently.

"Yes," she said with a slight wooziness to her voice. "I mean, no, I'm fine. I'm so sorry, Darnell. Thank you for catching me. I just had a dizzy spell."

"Are you sure you're well?"

"Yes, I'm fine, it's just—." She paused; seeing the rug on the ground, she exploited the chance to change the subject. "I see my laundry is not finished after all."

"I'm sorry I dropped the rug, Alexandra. I was just so startled when I saw you faint." He guided her to the steps of the house. "Come sit here. You must rest. Shall I send for the doctor?"

"No, Darnell. Really I'm fine. It's just dizziness. We must get the rest of the washing into the house. I thought I felt a drop."

"You stay here. I'll bring in the laundry."

"That's very kind of you, Darnell," said Alexandra, grateful for the momentary rest. "I'm sorry to burden you."

Darnell sat down next to her. Emboldened by their accidental embrace, he took her hands in his and looked into her eyes. "Alexandra, it is no burden to want to take care of you. And if it is, then I shall gladly bear it for a lifetime. You are a strong woman, but I can be strong for you as well. If only you will allow me."

Alexandra looked down at his hands grasping hers. His hands, his man's hands, were softer and cleaner than her own.

He doesn't work with his hands, she thought. *He works with his nodding head and with his scurrying feet, attending to the whims and wishes of the Barnards. It is not manual labor, but I suppose it is not easy work, either*, she acknowledged.

There were advantages to being a house servant, of course, but the job required a great deal of skill, tact, and resourcefulness. She knew she would not unhesitatingly trade places with him, nor could she think of others in the Barnards' employ who would want to hear what he hears, know what he knows, and be as trusting and discreet as his position requires.

Trusting. Discreet. Yes, Darnell was both, and these qualities, Alexandra felt, she would need at this time. She looked up at him and as rain began to fall intermittently, she began slowly to speak.

"Darnell. I know what you say is true, and I do appreciate it. You have a good heart and you are a good friend. I have burdened you with duty and now I would like to burden you with knowledge."

"I don't understand," said Darnell.

Alexandra paused, then spoke softly.

"Darnell, I have a secret and it is a shameful one. No, that's not quite true. Yet it—. What I mean is, I don't feel ashamed but others would think it a scandal and would judge me so. I haven't wanted to tell anyone, and of course I'm not sure it is a fact, but if what I feel to be true is true, then my condition will become obvious before long and I will need more help."

Darnell remained quiet. Their eyes remained locked. His hands tightened their grip on hers, prodding her to continue.

"I think I am with child, Darnell."

"Is Matty the father?"

"It is likely," she replied.

"Does he know?" Darnell asked.

"No," said Alexandra. "And as you said before, that is how it should remain. At least until I know for sure that I am pregnant."

"Do you believe he does not want the child?" asked Darnell.

"I don't know," she said. "I don't know how or whether to broach the subject with him. He is a free spirit, as you know, and though he may love me and may even love the child, I don't think that husband and father are roles he is eager to play."

"Then let me play them, Alexandra," said Darnell. "All that I have pledged you before I pledge again, plus this: I will have your child as my own. I will love and raise and teach that child, and that child will know me as its father, and you as its beloved mother, and we all shall be one family.

"You have denied me repeatedly, Alexandra," he continued. "And never have I lost my desire for you. No one need know that you are unmarried and with child. We can marry soon and preserve your honor. Your child need not be a bastard. You must consent to be my wife."

"Darnell," said Alexandra, "I don't want to marry out of necessity, if I even ever want to marry at all. At present, I am weak and tired, and you are kind and honest. It would be too easy to accept your offer right now. Please give me some more time."

Darnell released her hands and nodded silently. She grabbed his hands back, then kissed him on the cheek.

"Please know that I am grateful for your affection," she said. "And please know my affection for you increases."

Darnell blushed and smiled. He felt he finally had broken through. Certainly there was added urgency because of her condition. Yet she had admitted her affection for him. With Lady Barnard on his arm on Sunday, and the prospect of Alexandra as his wife, Darnell's spirits were high and his confidence strong. He felt like…well, like Matty must feel. Assured. In control. As the rain began to fall faster, he and Alexandra rose—slowly, in spite of the advancing precipitation—and climbed the front porch steps together as they brought the laundry into the house.

CHAPTER 7

After Darnell and Alexandra had rescued the laundry from the rain, an awkward silence arose between them. What else could be said after what had transpired outdoors? The silence, uncomfortable though it was, nevertheless was unfortunately short-lived, broken by Lord Barnard's bellicose call.

"Darnell! Are you there?" he shouted from the top of the stairs. Darnell smiled a wordless goodbye to Alexandra, then turned swiftly towards his master's bellowing voice.

"I am, Lord Barnard. Would you care to see me?"

"Yes, of course, that is why I have called," he answered impatiently. "Please come up."

Left alone, Alexandra returned to her regretful reverie, now made more complex by Darnell's knowledge of her condition and his continued pursuit of her. She knew that as much as Matty desired her, he would never force her into something she did not want. This was comforting to her, and she committed to him the same easygoing manner in their public and private relations. And yet, in her current situation, it took more restraint on her part *not* to make Matty feel he must accept responsibility for the child she believed she was bearing—and to chain his own future to hers simply because this one time out of many their passion had apparently been productive.

The Grave and the Gay

Perhaps, she wondered, *it is wrong for me to be more concerned for his feelings than for my own health. After all, he is a man, he leaves his mark and withdraws and is unchanged. Yet I am a woman, and woman is vulnerable to all sorts of horrors and inconveniences that men know nothing about. That is how nature intended it to be, I suppose. And so I must be strong and bear this. And I* can *bear it. But to see cracks appear in Matty's confident and contented face is more than my heart can stand to witness. I must know more, ashamed as I am to admit it. For I know that Matty would not want me to care so deeply for him. And would he—could he—ever care so deeply about me?*

This was not a question she had about Darnell. If he was to be believed—and when, after all, couldn't Darnell be believed?—he was ready to commit his life to her, and to the baby as well. Darnell had soft hands. She wanted her baby's hands to be soft as well. *It is well to work but hard manual labor is a station that is difficult to rise from.* She wanted more for her child. Could Darnell provide that? *When all is said and done, is a house servant's life so elevated from that of a stable hand? It is, I suppose.*

For his part, Darnell already had taken the well-worn path up the stairs and into Lord Barnard's study. He smirked at the thought that he had been jealous of Matty and in competition with him for the attentions of both Lord Barnard and Alexandra. Matty's looks might open eyes and doors, but Darnell knew that he and he alone possessed the empathy, manners, and discretion that ultimately would prove him to be the more valuable to his master and the more attractive to his beloved Alexandra.

A test, he thought, *if only there were a test, a challenge I could accept that would prove to both Alexandra and Lord Barnard that I was the better man.*

Yes, if only. Yet even Darnell knew that though his thoughts were emboldened this day, he was as likely as not to shirk from such a trial should it ever be presented; at least, in the past this was so. Maybe he could indeed embrace a new chance to demonstrate traits so deeply submerged in his personality that those who knew him best doubted they existed at all. *Maybe I could.*

Such a challenge would have to wait, however, since Darnell's thoughts were struck dumb by the sight of Lord Barnard standing sourly behind his desk, on which lay a leather valise and an assortment of papers in and alongside it. He had clearly been rushing around to get ready for his trip, as the chaotic condition of the room was a far cry from the fastidiousness that was more typical of his peculiar nature.

"Yes, my Lord," Darrell said when he entered.

"Close the door," Lord Barnard ordered. "Darnell, I have an important assignment for you while I am gone."

"Of course, sir. Just tell me what you would have me do for you, and it shall be done."

"As you know, I am leaving tomorrow morning on a hunting trip," Lord Barnard started, all but clipping the end of Darnell's response. "I suspect that Lady Barnard will want to go to church on Easter Sunday. However, I have forbidden her to do so."

"Yes, I see," said Darnell softly.

"In spite of my orders, I have a sense that she will attempt to go anyway. If she does, if she leaves the house at all that day, I want you to come find our party and tell me. Our camp will not be far away; I specifically told Quentin that I wanted to stay nearer to town in the event I needed to hurry back. While it is my hope that she will obey my wishes, should she choose not to I want to be able to return quickly and catch her in the act of defiance. I will then deal with her as I must. Do you understand?"

"Y-Yes, my Lord," Darnell replied. "But how will I find you?"

"Here is a map that Quentin drew up. I know you are not a strong rider but at a steady canter you should be able to reach us in an hour's time. The moment she walks out the door you are to seek us. If you don't tarry, we might succeed in returning home by the time church services have concluded."

"So, Lady Barnard is not to leave the house even to take fresh air, not even for a short spell?" Darnell asked.

"No!" shouted Lord Barnard. "I thought I made myself clear. She is not to leave the house at all. Not for a minute, not for a second. Not to attend church, nor to sit on the front steps. Now I ask again: do you understand?"

Hot blood rose to Darnell's face, though he was well-accustomed to modulating his voice in defiance of his inner feelings. Thus, though he felt a growing rage within, Darnell presented a calm exterior, saying simply, "I do." He took the map from Lord Barnard and walked from his office.

The bastard does not deserve the good woman who is his wife, he thought. And then he reflected on his use of the word "bastard." It was a slip of his mind's tongue, and he regretted it. He felt like a water bearer with a yoke on his shoulders: Alexandra and her unborn baby in one bucket, and the unfulfilled Lady Barnard in the other.

The sky outside darkened as the rain accelerated to a downpour and evening descended in kind. Lady Barnard, who earlier had heard the commotion yet not the content of her husband's shouting at Darnell, prepared pottage for dinner. This simple stew of cod, grains, onions, and turnips was well beneath them gastronomically. Minus the fish, it was what the poor people ate. (Had wild boar not recently become extinct in England, the forthcoming hunting trip might have yielded some of that tasty meat for a truly fine pottage.) Yet Lord Barnard preferred lighter meals and Lady Barnard had been raised on pottage and still enjoyed it. It was also easy to make and since the cook had been dismissed, ease trumped elegance.

The couple ate silently, the only sounds coming from Lord Barnard's impatient and overactive jaw. They drank wine, she three goblets to his one. After dinner, Lady Barnard summoned Darnell to clear the plates and invited him to help himself to a bowl of the pottage. Then the Barnards repaired to their separate rooms, leaving Darnell to wash the plates and put them away, after which he returned to his quarters.

Although there was excitement in the air throughout the village because of the approaching Easter holiday, the atmosphere within the house was stifling, as if it held too many people as opposed to just two morose people. All lights had been snuffed by nine o'clock, except for a lamp in Lord Barnard's study, and his was the only body to remain in restless motion deep into the night.

In spite of retiring late, Lord Barnard woke early the next morning. He got his own breakfast of hard cheese, crusty bread, and strong coffee. He carried his valise and a satchel of clothing, no more than a day's worth. So sure was he that Lady Barnard would flout his authority, he did not plan to stay away a second evening. Furthermore, there was business to attend to with his solicitor this night, so there would be little time to crouch through brush and shoot at animals. His clothes, therefore, would not be too soiled in the event he was able to wear them again on this trip.

Matty had been alerted the previous evening to have the horses ready by daybreak. He was securing the bridles when Lord Barnard appeared at the stable door.

"Good morning, my son," said Lord Barnard.

"Good morning," a sleepy Matty replied.

"I expect to return from my trip with good news for you. And a new life for us both."

"Yes, my Lord," Matty said darkly.

"As much as I look forward to making you my heir, Matty, I will miss your expert hand with the horses. They look as ready for a parade as for an outing. You've done a wonderful job, as always."

"Thank you, my Lord," said Matty.

"You sound tired, my son," said Lord Barnard. "You have been working hard lately. I suggest you enjoy my time away by resting and celebrating the season. But do not indulge too heartily, for when I return you will spend many hours by my side, as there is much to teach you about being a gentleman."

And without a response from Matty, Lord Barnard took the reins of his brown mare, Kayleigh, and led her out of the stable. Shortly thereafter, Quentin arrived, along with Dennis Upham the tailor (a small man with a high forehead and bushy moustache) and Thomas Gallagher the banker (fat, as befits a man who counts other people's money). Quentin was too busy with his client and his party to speak with Matty, though he offered a wave to his friend, who looked on impassively from the stable door. Finally, Basil Finster, Lord Barnard's solicitor, arrived. Tall and serious-looking, with a permanently furrowed brow, he also carried a valise,

The Grave and the Gay

and he and Lord Barnard conferred privately for a few minutes before joining the rest of the party and setting out on their trip.

"Are you able yet to talk about what's troubling you?" came a concerned voice from behind Matty.

Whirling around, Matty saw the familiar golden hair and inquisitive face of Alexandra. He smiled briefly, until he noticed the pale complexion of her sweet face.

"My troubles are my own matter," he said. "But what of you? Your face is white as bone. Are you not feeling well?"

"Bit of a sour stomach is all," she replied. "It happens. But you look to be of sour heart, which is most unusual for you. Come, Matty, what value is our friendship if you can only speak to me when you are gay? It has never bothered me that you share your bed with others, but I do not like it when you refuse to share your feelings with me. Have I not earned your trust?"

"Dear Alexandra," said Matty, taking her curls into his right hand, "I trust you as much as if you were my own blood. You are far too fine a friend—a lover—a woman—for the likes of me. I fear that the more you knew of me, and of what drives my desires, the less you would want ever to be with me."

"I care not about your past, Matty, and make no demands on your future," said Alexandra. "But I do want to know of today."

"All right," said Matty with trust in his heart yet resignation in his voice. "I shall tell you. But you must not repeat these words I tell you now."

"You have my vow," said Alexandra, her eyes wide and fixed in gaze at his.

Matty looked around to ensure they were standing a safe distance from Lord Barnard. He led Alexandra by the arm a few steps further along the side of the stable. In hushed tones, he spoke.

"Lord Barnard has plans to make me his legal heir," he said. "He will be making out the documents on this trip. When he returns, I shall essentially be his son."

Alexandra started to laugh, but Matty's expression told her that it was no joke—and his hand over her mouth reminded her that the subject of his secret was still on the property. Though Matty was known to tell tales, he could never make his audience believe something that wasn't true. In fact, as much as people enjoyed his stories, he loved them more himself. When he told a joke, his laugh was always the first and the heartiest. When spinning a yarn, his eyes and lips betrayed all the exaggeration of the narrative. Yet now, his stern expression made it clear to Alexandra that he was both serious and distraught.

"But what do you mean? How could this be?" she asked.

"The Lord is impatient at not having a child. You were right, I guess. It seems they don't bed together, and I'm not sure but I think it's because Lord Barnard is not right with women. So he wants to adopt me as his son and legal heir."

"Not right with women? What does that mean?"

"I don't know," Matty answered, "but I've heard from Quentin that he acts strangely on these hunting trips. Looks at the men quite a lot."

"Are you serious?" asked an incredulous Alexandra.

"Look, I told you I'm not sure of anything save for this: I do not wish to be his son," said Matty emphatically.

"Well, what will you do then?"

"I don't know," Matty replied, "and my dissatisfaction with my choices is what you have seen on my face lately."

"There certainly are advantages to being Lord Barnard's heir," said Alexandra, allowing herself to imagine a life with Matty as a man—and husband and father—of wealth and prestige. She realized this was unfair to Matty and unrealistic for herself, and so she quickly swept her statement out of the air where it had hovered between them with a new idea that was more sympathetic to Matty's plight. "Perhaps there is a way you can politely decline the offer?" she asked.

"If I do that, I'll tempt his ire and risk my job," said Matty. "And besides, who am I to disobey my master's wishes? He needs not my permission to make me his heir. I have no other family to claim me. He and

The Grave and the Gay

his solicitor make it so, and it is so. The only option I've considered is to do some awful deed that would make it impossible for him to carry through his scheme. Something that would bring dishonor to him if we were to be legally bound together."

"Yet if that ploy was successful, you would have to leave here forever," said Alexandra. "Are you prepared to do so?"

"It would sadden me immeasurably, not least for the distance between us," replied Matty. "But then roving is not unknown to me, and I would rather live elsewhere as who I am than to remain here and be something that is disgusting to me."

"Then it seems you are decided after all, Matty," said Alexandra. "What will be the deed and when will it be done?"

"I have no answer for either question, but it must happen soon, before Lord Barnard returns," said Matty.

"Would you dare to do evil on Easter?" she asked.

Alexandra wanted to say more but she sensed a catch in her throat, and she was afraid of betraying her true feelings about the news. Matty perhaps sensed as much, yet with genuine feeling he again held her curls and planted a kiss on her clenched lips.

"My dear Alexandra, with hair as fine as a bee's wings and the face of God's most favored angel, I would not go so far as the New World to escape Lord Barnard's wrath. He has not half my wiles, nor a tenth of my desire. I would find you and reunite with you under the shroud of darkness, no matter how many days I might need to travel to reach you. You will never be rid of me forever. And that is my promise."

With that, Matty kissed her again and Alexandra's heart filled. She did not doubt Matty's love for her in this moment. But could she trust it, come what may?

CHAPTER 8

Though neither could hear the exchange between Matty and Alexandra, both Lady Barnard and Darnell observed it, each staring out from a different window on the same wall and floor: Lady Barnard from her own room, and Darnell from Lord Barnard's study. In Darnell, the sight of the known lovers' earnest conversation, capped with a gentle kiss, produced anger; in Lady Barnard, who imagined herself in the place of the young and attractive Alexandra, the scene aroused passion.

For both lurkers, their visual eavesdropping served only to further enflame feelings they had already possessed. Darnell, still seething over Lord Barnard's cruel decree and incensed over Matty's lack of responsibility, felt protective of both Lady Barnard and Alexandra. Yet in truth, his attitude was not that of an altruistic benefactor, but rather of a frustrated suitor currently displaced in both instances by incumbents he loathed. To his chagrin, he knew that acting against either would be risky, and would not guarantee the ultimate objective he desired. Furthermore, Darnell was not a man of action. And so he reminded himself that patience would be required, for only if an opportunity for intervention presented itself—a test!—could he hope to advance his interests.

Lady Barnard, though flattered by Darnell's attentions, had not forgotten her first sight of Matty in the field. Rather than feeling jealous of Alexandra, the deserving wash girl confirmed Matty's handsomeness and virility. She began to feel a fluttering down below, her own imagination achieving more than her husband's fumbling hands were wont to do. She had Darnell to thank for opening her to the possibility that she could desire and be thought desirable. Yet the devoted assistant was not the one who could stoke her fire, who could strip away the years of unfulfillment and insert in its place a bounty of joy. She decided she must have Matty, even if it meant using her power and status in place of a more organic pheromone.

Darnell thought about Easter. He was to accompany Lady Barnard to church. To do so would be to conspire in defying Lord Barnard's orders. For both their sakes, he knew he should go to her and plead with her not to attend church tomorrow. But to please the master and thus displease the mistress struck him as foul, the exact opposite of what he desired to do. The alternative was to take her to church as planned, and then simply tell Lord Barnard that such never happened. The problem there was that Lord Barnard may have other spies in the village employed for the very purpose of catching them both in the willful act of non-compliance.

And if that be the case then so be it, Darnell thought with a bravado he could never speak. *What cad that would so seek to entrap his wife and loyal servant would be worth working for anyway?* Besides, he knew enough secrets that he could likely force Lord Barnard to maintain his employment for fear that he would tell all to the villagers.

Yes, Darnell in fact held something more powerful than mere position; he held knowledge, first-hand observations that he could use if need be to protect both his beloved Lady Barnard and his wages. They would go to church as planned, Lord Barnard be damned, and Darnell, the house servant who so often felt that the others envied and disliked him, who so long had been spurned by the object of his affection, he alone would have Lady Barnard's attention, if only for that one day.

Lady Barnard, too, thought about Easter. Surely this stable hand would go to church. All the servants would have the day free and she knew they enjoyed the chance to dress up and socialize among themselves.

I will go to church with Darnell, but I will make every effort to draw the attentions of this...this magnificent man, she thought. She quickly conceived a plan to meet and engage him: she would ask him to visit her that night and to guarantee his acceptance she would exert an influence she never had exploited before.

I will be bold yet confident. After all, I am a Lady and he but a keeper of horses. I could command him if he is at all hesitant about complying with my wishes.

And yet, once he came to her room that night, she knew it would be Matty who would have the power. She would willingly, most willingly, be submissive to his lead. He, after all, was the practiced lover, she the eager apprentice. Whatever his routine, whatever his rhythms, she would let him do to her what he does to Alexandra. He would direct her, tame her, mold her to his form and consume her, in ways she had never experienced before.

Intoxicated with her imaginings, she pulled herself away from the window and sat on her bed breathless.

Yes, she thought with a rare smile, *I will go to church in the morning and be saved in the evening.*

Darnell did not want to create a scene, here, the day before Easter, yet he felt compelled to interrupt Matty and Alexandra, if only to remind the latter that he was still a subject of interest, and the former that…well, that it is he who occupies a higher position and who therefore is due a level of deference. So he rather quickly descended the stairs, crossed the foyer, and stepped out the front door.

By this time, Lord Barnard and his hunting party, led by Quentin and his brass horn, had departed for the forest. Darnell crossed the yard and strode quickly to the stable. When he came upon them, Matty and Alexandra were no longer in embrace—and, in fact, were already moving apart from each other, he to the interior of the stable and she to the well.

However, while Darnell did not actually interrupt the two, his sudden bolting into view had the effect of startling the couple and drawing them nearer to each other in an instinctively defensive posture. He, in turn, was caught unawares when Matty, now recovered from the momentary surprise, was the first to speak—and to speak to him in such a cordial tone.

"Darnell, my friend," Matty called out, "you've a well-deserved rest from the Lord's demands. This holiday is yours to enjoy."

"Er, yes, yes indeed," Darnell stammered. "Of course, there is the Lady to attend to. I don't know if you've heard, but I am to escort her to church tomorrow morning. Her desire to attend church is in conflict with Lord Barnard's wishes so if you care for her well-being, you will not say a word about it."

"I am not one to gossip, Darnell, but I am certain that the two of you will make a lovely couple," said Alexandra in a friendly tease.

"I know so little about her, you know," said Matty, stepping nearer to the house servant. "She is quite shy, yes? Or maybe she prefers the indoors. I should like to hear more about her, and about the many important tasks you perform daily. We fieldworkers have no idea what it's like inside the house. What say you and I meet at the tavern tonight and talk over a few ales?" His strong hand now rested on Darnell's shoulder in a display of comradeship.

"What transpires inside the house, and especially with regard to Lord and Lady Barnard, is none of your concern," said Darnell with a slight tone of irritation. Matty touching him made him uncomfortable and Darnell's subtle shift of his shoulder failed to dislodge the stable hand's firm grasp. Still, he was quite surprised and a little flattered at Matty's invitation. "It suffices to say that it is an honor to walk to Easter services with Lady Barnard on one's arm, wouldn't you say?"

"Oh, indeed," replied Matty, withdrawing his hand now, with Alexandra nodding in kind. "I envy and admire your position, which I can only imagine is one that is intensely challenging."

"Why yes, it is," said Darnell, pleased to have the fact acknowledged—all the more so coming from Matty. "You don't know the half of what I am asked to do."

"Truer words have never been spoken," said Matty. "And that is why I should like to learn more about it all. Come, it is the day before Easter, the master is away, it is time to relax and rejoice. The tavern-keeper owes me a few favors, we can drink on my account. What say you?"

Turning towards Alexandra, whom he hadn't yet paid attention to because he was fixated on Matty's surprisingly collegial overtures, Darnell asked, "Would you be accompanying us to the tavern as well?"

"A fine place that is for a woman," said Alexandra with a false tone of hurt that Darnell took as genuine. "What would the talk be about me were I to enter a house of liquor on the arms of two men?"

Darnell, embarrassed for suggesting that Alexandra place herself in a compromising situation only so that he would feel more comfortable accepting Matty's invitation, was about to bluster out an apology when Matty, with a hearty laugh, broke in, "What could be said about you, Alexandra, that has not been said before? Does not the fairest woman in the village deserve to be doted on by two reputable and debonair gentlemen? We three shall be the class of the tavern."

Now Matty embraced both Darnell and Alexandra about their shoulders, his muscular arms drawing them to his body. Darnell had never been this close to Matty before, and his rival's workmanlike aroma required his utmost discretionary powers to bear with a smile. Alexandra giggled, knowing how uncomfortable Darnell must be and marveling at his decorum.

And with that unifying declaration and gesture, the three figures agreed to meet back at the same spot at eight o'clock and walk together to the tavern.

As they went until then their separate ways, both Matty and Darnell were quite pleased: Darnell at the respect shown him and the fact that a popular man like Matty, rake though he was, had desired to include him in his revelry; and Matty because he had been successful in getting Darnell to drink with him. Once the effects of the alcohol began to play with Darnell's senses, Matty would ply him with questions about Lord Barnard's intentions. Maybe then Matty could gain some information that could be used against his employer and thus compel him to nullify whatever legal document his solicitor would soon be fashioning for him.

Perhaps he also would learn some things about the mysterious Lady Barnard.

As for Alexandra, she knew what Darnell did not: that Matty was playing him like a lute. At this she was not a little uncomfortable. Never before in matters involving the three of them had she ever felt a divided loyalty. While she did not feel a passion for Darnell as she did for Matty, he had established himself as a decent man who clearly cared for her, even in her current situation—a situation she did not feel she could so much as discuss with Matty.

I know that Matty intends to use Darnell for his own purposes, she reasoned, *but I do not fear that Darnell will come to harm. If I thought otherwise, I would not be able to accept Matty's plan. In fact, my very presence may keep him from carrying the ruse too far, so I must participate. At the very least, I will have a chance to compare the two in a relaxed and neutral atmosphere. If nothing else, it will serve to take my mind off this pregnancy, which seems more certain with each passing day.*

CHAPTER 9

The area that Quentin had chosen for the hunting party's base camp was one he knew well. Though but a short ride due north from Lord Barnard's home, it was still largely virgin territory. Trails had been cut to reach a stream from which hunters and passers-by would let their dogs and horses drink. An associate of Lord Barnard's had been trying to encourage him to invest in a mill to be built on the banks of the stream, but Lord Barnard was unconvinced the venture was sound. One would have to clear the entire forest and construct a village around the mill to house the workers, he argued, which would take too long to build and make it far longer still to recoup the costs. The proposal was dropped.

Quentin had grown up about another ten miles northeast from there, and at age nine he and his family passed through the area on their way to the village to take up residence in his grandfather's house. His grandmother had died from influenza three months before, and the old man had proven incapable of caring for himself alone.

The "passing through" actually took three days, as Quentin's mother, pregnant to bursting at the time, began to have the child in the wagon just as it neared the stream. Quentin's father was a capable man and had delivered the last three of his four sons—the exception being Quentin, the oldest, who was delivered by an eccentric midwife who nearly threw the purplish squirming newborn into the basin because he was slow to draw his first breath.

Even so, Quentin's brothers had not developed quite as Quentin had and never seemed as bright, to the extent that some wondered if they might have fared better with the mad midwife. Whatever the truth, here in uninhabited territory there was no one else to whom they could turn. Quentin's father asked him to occupy his brothers in the woods while he attended to business in the wagon.

In the time it took for the sun to come from just above the treetops on one side of the sky to just above the horizon on the other side of the sky, Quentin and his brothers had run, skipped, climbed, hid, waded, dug, and rolled around nearly every square inch of land and water in the vicinity. Arriving back at the wagon as the dusk began to deepen, the boys were twice disappointed: first, to learn that they would not stay and live in these woods—though they had to stay put for a couple of days until Quentin's mother and the baby were strong enough to resume the journey—and second, that their newest sibling was a girl.

When, a couple of years later, Quentin was allowed to ride on his own, he began to return to the area to seek quiet relief from his chores. Still later, he would come to practice his marksmanship alone, as well as the challenging art of intimacy with girls whose layers of clothing seemed as dense as the woods themselves. He decided then that if he never was to live in these woods, he would like one day to die in them, to be buried beneath the moist soil of these sacred grounds.

Imagine, he wrote once in a letter to his father, *to be part of this rich forest floor, to decompose in this black earth, feeding the vegetation even at the expense of being fed upon by the bugs and worms who are fortunate enough to call this land their home. I would be among them and then forever I would abide in these woods.*

One night, several weeks after Matty had intervened in Quentin's fight with Phillip and his brother—during which interval Quentin and Matty had spent many nights at the tavern cementing their friendship with a mortar mixed of brown ale and barely exaggerated tales of their past—Quentin brought Matty to this place. There by the stream, they pledged brotherhood to each other. Quentin made a small gash in the meaty pad of his right thumb with a knife, then did the same to Matty's. They then shook hands, with thumbs erect so their blood could mingle. Finally, each licked the blended blood from his own thumb. By this ritual, consecrated by the trees and witnessed by the owls and the ferns and the snakes, Matty had finally gained a brother, while Quentin had finally gained one his equal.

Now, to nearly the same location, Quentin had led Lord Barnard's party. Camp was set on a small flat hill; from this relative high ground, one could see and hear the stream they had crossed and which trawled along lazily not more than two hundred paces away. Spring had thickened the foliage, which limited visibility yet created a lush green backdrop that was both calming and quiet. Arms they had, and sufficient in number to bring back as many kills as could fit in the wooden cart that Quentin's horse pulled along. As for the horses, they were tied to a tall oak tree, restricted to stare at its bark until they were loosened to visit the stream.

Yet hunting was not of primary interest for all this first day. Lord Barnard had sent Quentin to the stream to bring water for the camp, then instructed him to lead Upham and Gallagher out to find a deer or some rabbits for dinner. This he was happy to do, but Quentin asked Lord Barnard if he himself did not intend to hunt.

"Not today, Quentin," he said. "I have important business to conduct with Mr. Finster here. Hopefully we shall conclude by dinner. Tomorrow, I shall wish to remain near camp in case Darnell arrives with news. If he does not, then perhaps later in the day I shall try my luck."

Odd, thought Quentin. *Why come out to the woods to do business? Has the solicitor not an office? Is there something quite secret for them to discuss, something so private that they dare not do so in town lest someone should happen by the window and overhear?*

Well, it only served to confirm Quentin's idea of Lord Barnard that he was a strange duck. It was no matter to Quentin, after all. Here he was in his favorite location and if Lord Barnard would not point a rifle at prey, then that meant more shots for him. And so he took guns, powder, rope, and the tailor and banker, and walked deeper into the woods until to Lord Barnard and Finster they were no longer seen, and their footsteps—noisily walking on last autumn's detritus of brown leaves and twigs—were no longer heard.

The Grave and the Gay

The solicitor and his client sat on a fallen oak, quite an old one judging by the generous seating space it provided, felled some time ago by what must have been a wicked storm. Finster spoke first.

"So then, Lord Barnard, what business have you that it must transpire here, apart and alone from our friends and townsfolk?"

"Do you know of Matthew Musgrave, whom I employ to tend my horses?" asked Lord Barnard.

"I've not met him," said Finster, "but tales of his exploits are many. I know no details of any in particular," he hastened to add. "After all, I'm not one to listen to gossip, least of all to the prurient kind, but in the cumulative, they have made his reputation secure."

"Exploits?" asked Lord Barnard. "Of what kind?"

"Well, surely you must know. After all, he all but lives under your roof."

"Are you suggesting that he is the carousing sort?" Lord Barnard inquired.

"My good friend," replied Finster, "Matty Musgrave has made the intimate acquaintance of nearly every maiden in our town, not to mention the surrounding villages. And more than a few matrons, if the chatter is accurate. I shall not say more, for I do not indulge in this sort of gossip."

"Well," said Lord Barnard after a short silence. Another short silence ensued, broken by a clearing of his throat, through which next came, "He is a handsome lad, to be sure. Young and full of strength and vigor. But how would you judge his character? As a person, that is. Would you say he is a good, honest fellow?"

"As I've said, I don't know the man personally," replied Finster. "I should think, however, that he might require some lessons and refinement if he were to be introduced to proper society as an honorable man. When the citizenry in the street speak of a person, it is either because he is respected or because he is a rogue. In the former instance, the talk serves to build the man's character and reputation beyond its current standing. In the latter, a low man is brought even lower, because he is known only for his misdeeds. I suspect that is the nature of the scuttlebutt of Mr. Musgrave. But why do we speak thus of your Lothario, Lord Barnard?"

"Finster, I think I know Matty better than most, and I can speak with authority that he is both capable and kind. I agree with you that he is not now ready to assume the mantle of 'gentleman', but with the proper tutelage I believe he can become a most respectable and influential person. You see, because my wife is barren, I need other means to gain an heir. I should therefore like to adopt Matty Musgrave as my own son and legal heir, effective immediately."

"Adopt Musgrave?" Finster asked incredulously. "Have you gone mad? You are a man of position. How would your reputation and honor endure such an arrangement? It's one thing to have him in your employ, after all no one expects a gentleman to clean an animal and shovel its dung. But to make him as your own son? Why, that's inviting derision upon your good name. I shan't be party to it."

Lord Barnard was unaccustomed to not getting his way, which informed the tenor of his response. "I asked you here, Finster, not for the words you would speak, which are too many, but the words you would write," he said. "You are to draft a document that fulfills my wishes and I expect you to do as I say, for if you refuse our professional association shall be forever terminated, *effective immediately*."

And with that, Finster relented. Lord Barnard dictated the scope of what he desired in terms of his legal rights and the recognition of the town's governor that Matthew Barnard nee Musgrave was the son and sole legal heir of Lord and Lady Barnard. Finster asked questions, consulted a pair of legal tomes he had brought, and wrote out the document, the third draft of which Lord Barnard signed. Finster then affixed his signature as witness and executor, rolled and tied the document, and placed it within his bag.

This transpired as the day aged and darkened into dusk. In time, the hunting party returned. Quentin dragged a rope to which was tied two deer—one, a fine buck, he killed himself; the other, a faun, he had to put out of its misery as Upham the tailor's shot injured the young beast, yet not mortally. Gallagher the banker hit nothing but bark and earth. *Hands that count money are too soft and weak to make a good shot*, Quentin thought to himself on the walk back to camp. They feasted that night on the larger and older of the kills, and left the other in the cart to skin the following day.

All the while, back in town, Matty prepared for his night at the tavern with Alexandra and Darnell. He was unaware that he no longer belonged to himself, nor was the man he called himself. Though he had feared and may have suspected it, he could not have known that plans already had been made to relieve him of his duties attending to the horses upon his master's return, and that instead he would spend his hours in Lord Barnard's study, learning etiquette and matters of business, and leaving him little time and space free from the close gaze of his "father" with which to attend to the ladies of the town.

Yet as he changed into a clean shirt and smoothed his hair, his only thoughts were of what he could do to parry Lord Barnard's intentions. So preoccupied was he that he was startled back into the evening's plans only by Darnell shouting from outside.

"Musgrave! Are you joining us or have you a jug of your own by your wash basin?"

Matty took a few shillings from under his mattress and stuffed them into a small cloth pouch, which he then tucked into the waistband of his trousers. He called out as he walked towards the door, "Only the drunkard and the friendless drink alone." Joining Darnell and Alexandra in the road, he added, "Our party has convened. Let the merriment begin!"

So together, under a waxing moon climbing into a sky the dark green hue of ocean water, the three walked together to the tavern. Of the three, Matty was, not surprisingly, the most comfortable and confident. After all, he was in his natural element and had nothing either to prove or to hide. Darnell, on the other hand, felt alien and vulnerable in their company, like a ripe gooseberry in a bushel of hardy gourds. He did not trust Matty but did welcome the chance to spend an evening with Alexandra, fearing only that he wouldn't measure up against his rival's boundless charisma.

As for Alexandra, she was acutely aware that she and Darnell were in on a secret that Matty did not know, and worried that under the spell of alcohol the truth may come out. At the same time, she felt somewhat protective of Darnell because of the force of Matty's personality and the fact that she knew Matty sought to gain something from Darnell. Adding to these concerns, she did not feel well, had not much appetite, and tired more easily with each passing day. She intended to be more witness than participant in the frivolity and merriment sure to come.

The walk wasn't a long one but it was pleasant going, the calm elements of the day carrying over into evening, punctuated by a slight seasonal chill. Even before they were near enough to see the lamp lights emanating from the tavern windows, they heard the gaiety transpiring within. They spoke little to each other as they approached the building, but as he held open the door for his party, Matty quickly assumed the role of host. Thus, as the door closed behind him, Matty immediately raised his right arm and called for a round.

CHAPTER 10

"A holiday, a holiday! And the first one of the year! Here's to the grandest of companions with whom to celebrate it."

As he thus toasted, Matty raised his mug of ale, swinging it forward to clink against those held by Darnell and Alexandra with such gusto that rivulets of foam ran down the back of the vessel and onto the arc of skin between his thumb and forefinger. After taking a hearty swig, he slurped the bitter spill from his hand and laughed. "'Tis a shame that Lord Barnard is not present to have a drink with us, eh?"

"I shouldn't think he would share our table even if he weren't away hunting," said Alexandra, sipping from her mug, which contained a fermented cider known far to the south as scrumpy. "He's never been one to spend much time with the help—the two of you excepted, of course."

"Well, obviously, my position requires that I be in his company much of the time he is at home," Darnell was pleased to respond. "It is not often that he closes a door without permitting me to enter. Except," he tried not to frown, "except when he meets with you, Matty." At that, he gamely raised his glass, as if to compliment Matty on his own unique relationship with their employer. Taking the cue, Matty returned the gesture, and they drank again.

"As to your first statement, Alexandra," Darnell continued, "Lord Barnard is quite a sober man. Yes he takes the occasional drink, but never have I seen him do so to excess. So even if he were wont to pass the time with us in an informal setting, I doubt that the tavern would be his choice. Lady Barnard enjoys her wine—not in a bad way, mind you—but, of course, she is rarely permitted to venture far into town. I will thank you not to inquire as to why."

Devoid though it was of any trace of Lord or Lady Barnard, the tavern was a popular establishment this night. Even at an early hour, few were the jugs that held a cork for any length of time, and so the hops-scented air was thick with the festive din of hearty conversation, robust laughter, and unsolicited song.

Since his first day in town, when he wandered in and saved Quentin's life before even taking a drink, Matty had been a frequent visitor at the tavern. Which is not to say that he had a reputation as a drunkard because he did not. Truth to say, Matty was a frequent visitor to many places—church excepted—and was uniformly welcome wherever he went. Yet he did have a fondness for the tavern. He lived for companionship and made conversation easily with people of all stations, from the nobleman to the beggar. Further, given the smells with which he worked all day, he found the aroma of the tavern—an intoxicating concoction both yeasty and woody—a pleasing contrast.

The tavern was homey; in fact, it was the keeper's home. Informally (and secretly) for more than a year, Thomas Richardson had been brewing his own ale and charging visitors to drink it in his front room. For a few additional pence, he would play his fiddle for the patrons. Eventually, the authorities found out about his covert commercial enterprise and threatened to take his home unless he declared it a legitimate business and separated the serving area from his living quarters.

Richardson took a loan from the banker Gallagher and expanded his front room to comfortably accommodate as many as fifty people (though many nights, such as this one, half as many more were let inside). On the floor of wide wooden planks stood ten small tables, as well as counters built into the left- and right-facing walls. To the rear was the bar. On the other side of the wall behind the bar were the three rooms in which Richardson and his family lived.

Matty, Darnell, and Alexandra sat on high stools on the right side of the tavern, facing a window that looked out on the street. Matty was sure the venue was right for eliciting secrets from Darnell, but there had yet been sufficient time and liquor to loosen the house servant and cause him to speak with the freedom and frankness that Matty desired. Matty therefore playfully challenged Darnell to chug the remaining contents of their mugs, that they may be refilled with fresh brew. Uncertain, Darnell glanced at Alexandra, who smiled and nodded slightly. Though she knew she was abetting Matty's plan, she did truly believe that Darnell would benefit from being unguarded and relaxed this one evening.

With Alexandra's tacit approval, Darnell also believed that going along with Matty's sense of sport could only further endear himself to her. It was obvious that Matty and Alexandra were close; there was no benefit to being the odd man out. Having feared his ability to compare favorably with the stable hand, Darnell began to understand that Alexandra needed to see them together in order to realize more clearly what he offers that Matty does not. *She is not put off by the rascal in Matty*, he reasoned, *so I have license to be more assertive.*

"Not only do I accept your challenge," Darnell said at last, "but he who finishes last must pay for the next round." And then, when Darnell lost his own counter-challenge (as he knew he would; in fact, it took him a few seconds merely to catch his breath, find his voice, and wipe his chin), he said, "The penalty is mine, although I was set to procure the second round anyway since you bought the first." He raised his empty mug and waved it to catch Richardson's attention, and in short order a jug was brought to the table and the cups were refilled.

Darnell rose to inaugurate the second round with a toast. "I know my deportment is rather formal at times," he began. "It goes with the responsibility of my position, you understand. Yet while I am somewhat of a confidant of Lord Barnard's, I am not his colleague. I am therefore most pleased to mark this merry time with my fellow laborers, and may we enjoy many more such celebrations as this in the future."

Matty cheered heartily at Darnell's toast, not only for its literal sentiment but also because it was apparent that a single quaff had already loosened his inhibitions somewhat. Perhaps only two more and the information he sought would come dribbling out of Darnell's mouth like the saliva he'd spat when he uttered the word "pleased."

Alexandra was also heartened by the toast and by the fact that Darnell was indeed celebrating together with them. It was the first time the three of them had been together socially and she appreciated seeing

Darnell in quite a different context. Darnell's reasoning was proving true and effective, as Alexandra was very much enjoying his company—not because he was acting like Matty, but because he was acting like a man. Neither a gentleman nor a ruffian, but a simple, normal man who can both work and play, each honorably.

She began to feel less like a co-conspirator, and was moved to offer her own toast.

"I should like to add my own salute, if I may," she declared, and her companions responded enthusiastically with shouts of "By all means" and "Hear, hear." Alexandra didn't stand, but she held her mug with an outstretched arm at chin level, directly between Matty and Darnell, so that to look at the mug they must necessarily see each other.

"We three toil for the same people," she continued, "yet our places and our histories are varied. Darnell, you have been here the longest. You work inside and it suits your sense of order and propriety. Matty, you have been here just longer than a year and you work out of doors with the horses, for walls and doors can never hold your spirit. As for me, I work inside when the weather is cold and outside when it is warm. I make things clean," she said with a self-deprecating laugh, "yet they always manage to get soiled again.

"I have been here a while and I have seen people come and go. There have been times I have felt lonely and misunderstood, and there have been times I have received wonderful kindnesses."

She looked back and forth at the two men.

"The work is not easy and it's never done for good. My place in life seems set, and I can't say truthfully that this is what I imagined for myself even a few short years ago. And yet, while there are difficulties that we all face, I sit here tonight before the Easter holiday, and I am with two friends who care about me. We can have fun and be silly, and leave our work behind. This feels good to me, and I wish it could continue forever. And so I say thank you to both of you, for being wonderful and for being together with me this evening."

Alexandra began to sip her cider when she noticed that neither Matty nor Darnell had moved or spoken a word both during and after her speech.

Between the two, there was a blend of being touched by her words and her outspoken vulnerability, yet also a slight discomfort at the intimacy she had described all three of them all sharing, when neither felt it quite true.

"Heavens, have I sobered us so soon?" she asked in genuine concern. Darnell and Matty then quickly recovered, for her sake if not for theirs, with a chorus of "Amen" and "Well spoken." Matty clinked his mug against theirs and said, "We've just heard a lovely toast and so we must drink."

"Indeed," said Darnell, and then threw back his head and chugged the remains of his ale. "I've finished first this time," he said with unusual volume even given the setting, and Matty and Alexandra laughed gaily. When the next round was consumed, Matty decided it was time to begin fishing for useful information from Darnell's now-unguarded mind.

"I agree with Alexandra," said Matty. "I am most pleased that we all are here together. And I hope I'm not being too bold to suggest that I'm happiest yet for you, Darnell, for you seem to have less freedom to come and go as you would like."

"Yes, well, I'm often sent on errands, it's not as if I can never leave the house," replied Darnell. "But it's true that I am likely more constrained than the rest of the servants, by virtue of their need to have me close. The Barnards, I mean, not the servants." Darnell laughed at his silly joke.

"And how do you like their company?" asked Matty, allowing nary a second to pass since the conclusion of Darnell's ale-fueled chortle.

"How do you mean?" replied Darnell, composing himself.

"Well, I'm sure the nature of your work is such that some of it is quite interesting, yet some of it must be pure drudgery. Seems to me that's simply the nature of work itself. But apart from how you feel about the work you do for them, what is it like to be so frequently in the presence of Lord and Lady Barnard?"

"Come now, the experience is not unknown to you, Matty," said Darnell. "You've been in his office. He's come to visit you in the stable."

"Yes, true, of course, but I see him when he wants to see me," Matty replied. "He has a specific task or question for me and he gets right to the point, you know that about him better than anyone. Not one for idle chatter, right? But you, you see him in private moments, in rest and reverie. And the Lady, too, whom I see so rarely and know nothing about. How do you find them as people?"

"Well—," Darnell started, then hesitated, as he was unsure of what to say or how best to say it (he was, after all, still a little more possessed of discretion than he was possessed by alcohol).

"Mind you," Matty assured him, "I'm not interested in gossip nor would I dream of asking you to reveal any secrets. You're far too honorable for that and I would never attempt to compromise your integrity. Here, let me fill your cup again, nice of old Richardson to leave the jug, easier than trying to get his attention each time, isn't it? It's just that you know them so much better than I do, and I'm curious, that's all."

Darnell took another drink. "Well, I don't mind sharing my impressions of them. On the whole, they are kind and fair. They both enjoy music—though neither play, which is a shame considering the exquisite spinet they own. I rather wish I could play, then I'm sure they would ask me to entertain them on it. Lord Barnard is an avid reader; you've seen the many volumes in his study, no doubt. I can vouch for the fact that he's read every one of them. They are even-tempered for the most part, she more than he. In fact, I'll never forget the first time I experienced—in fact, caused—his anger...."

Just then, Darnell's face broke into a crooked little smile as his eyes seemed to run inward, watching a scene being replayed in his mind.

"Wait, what is this?" asked Matty enthusiastically. Perhaps a nugget he could use. "Your face betrays a tale that must be told. Out with it."

"Yes, please," said Alexandra. "If you're comfortable, that is."

"Yes, it's fine. It's more about me than him, actually," said Darnell. "When I first began working in the house, I was often quite flustered. Lord Barnard was a bit more brusque in his demeanor than I had been accustomed to. When he wanted something, he wanted it without delay, and I was not always aware of where the thing was, or how to do what he asked. Well, he'd just come in from a hunting trip and I guess he had lost a wager with someone in his party and needed to quickly write a promissory note. He was not at all in fair spirits and as I followed him into his study he commanded me to get him a quill.

"Well, I knew where they were kept but the first one I picked up had a rather dull nib and I decided it wouldn't do. As I reached in for another one, Lord Barnard again demanded the quill. I was so anxious that I thrust it towards him point forward, and in the same moment he was darting his hand out to receive it. The point lodged itself rather deeply into his palm, the fleshy part below the thumb, actually, and he cried out in pain. Had I not run out of the room quickly to fetch a cloth, I fear he would have beaten me with his riding crop."

Matty and Alexandra both laughed at the tale, Matty less heartily because it provided no clues as to what he should do about his own matter with Lord Barnard. But Darnell enjoyed the story as well, and was pleased to be regarded as so jolly by his two colleagues. He therefore drank all the more heartily, finishing the portion that Matty had drawn for him, and calling for more.

"I wonder," said Matty, "if Lord Barnard carries a scar on that hand to this day."

"He does," answered Darnell, "for that quill had been used once that day already and the ink that remained on the nib lodged under his skin. He bears a small black 'v' on his right hand. It's small all right, but plain to see if you know to look for it."

"How remarkable," said Alexandra. "I imagine Lady Barnard must have been alarmed by the racket."

"Indeed she was," said Darnell. "When I returned, she was there dabbing the wound with a cloth soaked with spirits. Lord Barnard was protesting that it worsened the pain, but she continued to tend to him as I looked on. Rather sheepishly, I must add."

"Is she handy with cures, then?" asked Alexandra.

Darnell paused, then sighed before responding, not actually addressing her question directly. "Lady Barnard is caring and kind as an angel," he said at last, in tones both of admiration and regret. "I wonder sometimes if Lord Barnard appreciates her qualities as he should. I mean, the very fact that he does not allow her to venture into the village at all. I mean, really. Why, if he even knew that I was escorting her to church tomorrow he would be blind with rage."

"Is that so?" said Matty, becoming quite interested in Darnell's testimony. It was obvious to both Matty and Alexandra that Darnell seemed protective of Lady Barnard. "Please do tell us more. She sounds like such a lovely woman, but how sad that she is kept like a caged bird by Lord Barnard. I envy that you know her so well. I'm not sure she even knows my name. I've never once seen her at the stable."

"She is fair, indeed," said Darnell. "Fairer yet when she smiles, which is all too rare, I regret to say." He paused. "Yes, serving Lord Barnard is my duty," he continued at last, "yet serving Lady Barnard is my pleasure."

"So much so that you risk Lord Barnard's wrath?" asked Matty.

"Without hesitation," replied Darnell.

"Tell me, then," said Matty, "what exactly do you think Lord Barnard would do if he found out you took her to church? And mind you, no word of this shall pass my lips while there is breath in my body."

"I imagine I would be fired and banished," said Darnell. "He would insist that I never pass before or onto his property for as long as we both shall live. And that would be fine with me."

This last remark surprised both Matty and Alexandra, yet they were unable to ask for clarification because just as he finished his sentence, Darnell's head fell forward onto the table. The ale had triumphed, and Matty's plan had worked perfectly: Darnell became more talkative as he became more inebriated, he unwittingly gave Matty the information he was seeking, and he would remember almost nothing of the evening when he awoke the next morning from his drunken slumber.

Matty and Alexandra arose, and Matty lifted the sleeping servant onto his shoulder. With his free hand, Matty tossed a few coins on the counter, and he and Alexandra walked back to the Barnard residence. In a few hours, the church bells would ring and none of the townspeople's cumulative joy would equal the pain and agony that the reverberations would cause Darnell as they clanged and echoed in his aching head. And yet he had an important job to do and would need all his wits and energy to do it well.

CHAPTER 11

It was an unusually quiet morning in the house when Lady Barnard slowly stirred herself awake. The rising sun, throwing its orange darts of light low across the village, was not blocked but rather recast in hue as it shot through her collection of colored glass that sat on the shelf by her windowsill, creating a kaleidoscope of bright, warm splotches on her still-drowsy face.

On a more typical day, the sound of Lord Barnard, ever an early riser, walking through a succession of rooms to find an item misplaced—a book, often; sometimes a letter or an article of clothing—would begin to rouse her. His inevitable call to Darnell to help with the search or to prepare his papers for work, and the loyal servant's prompt response, would complete the process of her awakening.

This morning, however, she rose on her own, as her husband was off in the woods and Darnell was still in the hold of a heavily liquored sleep. She sat up slowly in her bed, looked around with a questioning expression on her face, then became energized with the dawning realization that it was Easter Sunday, that she would be going into town, accompanied by Darnell—yet looking out for the handsome, virile stable hand.

Lady Barnard pulled back the quilt and swung her legs over the side of her bed. The silence in the house did not bother her, nor did the fact that she was alone.

It is worse to feel alone when you are in the company of others, she often thought, *than when you are, in fact, by yourself.*

Lord Barnard had once offered to hire her a servant of her own, a girl to help bathe and dress her, mend her clothes and make curtains, and any other tasks Lady Barnard may desire. Yet she would have none of it. She was too modest to allow a strange person to have such intimate contact with her, and she preferred to do her own sewing, one of the first skills she was taught. The wash girl Alexandra was sufficient for tending to the remaining textile management requirements.

She was glad she had no servant like Darnell—who, though he willingly served her, was clearly and primarily beholden to Lord Barnard—scurrying about her personal space all day looking to please her in myriad ways that were most unpleasing to her.

Luxuriating this morning in her temporary solitude, and truly inspired by the thoughts of what this day might bring, she removed her nightgown and strode nude to the wash table on the far side of her room. Separated from the rest of the room by a hand-painted screen given to her by a cousin of Lord Barnard's—which he'd acquired on a business trip to the trading port of Macao, the peninsula off the southeastern coast of China that the Portuguese had settled a century before—the wash table held on its marble top a large blue and white porcelain basin filled the previous afternoon by Alexandra with fresh well water. A looking glass was suspended from a hook on the wall behind it. A cake of scented soap lay waiting on a small silver dish to the right. A folded towel sat to the left. Atop the towel was a sponge.

Lady Barnard wetted the sponge in the basin water, then rubbed it against the cake of soap. She applied the foamy mass first to her shoulders. Streams of water ran down her collarbone and blazed a trail across her breast. She noticed the instant eruptions of goose pimples on her skin, dwarfed by the involuntary extension of her nipples. She was beginning to understand that her body was a living thing, that it responded naturally to certain stimuli. Touch, temperature, even thoughts created changes.

As much as Lady Barnard had suffered emotionally from a lack of interaction with people in the village, her body also suffered from its isolation, like a discarded dulcimer with unstruck strings or an indigestible bread made from dough insufficiently kneaded.

She wanted to bathe slowly, to revel in her awakening acknowledgement of her body's form and feeling, yet she also was impatient to get dressed and leave the house. She recalled the previous two Easters, when Lord Barnard grudgingly would escort her to church. It was apparent that people lingered in the street before and after the service, so as to see each other and make plans to celebrate the day together. Yet she had not been party to this social practice, as Lord Barnard made a point of arriving to the church just as Rev. Collins was closing the door, and heading straight back to the house as soon as the last refrain of the closing hymn was concluded.

Today, she hoped, would be different. She would arrive early, remain late, see and be seen, admire and be admired.

And so she bathed the rest of her body more rapidly, rinsed with the bracing fresh water, and toweled herself dry. She then opened the front door of the wash table and pulled out a rectangular wooden box that had been stained the deep brown color of a dark bay mare. Lined with crimson silk, it held her collection of scented powders and oils. The box had been untouched since last Easter, as she had long abandoned the notion that it mattered how she presented herself to a public she would never see. She applied powder to her face and oil behind her ears, within her cleavage, and, playfully, on her thighs and buttocks.

She dressed in equal haste, pulling on the frilly yellow vestment with decorative buttons made of ivory and a white lace trim to match that which had been sewn onto the bonnet she'd commissioned, delivered the day before by Mr. McDougall. He was very pleased with his creation, and Lady Barnard complimented him on it with great sincerity.

Of course, she did not have access to her husband's funds, nor could she ask him to pay for it, for she was not supposed to be going out this day and therefore should have no need for such a fine new bonnet. Instead, she offered Mr. McDougall a ring given to her by Lord Barnard on their intensely awkward first meeting, which she had always worn on her right hand. It was a simple band of pewter he had made himself—with his father's extensive help and persistent encouragement—but over the years it had become too tight on her finger and the constriction hurt her. She would be glad to be rid of it, and if Lord Barnard were to notice she would say it had fallen off while bathing and became lost beneath the floorboards.

McDougall accepted it with gratitude, and with the vow that he would not show or speak of it to anyone in public.

Now bathed, powdered, and dressed, Lady Barnard prepared to summon Darnell. His room was a small, low-ceilinged space in the basement, an area of the house she was not wont to enter. Yet with Lord Barnard not at home and none of the other servants working (due to the holiday, of course), she was forced to step gently down the cellar stairs (so as not to soil her clothing) and knock upon his door.

It was the third of an increasingly forceful series of three raps that produced the sound of movement from the other side of the pine door. Darnell, still in the clothes he wore to the tavern the night before, began to stir during the second series. At the end of the third series, he began steadily to realize his state, his location, and, by dint of the light he could see out of the narrow pane high in the wall that provided his only view to the world outside, the approximate age of the morning. The time obviously being late, Darnell thrust himself out of bed in a panic, his boot catching the blanket and causing him to tumble onto the floor—this the sound that Lady Barnard heard.

"Darnell, are you all right?" she called. "Are you ready?"

His head heavy and aflame, Darnell began a desperate dance of undressing, washing, and redressing, hoping to accomplish in seconds what he had planned to spend half of an hour doing earlier in the morning.

"My apologies, Lady Barnard," replied Darnell while throwing hand-wells of water onto his face. "I require just a few minutes more, if that's all right. I shall come up to get you the very second I am ready. I most deeply regret my delay."

"That's quite all right, Darnell," Lady Barnard lied. "I shall await you upstairs." With that, she turned to ascend the stairs, her earlier excitement giving way to anxiety at the prospect of missing anything.

For Darnell's part, there was only anxiety. He had but faint memories of the night before, none between Alexandra's emotional toast and his waking abruptly to Lady Barnard's knocking. He was unconscious when Matty and Alexandra walked him home, his ale-logged body slung over his rival's shoulder. When they arrived at the house, Alexandra opened the cellar door from which Darnell could come and go in his private hours without passing through the common areas of the house. Matty crouched through the opening so his burden would not strike against the frame. He dropped Darnell rather unceremoniously onto the bed and turned to leave. With hand gestures, Alexandra instructed Matty to go back and place the blanket over Darnell's body. He did so, then left Darnell to his drunken dreams.

Outside the house, Matty had invited Alexandra to spend the night in his loft in the stable. She politely declined, citing the lateness of the hour and her wish to rise early to prepare for Easter. So he walked her back to her cousin's house, then returned to the Barnard estate and went into his room in back of the stable. Matty slept well and rose early, taking a bathing swim in the pond behind the stable, where the horses would often take their drink. The crisp, cool water refreshed and invigorated his naked body, and he eagerly awaited the festivities of the day and the opportunity to enact his plan—one that he was sure would guarantee his freedom and independence from Lord Barnard. His only regret was not to have had a final coupling with Alexandra, for he was sure that he would have to leave for new environs once Lord Barnard found out what he had done.

Maybe, he thought, *I could try to live alone in that wooded area that Quentin favors so well. There was space and wood enough to build a fine little cabin, and a stream for drinking, cooking, and bathing. Maybe I could even ask Alexandra to go with me.*

As for that wooded area, it still was occupied by Lord Barnard and his party. All arose early that morning, none earlier than Lord Barnard himself. He was up before the sun and had to add desiccated branches and deep breaths to the gray, smoldering embers of the previous night's campfire. By the flickering yellow light of the resuscitated blaze, he sat and read. As the sun began its slow, steady ascent from beneath the verdant horizon, the rest of the party awoke to a spectacular panoramic view of the transitioning skyscape, with pink and orange hues in the east and violet and cobalt in the west.

Quentin took advantage of the fire to heat water for coffee. There was some deer meat left over from the previous night's feast, but the consensus was that a fresh woodland hare or two would make a more satisfying breakfast. Quentin offered to hunt them alone—preferred to, in fact—yet Lord Barnard, not having joined the hunt the day before and awake nearly three hours already, was keen to join him. And so while the rest of the party moved leisurely through their morning paces, Quentin and Lord Barnard took up arms and went after the small game.

The two walked in silence until they were well out of sight from the camp. This was necessary in order to hear the cautious footsteps of the forest's little creatures. Yet the quiet was also a consequence of the two men's differing attitudes towards the other.

For Quentin, he was here with Lord Barnard for purely practical reasons: he was hired to lead the party and would be paid well for his efforts. He had proven his worth over a number of excursions and though he disliked and mistrusted his patron, for matters both of pride and of necessity he was committed to continuing to earn Lord Barnard's favor. His lack of speech, therefore, was due to his focus on successfully shooting breakfast—or aiding Lord Barnard in doing so—as well as his disinclination to speak to him beyond the necessities of his role.

As for Lord Barnard, he was thinking less about firing at a rabbit or raccoon than he was about the paperwork he had completed the day before. Even he had to admit it was queer that a man's status as a person should be altered so drastically with just a sheet of paper strewn with legal jargon and made binding by two signatures rendered with quill and ink. Furthermore, the person in question was neither present nor definitively aware of when and where the course of his life had irrevocably altered. No one else in the hunting party had knowledge of what Lord Barnard and Finster had conspired to do.

This, too, gnawed at Lord Barnard. He wanted to share his news but felt that apart from he and his solicitor, Matty should be the next informed. Yet he wasn't here and the knowledge was ready to burst out of Lord Barnard's mouth like a shot from a rifle.

As they slowly walked and gently stepped, Lord Barnard's mind raced and pounded with the need to divulge his secret. And here he was with a young man he both liked and trusted. He weighed the consequences of breaking their silence, knowing full well that Quentin and Matty were friends. Yet Lord Barnard was of the mind that Quentin would be happy both for his patron and his chum, and certainly he could buy the skilled hunter's silence with a bonus pouch of shillings. At any rate, he intended to cut the hunting trip short and return at first light the following day in order to begin remolding Matty's life from stable boy to gentleman as quickly as possible.

And so it was that Lord Barnard was the first to break the silence, his outburst so sudden that Quentin heard three sets of scampering footsteps race away before he even understood what Lord Barnard was saying.

"Quentin, I have the most marvelous news to share and I simply cannot maintain my peace a moment longer," he said, as Quentin's eyes darted about to watch the trails of brush movements indicating where the game had gone. "I beg your attention for this concerns our mutual friend, Matty."

At the mention of Matty's name, Quentin's attention focused more clearly on Lord Barnard, and he looked at him quizzically.

"I have not known Matty nearly as long as you have," Lord Barnard continued, "yet I dare say I am as fond of him as are you. Though some think of him as something of a rogue, I see in him a rough jewel who is merely in need of refinement. I can help him to fulfill his potential as a gentleman, and so have worked it out with my solicitor to adopt Matty as my own son and sole heir. He is, for all legal purposes, Matthew Barnard even as we speak."

Quentin's mouth opened yet he did not betray the silence he had thus far maintained. Then his mouth closed and he looked down, as if something had literally fallen from his lips.

"Well, have you nothing to say about this?" asked Lord Barnard, impatient for a response after Quentin's pause. "Certainly you are surprised, who wouldn't be? But are you as excited for your friend as I am for both him and for me?"

Despite an additional few seconds of muteness, Quentin did finally find his tongue. "Is-is Matty aware of this? Has he given consent to be… adopted?"

The question displeased Lord Barnard. Aside from snuffing his excitement, it was an unnecessary query and avoided the question of whether Quentin approved. "If you must know," he said somewhat sternly, "I did speak to Matthew about this matter, however I did not ask his permission because I do not require his permission. He is not attached to family, nor has he anything—whether food, shelter, or clothing—that is not due to my largesse. I all but own his life and livelihood already. What is new is that he has my name as of today, and in the future will have my fortune as well. I should think any man would envy him."

"Oh, quite," said Quentin, realizing he was at risk of falling into disfavor with Lord Barnard. "In fact, my joy for Matty is rivaled only by my, uh, envy of him. I merely wanted to know if he might be celebrating his good luck even as we speak."

"He will know on the morrow when we return to the village. At that time, I will tell him myself and make suitable quarters for him in the house.

"Now listen well, my dear boy," Lord Barnard continued. "You are a man in whom I have placed my faith, and a large number of silver coins, many times. Never have you disappointed me. No one save you, Finster, and I know this information. No one else will know it until Matthew knows it, and only I will speak to him about this. Do you understand, and do you agree to utter not one word of this to anyone until I have done so first?"

Immediately upon uttering this last question, Lord Barnard placed a bag of coins in Quentin's hand. Quentin knew this represented a bonus—and a bribe. He did not know what ultimately he would do, but at this moment he had no choice but to accept it. "I do, Lord Barnard," he said, as his fingers closed slowly around the leather pouch. "I do. Thank you."

Lord Barnard smiled. "I shall be looking for a new man to care for my horses," he said. "I would greatly value your opinion should you know a suitable candidate." Just then, a hare darted out from behind a towering maple. Lord Barnard lifted his rifle and took aim. He fired once and the hare fell back. Lying still, with a trail of scarlet spilling onto its fair auburn coat of fur, was breakfast.

CHAPTER 12

Alexandra awoke in her cousin's house Easter morning with a stomach complaint akin to what Darnell felt. Yet while Darnell's condition was rare and acute, for Alexandra the experience was by now familiar and indicative of a longer-term condition. The conclusion was inescapable: she was pregnant. How far into her term she could not be sure; a month perhaps, maybe as much as a fortnight beyond that. She had no way to know for certain.

Of her condition, even when it was merely presumed and not known to be fact, Alexandra had been concerned and nervous, yet never upset or regretful. She'd never thought about bearing children, yet it was not something she very well knew how to avoid. She wished for luck and for years had been granted such. When finally it seemed that the curse of barrenness was not to be her fate, she accepted it, unashamed of her circumstance. Her only worries were about Matty: how would he respond to the news, would he maintain his affection for her, would he accept responsibility for the child she would bear?

This day, it being Easter morning, the concept of new life took on a deeper layer of meaning for Alexandra. She allowed herself to think well beyond matters of patrilineage and the immediate consequences of her situation, and to fantasize about what kind of a person this child would become. Male or female, no offspring of Matty Musgrave could help but inherit his compelling physicality, his unforced nonchalance, and his adventurous and playful spirit. Surely some of the rougher edges and wilder inclinations would be tempered by her own maternal influence, but one would never doubt, regardless of whether Matty admitted it or not—or was present in their lives or not—that he indeed was the father.

(The wonder, frankly, is how there could not have been scads of easily identifiable little Mattys scurrying about and making mischief in the streets of the villages he'd called home. Perhaps there were; he never stayed long enough to find out.)

What, then, would that mean for Alexandra should Matty abandon her and refuse to claim the child as his own? If, say, she accepted Darnell's proposition? Despite the previous night's drunken frolic, she knew he still detested Matty—would so even more given the unceremonious end of the evening and what she assumed was already an unsatisfactory start to his day. Would he, therefore, also detest Matty's child? Could he ever look upon the child not as Matty's but as his own, in not only a legal way but also an emotional manner? Or was Darnell's promise to compassionately father the child merely a ruse intended to win her hand?

Then, of course, there was the added intrigue due to Matty's impending new status. *Surely*, she had allowed herself to imagine, *as heir to Lord Barnard he would enjoy a comfortable life and would be able to give the same to his wife and child.* Alexandra also understood that his days as a lothario would be ended, as his "father" would never permit him to indulge in such behavior.

Although, she realized, *it is unlikely that Lord Barnard would approve of his son marrying a wash girl and acknowledging a child conceived prior to taking the vows of matrimony.* Indeed, it seemed unlikely she would ever be in line for an inheritance that would improve her station in life.

That knowledge served to sway her private deliberations back towards Darnell as being perhaps the best choice of husband and father. And yet—*my, how confusing it all is!*—Alexandra could barely imagine the reality of Matty commanding not only the man who would raise his child, but also the woman who carried it.

A large house indeed is Lord Barnard's, she pondered, *but can it accommodate Matty, Darnell, me, and a child sired by Matty who would possibly know only Darnell as its father?*

She realized that the complexities of her situation were far too much to contemplate on a day such as today. Desiring not to be late to church, and curious to see how the players in her intricate and intimate dilemma would behave the morning after—*Did Matty get the information he sought last night, has he a plan, and if so what is it and when will he enact it?*—Alexandra quickly bathed, letting her hair dry on its own, and dressed in a loose-fitting gown to hide her slight but noticeably convex abdomen, and headed out the door for the short walk to the church.

By this time, of course, Darnell had thrown himself together and run hastily up the stairs to Lady Barnard's quarters. His boots he held in his hands as he ascended the staircase, bending over to pull them onto his feet only after knocking on her door. And that is how Lady Barnard found him when she opened it. Sheepishly looking up at her with purple-lidded bloodshot eyes, he apologized a second time—this one he'd taken a few harried moments to prepare, knowing he would have her ire to soften.

"My Lady, I do deeply regret my delay this morning," Darnell uttered quickly from memory. "Not the least because I have missed several moments when I could have beheld your radiant loveliness. Forgive me if I speak inappropriately, but never before in my years of service to you have I seen you more captivating. Surely no angel attending to our risen Saviour is as exquisite."

Though blatant flattery, Darnell's words did have their intended effect, as Lady Barnard's expression relaxed into a smile. She was well-pleased that he found her attractive, though her ambitions this day went beyond the dutiful praises of the house servant. She wanted—needed—the attentions of, to her mind, *a man who knows about lovemaking; a man who has sampled widely and will show me why the wash girl should smile so sweetly when he pays her a visit.* That man was the stable hand, whom she still did not know by name. Yet soon that would change. Lady Barnard would see to that.

"Thank you, Darnell," she replied to him. "Now you are ready and so handsome, let us make haste for church."

They descended the stairs, he on her right, holding her hand at shoulder level to steady her while she used her left hand to hold up the bottom of her dress. For Darnell, despite the throbbing pain in his head, this was a moment of courage and triumph. The former, because of what he risked in defying Lord Barnard's explicit orders. The latter, because the oft-ridiculed house servant, so long all but emasculated by the unfair comparison to his Adonisian rival, had now the most well-known and mysterious lady in Lancashire county on his hand and by his side on this most special of days.

As soon as they reached the front porch, Lady Barnard could see the citizenry gathering in the street. She was eager to join them and all but pulled Darnell down the front steps with her. As they walked into town, Lady Barnard was entranced by the sight of so many people arrayed in their finery—or what passed for it, as few had the means to bedeck themselves in the elegant fabrics and jewels she had donned—and talking and laughing gaily in the morning sun.

They seemed to her like a bouquet of butterflies flitting and fluttering about. And when she passed through a throng, they scattered aside, not only in deference to her title, but also in awe of her clothing and overall appearance. It reminded her of how she would run through a flock of birds as a child and delight in how they would flee from her waving arms and stomping feet, then she would beckon them back to her by spreading handfuls of her father's grain on the ground.

This was what Lady Barnard had yearned for and needed. She was among the people, she had their attention, and they were both pleasantly surprised and soundly impressed by her beauty. Of course, this satisfied Darnell's wishes as well, and in spite of the pain and nausea that wracked his insides he held his chin high with rare feelings of pride and self-satisfaction.

For Lady Barnard, however, this was just the beginning of satisfaction. Her true desire was not to be above the crowd—separate from it, as she had been before—but truly to be part of it. And so she tried, a bit awkwardly at first, to converse with them, to wish them a good holiday, to compliment the better of the bonnets and dresses that she saw.

The Grave and the Gay

The result was more rewarding than she could have anticipated. The townspeople, sufficiently delighted at merely the rare sighting of her, were positively entranced to learn that she was open, kind, and curious. More of them crowded around her, slowing her progress to the church. Not a few noted that her demeanor, so different from past years, was all the more engaging now without the presence of her husband, a man many respected but for whom few felt affection—or even really knew. Their indifference to him had never quite been directed with the same fervor at Lady Barnard, partly out of pity for her, partly because not enough was known of her to form an opinion.

In truth, no one in the town had much direct contact with her, if any at all. The man on her arm this day, Darnell the house servant, was for all intents and purposes her agent in the village. He ran almost all of her errands, and communicated her requests to various vendors. The people did not think much of the fact that Darnell was her escort to church—many had heard that Lord Barnard was off on a hunting trip (though none knew he had prohibited his wife from leaving the house) and, after all, a servant does what a servant is commanded to do—though Darnell imagined that his stock among the people with whom he dealt daily rose significantly by virtue of his being seen with her in public.

Though she was impatient to actually get to the church for Easter Mass, Lady Barnard was only too happy to indulge her newfound admirers and she radiated pure pleasure at their close company. Darnell, however, took it as his responsibility to ensure that the primary objective was achieved, and begged the crowd to move along so that all may begin the holiday commemoration. Thus, their pace accelerated and soon the church, from steeple to steps, rose into view.

The church was set up on an elevation flanked by a dense grove of pine trees. The ornate mahogany doors and stained glass windows were imported from Italy (through connections of Lord Barnard's father, who also contributed a significant share of their cost), but the parishioners were proud to have done most of the construction themselves. The elder Barnard, in fact, had fashioned a number of the pews himself using the adjacent supply of pine.

The front lawn of the church was of a sufficiently low grade that it was easy to walk up to the entrance from the street. Lush green and clear of the towering trees that brought shade to the other sides of the structure, the grounds were a popular site for picnics and games. And if Reverend Collins noticed that there were more than a few who came often for recreation and rarely or never for spiritual reflection, he was heartened that they at least had come to pass their time on sacred ground.

When Darnell and Lady Barnard entered the church, they continued to attract the stares of the congregation. Swiftly, they walked towards the front pew. As they approached it, a man sitting on the end arose and offered the lady and her escort his seat. It was Matty, and he smiled and bowed at Lady Barnard with his most affecting expression. Her heart fell out of its rhythm momentarily and she nearly gasped at finally seeing from less than an arm's length away the man about whom she had fantasized. Recovering her composure, she nodded to Matty and proceeded forward into the pew. Darnell, at her side, came after, greeting Matty with a thinly veiled sneer.

When was the last time that damned Matty came to church on time, he wondered, *and when had he ever sat so close to the Virgin (or any virgin)?*

Indeed, having sacrificed his seat, Matty moved to the rear of the church. Lady Barnard turned to watch him walk away. Without removing her eyes from his departing backside, she leaned towards Darnell and inquired, "What is that man's name?"

"That is Matthew Musgrave, who minds Lord Barnard's horses," he replied, not without a trace of derision in his voice. "He is called Matty. I hope he has not tracked in straw that may soil your clothing."

Lady Barnard nodded with a wisp of a smile upon her lips. She might have turned back to steal another look at the object of her longing, but the choir launched into a hymn she only faintly heard as her attention turned inward to the theatre of her imagination, where the curtains were slowly opening.

Darnell looked around, saw Alexandra sitting off to the side, slightly apart from the others in her pew. *At least she is not sitting with Matty*, he thought. He had the sensation, real or imagined he couldn't tell, of Matty staring at him from the rear of the church.

Darnell wished he could remember more of what transpired the night before, particularly what he might have said while intoxicated. He suddenly felt very vulnerable and thought it ironic that he seemed to feel so much more secure on the street than he did here in church.

CHAPTER 13

Unbeknownst to both Darnell and Lady Barnard, Matty had left the church after giving up his seat. He had intended all along to make her acquaintance before the service commenced, and in fact had grown concerned when they were late in arriving. He was afraid both that he would miss his opportunity to make her introduction, and that he would be forced to endure the entire service from the front pew.

Fortunately, they arrived in time for him to make a quick impression and exit. He acknowledged, as he stepped aimlessly about the green lawn outside the church, that it likely was his fault they were tardy. Surely Darnell could have used a full day of rest after his rare evening of revelry. Matty smiled at the picture in his mind of Darnell, intoxicated to the point of unconsciousness, being flung onto his bed like a sack of soiled laundry.

He was pleased that his plan thus far was working perfectly. The first point had been accomplished last night: he learned how best to betray Lord Barnard. The second, getting the attention of Lady Barnard, was just realized. The third had to wait for the conclusion of the church service. He would be sure to stand in the open, so that when Lady Barnard walked out she would be able to find him easily.

As he stood looking at the door of the church, he was surprised to see it suddenly swing open. The service surely would not end until the sun was directly overhead. Indeed, it was not the entire congregation leaving the church, but just one person. It was Alexandra, her head down, her step brisk—though seemingly in discomfort rather than in simple haste.

"Ho there," Matty called out, not too loudly. Alexandra stopped and looked up. She was not pleased to be spied, as she had tried to leave discreetly, but was relieved that it was only Matty. Still, she was not in a mood to speak. The service had made her surprisingly emotional, and she felt somehow exposed sitting there among the townspeople. She wished to be alone until this sensitivity, this fragility, had lapsed.

"Oh, hello, Matty," she replied gamely. "How odd to find you not in church."

"Quite odder to see you sneak out of it early, Alexandra," he replied. "Are you not well?"

"Just a bit uncomfortable, that's all. Thought the fresh air would revive me."

"I hope it does," said Matty. "But as you have previously suggested to me, sometimes speech also can cure ills. You have been ailing for some time now, yet you have never revealed to me what is the cause."

"In due time, my dear friend," Alexandra replied. "I promise you that I have no fatal affliction. All I require is some rest." She turned to walk away but Matty continued to engage her.

"Have I done something wrong to you, Alexandra?"

She stopped, spun back slowly to face her fair questioner, and smiled wistfully. "No, dear Matty. You have never done anything to me that I did not desire you to do. There will be a time, soon, when I will tell you what is going on with me. At that time, all I'll need from you is the affection and the respect you have always shown me. But for now, I simply need to rest."

With that, she reached up to kiss his cheek, then they embraced. As Alexandra turned and walked away, resuming her original pace, Matty was left confused and concerned. He had thought she was cross at him and was relieved to find it was not so. Whatever the issue, it would have to wait as she clearly had no desire to take up the matter with him this day, and he had the rest of his plan to execute. So he continued to pace the lawn and waited for the great brass bell to ring and the doors to open.

After a time, the sun having risen nearly to its zenith, the doors did open, though the bell had yet to sound. Matty saw it was a group of about a dozen gents who slipped out quietly and trotted to the pine trees by the side of the church. There, they pulled out a number of sacks that had been stashed behind trees and began emptying their contents onto the ground. They appeared to be costumes and props.

Matty smiled as he knew that these were the pace-eggers, preparing to provide their entertainment in the street once it became filled with the villagers leaving the church. He recognized most of them; in fact it was the tavern keeper Richardson himself who was donning the guise of the Old Tosspot. This, of course, was the role Quentin was to have played before Lord Barnard hired him away for the present hunting trip.

Watching the players attempt to get themselves in order, a motley lot indeed, he could not help but think of his friend. He wondered what was transpiring out in the forest; what might have been discussed, decided, or done. He would have to speak with Quentin immediately upon their return, for no other person except Alexandra did he trust so well.

Quentin would give me a true account, he thought. *He also would have been a valuable source of counsel in my current undertaking.*

Kicking his toe into the soft verdant ground, Matty thought again about living in the woods where the men now hunted.

Would Alexandra ever go with me there, to live a life even less comfortable than the one she now endures? Could she bear a life with me at all? Either before today, or after?

His thoughts were broken by the pace-eggers, who took positions just behind him and to the left. He didn't want to be lost in the crowd that would assemble around them, so he moved farther off to the right. Just then, the church bell rang and the doors opened. Lady Barnard and Darnell, being in the front row, were among the last to leave, and in spite of Matty's attempts to be slightly apart from his fellow citizens, he was well-ensconced by the crowd by the time he spied the mismatched pair.

Matty began to navigate through the crowd to get near to them, yet Darnell saw his approach and tried to direct Lady Barnard away. She protested, however, as Lord Barnard had always insisted on a hasty exit in the past. Buoyed by the reception she enjoyed as she walked towards the church, she was in no hurry to get back to the gaol in which she lived.

Further, she intended to meet up with Matty and looked for him, not knowing he had her in his sights already.

Darnell was left with no option save to attempt to intercept Matty, but he was no match for the stable hand's determined stride into Lady Barnard's company. Matty bowed once more to her, finally addressing her directly.

"Lady Barnard, may I say what a privilege it is to see you on this most joyous day. I've never seen a bonnet to match yours, nor a lovelier face for it to adorn."

Lady Barnard smiled and blushed, then forcibly removed her pleasure from her face. "You are called Matthew, is that not so?" she asked with an air of nobility she had rarely displayed before, and could barely pass off as genuine.

"By my friends I am known as Matty, and I am your grateful servant, my lady," Matty replied.

Darnell began to interject, but was cut off by the pace-eggers, who announced that their production was about to start. Lady Barnard inquired to Matty what was to come, but Darnell quickly answered instead.

"It is a coarse and farcical presentation, Lady Barnard," said Darnell, "quite beneath the standards of someone of your taste and stature. Perhaps now would be an appropriate time to return to the house."

Darnell not only wanted to keep Lady Barnard from Matty, he also was concerned about Lord Barnard returning early to find the house vacant. He had tempted chance sufficiently just to bring her to church, and the reward having been worth the risk thus far, he was eager to mitigate the very real chance that his luck—and his livelihood—may soon run out.

"No, I should like to see it," said Lady Barnard. "Matty, will you stand with us to watch this play?"

"I should be delighted," he answered, and took his place on her right side. "Hear now, they will start with a tune, introducing each character in kind. Watch this rascal here with the needled tail. He'll give you more than a scratch if you've not some coins or eggs to give him."

Lady Barnard laughed and stared with eyes agape as the players took their places, and presently fiddle, whistle, and drum combined with voices into song:

Here's one, two, three jolly lads all in one mind
We have come a pace-egging and we hope you'll prove kind
We hope you'll prove kind with your eggs and strong beer
For we'll come no more nigh you until the next year

And the first that comes in is Lord Nelson you'll see
With a bunch of blue ribbons tied round by his knee
And a star on his breast that like silver do shine
And I hope he remembers it's pace-egging time

And the next that comes in, it is Lord Collingwood
He fought with Lord Nelson till he shed his blood
And he's come from the sea old England to view
And he's come a pace-egging with all of his crew

The next that comes in is our Jolly Jack Tar
He sailed with Lord Nelson all through the last war
He's arrived from the sea, old England to view
And he's come a pace-egging with our jovial crew

The next that comes in is old miser Brownbags
For fear of her money she wears her old rags
She's gold and she's silver all laid up in store
And she's come a pace-egging in hopes to get more

And the last to come in is Old Tosspot, you see
He's a valiant old man and in every degree
He's a valiant old man and he wears a pigtail
And all his delight is a-drinking mulled ale

Come both ladies gay and dear sirs so refined
Put your hands in your pockets if you're of the mind
Put your hands in your pockets and treat us all right
If you give naught, we'll take naught, farewell and good night

If you can drink one glass, then we can drink two
Here's a health to Victoria, the same unto you
Mind what you're doing and see that all's right
If you give naught, we'll take naught, farewell and good night!

Lady Barnard delighted in each successive character more than the one who'd come before. To Darnell's consternation, she and Matty laughed together, pointing at the players' fantastic antics. When Old Tosspot Richardson came around with a pail for favors, Lady Barnard—well warned about his sharp tail yet happy to pay for such spirited entertainment—scampered about herself, looking for something to give. Though she was the wealthiest person in attendance this day, without her husband beside her it was not appropriate for her to carry money.

Darnell, with neither a will to give nor anything to offer, had backed up a few steps to avoid being struck should Old Tosspot wield his weapon. Matty, better prepared and intent on impressing, had kept a couple of pence in his pocket, which he casually and accurately pitched into the pail. Refusing to be excused, Lady Barnard settled on the only thing of value besides her jewelry with which she could part: her bonnet. She held it out to Old Tosspot, who accepted it with a deep bow and delighted the crowd by donning it himself.

Within a few minutes, the entire crowd had been solicited, the eggs and coins collected, and all had escaped being pricked. The townspeople began to scatter, as holiday lunches were ready to be served. Darnell stepped forward to take Lady Barnard's arm, yet was rebuffed.

"Thank you, no, Darnell," said Lady Barnard. "I wish to discuss some matters with Matty." She laughed at her unintentional play on words, and enjoyed saying his name. "I shall see you later back at the house."

Darnell began to protest, but realized he had no argument. "As you desire, Lady Barnard," he said quietly.

Lady Barnard addressed Matty next. "The noonday sun is hot, Matty, and without my bonnet my head feels afire. May we sit under those trees?" She pointed to the pines where the pace-eggers, now on their way to the next village, had earlier assembled their costumes and props.

"Let me lead the way, Lady Barnard," said Matty. As they walked together towards the trees, neither noticed that Darnell, having started down the road towards the Barnards' home, had turned back and walked around the rear of the church, emerging near the spot where Matty and Lady Barnard sat. Matty removed his jacket and laid it on the ground so that Lady Barnard could sit without soiling her dress. Staying out of sight, Darnell tried to listen to their conversation.

"I have noticed you in the yard, Matty. Yet I don't know why I haven't met you until now."

"Where I work is not a place for such a fair one as yourself," Matty responded. "The horses are lovely, yet their smell is offensive. Quite unlike you, my lady, whose perfume is as delightful as her face."

Another smile, another blush, but an air of vulnerability now served to color her words. "Matty, I have been inspired by the season to begin my life anew. I want to dissolve the habits and routines that have kept me from truly experiencing the joys of living. There are things I've only begun to feel and I want to know them fully realized, rather than as fantasies in my imagination. Do you understand my meaning?"

"If the honor of sitting alone with you is part of this process of renewal, then I wholeheartedly support your efforts," said Matty. "I have often seen you in the window looking out"—at this Lady Barnard dropped her head, feeling exposed and embarrassed—"but never could I have imagined your true beauty until I met you today face to face."

"I dare say I have never been so bold, Matty, but my desire is great and my time is short. As you know, I could order you to do what I command, but I prefer to ask you as a favor. Matty, I should like to be alone with you this evening. In my home, in my quarters. In my bed. I know very little about what goes on in this town, but I know you are well versed in the practice of…of…intimate relations." A pause and a swallow. "I want you to do that with me."

To Matty, this was almost beyond comprehension. Lady Barnard was doing his scheming for him. He had planned to use all his powers of romantic persuasion to try to bed Lady Barnard, and here she was all but throwing herself at him with lustful abandon. It was almost as if someone were laying a trap for him, yet his intention was to be snared anyway, so what could it matter should it be true? Still, it was important to ensure her consent, so he decided to parry with some of the mild protestations he so often had successfully fended off himself.

"Lady Barnard, your request is so grand it should be sufficient to satisfy all my dreams and desires. But surely, you are Lord Barnard's wife, as the ring on your finger—", and with that Matty saw that Lady Barnard's ring finger was barren. "Well," Matty continued, "as you are Lord Barnard's wife, surely it wouldn't do for a stable hand to be seen accompanying you into your house."

"Matty, just as well as you know that I am Lord Barnard's wife, you know that Lord Barnard is not at home. Nor is he expected for another day. Furthermore, it is common knowledge that Lord Barnard favors you and has had you in our home many times. So you will know where to find me. The only remaining concern is when. Surely evening would be better, yet not too late for I will need time to make sure all is right in the house before morning. When you count three stars in the sky, come to the rear door. It will be unlocked and no other servants will be about. Are we agreed?"

Matty smiled, took her hand, and gently kissed it. Then he rose and helped her to her feet. He picked up his jacket and brushed the dirt and grass from the cloth. "My lady, I will do everything in my power to make this night one you will long remember. May I now escort you home?"

Lady Barnard made a small curtsy and held up her hand, awaiting his arm. Together they began walking towards the Barnard residence. When they had traveled out of view, Darnell emerged from his hiding place in the wood. He had not heard everything—was not close enough and his head still hurt from the night before—yet he had heard sufficiently to be shocked and appalled. His long resentment of Matty, so briefly transformed into a bemused tolerance, was instantly inflamed into a searing hatred. His ire caused him to tremble and he threw himself to the ground in a bitter stew of anger, hurt, and a blistering desire for revenge.

After a few moments, his emotions had peaked and he was soon capable again of rational thought. He knew what he must do, and it not only was his duty as Lord Barnard's trusted servant, but also the ultimate strategic assault in his long, losing war with Matty, the thing that would be most likely to earn him the spoils he sought: a higher position among the Barnards, a greater reputation among the citizenry, and most important of all, Alexandra and her baby. Yes, he knew what he must do.

I must find Lord Barnard and tell him about this horrific conspiracy. That surely will prove the end of Matty's tenure in the village. But what about Lady Barnard? She will be hurt as well. Yet she, too, has betrayed me, used me to get to that detestable rogue. She, too, is guilty. She, too, must suffer.

However, Darnell was not a rider—even if he were, to get a horse he would have to get one from Matty, which would be impossible (and a complication Lord Barnard could not have foreseen when he instructed Darnell to ride to him). Therefore, to get to the hunting party in time for them to ride back into town and catch the would-be lovers in the act, he would have to run, walk, and swim as fast as possible.

This, then, is my test, he thought. *But first I must change into clothes more appropriate for athletics and eat something to give me energy.*

Darnell then rose and headed quickly back to his room in the cellar of the Barnards' house. Once there, he opened a small icebox and took out half a loaf of bread and a block of cheese and placed them on his table. He filled a skin with water, then removed his Easter clothing. Donned whilst in a pained panic, his wardrobe had seemed like royal robes as he and Lady Barnard traveled to church. Now, they lay hastily strewn in a pile on the floor, ill-suited to the task that awaited him.

Darnell dressed in lighter pants and a woven wheat-colored shirt. He replaced his finest shoes with worn leather boots cut low below his calves. He stuffed a handkerchief in his pocket and quickly tore off pieces of bread and chunks of cheese. He ate noisily and with as little contentment in the flavor as he felt about the recent events.

While he chewed, Darnell rehearsed what he would say to Lord Barnard, knew he would have to speak quickly and clearly, and with such urgency that his master would not think to question him about whether Lady Barnard had been to church. If he did, Darnell knew he would have to construct a story that absolved himself of all blame.

Not that he was unwilling to accept any consequences for his role in breaking Lord Barnard's rule, but it was more important that Matty be disciplined. He assumed that Lord Barnard would ultimately feel obligated to reward him for revealing this plot. And even if not, even if Darnell's loyalty only tempered the severe decree his master would issue him for taking Lady Barnard to church against his orders, with Matty gone at last Darnell knew he could more easily endure Lord Barnard's wrath.

The bread and cheese consumed, Darnell swallowed the contents of his skin, then refilled it and placed it over his head and onto his shoulder for the journey. Taking Quentin's hand-sketched map, he wiped his mouth, shook crumbs off his clothing, and drew a deep breath, visualizing the challenging journey that awaited him. Finally, the loyal house servant left his dark quarters and set off at the sun's height for the deep woods.

CHAPTER 14

After Lord Barnard shot the hare, Quentin killed two more and the men walked back to the camp in silence. As before, each indulged the comfort and company of his own individual thoughts.

Quentin was consumed with concern for Matty and wished he could leave the hunting party and ride back into town to warn his friend about what had transpired. He would gladly conspire with him on a plan of escape. Quentin knew the forests bordering the town, and some well beyond, better than anyone he knew. He could help to provision and protect the man who once had saved his life. If only there was a way to reach Matty before Lord Barnard returned. Yet that would call for potentially drastic measures he wasn't comfortable undertaking, at least not until he had had a chance to speak with Matty himself.

As for Lord Barnard, he was wading within two streams of thoughts: one, of course, involving Matty and how he would begin his tutelage and thereby transform the rough-hewn stable hand into a gentleman as respectable in his comportment as he was fair in his features. The other stream involved his wife. If his orders were being heeded, she would be in the house while the townspeople, having survived Reverend Collins' judgmental harangues, would take in their inane entertainment in the village square. He fully intended to hold Darnell responsible should she venture outside, though surely there should be a severe punishment for her as well, if indeed she dared to flout his authority.

Lord Barnard had long assumed that he would grow to love his wife, and that they would have more successful and productive relations. Instead, he found her increasingly withdrawn, unresponsive, and bitter. Though he knew she was attractive, and was at heart a kind person, he did not enjoy being in her company; did not know, perhaps, how to engage with her socially. She knew nothing of his work and his interests, and he never thought to inquire about hers.

The plain fact, which he perhaps could not acknowledge or articulate, was that Lord Barnard simply preferred to be alone. Having largely been left by his childhood peers to amuse himself, he had never fully developed the attributes of empathy and patience that true friendships require. The one time he came closest to having such a relationship—with Peter Williams—fate callously took it away from him.

It was not all his wife's fault, he knew. But this was their life together and though it be unsatisfactory, it was something they, each in his or her own way, had to endure. Thus, Lady Barnard remained his wife largely because a nobleman requires a wife and she at least was compliant, generally being as invisible as he wished her to be. Yet lately she had seemed even less content, more complaining than was her wont, which is why he was concerned, for the first time really, that she would defy his order and go to church. Was this prescience or paranoia, of which Finster had once accused him when his client spoke of his distrust of the citizenry and their presumed gossip about him?

Well, he reasoned to himself as they reached the camp, *it is Easter morning and I should know some short time after we have consumed breakfast whether or not my orders have been obeyed—assuming, of course, that Darnell comes without delay as instructed.*

Quentin stoked the fire and prepared the hares. Using his sharpest knife, he removed the heads and feet, then made a slit in the belly and carefully cut around the midsection. With a tug, he removed half the animal's pelt over its hind legs, finally cutting off the tail to separate the fur from the rear. Then he turned the carcass around and did the same with the front half of the pelt. (Only Lord Barnard observed Quentin's skilled work, the others being put off by the blood.)

Reclaiming his knife, Quentin gutted the hares, pulling out the innards. Before bringing the stripped, disemboweled animals to the stream to wash them, he dug a hole about fifty paces away from the camp in which to bury the heads, feet, skin, and organs. Then he washed the carcasses in the stream, peeling off bits of silver skin and tossing them into the water.

Back at the fire, Quentin placed a grid of live, wet branches over the fire and laid the hares on top. They took long enough to cook for the men to regain their appetite and enjoy the fresh, tasty meat. After the meal was finished, the bones were placed in the hole Quentin had dug and the men went to bathe in the stream. With no sight nor sound of Darnell noted by any of the party, Lord Barnard finally had reason to believe that all was well. In fact, Darnell's absence so pleased him—for numerous reasons— that he vowed to make the most of their last full day in the forest. He suggested that they venture deeper into the woods in search of larger game, and asked Quentin to lead the way.

Quentin was uneasy about going farther away from town when what he most wanted to do was to get back at once. Yet he had no choice so, standing on the grassy hill where Lord Barnard and Finster had consummated their legal *coup d'corpse*, as it were, he raised a spyglass to the green depths that lay before them. Quentin saw that in one direction they could reach a clearing only about half as far from their camp as their camp was to the town. From there they would have good visibility. He could lead them there by a circuitous route, making it seem farther than it actually was in the event he was able to escape. He would then take the more direct route back and be able to place distance between himself and the others so as to reach Matty first.

Quentin got supplies and ammunition together, and organized the men for the trek.

For her part, Lady Barnard returned home breathless and burning with anticipation. She did not believe she could wait until Matty arrived. She could not, in fact, believe the day had gone so harmonious with her desires. Never had she conceived such a complete plan of action and executed it so well. She boldly and confidently walked the streets of the town, gathered a crowd and kept them with her beauty and charm, and also succeeded in attracting the attention of the handsome stable hand. From one perspective, the hardest part of her strategy had already been completed.

And yet, the consummation of her plan would, she knew, in fact be the most difficult. For she, who had long experienced lovemaking to be a monotonous duty, would be paired with one expert in the full palette of sexual hues that only a true artist would know how to apply. She feared her inexperience and lack of sophistication would show, that she would not know how to please a man who had been with so many knowing and vivacious maidens.

Though I arranged this tryst through the influence of my power over Matty, she acknowledged, *I know that once in bed, I will be the servant and he the master.*

In any event, her concerns and fears only heightened her excitement and impatience, for this evening she would feel the pleasures of the flesh as never before. She would experience a reawakening of herself as a woman, as a person capable and deserving of giving and receiving carnal joy.

I will at last know what other women experience, what all—most—men desire, what has been kept from me for all these years.

From the heat of the day and that which she felt from within, she was fairly drenched and so she drew her own bath—how she loved being alone at last! It was hard work heating well water in the laundry cauldron and bringing bucketfuls up the stairs to fill her footed porcelain tub, yet when she finally disrobed and penetrated the clear, steaming water, the reward was more than sufficient to justify the effort.

Lady Barnard did not bring a cake of soap or a brush. She simply reclined in the tub, let her head fall back, half her hair falling in the water and half draping over the side, and let herself be consumed by liquid. She felt light—*Even my breasts are floating!*—clean, and pure. She imagined herself a fish, gently propelling herself along with graceful and fluid movements. She was smooth, colorful, curious. No longer was she Lady Barnard; rather, she was the woman she was before she married Lord Barnard. She was, simply, Mary. Her eyes were closed. Her body was wet. Her heart was full. She remained in the tub until she became cold. Then she rose, dried her body, applied perfume and powder, donned a robe, and waited for the sun to set. Waited for Matty.

Unlike Lady Barnard—unlike even himself—Matty was anxious. Sitting on a bench in the stable, he felt an odd uncertainty. It all had gone so well thus far. *Could my luck continue?* he wondered. The only task still awaiting him was one he was exceptionally adept at, one he enjoyed and experienced more than most. Yet it always was an activity he had initiated with someone who had captured his fancy. Lady Barnard was certainly an attractive woman for her age, had all the finest clothes, jewelry, and perfumes to enhance her appeal. But she was no rugged beauty like Alexandra, nor had she a face or a figure the likes of which he had been drawn to and had frequently pursued in this and other villages.

Still, pleasure is not the goal of this love act to come, Matty assured himself. *All that was important was that the act should occur. And that Lord Barnard should soon learn of it.*

Oh yes, Matty was well aware that Darnell was within earshot of his conversation with Lady Barnard after the pace-eggers had left the square. He knew that Darnell would be loyal to Lord Barnard if for no other reason than it would serve to eliminate the stone in his boot that Matty so enjoyed being. He could envision Darnell meeting Lord Barnard at the door as he always would, then requesting a private audience with which to address an urgent issue. Matty would wait in the stable with a saddlebag packed for Lord Barnard to come out and banish him. He would leave word for Quentin to meet him in the woods and help him get settled. He would stay there a month or so until the talk ebbed. Then he would send for Alexandra. And then?

Another town, another life, another new beginning. Just as before and, who knows, as it may one day be again.

He did not want to leave the village, but could not bear to stay as Lord Barnard's son. He did not even want to hurt or disappoint Lord Barnard, but he knew he could not reason with him nor argue his desire away.

I have no position from which to fight, and no will merely to run away and risk capture, Matty acknowledged. *I will not resort to violence, but neither will I be cowardly or complacent.*

What he could do—would do—is to be the rogue his reputation had insisted he be. In that way, Lord Barnard would be confronted with and forced to admit the folly of his scheme. To save face, he would have no other choice but to send Matty away.

Perhaps it would even prove beneficial for all involved. Matty might inspire Lady Barnard to improve the quality and frequency of her lovemaking with her husband. Perhaps they would be able to conceive their own child, which surely would be preferable to adopting a full-grown man and posing as if he were their true offspring. Darnell would be better off without Matty, maybe even Alexandra would, too, if she chose not to join him in exile.

Maybe the change, the chance to be alone, would be good for me as well, he thought. *Maybe a new beginning was needed by all, and by fate it was left to me to orchestrate the renewal, to set these transformations in motion.*

Contemplating that this all was necessary and that he had no choice but to serve fate's decree, Matty began to feel less anxious. He had a job to do for which he was uniquely well-suited. And believing that this would be his final conquest in the town, he decided it should be enjoyed to the fullest. He thought again about Lady Barnard, that perhaps there was something appealing about the vulnerability she barely could conceal behind the façade of her presumed power, something irresistible about this particular trophy, to bed the wealthiest woman around, his employer no less, while her husband hunts game less than half a day's ride away. And as he saw her fair features in his mind, his pulse quickened, and he began to wish away the moments that stood between his growing desire and its eventual fulfillment.

No place in his mind just then was Alexandra and her mysterious ailment. Yet she was in mind of him. Having left church early in haste, she went directly to the pond where Matty liked to bathe. Sitting on the edge of the water, she watched as gulls and hawks flew low over the flat, glistening surface looking for the perch and lake trout that called this serene body of fresh water home.

The pond was not a place Alexandra came to often by herself, other than to fetch water for the wash when the Barnards' pump was in need of repair. Matty tried a number of times to entice her into the water with him, yet she always refused. As a girl, she had seen a playmate drown in such a pond. She remembered seeing her face when she was taken from the water. It was blue, the mouth agape, her expression frozen in a state of surprise. *At what,* Alexandra wondered for days. Since then, she had never gone into a body of water deeper than her finely formed calves—though she did occasionally enjoy watching an unclothed Matty swim.

Staring at the pond, she thought of her baby, who, like her childhood friend, was completely immersed in water. The thought of it frightened Alexandra, more than the pond itself threatened her own sense of well-being. The prospect of having a baby had concerned but not pained her. Now, the very idea, the sickening image, of a dead baby inside of her brought forth a wave of nausea. She closed her eyes and drew a deep, slow breath. The feeling departed, though she kept her eyes shut, desperately seeking to regain control of her senses.

Now she tried to imagine her baby again; not dead, asphyxiated by fluid inside her body, but rather alive and outside of her. She had done this before, of course, but now, for the first time, she continued to feel a dread. Would this child's father claim patrimony? Would another man love the child as his own? Would she be able to bear the stares and the gossip of the ladies of the town? Would the child grow to feel wanted and accepted, both in its home and in its community?

Alexandra began to despair. She opened her eyes and looked again at the pond. It was still. Not a ripple, nor a bubble. No fish kissed the surface, no birds pecked the barrier where the air gave way to water. She looked around her. Rocks, sticks, greenery. She had heard of an herb that a woman could chew if she wanted to end her pregnancy. There were a variety of plants growing at the shore near her. She grabbed a few, tore them desperately from their stems, and stuffed them into her mouth. She chewed quickly, but they were bitter and she gagged. Most of what she had tried to eat came out.

Now came the tears. Water again, this time coming out of her eyes, running down her face, dropping to the ground. They were the first she had shed. And the last she would allow. She was not, after all, a helpless victim. Would never permit herself to be one, nor to feel as one.

I carry inside of my body a life, and if that is a large responsibility—and surely it is that—then I will have to be as large, if not more so, she commanded herself.

If for whatever reason she never saw Matty again, his presence would still be palpable within her child. She would draw strength from such reminders of him, even as she lent her own to her baby.

There is a reason this has happened, she was convinced. *I must be equal to the challenges that await. I owe it to myself. To my baby. To Matty.*

She rose and walked back to her cousin's house to rest. The holiday would soon be over, and tomorrow there would be fresh washing to do.

CHAPTER 15

Darnell was lean in body, but no athlete. The midday sun and the weight of his skin of water bore heavily on him as first he ran, then, breathless and perspiring, slowed his pace to an urgent walk. Twice before he reached the edge of the woods he stopped to drink. After the second time, upon resuming his pursuit of the party he developed a cramp in his side. The pain was sharp, as if a colt unwilling to be shod struck him with its hoof. Again he stopped, wiping his face with his handkerchief. Soon he would be covered by the forest's canopy; the cool, moist, mossy air would comfort him. That thought, and the importance of his mission, drew him forward once more.

His mission, in effect and in truth, was to bring down his enemy. Darnell knew he could never defeat Matty in terms of physical force, or of beauty or personality. Instead, he would leverage his own strengths, among them responsibility, propriety, loyalty.

Surely Alexandra can understand that these qualities are the more important, he assured himself. *Particularly now, in her present situation, needing as she does a reliable man who would be a faithful husband with stable employment.*

Darnell laughed to himself at his inadvertent pun on "stable."

At the very least, he thought, *the child wouldn't have to grow up with a father who smelled of horse dung. How fair Alexandra could desire someone who worked with horses is beyond my powers of comprehension.*

In truth, Darnell was rather afraid of the beasts, a trait he knew he shared with Lady Barnard. She, too, would be injured by his mission. But so be it. He'd indulged his fantasy of having her on his arm, and had done so at considerable risk. He owed her nothing and in reality there was no chance of her ever giving herself to him. Darnell's choice was clear, and his chance was now.

By eliminating Matty, I am almost assured of having Alexandra. He pressed on.

The forest terrain grew more uneven now. He tripped on thick cords of roots that lay tangled among the carpet of half-decomposed mahogany-colored leaves. Branches tugged at his clothing and scratched his cheeks. The sameness of the scenery—greens and browns, everywhere greens and browns—made him disoriented. Though Darnell had verbal directions and a hastily sketched map to guide him, he grew unsure of the way. He looked up to the sky to gauge the position of the sun, to find an afternoon star, yet it was a futile effort as he was ignorant of how to navigate by celestial points.

Darnell brought his gaze down again. Before him, a steep rise. The quill-and-ink lines on the map held no topographic information. Had they taken this hill? Could horses climb such a grade? Was it even so steep as it appeared, or was his weariness and uncertainty generating unfounded doubts?

At his feet, a long stick. Darnell bent down for it, holding it vertical in front of him. The tip reached his collarbone. He would use the stick to provide balance and leverage as he climbed the hill. It seemed to work. Darnell was surprised to find the going none too strenuous. At the highest point he was able to see his position with greater clarity and perspective. In fact, the ground did not slope down much at all on the other side. Where he had been before was not the true level earth, but rather a low-lying valley. From his new vantage point, Darnell had a better view of the landscape and a surer sense of his footing.

He moved ahead.

By the angle of the sun's rays through openings in the forest canopy, even Darnell could tell that the day was waning into late afternoon.

Before long, it would be dark. He would need to find the camp quickly. He stopped for another drink from his skin of water. Two gulps were all that remained. Still parched from his previous evening's alcohol consumption, it was insufficient to quench his thirst and quell the throbbing in his head. He sat down on a fallen oak to rest and think. Surely, the camp must be nearby. Darnell's head and legs ached. His back and feet were sore as well, and his clothes, soaked now with perspiration, hung heavily on his weary body.

If the camp is not near, he thought, *I am more likely to die on this very spot than ever to complete my task.*

At the nadir of his deepening despair, Darnell heard in the stillness that surrounded him the sound of water slapping gently against rocks. The stream! He reached for the map and saw the parallel horizontal squiggles that Quentin had drawn to represent the crossing. Close above it was an "X". The camp! A surge of adrenaline seemed to expand his veins and animate his limbs. Quickly he rose to his feet, and he followed his ears to the source of the luscious liquid sound. Running again, he soon saw the water, and it may as well have been the River of Jordan come to take him to freedom for the prayers of gratitude it elicited in the servant.

Finally he stood before it, almost disbelieving that he had actually reached this critical landmark on his arduous journey. Gurgling continuously with neither pause nor impatience, the stream was blissfully, peacefully oblivious to the frantic, desperately relieved form on its bank. Darnell dropped to his knees and all but thrust his head into the cool water. He cupped his hands and drank the most delightful brew he had ever been served.

Wiping his eyes and forehead, Darnell looked ahead and saw the small hill that he knew must be the site of the camp. Though he wished to remain and refresh himself longer, the target being so close he dared not delay a moment longer. He took one last drink, filled his skin with water, and then began to ford the stream, which was approximately ten horse lengths wide.

Midway across, it became deep enough to warrant a few swimming strokes. The current carried him somewhat, but he was able to maintain his direction. As he neared the other side, his sore feet—soaked and glad to be so—returned to the bottom and took him in labored strides towards and up the far bank. Again, Darnell silently expressed gratitude for the water that served him as both curative and compass.

As Darnell climbed the hill, leaves and dirt and twigs clung to his boots and legs as though he were a tree oozing sap. His profoundly improved spirits helped propel him quickly to the top where, sure enough, there was visible evidence of the camp: the rock-lined fire pit, the canvas tenting and blankets, personal effects in small, scattered piles. Yet there was no sign of Lord Barnard or the others in his party.

Perhaps they are still out hunting, he thought. He cocked his head to listen for gunfire but heard none. There was no way for him to tell how far and in which direction they had gone.

His mission was still incomplete, yet Darnell felt he had accomplished much simply by finding the camp before dark. The sun was less than a hand's breadth above the horizon.

The best thing to do is to stay here at the camp and await their return, he reasoned. In any event, he was too exhausted to search further. He laid his water skin on the ground and sat on a rock. It was hard and unfriendly.

Darnell turned to see the blankets sprawled on the ground around the fire pit. They looked far more inviting. Despite being soaking wet, he went and sat on one. He removed his boots, took off his shirt. He leaned back, supporting himself on one elbow. Soon he was lying flat.

The forest looked calm and beautiful. Darnell was pleased to have endured such an arduous adventure. He had met the demands of his test! He closed his eyes. He listened again for sounds from the party, but heard only the stream. He imagined himself lying on a raft in the middle of the stream. Birds singing, the water lapping, his breathing soft and slow. He had never felt so relaxed. He had never felt so safe. The raft floated gently downstream. Cradled by the earth, calmed by the violet sky, Darnell was at peace. And in seconds, he was asleep.

No gunshot ever awoke Darnell, for the party found nothing worth spending the powder on. There were rabbits, woodchucks, and squirrels a-plenty, to be sure, but Lord Barnard's hunger was for larger prey. He wanted a trophy, a light meal wouldn't do. Yet nothing suitable was seen.

No deer, no elk, no moose. The men rode on in hopes of finding game. Quentin was forced to go deeper into the woods than he had intended. And though it was essentially his responsibility to facilitate a successful hunt, Quentin was anxious to suggest that they cut short the day and head back to town.

Lord Barnard, however, was keen to continue. So much else had thus far gone so well that he insisted on pressing his luck. Surely a beast of some sort would spring into view. He would raise his firearm and with sure aim press the trigger. Two explosions—from the powder in his gun and from the tearing of the creature's flesh—would signify success. A third explosion, in his heart, would throw throbbing streams of blood throughout his body at the excitement of the kill.

This strange man, stranger yet when he was younger, when he was too refined and aloof for the rough play of the boys at his school, those boys who teased him, those boys he had neither the strength of body nor the resolve to fight, this strange man, now with a gun in his hands, felt strong, virile, unconquerable. It was a rare feeling and he would not release it willingly.

It was not blood that Lord Barnard was after. He loved the hunt because it produced trophies, physical proof of his manliness. The gun was his great equalizer. His wealth gave him leverage in his business relationships, but he was easily intimidated in social engagements. The unhealed scars of his youth he not only felt inside but also thought were obvious to others, as though they were a physical mark on his forehead—easy to spot and easy to disdain. But here, out in the woods, he could prove himself superior to his prey. With his intelligence and his sure trigger finger—and, of course, Quentin's keen eyes and unimpeachable instincts—he could compete, man against animal, and most times would emerge the victor.

No, to Lord Barnard a measly hare was insufficient spoils for his first hunting trip of the spring. It would never do. They must press on.

"Quentin," said he, "I have charged you with finding for us some game to hunt. Can it be there is no animal left in these woods that weighs more than my boots?"

"Surely it's quite odd, Lord Barnard," said Quentin. "Yet we have had enough for both dinner and breakfast. You supplied the latter yourself. May I suggest we call the hunt complete and head back to camp early?"

"I'll not hear of it," said Lord Barnard, "until I have shot something that stares at me with eyes as large as my own. I came to this spot to conduct some business in private and to hunt with my friends. The business has been concluded. The hunt has yet to be."

So Quentin led the party deeper into the forest, though he knew that it was getting too late in the day to find good game. He decided it would do no good to quarrel with Lord Barnard, who surely was experienced enough a hunter to come to this realization himself, once he surrendered his stubborn position. He finally did so as dusk descended, though he was unhappy about it and remained silent as they began to return to the camp.

Shrouded in a darkening veil, the day was too old, Quentin thought, to return to the village. They would have to bed down at the camp one more night and return in the morning light. Yet as they approached the high ground, the unexpected sight of Darnell's sleeping figure signaled that all was about to change.

CHAPTER 16

Matty changed. He washed himself, dressed in fresh, clean clothes. Additionally, he embraced his new attitude about the evening that awaited him. Or rather, he reclaimed anew his traditional attitude about romantic trysts. He felt bold, desirous, adventurous. He erased any lines drawn in his conscience around good and bad, right and wrong. He had composed a script that thus far had played out perfectly, and now he was ready to accept his cue to come on stage and fulfill the exciting final scene.

This is who I am, he told himself with no trace of modesty or shame. *This is what I do and I do it, as ever, for me and for my doomed brother as well.*

Leaving his room, Matty stepped behind the stable into the woods, just a few paces so as to pick some of the purple wildflowers that came up each spring. He carefully broke the stems, leaving white drops of succulence on the torn tips. Matty brought the flowers to his nose; satisfied with the scent, he walked towards the Barnards' house.

Lady Barnard, at her familiar place beside her window, sat in her silk robe and watched Matty's approach. She smiled, spying the flowers in his hand. Soon she would be the flower in his grasp. She prayed that her sight and scent would be as pleasing to him as the purple petals he now held. Her pulse accelerated, she felt the robe itself was pounding in time with her heart. Between her legs, a moist heat arose. He was nearly at the back porch, so she left the window and hurried down the stairs to meet him.

The Grave and the Gay

Halfway down, she stopped herself. She didn't want to be breathless and impatient. She was the Lady, he the servant. She must not betray her intense need, must at least feign the appearance of being in control. She took a deep breath, then saw the door handle turn. Lady Barnard elected to remain on the stairs, and struck a pose that was at once authoritative and inviting.

Matty, while crossing the yard to the Barnard house, had seen her sitting by the window. He had become accustomed to her looking at him, and had trained his upward peripheral vision to gaze back at her while appearing to look straight ahead. He could recognize a woman rabid with desire. Recalling Alexandra's testimony about the Barnards' bed sheets, he realized just how desperate Lady Barnard really must be for a man who could please her. It was just the sort of challenge on which he thrived—and just the sort of situation on which he had made his reputation.

He took the final steps to the door with the same measured pace at which he had been walking. Without hesitation, he reached for the doorknob and turned it. The last time he did so it was on the orders of Lord Barnard. Now it was on the invitation of Lady Barnard. What had Lord Barnard ever offered in return for his service? Money, of course. Some favors, gifts, food, clothing. A nice room built just for him in the rear of the stable. Useful things, to be sure, but they paled in comparison to what Lady Barnard, standing on the staircase with her right hand on the rail and her left upon her hip, was about to tender.

He is beautiful, she thought, barely able to hide the short gasp of a breath she took as he closed the door behind him. *How shall it be,* she wondered? *Shall we sit and talk for a while? Are we to go immediately to my quarters? Would he carry me there? No, I mustn't wonder. I must be in control. I must initiate what is to be.*

"I am pleased you are punctual, Matty," she said, trying desperately to disguise her lust.

"The time since last we spoke has crawled as a snail, my Lady," Matty replied. "It was all I could do not to leap into the sky and draw the sun back down with me."

Matty walked over to the stairs. He stopped at the bottom, looking up at her. With the light from the chandelier candles casting an amber glow upon her, the thin, smooth material of Lady Barnard's robe outlined her figure. Matty could see that the robe was the sum total of all the clothing she had on. His blood, too, began to race. He wanted to leap up the steps to her and have her right then and there, but he knew he needed to demonstrate caution. This was a Lady in her house, and to ensure that any shred of what was to happen might possibly be defensible, he needed her to make the first move.

"Come here, Matty," said Lady Barnard.

Matty complied, more slowly and deliberately than either of them wanted. When they were standing on the same step, she turned, her right hand releasing the rail. Matty could wait no longer and took the slight change in her stance as an invitation. He took her in his arms and kissed her, powerfully, deeply, all the while their pounding hearts—now pressed together—kept time of each exquisite moment of their embrace.

When their lips parted, Lady Barnard's whole face—from brow to chin—was moist with saliva, desire, and sweat. Over her entire body, she felt her skin was alive, pulsing, afire. She felt as though she was close to tears and her mind could not focus.

"I don't know what to say," she whispered, which was true; yet what she also was trying to express was that she did not know what to do. Matty understood and was more than ready to take control.

"Let us say nothing, nothing more," he said. "We must let our bodies speak for us to each other."

With that, Matty, emboldened fully both in his mind and in his groin, lifted Lady Barnard into his arms and carried her up the steps, the purple wildflowers falling onto the space the two lovers-to-be had occupied. Lady Barnard was sure she should faint before they reached the top of the staircase. She hugged Matty around his neck and buried her head in his chest. She was his prize yet the reward would surely be hers.

Taking the final step, Matty turned and carried Lady Barnard past the sword rack directly to her room and placed her gently on her bed. A candle she had lit and placed on a small round table by her bedside flickered its greeting.

Lady Barnard had yet to release Matty's neck and drew him down to her that they might kiss again. This time, Matty's hands glided down the outline of her body that her robe had so teasingly revealed on the stairs. She felt his hands on her shoulders first, and tiny shocks such as one felt in winter when walking on the carpet shot off throughout her being as he felt the sides of her breasts. His hands continued to her waist sloping inward, then out again at her hips and down her thighs, which she parted slightly not only in invitation but also to welcome in cooler air to offset the blazing heat that seemed to be melting her from the inside.

Matty then broke the embrace, rose, and saw the pleading and yearning in Lady Barnard's eyes. He began to remove his clothing and she watched him, her need banishing any embarrassment she might otherwise have felt. He soon stood naked before her, his blood-engorged penis jutting perpendicular from his body. In all their fumbling attempts to copulate, Lady Barnard had never seen with such clarity her husband's organ the way she now took in Matty's. Throbbing, bobbing, it seemed to have a life and will of its own. She wondered what it would do inside her. Unselfconsciously, instinctively, she spread her legs further apart.

Yet her robe was still a barrier between their bodies. Matty sat on the edge of the bed, reached over and untied the sash that kept the folds of her robe closed. Slowly, gently, he opened them, and Lady Barnard's pale nakedness glowed upon his face like a treasure revealed. Now it was his turn to gaze and Lady Barnard swore to herself that she could feel his eyes as fingers on her breasts and belly.

"I must have you," she said.

"And I you," he replied.

Matty lay beside her, on her left side, and burrowed his right arm beneath her neck. With his left hand, he traced the arc of her eyebrows, his fingertips barely brushing her skin. From there, they glided down the gentle curve of her nose, then pressed against her lips, which pursed and kissed his skilled, strong hands. With his first finger, he drew a circle around her chin, then tickled her throat, finally settling high on her chest, where the soft mounds of her breasts began. They heaved with her deep and rapid respirations, and he let them move against his open palm, occasionally bringing his fingers forward in a gentle squeeze.

He drew more circles, one on each areola. Her cinnamon nipples pointed like spires to heaven and he bent down to kiss and suck each one in turn. Lady Barnard could barely keep from shouting, such were the sensations pulsing from within her, her blood coursing like river rapids. She prayed he soon would reach her molten core, yet each slow second was agonizingly delicious.

Indeed, Matty quickened his pace and gave scant attention to her belly, nestling his fingers in the small hill of hair a hand's breadth below her navel. It was moist like morning dew, fragrant like marsh grass, and led to a warm, wet opening with thin petals splayed apart, welcoming him inside to seek its nectar. Matty's fingers explored her slick interior to their full length, taking stock of her feminine architecture, the sloping walls, deep passages, and sensitive spots in places never before sought and never before found.

Now Lady Barnard's eyes closed. Her right hand went to her mouth and she bit down hard on the meaty part of her thumb. Matty's glistening fingers led her left hand to his member, and she could feel the life surging through it. She traversed its length, gripped its girth, and marveled at the hard muscle he managed to keep hidden in his trousers.

Lady Barnard was on the edge of unconsciousness, Matty on the verge of climax. He rolled on top of her and guided his insistent sword into her sopping sheath. Lady Barnard was silent no more. Of just how she expressed herself she had no sense; it was moaned gibberish and guttural breaths that filled the room, yet all she heard was her own blood rushing through the tiny vessels in her ears.

Matty gave two gentle pokes, embedding himself halfway and withdrawing nearly fully each time; on the third thrust he plunged to the hilt. Lady Barnard's vagina took his length, smothered and embraced it, moistened it, and let it go, only to draw it back in again. Her heels rested in the pits behind his knees. She kicked him forward into her as a desperate rider drives his boot heels into a horse's ribs. Her arms squeezed his neck, pulled his hair. With his left elbow driven into the mattress to maintain his balance and position, Matty was able to reach his right hand around to pull and squeeze at her buttocks.

He, too, grunted and wheezed, yet there were more sounds emanating from the couple than those that flowed from their mouths. Her wetness was sufficient to make slurping, slapping noises with each stroke in and out. Their sweaty bellies clapped with each thrust and the bed itself seemed to squeal with delight. The primordial aroma of lovemaking wafted everywhere. Matty's pelvis pivoted more quickly, Lady Barnard's met each parry. They began pounding against each other faster and faster, then Lady Barnard thrust her buttocks off the mattress and emitted a shrill cry. Her vagina gripped Matty's penis as a milkmaid works a teat, and Matty shouted as his seed shot in rapid spurts deep into her canal.

Where once had been a chaos of movement colored by wordless grunts and breaths, now was all stillness and silence.

"Let us say nothing, nothing more," Matty had advised on the staircase. To this they remained true as they concluded their coupling. Their eyes met, their lips came together in a final, gentle kiss, and as Matty slipped out of her and off of her body, the two lovers' heartbeats began gradually to slow to their normal resting rhythms. Matty drew the coverlet over their bodies and he tenderly stroked her belly.

For the first time in her life Lady Barnard was fully satisfied, yet she was still too consumed by the aftershocks of their lovemaking to speak or show her gratitude to Matty. No matter, for within minutes the two lovers were asleep. To this extraordinary performance, there would be no encore. The act was its own reward.

CHAPTER 17

The footsteps he heard clearly enough, but were they real or a part of his dream? On the cusp of consciousness, Darnell slowly opened his eyes. Despite the dark sky in the background, he quickly understood that it was the end of a rifle he was looking into. Directly behind the weapon's black shaft he could see Quentin's squinting face. Again unsure whether this was true or illusory, he wisely chose to remain still, testing the persistence of the image by closing his eyes and opening them again.

At the same time that Darnell concluded he was indeed trapped at gunpoint, Quentin recognized the strange figure asleep at their camp site as his client's house servant. "It is Darnell, Lord Barnard," Quentin reported.

"Darnell?" Lord Barnard responded, in a voice at once shocked, irked, and concerned. He pushed his way past his friends, whose craned necks peered over Quentin's shoulders even as they kept their bodies safely behind the armed guide. From Darnell's dazed perspective, this gave Quentin the appearance of being a many-headed beast. Finally, Lord Barnard and Darnell were face to face. This was the moment at which Darnell's courage and resolve were to be most strenuously tested. Fail this test, he knew, and no other would matter.

"Well? What is it? What brings you here, and why now?" Lord Barnard's words came quickly and with rhythmic emphasis. Darnell was ill-prepared to deliver the news under such intense inquisition, yet he knew he was not to lead this conversation. Still, he managed to raise himself onto his elbows to better give himself breath and a little more space with which to speak his testimony.

"I have traveled a long, hard journey on foot to tell you urgent news regarding Lady Barnard and Matty Musgrave," Darnell began in measured tone and meter. Looking at the mute gawking faces, he added in a softer voice, "Perhaps we should speak alone."

"Out with it!" Lord Barnard commanded.

Thus chastened, Darnell continued at a more rapid pace. "I am sorry to report to you, sir, that they have conspired with each other to undertake a tryst that likely is happening at this very moment. In your own house," he added for emphasis.

Lord Barnard's eyes grew to wide white circles that the growing darkness was helpless to obscure. He plunged his arms down, grabbing Darnell's shoulders with both hands and raising his servant's upper body off its elbows. Lord Barnard stared intensely into Darnell's eyes as if they were broadsides pinned to his face. The master's pursed lips held back a bilious screech, even as a couple of drops of spittle eked through. Several silent moments ensued, with no man daring even so much as to exhale.

Finally, Lord Barnard released Darnell, who fell back flat, then quickly brought himself up to a sitting position and put on his still-damp shirt.

"Fetch a torch," Lord Barnard finally ordered. Two of the men scrambled in the darkness to find a thick branch, then flailed about trying to light it aflame. When they succeeded in getting it lit, they brought it back to where Lord Barnard and Darnell remained mute and unmoving.

"Tell me exactly what has occurred, Darnell," Lord Barnard demanded.

"I overheard Lady Barnard and Matty speaking this morning. He was flirting with her, and she with him. I heard them make plans to meet in your house this evening."

"Where did they speak to each other?" inquired Lord Barnard. "Did Lady Barnard leave the house against my orders?"

Now Darnell had to tread carefully, for to admit that she did would only incriminate himself. He knew he might not escape punishment, yet he did not want to dilute the blame that Lord Barnard must find with Matty primarily, and his wife secondarily.

"Yes, Lord Barnard, but under my very careful guidance," he said. "She so wanted to see the people all dressed up and therefore I escorted her to the front porch. Merely to watch until they had traveled beyond our view to church," Darnell was quick to add. "It was not my intention that she should speak with anyone, but Matty saw us and came over. I didn't believe that Matty meeting us on the porch would violate your orders, yet when they began to make their plans, I knew I must come to you at once. Had I a horse and could ride competently, I would have arrived here sooner. But if you hurry back to town, back to your house, I am certain you will find them together in the most profane circumstances."

It was a good lie, plausible, and rendered quite believably by Darnell. The moments of silence during which Lord Barnard fought to maintain his composure had enabled Darnell to compose himself as well, yet he was unsure whether the lie was accepted, as Lord Barnard committed himself to no verbal response for several moments longer. Finally, he called his solicitor over.

"Finster. Bring my satchel." Finster did as he was told. Lord Barnard grabbed the bag from him and pulled out the papers the two had prepared the day before.

"You see this document, Darnell?" he asked his servant. Darnell nodded. Lord Barnard continued. "By this document, I have made Matthew Musgrave my legal heir. He is to be my own son, do you understand?" Again, Darnell nodded (what else could he do?). Again, Lord Barnard resumed his declaration.

"If what you say here is true, I will cross out Matthew's name and write yours instead. Finster here will witness and notarize it, and my fortune will in time pass to you instead of to him. However, if what you say is a lie, I will kill you. With neither hesitation nor remorse. Do you understand that?"

Darnell swallowed hard, but spoke firmly. "Lord Barnard, I have ever been loyal to you. As much as it pains me to bring this news to you, you who already have been as a father to me, I swear to you that what I tell you is true, and that you will have proof waiting for you in your own home, if only you will hurry to it."

"Quentin, gather our horses and all our belongings," ordered Lord Barnard. "We are returning to town at once. Finster, get a pen and ink." With that, in front of Finster and Darnell, Lord Barnard did as he promised. He substituted Darnell's name for Matty's, and Finster signed the document again. "Hear this, Darnell," warned Lord Barnard, "if you are wrong, you will hold this paper over your heart, and I will thrust my sword through its center until my blade exits through your back. If you are right—and I have known you long enough to believe that you must be—this paper guarantees that you are heir to my estate."

"You must hurry back if you are to view the evidence, Lord Barnard," said Darnell. "You will then see that I am speaking the truth."

"Indeed we shall," said Lord Barnard. "Quentin, are we ready?"

"Yes, Lord Barnard," Quentin replied. Stunned by Darnell's words, and fearful of what may come to pass, Quentin realized there was nothing he could do to save Matty from his fate. No matter how quickly or expertly he rode, he could not arrive back in town long enough before the others to help Matty make his escape. His only hope was to warn him in advance of their arrival, and the only way to do that was to use his horn when they emerged from the woods. But to do that would surely result in a severe response from Lord Barnard.

Quentin was torn, and not in the least because he knew his friend so well. Matty courted danger just as surely as he courted women, and he could neither be changed nor dissuaded from who he was and what he chose to do. Never had Quentin known a man whose destiny seemed so much of his own making, and while that made Matty all the more appealing—to Quentin as a friend, and to countless women (of every class) as a lover—it also necessarily left impotent any friend of Matty's who might hope to wield an influence on him.

"Darnell, you will ride with Quentin," Lord Barnard ordered. "Everyone else, mount your horses and stay close, for we shall wait for no one. True, it is dark and the woods are thick, but we must make haste."

Clumsily, Darnell tried to mount Quentin's horse but needed the concerned guide's assistance to get on securely. "Hold on tight, it will be rough going until we reach a clearing," advised Quentin.

Then at once, the entire party plus Darnell shot out towards the town, Quentin necessarily in the lead as he best knew the way, with Lord Barnard just half a length behind. No one spoke as they rode, yet all understood that something quite scandalous had occurred, involving Lord Barnard's wife. Improper a topic as it would be for public discussion or even with their own wives, it would be something to snicker about in private with customers, colleagues, and friends. Knowledge of this inflamed Lord Barnard's paranoia, while adding heat to his raging anger.

Finster, though he was well aware of Matty's reputation, still was shocked to think that he would have the pluck to ply his romantic trade with his employer's wife. Though he did feel some satisfaction in that he had held the correct opinion about Matty's suitability as an heir, he had not much higher a regard for Darnell. Had the circumstances been quite different than they were, Finster would have felt compelled to caution his client about the change made hastily on the legal document.

Darnell, his arms wrapped tightly around Quentin's torso, felt such an exhilaration that his loyalty was to be rewarded that he momentarily forgot his fear of riding on horseback. In fact, he had barely the clarity of mind to realize what Lord Barnard had meant about this document he had defiled with a quill, applying the brute force one might use to gut a deer.

Crossing out Matty's name and writing my own, what did he say? Legal heir? Own son? Me? This is to be my reward? And had I not acted, what then? I would have had to serve Matty? What insanity had come over Lord Barnard anyway?

Difficult though it was to make sense of the details, Darnell seized upon the end result: he would stand to inherit Lord Barnard's estate. He would be a servant no more. Surely Alexandra would have no choice, no other desire, than to devote her life to him.

My enemy gone, Darnell thought, *my love won, and a fortune as well. Victory is mine. At last, I have prevailed!*

Quentin, navigating through the darkened woods at quite a quicker pace than he would otherwise advise, gave no thought to—nor really felt—Darnell's arms clasping him tight around his belly. He thought only of Matty, tried to imagine the situation in which he would be found, and despaired of being able to help the man who once had saved his own life. Quentin resolved that whatever Matty's punishment (banishment he assumed; to bring charges of adultery would only further bring shame and scandal to Lady Barnard), he would bear it with him. Together they would go elsewhere, perhaps back to these woods that he knew so well.

My son, Lord Barnard lamented to himself, *how, my son, could you have so abused my love for you? I have always treated you fairly, favorably even. I was prepared to give you all I own, yet you have taken the one thing most rightfully mine.*

He imagined Matty lying in bed with his disloyal wife. He could picture the scene, but had no frame of reference with which to assign a look of blissful fulfillment on her face. Yet he knew somehow that Matty could do—likely had done—what he himself had never been able to accomplish. And the hurt and disappointment he'd been feeling were swept away by a fresh torrent of anger.

He tightened his grip on his reins. A flash of red appeared before his eyes—perhaps a surge of blood flowing through his veins. He replayed these thoughts in his mind repeatedly, unable to shake it free so as to enable a new idea to enter. Before long, however, the approaching border between the woods and the village sharpened his focus on the here and now, as opposed to what may already have occurred.

Suddenly, a keening wail was heard, jarring him from his perseveration. Lord Barnard cocked his head to identify the source of the sound. Again he heard it, though now he looked ahead and saw it was Quentin, his brass horn to his lips. *He is trying to warn Matty*, he realized. Each gallop bringing the party closer to his house, Lord Barnard would not allow a third blast from the horn.

He reached for his gun, which had held an unused shot for hours now. Darnell was hunched over, looking down, leaving Quentin's head in full view. Lord Barnard saw him draw another breath, then he pulled the trigger. Quentin's breath never reached the horn. Instead, his head swung back, his left arm, with which he held the horn while using the right to control the reins, flung overhead, the horn itself becoming a projectile that hit Upham square on the forehead. Though stunned for a moment and bleeding, the tailor managed to maintain his mount. Now Quentin's upper body jerked forward, slumped over his horse's neck. Slowly he began to slide off the horse to the ground, lifeless as the cold dirt that awaited him.

The only thing momentarily keeping Quentin on his horse was Darnell, who had yet to loosen his grip. But when he raised his eyes to see streams of blood flowing down Quentin's back, he drew his arms back quickly (nearly unsteadying himself) and watched in horror as Quentin fell off. He could hear the horses behind him kicking and stepping on Quentin's body as they passed it, as if it were no more consequential an obstacle than a branch or stone.

Instinctively, Darnell grabbed the reins and secured himself on the horse. Frightened as he was to find himself in control of a galloping horse, he was more stunned still by Quentin's ghastly murder, evidence of which dripped down Darnell's face. (Had he not mistaken it for sweat, surely Darnell would have fainted and fallen to the ground to be trampled to death.)

Dear God, he thought, *if this is how Lord Barnard punishes Matty's friend, how much more savage a sentence must await Matty?*

Darnell had not considered that Lord Barnard's rage could turn lethal. He began to fear the confrontation to which they raced ever closer. True, Darnell wished to be rid of Matty yet it was not his death he desired; expulsion would have been more than sufficient. Yet it was clear to him that it was impossible to challenge Lord Barnard in his present emotional state.

Now at the head of the group, and with his house in sight, Lord Barnard gestured with his right arm for all the riders to slow down to a trot. Though Darnell lacked the skill to control Quentin's horse, the well-trained beast instinctively followed the pace of its peers. They stopped at the edge of the property to the rear of the house. Lord Barnard asked Finster and Darnell to follow him but to wait downstairs. He gave leave to the others to return to their homes. Slowly, silently, the three approached the house, Darnell shivering with fear, Finster carrying his client's satchel, Lord Barnard loading new bullets into his gun.

The house was still and silent.

CHAPTER 18

In the beginning, there was darkness. The end, presumably, is encased in darkness as well. But no matter how deep and absolute a darkness may be, it inevitably is overcome by light. Not all at once, but slowly, gradually. As one advances, the other recedes, and the one coming into power will in time be the one to surrender.

Such are the cycles of the days. Such are the cycles of life itself.

Picture a figure lying in blissful unconsciousness. To him, light and substance are not merely hidden, they are infinitely void, like a starless sky in the deep black of space. Yet from this vast emptiness, this enormous absence, slowly builds an awareness. A subtle change in tone and hue. The blackness gives way to warmer shades. Now it is brown, like a horse. Then red, like blood. Now orange, like the morning sun. Then yellow, like candlelight.

Candlelight is familiar. It has not only luminescence but a scent as well. Stirring two senses now, it acts upon the prone figure of a man. Consciousness rises, sleep subsides. The eyes slowly open. There is the light. And there, in front of the light, is a figure. Because the light is behind the figure, no features are visible. A featureless figure can well prove to be a figment of one's imagination, and so the eyes close again, then reopen. The figure remains. The eyes open further. They focus more sharply. And within the dim nimbus, the figure soon becomes recognizable. It is Lord Barnard, standing at the foot of the bed and pointing a gun directly between those eyes.

The Grave and the Gay

Those eyes, of course, belong to Matty, lying still in Lady Barnard's bed. To his right, in his arms, is the naked figure of Lady Barnard herself. Warm, soft, sleeping, she is a study in bliss. In front of Matty stands a present danger. At his side, a sweet memory. Becoming clear-headed again, he understands the situation. He had schemed for such a confrontation, though he had expected it would happen later, on more neutral ground. When he was better prepared and when he was clothed.

So, the final scene is to be played here, now, in full view, thought Matty as he surveyed the scene. *I had hoped it would be enacted on the morrow, in daylight, standing, face to face, eye to eye, man to man. Yet it is just as well that Lord Barnard need not rely on rumor or hearsay. The evidence of my offense is laid bare before him. The next move is his to make. Then it will be mine.*

"Tell me, Matthew," Lord Barnard said with mock generosity. "How do you find my feather bed? My pillows, my sheets? Are they comfortable? Are they well to your liking?"

Sitting up, Matty would concede no disadvantage in this remarkable situation in which he found himself. "I do like your feather bed, Lord Barnard," Matty replied confidently. "The pillows are soft and the sheets are warm. I've not known such comfort before."

"And tell me further, Matthew," said Lord Barnard, now raising his voice and speaking with clenched jaw, "how do you enjoy my lady, asleep beside you? How is it to lay with my *wife*?"

Matty spoke calmly and slowly. "In truth, Lord Barnard, many fine women have I known in the past. Yet your lady gay stands alone for the sheer depth of her desire and the tenderness of her caresses. I do envy you…master," he said half-tauntingly.

"Arise, you scoundrel," shouted Lord Barnard, waking his wife. "For this insult, this gross disrespect, you will die!"

At the sound of her husband's voice, Lady Barnard sat up quickly, her breasts falling on the blanket that covered her only as far as her belly. Feeling the night air on her exposed flesh, she hastily drew the blanket up to her neck. She attempted to speak, but Matty bade her to hold her peace by placing his hand on her still-exposed bare shoulder.

"If you so desire to kill me, you need only to pull your trigger, Lord Barnard," said Matty, doubting Lord Barnard's resolve in light of the affection he had always shown his trusted stable hand.

"It shall never be known in fair England that Lord Barnard slew an unclothed man," replied Lord Barnard. "Now, get up and get dressed."

"And then what?" challenged Matty. "Will you do greater honor to yourself in shooting an unarmed man simply because he is not naked?"

Lord Barnard walked out the door of Lady Barnard's room and into the hallway, where his sword rack was stationed. He removed the top two—the finest two, which he himself had bought yet never planned to use—and returned to the room.

This action was observed silently by Darnell and Finster, who had dutifully been waiting downstairs. From there they had heard the confrontation coming from within Lady Barnard's room. Now, seeing Lord Barnard take weapons for an apparent duel, they felt compelled to risk his ire and ascend to the second floor to try to avert another murder. (For his part, Finster was already conceiving a defense of Lord Barnard for his shooting of Quentin.) On their way up they stepped on the fallen purple wildflowers that lay scattered on the stairs.

"It is true you have nary a pocket knife," Lord Barnard said to Matty, "against such fine long beaten swords as these. But you shall have the better of the two and I the worse. Thus you have your chance not only to survive but to succeed. But I say that my skill shall triumph over your pluck, and this dishonor you have brought to me and to my wife shall pass away even as your blood shall leave your body with every last beat of your roguish heart."

At this point, Darnell and Finster reached the doorway. Lord Barnard sensed their presence but rather than turn away from his opponent, he merely waved his sword at them to keep them in their place. With his left hand, he held out the sharper, shinier sword to Matty, who arose from Lady Barnard's bed and side, donned his pants and shirt, and took the weapon reluctantly, for no swordsman was he.

Has it come to this end? Matty thought anxiously. *Has my plan worked too well, or not at all? I have never dueled another man in my life, and now am I to die before the eyes of the hated Darnell and the barrister chap? Where are the others in the party?* he wondered. *Where is Quentin?*

"Here is how it shall be," said Lord Barnard. "You will have the first blow, and I'll defend it if I can. If so, I shall take the next blow, and a fatal one I intend it to be."

"You would pierce me with your blade, Lord Barnard," asked Matty, "you who have claimed to love me?"

"I *did* love you!" shouted Lord Barnard. "I wanted to give you all that I have; all I have that is precious and of value would one day have been yours. But you were not satisfied, not grateful for my love and my generosity. No, you took the one thing I could not give you, the one thing both God and the Crown understand is mine. Mine and mine alone!"

Lord Barnard's emphatic rationale bellowed through the open windows and began to attract a small crowd outside the house. Upham and Gallagher were closest to the door; they never continued on to their homes, but waited at a distance until they saw Darnell and Finster enter. Now they were joined by others, and the stirring outside the house was also soon noticed by Alexandra, who was out walking in the hope that the fresh air would clear the nausea and lightheadedness she felt.

"When the sun still shone overhead, you were my son in deed and in fact," Lord Barnard continued. "To kill my own son is a repulsive thought. But no son who lays with his father's wife can go unpunished. And as it is you who have shown hatred and dishonor to me, I will kill you not as my son, but as my enemy."

Suddenly Finster broke in. "Lord Barnard, I must protest. No good can come of this action. Let us retire to discuss a more rational resolution to this unfortunate situation."

"Silence!" ordered Lord Barnard. "As a businessman, I will negotiate many things, but never my honor. I'll hear not a word from you, nor from Darnell. Nor," addressing Lady Barnard for the first time, "from you. Now, Musgrave, raise your sword."

Matty did as he was told. Resigned to a fate he had so long eluded, he thought only briefly of how he would attack. Holding the sword in his right hand, he crossed his arm over his chest and drew the weapon back over his left shoulder, as if to take a backhanded course. He then swiftly circled the sword above his head and came down instead with a forward blow from the right.

Lord Barnard parried the simple attempt at deception, and with a turn of his wrist drew Matty's sword hand back. Matty's front fully exposed and vulnerable, Lord Barnard lunged his right arm forward, his sword plunging into Matty's belly, and the collective gasp and cry of the observers in the room masked the fact that Matty took his wound silently.

Outside the house, Alexandra came upon the small crowd, finding all ears cocked to hear the goings-on within.

"What is the matter?" she asked someone at the rear of the group. "Dunno," came the reply. "Bit of a row going on up the stairs."

Alexandra pushed forward to the front of the throng, and posed the same query to Upham.

"Lord Barnard has challenged Matty to a duel," Upham replied.

"What? Whatever for?" asked Alexandra.

"It's not my place to say, madam," said Upham. "But I'd wager that old Matty's days of wooing in this town are no more."

Alexandra ran up the porch steps and let herself in the front door. The downstairs was entirely dark, the candles having long since extinguished themselves, but at the top of the stairs she could see the backsides of Darnell and Finster outside of Lady Barnard's room. She bounded up the stairs and pushed through the two men, entering the room in time to see Matty slumped to his knees, head bowed, as if offering a prayer to Lord Barnard's sword, dripping red before him.

"Matty!" Alexandra screamed, running to her long-time lover. Lord Barnard held her back with his left arm. In his right, he still held his sword, point facing down, inches from where it had entered Matty. Slowly Matty looked up at Alexandra, mouthed the words, "I'm sorry," and fell forward onto the floor, dead.

Darnell came forward and pulled Alexandra back, away from the violent scene, yet she refused to leave the room where the father of her unborn child lay lifeless. Lady Barnard, now on her knees, blanket fallen and naked to the room and all its inhabitants, also screamed, yet her sorrow was nothing compared to the anger she felt to her husband, who had taken from her the one man who had taught her joy, brought her bliss, and made her feel for once grateful to be a woman.

The screams of the two women brought forth a rush up the stairs of all who had been eavesdropping outside. Finster allowed Upham and Gallagher in, then the three blocked the way of the others, preventing them from fully satisfying their prurient urges.

Oblivious to his growing corps of observers, Lord Barnard grabbed Matty's head by the hair and dragged him over to the edge of Lady Barnard's bed.

"Well, my Lady," he said. "You've had my company for nigh on ten years, and you've had an evening with him. So I ask you now: who do you like the best of us, Matty Musgrave or me?"

With all eyes on Lady Barnard, this mysterious woman of whom little was said, from whom little was seen or heard, about whom little was known, this woman who had earned the sympathy of those who knew and disliked her husband but had never felt loved or understood before this night, spoke up now, loud in volume, clear in conviction, freely from her heart, and with angry resolve in her eyes.

"My husband," she said, "hear this and know it to be true. You have given me comfort but never care, pearls but never pleasure. The one manly thing you've ever done has only extinguished my sole chance for happiness in this life. And now you ask me to choose between you and he? Then here is my choice: I'd rather a kiss from Matty's cold, dead lips than to spend another day with you or your meaningless wealth."

Lord Barnard stood transfixed. Never had he heard Lady Barnard speak with such force of opinion, with such ire, with such disparagement of him. Suddenly, he became aware that her outburst, painful as it was to hear on its own, was heard by several others: friends, servants, commoners. His right hand—which had gripped the handle of his sword with such strength for so long that it was sweaty, with blood drawn away from the taught, bent knuckles—had thus far killed two people he once had loved.

Despite the horrible work it had carried out thus far, his hand could not yet rest.

And so again it was raised, again it thrust forward, again a cry went up in the room. For Lord Barnard's sword again found flesh, this time its point piercing Lady Barnard's heart—Darnell could feel the prick in his own chest—its shaft protruding from the center of her cleavage, one pink breast hanging at either side.

As Lord Barnard withdrew his sword, the force of his action caused Lady Barnard to fall forward, tumbling off the bed, and onto Matty's still body.

"Finster," called Lord Barnard, without looking his way, "I shall need a grave, a large grave, of sufficient size so as to contain both these lovers. But make it deep not wide, and bury my Lady at the top, as she is now, for she was of noble kin."

With that, Lord Barnard tossed his sword on the floor. His right hand at last flexed and relaxed. But Darnell, overcome with shock and grief, suddenly tensed and sprang into action. All but leaping over Alexandra, who was wailing and slumped on the floor before him, Darnell grabbed the sword Matty had used in vain, and swung it madly and clumsily at Lord Barnard, slicing his neck. Lord Barnard reached for his wound and fell backwards. Darnell regained his own balance and stabbed Lord Barnard repeatedly in the abdomen, until Finster and Upham restrained him and removed the weapon from his hand.

Darnell, however, felt himself filled with the strength of ten men, and freed himself from their grip. Standing over his master's lifeless body, quickly draining itself of its blood, his mind now was clear and his voice was firm and strong.

"Finster," he said, "you have papers to the effect that I am Lord Barnard's sole heir, is that not true?"

"It is true," Finster replied, "but it is not valid if you take his life yourself."

"All I've done is stop a madman who had murdered three people in barely an hour's time," said Darnell. "Surely you've a sufficiently skilled

The Grave and the Gay

legal mind to clear me of fault and entitle me to my claim. There is no one else alive with as much right to his estate as have I."

"In light of the extraordinary circumstances, Darnell, I'm inclined to agree with you," said Finster, coming to his conclusion while surveying the ghastly scene. "And the sooner we can bring these tragic events to closure, the better for all. I'll take on this case first thing in the morning. But first, we must take these bodies and prepare them for burial."

Gallagher, now the only one blocking the doorway, allowed a few of the gawkers in for the purpose of removing the bodies. Finster directed them to lay the corpses on the cart that once had carried deer from the hunt, and told them to take the path into the woods so they could recover Quentin's body as well. All four victims were to be brought to the mortician, whose studio was located just past the tavern. There, in the morning, Finster would make the necessary legal and burial arrangements.

Orders having been given, and a long night ahead for some, the house soon was emptied of the living and the lifeless alike, leaving only Darnell and a still-weeping Alexandra. Since Darnell's bold speech, neither had said a word. All they could muster was the strength to embrace, to bind themselves together so as to block out the terrible spectacle of the murderous rampage that had just taken place.

"My dearest Alexandra," said Darnell at last. "A more horrible night is unimaginable. I am fearful of what effects there might be for you in witnessing this carnage."

Alexandra looked up at Darnell, her face contorted with grief, her cheeks slick with sorrow. "I cannot believe Matty is gone. I cannot believe any of it. And yet you, Darnell, you were the only man brave enough to act against Lord Barnard. I'm proud of you. And how awful it must have been for you, for I know that you cared for Lady Barnard as well."

"Hear me, Alexandra," said Darnell. "The only person I care for now—and forever—is you. You and your child. Let him be our child. Marry me, Alexandra. You have no reason to say no. Matty is gone and I am no longer a servant. We'll be wealthy, Alexandra, and we'll have our own servants. Please say yes."

"Oh, Darnell, at such a time as now, how can I say yes with a sure mind and a full heart?" asked Alexandra. "I pray you, ask me again a month from now and I promise my answer will be pleasing to you. But I need you to swear something to me. This child I have inside me, you know that it is Matty's child. And whether male or female, this child may look like Matty, make his faces and his gestures. Matty's soul and spirit will live through this child. You must promise me that you will love this child and not hold your hatred of his father against him."

"I do swear this, Alexandra," said Darnell, taking her hand and squeezing it firmly. "Though Matty and I were ever at odds, we now shall forever be linked, and it is because of our shared love for you."

Darnell and Alexandra kissed, then turned away from the bloody chaos in the room and went out the door, down the stairs, and then down again to Darnell's basement quarters. Though the images and events of the evening left them restless and anxious, eventually they fell asleep and there spent the night in a silent embrace, all now still and serene, save for the gentle kicking of Alexandra's child in her womb.

CHAPTER 19

Nearly a fortnight passed before Finster completed the burials and all the legalistic maneuvering required to give Darnell title and deed to the Barnard estate, as well as ownership of all the Barnards' assets. Much was done by Finster as the law required it be done, though wherever subjective interpretations of events could be proffered, discretion most often won out over cold, objective facts. After all, the once-honorable Barnard name already had been besmirched by the bloody affair; it would do no good to further inflame outrage and controversy by making some of the more sordid details a matter of public record.

Finster served not only the rule of the law but also the will of his new clients, Darnell and Alexandra. For example, Lord Barnard's final order, that Matty and Lady Barnard be buried together, was, like his order forbidding his wife to attend church, disobeyed. Darnell and Alexandra both were insistent that they be buried in separate coffins, and that the remains of Lord and Lady Barnard be interred adjacent to each other, while Matty's final resting place be near the pond behind the stable where his presence in life was a familiar one.

Quentin's family, aware of his connection to the woods at the edge of which he expired, buried him beneath a mammoth oak near the stream.

Darnell and Alexandra also both agreed that they desired not to be master and mistress to a house full of servants. However, given the emotional turmoil they had recently endured and the challenges that lay ahead with Alexandra's pregnancy and Lord Barnard's business affairs, having a cook and a housecleaner would be a great help. And so Finster was asked to rehire those that Lord Barnard had earlier dismissed. The cleaner would handle Alexandra's former laundry chores, enabling her to rest and to get strong and healthy again.

No replacement for Matty as caretaker of the horses was hired. As neither Darnell nor Alexandra were riders, there was no need to keep all four beasts. One was given to Reverend Collins for his personal and pastoral use, and one was given to Quentin's family as compensation for their loss. The remaining two were used to start a private coach business located off the property. Darnell hired Francis Richardson, younger brother of Thomas the tavern keeper, as the driver and manager. Darnell and Alexandra would have use of the coach for their own travel needs, and when they did not require the service it would be hired out to others.

Finster completed the business arrangements, including overseeing the construction of a new stable and office just beyond the church.

For Darnell's part, though he was legally Lord Barnard's heir, he sought to distance himself from his former master. He rejected the notion he'd been adopted by him and refused to take his last name. He would take the man's house and his money, yes, but would not adopt for himself Lord Barnard's cruelty and paranoia. Darnell had earned newfound respect from the citizenry and vowed never to be aloof around them or to place himself and his priorities above theirs if he could help it. He never did return to the tavern, however, which suited Alexandra well.

As she had requested, a month after the horror Darnell proposed again to her and this time she accepted. Yet not without conditions. First, Alexandra insisted he reiterate his pledge to be loving to her child, to raise the child as his own, and to never speak ill of Matty. She also strongly encouraged him to remove the shackles of his former position and the comportment it required, and to be more carefree and passionate. She was genuinely impressed with his bold actions that night in Lady Barnard's room, yet that was not the type of passion she desired of him. Alexandra neither expected nor wished for Darnell to become like Matty; she only wanted him to enjoy his days—and if he could, she would help him to enjoy his nights as well.

The Grave and the Gay

As for Lady Barnard's room, the site of three bloody murders, it was thoroughly cleaned, from the floor and the walls to the linens and the furniture. Then Alexandra asked that the doors be bolted shut, that no one should ever again enter or use the room, and so not to have the awful memory of that night relived each time one made use of it.

At first, Darnell was reluctant to comply, for there were valuable items in her room and it had always exuded a warm, appealing femininity so lacking in the rest of the house. Yet he acceded, for he knew well that he could not be sure of his own ability to remain stoic in that space, given his prior history there in Lady Barnard's presence, and the carnage he witnessed and contributed to only a month before.

As summer dawned, Darnell and Alexandra were married in a small, private ceremony performed by Reverend Collins. Only Finster and Alexandra's cousin Andrew attended. With the warmer weather, Alexandra donned lighter dress and her pregnant state was becoming apparent to observers. She had long recognized that she stood to be an object of scorn among the villagers; indeed, she knew there were whispers about her from those aware of her liaisons with Matty—in particular from those who knew that Matty favored her among all his other conquests, for if she was the most favored then she must also be the most experienced.

Yet Darnell was uncomfortable, self-conscious even, about the gossip. On his many trips into town on behalf of either Lord or Lady Barnard, he'd learned to keep a sharp ear tuned to rumors, never once betraying by his expression that he was eavesdropping on those who always regarded his presence in town with curiosity. For after all, only he knew the truth behind their suppositions, and what a blessing and a curse it had been to hold such intimate knowledge about such an enigmatic couple.

Now, with Alexandra clearly pregnant longer than married, he was sensitive to chatter, and he confided as such to her one night.

"Alexandra, I am deeply concerned with what I hear in town about your...your status," he said.

"Ah, pay them no mind, dear one," she replied. "If they've nothing better to occupy their minds with, that says more about their status than it does mine."

"Nevertheless, I hear it in town and it makes me angry," he said. "It makes me want to confront them, but I don't, and then I feel I am failing to uphold your honor. I just think it would be better for us—for all of us, the baby as well—if we lived elsewhere."

"Lived elsewhere? What do you mean? Are you suggesting we leave here, our home for so many years, a home we now own rather than work in, simply because of idle gossip?"

"I'm not suggesting it, Alexandra," Darnell backpedaled. "I've just been thinking that…that it would be a good thing for us to start over. In a new county, perhaps."

Alexandra stared at him, trying not to show anger. She knew his intentions were good. Yet she also wondered and worried about whether Darnell had yet attained the strength and resilience she hoped he was accruing in the days and weeks since he so boldly and instinctively wielded Lord Barnard's sword. Further, she had heard Darnell, no longer held by the duty and discretion of his former position, tell her of Lord Barnard's maniacal obsession with what the villagers thought of him. Could Darnell be adopting such an attitude as well?

Finally, she spoke, in soft, measured tone, with her hands upon her husband's arms.

"I am sorry, Darnell, that you are hurt by what others may be saying about me. But please let me assure you that I am not bothered by it. And surely they will soon find something else to talk about. I want to stay here. My cousin is here, and he is the only family I know anymore." *And I cannot leave Matty's grave*, she kept to herself.

"I am not deaf to your wishes, my darling," said Darnell, "yet all I desire for us is a fresh start, a new beginning, as we prepare to welcome our child into our lives." *And in leaving we would not have Matty's grave so close by to serve as a constant reminder*, he added in thought.

"Darnell, every day we are making a new life for ourselves," she replied. "This is all new to us. We are new together. Newly married, learning our way around each other. Soon to be parents for the first time, not knowing what to do. Our home is the one familiar thing we possess, the one source of stability we have. We must cling to it, not desert it. If we leave here, we will be strangers no matter where we go. I won't have it," she insisted. "I'm sorry, Darnell, but I won't."

And with that, he relented.

To help Darnell face his fears and increase his comfort in their new life and their current home, Alexandra insisted nightly that they walk into the village, visit the shops, be as visible, social, and unselfconscious as possible. In time, the citizens came to view them not as former servants but as masters of their own lives, not as undeserving lowlifes who fell into fortune but as kind, pleasant, and polite people who were generous with their time and friendship. Her plan worked, and Darnell—though still immutably aloof and unnecessarily formal—indeed became more comfortable and never again raised the notion of leaving Lancashire.

Summer passed, its heat carried off by the cooler breezes of autumn, which rustled the fiery leaves of orange and gold and broke them from the trees. The more agreeable weather suited Alexandra, easing the growing burden she carried in her abdomen. Thus she retained her energy and vigor through the middle of November before the imminence of her baby's birth finally forced her to rest and await the pains that would bring the nameless child into the world.

Ultimately, it was another fortnight before the baby began to wend its way from its warm, secure home inside Alexandra's body to the cold, uncertain space of Lady Barnard's room. Yes, Alexandra had lately changed her mind about keeping its door bolted shut, believing that by doing so she had been preserving it unchanged as a room of death. By giving birth in that room, she would restore it to one of life. And the baby's first breath would take place mere inches from where its father took his last.

So it was that in the early hours of December, with encouragement and guidance from the village midwife, and Darnell pacing the floor downstairs, Alexandra gave birth to a son. Healthy and well-formed, the boy's robust cry brought Darnell bounding up the stairs and into the room. As he held his son, Darnell looked at the face and saw reflected back the dark hair and eyes of the father, and the sweet nose and lips of the mother. He was instantly smitten.

Alexandra wanted to name him Matthew but out of respect for Darnell's feelings she instead suggested Henry, for no other reason than she liked the name. Darnell, his heart open, his dream fulfilled, his life now triumphant with a beautiful wife, a darling child, a stately home, and wealth enough to ensure the long-term comfort of all, agreed.

"Welcome, Henry," he said. "Know that you are loved. From love were you made, in love shall you be raised."

Alexandra smiled. She was content. Henry cried. He was hungry. Outside—visible through the window in the room that had been Lady Barnard's view of the world—a light snow, really just a frozen mist, began to fall. The cold of winter was returning, and yet the sun was rising, casting an orange glow on the pond behind the empty stable, on the stone marker on Matty's nearby grave, and on the once-unhappy house that now was a loving home to three people at peace, together in embrace on a bed with languid hues of light through colored glass gently creeping over them.

ACKNOWLEDGEMENTS

With this volume compiling both *King of Kings* and my first novel, *The Grave and the Gay*, I have the opportunity to acknowledge some people I failed to recognize the first time out, as well as people who have earned my gratitude since then for their help, support, and love. To begin with, the writing style I employed in *TGATG* was strongly influenced by my friend and former colleague and collaborator Ellen Kushner, via her marvelous book, *Thomas the Rhymer*. Dawn Blanchard was kind enough to publish *TGATG* in 2012, ending a lengthy run of rejection notices from agents and publishers alike. Ose Schwab has graciously sold the book at her store, The Gallery, in Malden, Massachusetts, and her husband, Marcel, inadvertently guilted me into finally finishing *KOK* so I would have new product to sell there. Former colleague Sarah Jensen dared me to write *TGATG*, edited *KOK*, and in between acknowledged me in her book, *A Perfect Union of Contrary Things*. Christina Ramirez from BookBaby was a kind guide to getting this volume published. My daughters Hannah and Stella have never read my books but they bring me joy all the same. And Naomi Kahn, who unintentionally offended me by saying that *TGATG* was "an easy read," has nonetheless been an inspiring, loving, and fun companion the last few years, during which time I was able to finish *KOK*.

This is for my mother.